Skater Boy

a novel by
Kay Manis

Chris Chann's Tricks

1) nollie pressure late flip
2) kickflip late flip or Do it
switch if you can actually do
it
3) Switch Double Checco Bird

ISBN-13: 978-1492235750

For more information about this book or others in
the X-Treme Boys Series please visit:
www.KayManis.com

Dedication

This book is dedicated to my beautiful daughter
Kimberly, who, with four small words, changed
the course of my life forever.
"Just write it Mom!"
Thanks for *always* believing in me.

Chapter 1

~ HINDLEY ~

My fingers fumbled with the straps on my shoes as I desperately tried to catch up with the other girls. You would think, given my history, I'd be able to slap on these stripper heels in record time. But no, of course, today I'm all thumbs.

"Alright ladies, let's make our way around the center pole."

I raised my head and saw the other girls begin to migrate towards the instructor. Their idiotic giggles and smirks made me nauseous. Who the hell has a Bachelorette Party at a pole dancing studio anyway? *The dim-witted, shallow, and pretentious Geneva Barton, that's who.*

"Is everyone here?"

I looked up and saw Geneva's eyes boring into mine, her face riddled with disgust. "Come on, Hindley!" She half shouted, her words echoing throughout the small studio.

"Everyone's waiting on you." Her voice was laced with hate.

"I knew she'd ruin this for you," Wendy, her idiot friend chimed in. *I can think of a million ways I could ruin this night for Geneva, you dumbass, but trust me, being late for your stupid party isn't one of them.*

I wasn't naive enough to believe I'd been invited to Gen's party because she liked me. The only reason they'd sent me an invitation was because Geneva and I were sisters. Well, not technically, thank God. We were just step sisters, although my mother always tried to introduce us as real siblings, more for my benefit than Geneva's. As if being blood related to Geneva Barton would somehow make me more appealing to the opposite sex. Gen barely acknowledged me as family in public and that was just fine with me. I had no desire to be related to her either. I only showed up tonight because my stepfather, Geneva's father, had begged me to.

I secured the last hook and pulled on the strap just to make sure the shoes were snug. I knew how dangerous it could be if your shoe slipped off mid-performance and I didn't need that kind of attention tonight. My goal was to stay as invisible as possible and just make it through the night unscathed by Geneva's piranhas.

As I walked over to the group of girls, I remembered that none of them knew about my past. I could not look as confident and brave as I knew I was in this setting. To these superficial twits, I was still Geneva's gangly, older step-sister stuck in our high school days wearing braces and head gear, a book nerd and hopeless geek to the core. Forget that I now had a Bachelor's degree and a Doctor's of Jurisprudence certificate hanging above my desk at work, they still saw me as shy, uncoordinated Hindley Hagen, geeky older sister to the effervescent, outgoing Miss Hawaiian Tropic 2004, Geneva Barton.

Well tonight, I would personify that geeky older sister if it killed me. I pushed my glasses further up my nose and gave my ponytail one last pull to tighten the holder as I slowly made my way to the class, trying to look as uncoordinated and disinterested as possible.

"Uh! Finally," Gen sighed. "Can we start now?"

"Be my guest." I motioned to the instructor.

"Hi ladies, welcome to Miss Understood Dance Studio." *Miss Understood? For real? That's the name you actually chose for this place? Miss Understood?* I wanted to hate it but actually, I kinda liked it now that I let it roll around through my mind a little. *You're too cerebral, you think way too much.* "My name is Sadie Sunnydale." The instructor was tall and lean and oozed sensuality with her long scarlet colored hair and emerald green eyes.

"Wow," Wendy let out. "What a name."

Sadie laughed. "It's actually my stripper name."

"You're a stripper?" Geneva asked, her voice dripping with disgust. *Hater!*

Sadie's face twisted up like she'd just sucked on a lemon. "Oh no, honey." *Another hater. These bitches are so judgmental!* "I'm a real dancer." She said it with such audacity, such superiority. People like her made me sick.

Geneva brought her hand to her chest in relief like she'd just heard her credit card wasn't declined after all. "Oh, thank God!"

"You'll each come up with your own stripper name," Sadie explained.

Geneva began to rub her hands together so hard and fast, I thought she was going to spark a fire. She looked like she was about to be served a five course meal, which was kind of funny considering I thought she might be semi-anorexic, if that's possible. "Oh, this is going to be so much fun."

"Wait!" Sadie stopped all the girls mid thought. "There's a special way you come up with your name."

"How?" I heard someone ask in the front of the group. I looked up and saw it was Marabelle, Geneva's best friend from high school. It was easy to spot her, she stood a head taller than the rest of the girls, quite modelesque. She was the only friend of Geneva's I could even remotely stand to be around for more than a nanosecond, probably because she didn't play into all of Geneva's bullshit, just some of it.

I say Marabelle was Gen's high school best friend because according to Gen, best friends change every four to five years, whether you needed them to or not. Marabelle was High School Best Friend, Wendy had been College/Sorority Best Friend, and now, Isadora was Professional Best Friend. Having had only one best friend my entire life, I didn't understand the concept at all. But Geneva was superficial in every aspect of her life, so why should friendship be any different?

Sadie continued. "First, we'll begin by selecting the name of your very first pet."

The girls erupted into giggles again, talking about all the pets they'd owned over the years. I'd had two. Harold was a gerbil I had when I was five. My mom left him in the garage over Christmas break and he ended up as a New Year's Eve popsicle. I didn't' think the story or the name would make for a good stripper persona.

Thinking of my second pet brought tears to my eyes. He was a stray dog I'd found a few months after Harold died. I think my mom felt guilty about my hamster and let me keep the dog, even though he wasn't allowed in our rented duplex. I named him Rocky because I loved the movie and because his front two paws were black and looked like boxing gloves. Two weeks after I found him, the landlord knocked on the door and told my mom if we wanted to keep the dog, she'd have to fork over another five hundred bucks for a pet deposit. The ride to the animal shelter was the longest of my life. There was no way my stripper name would be Rocky either.

Sadie continued with the instructions. "Then, your last name will be the name of the street you grew up on." *Uh, which one, dancer lady? I have like a zillion to choose from.* This assignment was getting dumber and dumber by the moment. I decided to go with the name my friends from law school had given me. It was really good and made me laugh every time I thought of it.

"Does everyone have their name yet? There's a prize for the best one." The room erupted in cheers and hoots and hollers and suddenly, everyone really started concentrating. I couldn't believe this lady was going to make us go around and say our names. There were almost thirty girls here. It would take half the night.

"You only have to tell us if you want to," Sadie said. I thought it was funny that I kept referring to her as Sadie, as if that were her real name. Of course, everyone was going to compete. Everyone but me.

"Now what I want you to do is take hold of the pole like this." She reached up and grabbed the pole high above her head. "Then kick your leg out and bring it back in and fall down as you swing around like this." She kicked up her right leg high into the air, almost touching her ear, then in one fell swoop, let it fall and curled it behind her as she made a beautiful swan circle around the pole. "My name is Sadie Sunnydale," she blew out, her voice smooth and sexy as her body came to a gentle stop. *That's the best you got Sadie Sunnydale? You'd never make it two seconds on the stage.*

All the girls started laughing and giggling and clapping like they'd just seen a member of their favorite boy band. I thought I actually might throw up.

On cue, each girl took their turn and I wasn't surprised to hear that their names were just as atrocious as their kick turns on the pole. I knew I said I would keep it low key but I just couldn't help myself. Growing up, there was absolutely nothing I did better than Geneva Barton. But this was one thing I knew I was better at. *The fact that you have no student loans after three years of law school proves just how good you are!*

"Alright, let's see what you ladies got," Sadie said motioning toward me, almost daring me to be worse than the others.

I rubbed my hands up and down on my shorts then blew on them out of habit. I hadn't even started and already I had all the girls' attention. I grabbed the bar with one hand and kicked my leg straight up in the air, completing a perfect aerial split, gently touching the pole on the other side. After holding the pose for a few seconds, I let my leg fall toward the ground as the momentum effortlessly swung my entire body around the pole two full revolutions. I came to a stop, doing a complete back bend with one leg on the floor and the other wrapped around the pole. I mustered the sexiest voice I could find. "Hi! I'm Cookie Waterbrook." The entire studio was silent except for one lone giggle. Mine.

~

"No way, no how, Paul!" I screamed into my phone.

"Please Hin, for me, your old man."

"No, not even for you Pop."

"But, she's your sister."

I started laughing. "Not technically."

"Come on Hin. She needs you."

"She's never needed me Paul, and you know it."

"Well, I need you."

Those three words, 'I need you,' coming directly from my stepfather's mouth instantly made me stop arguing with him. Paul Barton didn't need anything, not money, not power, not fame, not love, not accolades. He had it all. Yet, here he was, hanging on the phone at my mercy, begging me for help. He needed me. How could I refuse him?

"You're not playing fair now. Why do you do this to me old man!"

"Because I know you love me and you'll do anything for me."

"Ugghhh." He was right. There was almost nothing I wouldn't do for him, even babysit his ignorant daughter tonight. "Sometimes I hate you."

"I know," he laughed, his baritone voice vibrating through the airwaves. "But most of the time you love your old man, don't ya?" I nodded my head in silent agreement, knowing he knew the answer. "And most of the time, I love you, too," Paul added. "Well, actually, that's a lie." I gasped in shock, believing for a split second that he really didn't love me. "I love you *all* the time, Hinny Bin." I smiled at his term of endearment.

Hinny Bin was Paul's nickname for me. When anyone else tried to use it, they usually got a swift kick in the ass from me. The words grated on my nerves. But coming from Paul, the name had always been special to me.

Even though Paul was only my stepfather, he was the only father figure I'd ever known and perhaps one of my best friends.

Paul met my mother when I was in eighth grade and his daughter, Geneva, was in seventh. We went to different schools, mine public and Gen's private. Our families were polar opposites, literally from separate sides of the track. Paul was a rich, successful real estate broker and developer and instantly fell in love with my mother the moment he showed her the five bedroom semi-mansion he had for sale. She and I both knew she couldn't afford it but that wasn't going to stop her. It had been a set-up from the start and Paul had walked right into my mother's trap. Not that I would ever admit that to him.

My mom and I had been on our own since I was born. She'd become pregnant in high school and had always told me she didn't know who my father was, claiming she was a real slut in school. She said it could have been any number of guys but I think the truth was she knew exactly who my father was, she wasn't the promiscuous type. I think my birth father bailed on her when he found out she was pregnant and she just didn't want to admit that any man had ever left her.

Her parents tried to talk her into an abortion when they found out she was pregnant, even threatening not to support her if she kept me, but my mom refused to succumb to their pressures, fully believing that once I was born they'd change their mind. She was wrong. To my mom's surprise, and mine now that I was a grown woman, they stuck by their threat and kicked us both out of the house when I was just two months old. They said they were two old to raise another child. Their mindset baffled me. What kind of people do that to their only daughter and granddaughter? *Assholes, that's who.*

My mom was a knock out, a real looker. She was tall and slender with long blonde hair, big boobs, a teeny-tiny waist, and a butt you could still bounce quarters off of. Women around the world paid hundreds of thousands of dollars to look as stunning as she did naturally.

Caroline Hagen-Barton knew she was gorgeous and used her looks to get us through tough times. She could sell ice to an Eskimo. One time, they actually hired her as a nurse at an old folk's home, even though she'd never even finished high school. The manager was an old fart, just a few years away from residing in the facility himself, but he fell in love with my mom the instant he saw her. I couldn't blame him, there wasn't a man alive immune to her good looks and charm. The poor sap hired her on the spot, never asking for any transcript or diploma or anything. *Men are idiots! Have I said that already?*

I envied my mom in many ways. What I had to work years for came easy for her. Men were putty in her hands. For me, they were rocks, hard and unyielding. Most of the men in my life had done nothing but use me for their own selfish gain then cast me off once they'd realized how hopeless and damaged I was.

My mom had seen Paul's real estate advertisement in a local newspaper and proclaimed, "I'm gonna marry that man and he's gonna be your Poppa!" She called him immediately and arranged for a private showing of a five thousand square foot mansion under the pretense of buying it, even though she knew she couldn't have even afforded the electric bill, let alone a $750,000 mortgage. She said Paul didn't need to know everything about us but somehow, as soon as I met him, I knew Paul was smart and probably onto us. He showed her the property anyway, even spending an hour and a half walking around the mansion just to be able to spend more time with her. *Men are idiots!*

Paul Barton was a goner the instant he saw my mom's emerald green eyes and hour glass figure. And my mom had fallen hopelessly in love with him, too. But not for his money like some people in his high society circle thought. She fell in love with his heart, which was made of pure gold. They'd pretty much been inseparable ever since. He'd made it his life's mission to give my mom everything she ever wanted, even if what she wanted wasn't good for her. And Paul was equally as devoted to me.

As easy as their relationship had bloomed, Paul's daughter and mine had not. I never like to say I hated people, I always wanted to think there was room for everyone to redeem themselves, but Geneva Barton was very close to one hundred percent on my hate-o-meter. I never knew why she didn't like me. It wasn't like I was a threat to her at all in any area of life. She was beautiful like my mother and they're relationship grew just as fast and as tight as Paul's had. Sometimes, I felt like my mother loved Geneva more than me. But the thought never made me jealous or act out toward her. It was always hard for my mom to relate to me, given the fact I wasn't drop-dead gorgeous like she was. I was actually relieved she had a beautiful stepdaughter she could finally relate to, someone to pass on her golden nuggets of beauty and fashion wisdom.

Geneva had tons of friends, went to the best schools, had the trendiest clothes, and dated more boys than you could shake a stick at. One of the things that irked me the most though was that Geneva was actually really smart. I would never admit that to her or anyone else though. Unfortunately, she'd never developed her brain, choosing to skate by on her good looks rather than apply herself.

The only reason I could think of why she hated me was because of my close relationship with her father. Paul wasn't just *like* a father to me. In my heart, he *was* my father. He had pulled me out of a dark place and protected me, even when the law and my own mother couldn't. He'd motivated me over the years to do more with myself, pushing me past my own limits, even encouraging me to go to law school when my college grades had been sub-par. Any good thing I accomplished in life, I always attributed to him. And he was equally as smitten with me, often asking for my opinion on all kinds of issues from the most mundane like what tie to wear, to the more serious like what piece of real estate to invest in next. He truly valued my opinion, relying on it sometimes, and I think Geneva resented that most of all.

Everyone who knew Paul knew I was just as much his daughter as Geneva and I think that was another motivating factor in her hatred of me. There wasn't anything Paul and I wouldn't do for one another. Looking back over the years, I could see that perhaps I was actually closer to Paul than his own daughter and something told me she knew it, too.

"I can't believe I'm doing this. You know I hate clubbing," I groaned into my phone.

"But tomorrow is her wedding, Hin, and I've shelled out a small fortune for it, money I don't have right now, just to make her and your mother happy," Paul groaned. "I don't want her to show up at her own wedding hung-over and half-drunk from her Bachelorette party. It would kill your mother."

I felt bad. I knew Paul had taken a big hit when the real estate market tanked four years ago. That was one of the reasons I'd decided to put myself through law school, even though he assured me he could help. I was blown away that Geneva was so selfish. She knew Paul's financial situation was still rocky, even though he was rebuilding his company. Most of the real estate he owned was still mortgaged to the hilt trying to stay afloat. But his business was making a surprisingly successful comeback and he had high hopes. Fortunately for Paul, the real estate market in Texas hadn't been hit as hard as the rest of the country. My mom and Geneva had been blissfully unaware of the financial pressure Paul had been under the last five years. Either that or they'd chosen to purposely ignore it. Asking for such an elaborate and costly wedding had made Gen jump up at least ten points on my Bitch-O-Meter scale. I wasn't pleased with my mom's demands for Paul to shell out more money either.

"I know Pop. I'm sorry about that."

"Don't be sorry, it's my fault. I just can't seem to say no to you girls."

"Well, I don't have a problem telling them no."

"I know Hindley. You're much stronger and smarter than I am. You're my only voice of reason most times. I don't know what I'd do without you."

There was silence on the line as I let his loving words soak in. Even though Paul was asking me to do something he knew I hated, his words weren't being offered up as bribery. He was nothing if not honest with his feelings. Paul wasn't a liar, he was true and honest and genuine. I thanked God almost every day that my mom fell in love with his photo in that real estate ad twelve years ago. Without Paul, I knew my life would have been drastically different.

You have to do this for him, Hindley. You owe everything good in your life to Paul Barton.

"What exactly do you want me to do?" I tried to sound enthused but my words came out with a heavy heart.

"Just go out to the clubs with them, make sure she doesn't drink too much or get into too much trouble."

"She'll never listen to me. Hell, she probably doesn't even want me there."

"She listens to you Hindley, more than you know."

I knew he *thought* his words were true but in reality, Gen could care less what I had to say most of the time. And I knew for a fact she thought I was a complete idiot on most of life's subjects. Thankfully, I'd never needed approval from others to fill up my self-esteem tank. Gen, on the other hand, thrived on attention, needing other's words of affirmation like vampires needed blood.

"Fine," I blew out, exasperated. "But the minute she starts acting like a bitch to me, I'm gone."

"Deal!"

I put the phone on my shoulder and balanced it on my ear as I dug around in my trunk. "Shit!"

"What?"

"I don't have any clubbing clothes."

"Do you want my credit card?"

"No, there's no time. The outrageously expensive Hummer limo you rented for the blessed event just pulled up. I'll have to wear my yoga pants and sports top. Seriously Paul, what were you thinking, a Hummer?"

"I love you Hindley."

"Whatever. You so owe me!"

I hit the END button and slammed down the trunk, shoving my phone into the inside pocket of my pants as I glanced over at the limo parked a few feet away. *That thing is friggin' ridiculous. She's such a bitch, always asking for more, never satisfied with what she has.*

I checked myself in the side mirror of my car. My reflection was awful but there was nothing I could do about it now. I stood up straight and smoothed out my clothes as if that would magically make me more presentable knowing all the while Geneva would revel in my haggardness. *This is going to be one fucked up evening!*

~

We were at our third bar of the evening and despite what I'd told Paul, I was not keeping a watchful eye on Geneva. In fact, I myself was quite good and liquored up. I usually didn't drink, at all, but being around Geneva's gaggle of gal pals had driven me to the extreme.

"Do another!" Wendy shouted above the blaring hypnotronic music as she shoved a shot glass full of Tequila into my hand.

If I didn't know better, I would have sworn they were all trying to get me completely smashed. At this point, I didn't care. I'd do just about anything to numb myself from their mindless jabbering about last minute wedding details to take care of tomorrow before the blessed day.

Geneva had been planning this wedding for over a year, which was twice as long as she'd known her fiancé when he proposed. They'd met at one of my mother's numerous charity events. Even though my mother grew up basically broke as a joke, she'd had no problems fitting in with Paul's high society friends, hosting galas and charity events galore. My mom usually had a heart of gold, even though she'd suffered from a Princess Complex most of her life. Meeting Paul and being introduced to some of Austin's most elite had been a dream come true for her. For me, it had been yet another reminder of what an outcast I was.

Gen's fiancé, Stanley Winston III, or 'Third' as I affectionately called him, came from money and that's all Gen needed to hear when they were introduced eighteen months ago. She'd spent more time with her friends in the last year planning this stupid wedding than she actually did with Stan.

Stan was a good looking guy by most women's standards, but nothing compared to Gen's boyfriends in the past. We were all a little surprised when she told us she was engaged to him. I expected her to bring home a super model or Hollywood beau-hunk but instead, she'd brought home a man only a few inches taller than herself with a full head of hair that was clearly thinning and a solid jaw line you knew would sport a second chin within the next decade. I thought Geneva was probably more in love with Stan's money than with him and the realization killed me. Stan had his moments but for the most part, he was a decent guy and deserved a woman who adored him. Geneva Barton was not that woman. I'd spoken my peace to my mom, to Paul, and even to Stan a few months back but it was to no avail. Instead, everyone buried their head in the sand and pretended like Snow White had met her Prince Charming. Who was I to question Walt Disney?

"Give me another one!" I shouted, slamming the shot glass on the bar, disgusted with the fact that I was actually going along with this charade.

The bartender leaned over trying to shout directly in my ear. "I'm afraid you've had enough for this hour."

"What the fuck! You're cutting me off? That's bullshit!" I didn't know they even did that. I figured as long as the credit card said 'approved', they'd keep pouring.

Gen grabbed my arm and pulled me away from the bar. "Calm down, Hindley, you're making a scene."

"I thought you wanted me drunk."

"I do, but not belligerent."

Well, there you go. She'd admitted it. For whatever reason, she wanted me plastered tonight. "Screw you Geneva. I'll scream whatever the hell I want to!" Those were the words I tried to get out of my mouth but I knew they came out garbled and slurred and probably sounded like some kind of foreign expletive.

"Let's dance!" Mirabelle shouted, hooking her arm through mine and pulling me toward the dance floor. Geneva and a mass of her friends followed us and I rolled my eyes. This was not a good idea because I was already three sheets to the wind. I tried to stop to right my spinning head but Mirabelle drug me on.

"Come on!" Geneva barked pulling on me, too. "The dancing will make you feel better." The smile on her face was in direct opposition to her words. She had no intentions of trying to make me feel better. But I was too drunk to care.

Our small group of party goers was able to part the dancers on the floor like Moses did the Red Sea. We took over most of the dance floor and all began jumping up and down like we were at a Bon Jovi concert. I could feel the vibrations of the music all over my body and the flashing multi-colored lights had me feeling euphoric, like I was on top of the world. I had to admit I was having fun. Rarely did I let my guard down. During college and law school, I'd been busy studying and now that I was at a law firm, I was too busy working. I'd never done most of the things kids my age did, like drinking, dancing, partying, having random sex with random guys, all the things that Gen did. Instead, I'd been too busy preparing for the future as she was completely infatuated with making the most of every single day, filling her senses to excess, supported by her father's wallet. I was jealous of her lackadaisical attitude and tonight, I made up my mind that I wasn't going to give two shits about anything, least of all Geneva Barton.

After what seemed like an eternity of dancing, a slow song finally came over the surround sound speakers and I couldn't have been more thankful. My legs were already weak from the Bachelorette pole dancing party and jumping up and down like a spastic dog for the last thirty minutes on the dance floor hadn't helped any. Not to mention what the constant gyration had done to the alcohol in my stomach. The room was starting to spin and I could feel rumbling somewhere within my gut.

I reached out to grab Gen's hand to steady myself and let her lead me off the floor but suddenly, someone's arm wrapped around my waist and pulled me close. When my hand fell out of hers, she looked back at me and gave me the biggest shit-eating grin. "Have fun," she mouthed. I knew her words were sarcastic but I didn't care. I hadn't felt the embrace of a man in a long time and I was too drunk to fight it anyway.

When I turned around, I saw a semi-decent looking guy, undressing me with his eyes. I was surprised he was interested because I knew I looked like hell. I was still wearing my yoga pants and tank top from the party and my hair was twisted up in an awful bun. All of Gen's friends had brought a change of clothes for the club but Wendy had conveniently forgotten to tell me we were going out dancing after our class. By all accounts, I was a certifiable mess. But hey, if this guy was game, so was I.

He was tall, really tall and good looking in a Gap commercial kind of way. His khaki Docker's and starched blue polo shirt stood in stark contrast with the fashion of the hipster crowd in the bar. His jet black hair was perfectly groomed and parted and his hands were professionally manicured. I knew this right away because he immediately glued them to my chest, just above my boobs, as if he was being coy. I wanted to move them but honestly, I was too drunk to even put one foot in front of the other, let alone defend my honor.

"Come here often?" he whispered in my ear. He was trying to be seductive but his tenor voice just came across as creepy. Only a guy with a voice like Johnny Cash could pull off such a cheesy line.

I rolled my eyes again and that was my undoing. Whatever I'd been holding back in my stomach now decided it wanted out of my body. I pushed past him and ran straight for the bathroom, barely making it to the first stall before all the contents of my stomach were fully hurled into the toilet.

"Ouuuhhh!" I heard a few girls scream. "That's disgusting."

I'd heard of people praying to the Porcelain God but never quite understood the religious connotation until now. Real or imaginary, I was thanking this god of the toilet right now that my hair was already pulled back in a ponytail and promising him my eternal allegiance if he'd just make this wretched heaving stop.

A random stranger came up from behind and put her hand on my back. "Are you alright, sweetheart?" She had a deep southern drawl and I knew she was from Texas. Partly because of her accent but mostly because the people in Texas had a way of caring for complete strangers like no one I'd ever encountered. "Here doll." She handed me a wet paper towel and I used it to wipe up the putrid string of bile hanging from my lips. I leaned back against my heels trying to catch my breath and prepare for round two, which I knew was coming at any moment. Suddenly, I saw her foot extend past me as it hit the handle of the toilet, sending the contents inside down into the bowels of the Austin sewer system. "Let me help you up." She braced me under my elbow and pulled me up effortlessly. To me, she was a goddess in a sea of vipers.

"Thank you," I whispered. I don't know why but I leaned my head against her shoulder as if we'd been soul mates for life.

"You need some fresh air, sweetie. Come on." Without hesitating, I followed her through the crowd. I noticed Gen sitting at the bar in between two gorgeous men, both of whom had to be either strippers, male models, or both. She was batting her eyes and flirting beyond belief and I saw one of the guy's hands resting on her bare thigh. Her skirt was so short, it should have been illegal and I knew there was no way Stan had approved this outfit.

"I'm going outside!" I shouted as we walked past them.

"Don't forget, eleven o'clock at the restaurant tomorrow for my bridal luncheon." I nodded my head, not fully understanding what she had just said. "Don't be late Hindley, or I'll kill you!" That I understood completely.

My mystery goddess laughed as we strolled past Gen and her man candy. "Wow, she's a pistol."

"You have no idea."

Finally, we made it to the exit of the club and the doors flew open as a gust of cool air hit my face. Instantly, I felt better. My goddess must have felt me capable of standing on my own as she released me from her vice grip.

"You okay now, hun?"

"I think so."

"I've got her." An all too familiar arm snaked around my waist again and for some reason, dread filled my entire body. It was Gap Boy from the dance floor.

"Is he with you?" my goddess asked, looking at me.

"I said I've got her!" he snapped back at her.

"Are you sure you're gonna be alright, sweetheart?" Her eyes beseeched me for an honest answer but I couldn't give her one. I had no idea where I was and absolutely no clue who this guy was man-handling me. I'd never felt so out of control in all my life. All I could do was look at her and smile. She mistook my silence for assurance that I was going to be alright in Gap Boy's care.

"Stay outside until you feel better, okay hun." She instinctively began to rub my back again and a thought occurred to me even in my drunken stupor. I'd never felt anything so soothing in all my life. *Wait! Don't leave me Mystery Goddess, please!* "Take care of her," she instructed Gap Boy, her words imploring him to do more than she knew he was capable of.

I stood in silence and partial paralysis as I watched her walk back into the club, the sound of the door clicking closed a sobering reminder to me that I hadn't kept my promise to Paul to keep an eye on Geneva. A sick feeling washed over me as I realized Geneva's safety was the least of my concerns right now. Looking into Gap Boy's darkening eyes, feeling his hands start to roam about my body, I suddenly realized my own safety was in jeopardy.

Chapter 2

~RORY~

I stood outside the noisy club, my back leaning against the building as I faced the busy downtown street wondering why I'd let Leif talk me into going out tonight. I needed to rest my body in preparation for next month's competition. But I laughed at myself, looking down at the glowing cancer stick in my hand. A night of drinking, partying, and rough sex was nothing compared to the damage I was doing to my lungs with this cigarette. My sponsor had specifically forbid me from smoking but I was still a few days away from officially signing with them. *What they don't know won't hurt them.* I took another long drag off the no filtered Camel. I figured if I was going to scar my lungs, I might as well choose the most deadly of brands. *Maybe Camel will sponsor me one day and I won't have to hide my addiction.* The thought made me laugh out loud.

Suddenly, the club door swung open with a bang and two girls came stumbling out. One girl had her arm wrapped under the other's, obviously trying to balance her. It was clear her friend was pissing drunk and I couldn't help but smile. I liked when girls were drunk, they lost their inhibitions and it was easier to get them to do all kinds of kinky shit. But this girl was beyond drunk, she was damn near comatose.

"You okay now, hun," I heard the smaller girl ask.

I was surprised she could even hold up the drunk one, she was so much smaller. I looked Drunk Girl up and down. She was dressed completely inappropriate for club life, her outfit reeking of Pilates or some other kind of bullshit work out that snotty, rich, bored, white girls did. And she obviously didn't know how to handle her liquor. Both observations had me thoroughly disgusted with her and I had no idea why. Why did I even give two shits about this girl? I flicked my cigarette into the street and pushed off the wall, about to make my way back inside.

"I've got her!" I heard a man shout behind me.

I looked back over my shoulder and saw a tall, lanky dude wrapping his arms around Drunk Girl like she was a gold medal at the X Games. I couldn't make out any more of their conversation but her body language said it all. Drunk Girl was definitely not okay with this guy. *A good friend should know that.* Then it dawned on me. The woman helping Drunk Girl wasn't her friend at all. The hair on my neck stood up as I realized Drunk Girl may be in trouble. I decided to hang out a while longer and smoke another cigarette, just in case. *Who gives a flyin' flip about these girls man? She's too drunk to offer you any fun at all.*

My eyes rolled over Drunk Girl again. I knew I had to stay. If anything happened to her, I'd never forgive myself. I mean I didn't *really* hate her, but there was absolutely nothing special about her, at least from my point of view. But Frat Boy sure was into her and I found myself getting territorial, almost jealous of the way he was touching her. *You're a complete moron, man.*

The small girl examined Frat Boy from head to toe, not quite convinced Drunk Girl would be alright but decided to leave her in his care anyway. As her petite frame breezed by me, she nodded her head toward the couple.

"I gotta get back inside before my boyfriend starts freakin' out. Keep an eye on him, will ya? I don't trust him." Before I could ask any questions, like why I should care or if she even knew Drunk Girl, she disappeared back inside the club.

Well, shit! Now I was stuck. The little wench had involved me in a situation I had no desire to be a part of. If this scene went to hell, I would be responsible. Why hadn't I just stayed inside with all the other guys? It seemed that tonight, cigarette smoking had become more hazardous to my health than I realized.

I approached the girl and stuffed my hands in my pocket as a sign to Frat Boy that I didn't want any trouble. "You two know each other?" I asked.

He pulled Drunk Girl closer to him, his hands running up and down her body. My temper began to flame and I had no justifiable reason why. *Pull yourself together, for God's sake. You don't even know this chick.*

He cocked his head to one side and narrowed his eyes. "What's it to you?"

I raised my eyebrows in disbelief at this asshole's comeback. He could tell by my expression he'd already started to piss me off. I wasn't huge or anything but I knew I could kick this douche bag's ass from here to New York City.

"It's not really." I answered truthfully.

"Then why you askin'?"

"Is she your girlfriend? Looks like she's pretty smashed."

His face lit up like this girl was the best present he'd ever received. "I know, right."

My guard went on high alert. This dick face was seriously going to take Drunk Girl home and fuck her ninety ways to Sunday. *Don't get involved man, you don't even know her.*

"What's her name?" I asked him.

"Fuck if I know. Drunk-as-a-Skunk is what I'm callin' her tonight."

Suddenly, Drunk Girl came to life. "What the hell did you just call me?" she screamed, pushing him away from her body with such force that even I was amazed the douche bag didn't fall on his ass. Obviously Drunk Girl's Pilates class was paying off. She had skills.

A cab slowly pulled up to the curb as the driver stepped out. "Somebody call a cab?" he asked.

"I'm sorry, sweetheart," Frat Boy said to Drunk Girl, trying to appease her and get back in her good graces, or into her panties. "Why don't we just get in the cab and I'll take you home." Drunk Girl rolled her eyes and I saw her face turn ashen as she lunged her body forward and puked all over the sidewalk, vomit splattering on all of us.

"Shit!" Frat Boy screamed. "You got vomit all over my new loafers, you stupid bitch!"

I was about to light Frat Boy's ass on fire when I looked down and saw Drunk Girl had fallen down onto the sidewalk on all fours, dry heaving. The scene was disgusting and heart breaking all at the same time and I couldn't help but feel sorry for her. *Don't do it man. Don't get involved. Just walk away now.*

I heard the door clank shut again and looked up to find Frat Boy was gone. Here I was now *all* alone with this vomiting, pathetic creature. *Fuck! I'm never smoking again!*

"Do you live around here?" She shook her head. "Did you drive here?" She shook her head again. "Are your friends inside? Maybe we could go back and get them."

"I don't have any friends inside."

"You came to a club all alone? What's wrong with you? Why would you do that?"

"Spare me a lecture, asshole. I'm sick as a dog here, as if you can't tell. I just wanna go home."

I took in a deep breath, wondering what to do. I just wanted to walk away but suddenly, I was scared for Drunk Girl. *What's wrong with you, man? She's just another drunk chick. Put her in the cab and send her packin'.* But what if another douche bag approached her and took her home? I couldn't take the chance.

"Get up," I said, pulling her to a standing position as I opened the back door to the cab. "Get in." I hadn't been forceful up until this point but she started fighting against me trying to pull away so I pushed her body inside careful to duck her head down. The last thing she needed to be doing was roaming around the streets of downtown alone and drunk.

"But wait, I don't have any money!" she begged from inside the cab.

"Scoot over, I'll pay. You can thank me later." I pushed her all the way over to the other side of the cab as I pulled my long legs inside the cramped space.

"Where to?" the driver asked.

I turned to Drunk Girl. "So where do you live?" She looked at me with crocodile tears in her eyes.

"Why? So you can take me home and screw me like Gap Boy?"

"What the fuck are you talking about?"

Before she could answer me, her eyes slammed shut and I saw one lone tear roll down her cheek as she fell into my lap, passed out cold. *Oh, great, what the hell kind of messed up shit have you gotten yourself into now, Rory Gregor?*

~

"What's the address, son?" I looked up from Drunk Girl's comatose face and saw the driver, his body completely turned around, staring at me.

"Um, give me just a minute."

"One minute and I start the meter."

I shook the girl as hard as I could but it was obvious she was out for the count. "Shit!"

"Does she have a phone?"

"What?"

"Maybe you can find her address on her phone."

I felt around her shoulder and didn't find a strap or a purse.

"Sometimes chicks stuff them in their bra." I raised my head and saw a small smile on the driver's face. "No, seriously, chicks do that all the time," he continued. "That's where my girlfriend stashes hers when she doesn't have pockets."

"I'll look for pockets first, thanks." I pushed her off my lap and looked down at her pants. *Shit! Exercise pants.* "She has on stretch pants."

"Look on the inside of her waistband. Sometimes they put a secret pocket inside for them to stash shit."

"How do you know all this?"

"I've got a girlfriend, a mom, and six sisters. I know everything about women, dude."

Judging by his pudgy belly, crooked teeth, and over grown man bushes he called eyebrows, I was pretty sure he didn't know *everything* about women. But, I had to trust him on this one. I slowly rubbed my palm around her waistband, hoping to find something that identified this mystery woman. As my hand moved around her back, my fingers grazed her bare skin. I felt a slight tingle and immediately pulled away when I noticed my body respond inappropriately. *Cool your jets, tiger, she's three sheets to the wind. You don't need a rape charge added to your rap sheet.* I cursed myself for being a pig but realized I had to trudge on, no matter how weak my body was. Just as I was about to give up hope, my fingers ran over a bump in her waistband. Slowly, I slid my thumb and forefinger inside, careful not to touch anything I didn't have to.

"I found her phone," I cried in victory, holding it up in the air. "Now what?"

"What cell service does she use?"

"How the hell should I know?"

"Go into her settings and find out who her network provider is."

"I have no idea what you're talking about."

"Here, give me the damn thing." I watched as he frantically pushed buttons and within a matter of minutes, he produced her address.

"How the hell did you do that?"

"Sisters," he laughed, handing me the phone back.

"I don't even want to know, do I?"

He put the car in drive shaking his head as he looked back over his shoulder to check traffic. "Nope, probably not." Without another word, the cab pulled out into the night.

After a short drive, he pulled up to a small house. "This is it. Now what? How ya gonna get in, Ace?"

Oh shit, I hadn't thought this one through. *She's probably dumb enough to put a key under the mat. Check there.*

"Hey," I said shaking her shoulders trying to jar her.

"Hummm."

Thank god, she was responding. "We're at your house. Where's your key?"

"What key?" she mumbled.

"The key to your house."

"Where's my car?"

"I have no idea. We need to get you inside right now. You can worry about your car later."

Suddenly, she sat straight up like she'd been hit by lightning, darting her eyes from me to the driver then back to me. Maybe I wouldn't have to carry her in after all.

"It's not locked," she said flatly, then just as quickly as she'd recovered, she closed her eyes and fell back into my lap, knocked out cold again.

"What the fuck was that?" I asked to no one in particular. The driver shrugged his shoulders, obviously hearing my question. "What? Your sisters never got drunk?"

"We're Catholic, we stay drunk twenty-four seven. Why don't you try the door? Maybe she's right, maybe she didn't lock it."

"No way. What woman doesn't lock her door?"

"Maybe she's dumber than she looks."

I looked down at her face lying in my lap. On further inspection, I could see she possessed a natural beauty I hadn't noticed before. She had full red lips and a button nose that fit her face perfectly. She was void of any tacky make-up, despite being at a club tonight. I couldn't remember what her eyes looked like but I knew this girl was anything but dumb.

"Keep an eye on her, I'll be right back."

"Meter's still runnin', guy."

I shut the door and half walked, half ran to the front door. Shit! There were two. This was a duplex. How the hell was I supposed to know which one was hers? I noticed the lights were on in the windows to the right so I decided to approach that side first. I walked up to the door with caution, knowing that in Texas, people shoot first and ask questions later. I looked at my watch. It was a quarter til midnight, way too late for someone to be coming to your door for a visit. I turned back at the cab behind me and realized I had no choice. I had to knock. My knuckles made contact with the aluminum door and I heard the soft banging ring through the silent night. Without a moment's hesitation, the door swung open. *What is wrong with people? Didn't they lock their doors or check their peepholes?* Texans were way too trusting.

A small, red-headed woman, probably in her mid-twenties like me, answered the door. I saw a large muscle-head man sitting on the couch behind her, glaring at me as he nursed a beer. I was surprised he'd let the girl answer the door. Obviously, he was a lazy asshole, putting his girlfriend in this type of vulnerable situation. I could be anyone, a serial rapist for all he knew.

She put her hand on the edge of the door and cocked her head to the side. "Yes?"

"Umm, I'm sorry to bother you so late."

She looked me up and down, her eyes examining every nook and cranny of my body. "Oh, no bother sweetheart." Her words were steeped with sexual innuendo and I tried to keep my eyes focused on her face and not on the revealing halter top that exposed her massive, fake boobs. The last thing I needed was a fight with Mr. Ultimate Fighting Champion on the couch.

"I was just wondering if you knew the person who lives next door."

"Who? Hindley?"

"I'm not sure."

"What's going on?" She stepped out onto the porch and looked up and down the street. "Look, we paid our balance off and we've been on time for the last three months. I don't want no trouble."

"What?"

"You're not here collecting?"

"Collecting what? No. I found this woman drunk and passed out outside a club downtown and I'm trying to bring her home. Her phone says this is her address."

"She in the cab?" Red nodded toward the car waiting at the curb.

"Yes."

"I can guarantee you, if the little chicky in that cab is drunk and passed out, then it sure ain't Hindley."

"Would you mind coming to take a look for me? I just want to get her home safely."

"Well, aren't you Prince Charming." She began shamelessly staring me up and down again, giving herself permission to eat me alive. I felt my body go red with embarrassment, a new emotion for me. On any other night, I might have given her a chance to get into my boxers, but tonight, I was worried about Drunk Girl and needed to make sure she got home safely.

"Would you mind looking at her?"

"Why not." She turned back to gorilla man. "Back in a minute, hun." She walked along side me as we made our way toward the cab, popping the bubble gum in her mouth the entire way. The sound irritated the shit out of me and whatever male animal lust I had felt for her earlier completely evaporated. I opened the back door to the cab and tried to raise Drunk Girl up so Red could get a good look at her.

"Holy shit! That *is* Hindley!" She shouted. "I can't believe it! That chick never gets hammered. Where did you say you found her?"

"At a club downtown."

"She was out clubbin'? Who knew Hindley had it in her."

"She doesn't normally act like this?"

"Hell no! She's the most straight-laced, uptight chick I know. I wonder what happened to make her tie one on like this?"

I remembered Drunk Girl's words outside the club earlier. 'I don't have any friends inside.' I wondered if she had any friends at all. "Do you have a spare key to her place?"

"Hindley never locks her door."

"Why?"

"Beats the hell outta me. She says people may need something inside her house and she doesn't want to be the one to stop them."

"That's the dumbest thing I've ever heard."

"I know, right? She locks it when she's home though."

"Well, that's good." *What the fuck, Gregor? Why do you care if this chick keeps herself safe and secure or not?*

I reached in and took Drunk Girl's arm and wrapped it around my shoulder, trying to shake away the thoughts in my head. As I pulled her out of the cab, I noticed her shirt had ridden up and was hovering just under her breasts. I reached over to pull it down but as I did, my fingers grazed over her bare abdomen and I felt a pain in my pants. *Quit being a dick, Rory. And quit thinking with it, too. This chick is drunk. Forget about it. Dump her ass and get back to the club. The guys are waiting on you.*

I swept her body over my shoulder and was surprised at how long she was. Her legs went on for miles and she had an ass that wouldn't quit. Maybe there was something to Pilate's classes after all.

"Will you get the door for me?"

"Sure." Red turned the knob and shock ran through me as I realized Drunk Girl really did keep her door unlocked. *She is dumber than she looks.*

I walked inside the small living room and plopped her down on the first piece of furniture I could find, an oversized chair.

"Will you keep an eye on her for just a minute while I go pay the cab?"

"Just for a second. Robby doesn't really like me hanging out with Hindley, says she fills my head with too many dumb ideas."

"Who's Hindley?"

She threw her thumb over her shoulder and motioned toward Drunk Girl. "You really don't know her?"

"Nope."

"That's funny."

"Why?"

"If you knew Hindley, you'd know why."

I walked out of the duplex, pulling money out of my wallet, trying to figure out what Red's comment meant. Obviously Drunk Girl's behavior tonight was very out of character for her. I wondered what had made her go to such extremes. *Who cares? Get back in the cab, go back to the club, and find someone willing AND able. Red can take care of her now.* In my gut, I knew I was lying to myself and my stomach started churning as I realized the thought actually worried me. *Why the fuck is this girl suddenly on my 'Give a Shit List?'* Skateboarding, drinking, and chasing tail were the only three things important to me for most of my life. But now, in walks this tall, drunk drink of water and suddenly, I'm adding 'Caring for Drunk Girl' to my list. *Asshole!*

I reached the cab and handed the driver a hundred dollar bill. "Thanks for all your help, man."

His sobering face curled into a soft smile as he realized the denomination of the bill. "Anytime, my friend! Anytime! Good luck with her."

"I think I'll need it."

"You're doing the right thing. If this happened to one of my sisters, I would be happy as a hell that a man like you found her." He leaned over the passenger seat and rummaged through the glove box then turned back around and handed me a piece of paper through the window. "Hey, here's my card. When you're ready to go home tomorrow, give me a call. I'll drop you off anywhere you want. No charge."

"Tomorrow? What makes you think I'm spending the night?"

"You're not quite the bad ass you think you are, Ace. I know a good guy when I see one."

"I may not be a total bad ass but I'm definitely not a good guy either."

"We'll see. Call me tomorrow when you're ready to go home."

I walked back toward the house staring at Raul's business card, completely affected by his words. *Fuck him, man. You are a bad ass. Dump this chick and prove it.*

When I walked back in the duplex, Red had a lamp on and was pulling Drunk Girl's hair down and wiping her face with a wet rag. From this angle, I could tell that in any normal circumstance, she really was beautiful. *Dude, who are you kidding? Look at her, blonde hair spilling over those perfect tits. Man, she's hot, even plastered. Maybe we should stay after all.*

"I think she's out cold. She looks awful. You stayin'?" Red asked, looking up at me.

Was I? I hadn't planned on this at all. Suddenly, my phone rang.

"Hey listen, I gotta go," she said stepping over Drunk Girl's long legs as she darted around me and out the door.

"Wait! What did you say her name was?"

"Hindley. H-I-N-D-L-E-Y" she spelled out. "Hindley Hagen." I furrowed my brow in confusion. "I know, right," she said, trying to answer a question I hadn't asked. "Apparently it's a character from a famous book. I don't really read much."

"Me neither."

"Knock if ya need anything. Night, Lover Boy!" I watched as she blew me a kiss and waved each individual finger in succession before quietly closing the front door.

I turned my attention back to my phone and saw the missed call was from Leif. I knew he'd be worried but I had no idea what to tell him. He would call me a pussy for sure if he knew I pulled a chivalrous act and brought a girl home without bangin' her. I couldn't jeopardize my reputation as a ladies man. But now, as I sat here gazing at this comatose damsel in distress, I couldn't imagine letting anyone think I'd taken advantage of her. Especially if her drunken stupor was truly out of character for her.

What the fuck are you saying, man? Have you lost your ball sack? Call the cab man and tell him to bring you back to the club. This chick is home safe now, no one's going to attack her, least of all you. You've done your duty so let's go!

I looked down at my phone and debated whether to call him back or not. If I was a normal person, I would just text him and save myself the embarrassment. But who was I kidding, I was anything *but* normal. I pushed the 'Call Back' button and waited anxiously, trying to figure out what I was going to say.

"Dude, where the fuck are you? This place is crawlin' with hotties."

I decided I had no choice. I had to sacrifice Drunk Girl. My reputation was on the line. "I'm with a chick, man." *Well, that's not a lie, technically.* "This better be good. You're interrupting me."

"I don't know how you do it, man. Girls will do just about anything for you."

"What can I say? Chicks dig pro athletes." He began laughing hysterically and I hit the 'End' button. *Asshole.*

I looked at Drunk Girl. *Her name's Hindley, remember, genius?* Her body was slumped over the side of the chair and I knew if she stayed that way all night, she wouldn't be able to walk for a week. I scooped her up in my arms, surprised at how heavy dead weight really was. If I didn't find her bed soon, I was going to drop her right in the middle of the hall. Thankfully, the first room I came to had a bed and I let her fall onto the white blanket, watching her unconscious body collapse in a messy heap of limbs and hair. I surveyed the damage and realized her tennis shoes and pants were spattered with vomit. As much as I didn't want to do it, I knew I'd have to undress her.

I untied her shoes and pulled them off her feet, along with her socks. I noticed her toenails were painted a bright blue color and for whatever reason, her polish selection shocked me. From what Red told me earlier, Hindley seemed like an uptight girl. Blue toenail polish was not an option for neurotic, self-controlled women. Hindley had a playful side. For the first time tonight, a genuine smile spread across my face as I thought of the possibilities. *There may be hope for you yet, Drunk Girl.*

Chapter 3

I couldn't tell if the pounding in my head was real or a dream. The throbbing was nauseating and I felt like I was on the Merry-Go-Round from Hell. I tried to swallow but apparently, sometime during the night, someone had dumped an entire container of Elmer's glue inside my mouth, making it almost impossible to swallow, let alone speak. The stench of cigarette smoke filled all my senses and I could feel my throat constricting. I tried desperately to open my eyes but they were swollen shut and I knew I probably looked like I'd gone ten rounds with Muhammad Ali. There was no way this could be real. I had to be in the middle of a dream, maybe even a nightmare.

What the hell happened last night? Come on Hindley, think!

Suddenly, images flashed through my mind, pole dancing, Tequila shots, Gap Boy, and vomiting, lots of vomiting. Oh shit! All the sudden, my door flew open with a bang as the doorknob hit the wall.

"What the fuck is going on in here?" Dana screamed. Each syllable she uttered felt like daggers piercing my head. "Holy hell! You finally got laid!"

Dana Di Grazio was my best friend and I could always count on her to be as blunt as a sailor, with a mouth like one, too. But for better or for worse, she'd stuck by me through some of the most traumatic times of my life, even when others walked away.

The best thing about Dana was she never judged me. No matter what I did, who I dated, or where I lived, she just let me be me, knowing eventually I would right myself if I took a misstep. I loved her for that.

Dana and I met in second grade when Ms. Alferia paired us together for badminton during gym glass. Despite countless moves, different colleges, feuding boyfriends and more, we'd still managed to stay best friends through all these years. She was my one true confidant in life. I shared everything with her and I knew I could trust her with my life. If I was being a turd, she'd call me on it. If someone was taking advantage of me, she'd stand up for me, something I had a hard time doing myself. And if I needed a shoulder to cry on, she'd come, no questions asked.

One time in college, when Chris Putman broke my heart by dumping me at his fraternity's Valentine's Day dance in front of half the student body, Dana left her college two hundred miles away and drove four hours one way just to bring me ice cream and hold me as I cried my eyes out. She understood that my tears were more from humiliation than lost love.

We were polar opposites in every way. Where I was tall, lean, and quiet she was short, curvy, and boisterous. I was a fair skinned German with long blonde hair and generic brown eyes. She was a dark skinned, saucy, Italian dynamo with curly jet black hair and arctic blue eyes that could stop traffic. She was the Yin to my Yang. We were a natural fit. Always had been, always would be.

I stretched my arms above my head, feeling every muscle in my body scream in agony. "What the hell are you talking about Dana?"

"That hottie next to you!" I stared at her in disbelief . "Look!" She said pointing to the other side of my bed. *Oh shit!*

I turned my head to see what Dana was pointing at and gasped in horror when I saw a man's face less than a foot away from mine. I shot straight up in bed, pulling the covers up to hide my body as I tried to push as far away from him as I could. My bed was only a full size so I didn't get very far.

"Holy hell!" Dana laughed. "You finally screwed some random dude from a bar."

"I did not!"

She approached the bed as if she were going to rip the covers off. "Do y'all have any clothes on under there?"

"Dana, stop!" I shouted as I held the blanket tighter. I slowly lifted the covers and peered underneath, afraid of what I might find. I blew out a loud sigh as I saw I still had my tank top on from last night. And my bra! *Oh, thank God!*

Obviously not pacified by my examination, Dana grabbed the blanket from the bottom of my bed and gave it one quick yank, pulling it from my grasp, completely exposing me and the mystery man next to me. I was mortified to find I had no pants on, but at least I was still wearing underwear, not very sexy ones though. I was too scared to look over at the man lying next to me. Instead, I looked up at Dana to gauge her reaction to see if it was true. Had I been a complete slut last night?

Her lips turned up into a seductive smile, revealing two massive dimples on either side of her face. Her eyes were glowing and I could tell whoever was lying next to me had to be pretty good looking. Even though I was somewhat relieved, I still couldn't find the nerve to turn around and really check him out good.

"Damn girl! You held out for a fine one, didn't you! I'm completely jealous, you slut."

"Dana, please give me the blanket."

"Uhnt uh," she said shaking her head. "I wanna look at this hottie all day."

I couldn't take it anymore. I had to see this mystery man who'd shared my bed all night. With great apprehension, I finally turned my head to inspect my one-night-stand. I did a quick sweeping survey from head to toe and was happy to find he was at least wearing underwear. Maybe we hadn't had sex after all. Or maybe we had and he just didn't like to sleep in the nude.

His body looked like a bronze god and stood in stark contrast to my pasty, pale, white legs. His face looked like an angel as he slept. It was perfectly sculptured with a strong jaw that I sensed probably got him in more trouble than I wanted to know about. His hair was dark brown with streaks of golden blonde that you could tell came from being in the sun. He must work outdoors.

He was lying on his stomach, holding on to one of my throw pillows like it was a life preserver. I found the entire scene adorable. He looked like a lost little boy and my heart skipped a beat, feeling like he needed to be rescued. Suddenly, I felt like I wanted to be the girl who did. *Where did that thought come from? You don't even know who this guy is.*

His well-defined biceps were flexed around the pillow and his back was rippling with muscles I didn't even know existed. Dana was right, this guy was super hot. No matter what I did or didn't do with him last night, I could rest assured that I'd at least picked a cute man to spend the night with me.

I'd never had a one-night-stand before so I didn't know whether I should be ashamed or impressed. It wasn't like I was a virgin or anything but according to Dana, I hadn't had as many conquests as someone of my youthful twenty-five years should have by now. I couldn't help it, I just wasn't into cheap, meaningless sex. When I was intimate with a man, I wanted to at least know his name. *Do you even have the slightest clue what this guy's name is?*

I let my eyes take in the rest of my one-night-stand man. His boxer briefs showed off the perfect form of his butt and his long, lean muscular legs stretched out all the way down past the end of my mattress. I smiled, realizing he must be a very tall man. Just as I was about to finish my perusal, he stirred and I backed up, paralyzed. He raised his arms over his head to stretch as his entire body began to roll over. *Holy crap, I hope he doesn't have a hard on! Or, maybe we do.*

He completed his turn, which was quite a feat in my tiny bed, and was now entirely on his back. I tried to push myself even further away but it was no use. I knew I should jump out of the bed and get as far away from his as possible but for some inexplicable reason, I didn't want to move. I needed to be near him. His mouth opened up in a huge yawn and I saw perfectly straight, white teeth. He was obviously still asleep so I let my eyes rove further down his body. His chest was broad and muscular like most women fantasize about. But what really took my breath away was the massive tattoo taking up half his abdomen.

"Holy shit, he looks even better on his back," Dana laughed. "And look at that massive ink on his stomach. That's awesome!" Dana and I both leaned over his torso to look at the artwork that covered his entire right side and wrapped around to his back and down his hip, disappearing into his underwear. It was a picture of a man skateboarding in some kind of park. The skater was in mid-air, skateboard glued to his feet with the bottom of the skateboard completely visible. The skateboard ran diagonally across his ribs and the words 'SK8R BOY' were tattooed on the bottom of it. I normally wasn't a big fan of tattoos, but I had to admit, this was true artistry. Even though I knew absolutely nothing about him, I could tell the tattoo fit him perfectly. Skater Boy.

Dana reached out her finger almost touching Skater Boy as she traced the tattoo just above his body. "That ink is bad ass." *She ought to know.* Dana had several tattoos littered all over her body. Most weren't visible unless she was fully undressed but that never stopped her from showing them off. "And look at his chest. You could serve a five-course meal on those rock hard abs." She flattened her hand, about to start rubbing his bare chest, when I reached over and swatted her.

"Stop it!"

"Stop what?" I heard a deep voice grumble. I diverted my gaze from his muscular chest up to his eyes. They were a mesmerizing mix of copper and blue I'd never seen before. A slow tingle ran up and down my spine as I watched him pull his arms up over his head then interlock his fingers and rest them comfortably behind him. His pose showed off every rippling muscle in his upper body and I beat myself up for not remembering being intimate with him last night. "Good morning Drunk Girl. Enjoying the view?" His words were sweet and seductive and I wanted to hear him talk more, but I was mortified he'd caught me checking out his body.

"Very much," Dana answered with no hesitation.

"Dana!" Suddenly, I became hyper aware of my own nakedness, embarrassed that I had on white cotton Granny panties. Why couldn't I be wearing something sexy? *You don't have anything sexy, you moron!* I bolted straight up out of bed, grabbing the blanket from Dana's hand and wrapping it around my body. The smell of cigarettes suddenly invaded my entire respiratory system. I pulled the blanket up to me and felt even more nauseous as my head began to spin.

"Did you smoke in here?" I was highly allergic to cigarette smoke and the thought that he may have lit up in my house really pissed me off. But my pounding headache made it difficult for me to scream.

He pushed up to a sitting position, propping himself up with one arm, obviously comfortable in his own skin and in my bed. He looked like a centerfold in a slutty magazine and I couldn't take my eyes off of him. *You want him, just admit it.*

Dana's voice broke the silence. "Damn dude, you're fine." I looked over and saw she was actually having sex with this guy in her mind. A jealous rage ran through my body and I couldn't understand why. *You like this guy. A lot. But look at him. He's too confident, too poised, being in a bedroom with two women. He's a player. Let him go.* I shook my head, trying to clear my thoughts but the movement made me nauseous.

Skater Boy was completely unaware of Dana's assault on his body. Instead, he continued to look me up and down with a sideways grin that had me feeling like a giddy school girl. I wondered if I affected him the way he did me. I could kick myself for not remembering my night with him.

"Did we, um," I pointed my finger from my chest to him and back to me again, trying to insinuate sexual contact.

"What? You don't remember the best night of your life? Well, that's what you said it was for you. Honestly, it was for me, too." He looked directly at me and winked as his mouth turned into a sideways smirk. In any other situation, it would have been adorable.

I felt my eyes grow ten times bigger and my face glow with red. Oh my God, we had done the dirty deed. And I didn't even remember it. *Dammit! You're such an idiot!*

"You screamed out my name over and over again, begging me for more."

"Well, alright!" Dana hooped and hollered from the door way.

I could feel tears begin to sting my eyes and I needed to escape.

"Hey, hey, wait, don't get upset," he said, reaching out toward me. "I'm just kidding. We didn't do anything, I swear. You were drunk as a skunk and passed out the entire night. I brought you home and put you to bed. I tried to sleep on that shitty couch of yours in there but it killed my back and I can't afford any injuries right now so I decided to sleep in your bed. On top of the covers!" My eyes slowly returned to their normal size but I could still feel the heat on my face from embarrassment. "But apparently, somewhere during the night, you allowed me under the blanket. That was you're fault." His smile returned and I was surprised to feel one growing on me as well. "That's it, that's all that happened. I swear." He held his hand in the air as if he were about to testify in front of the Supreme Court.

I could tell by his face he was telling the truth. He was trying to make me feel better and it was working. But I was still furious with myself for getting so drunk last night that I didn't even remember a complete stranger bringing me home.

"Well, shit!" Dana interjected.

"What?"

"You're not the slut I thought you were born to be. So much for random sex. But, there's always tonight, right?" Her rueful smile made me laugh.

"Oh crap! Tonight! What time is it?" I began to panic, remembering Geneva's demand last night. 'Don't be late.'

"It's ten-forty," Dana answered. "Why?"

"Shit! I have Geneva's bridal luncheon in twenty minutes. She's gonna kill me."

"Who gives a shit about that bitch?"

"Lord knows I don't. But I promised Paul I'd keep an eye on her last night. I can't even remember what I did last night, let alone Geneva."

"Who's Paul?" Skater Boy asked. I noticed he sounded a little jealous and I liked it. *Controlling, possessive men are a recipe for disaster. Remember that.*

"Paul's her dad," Dana answered.

"Step dad," I corrected. Dana flashed me a sideways grimace. "He's my step dad but to me, he's like my own father." I don't know why I felt the need to clarify to Skater Boy but for some reason, I did. I began digging through my closet, looking for anything presentable to wear. I looked over my shoulder. "You coming?"

"Who me?" Skater Boy asked. His entire face scrunched up in confusion. He looked absolutely adorable.

"Not you," I laughed. "Dana, are you coming?"

"To a boring ass bridal buffet with some of the snootiest women in town? Hell no!"

"I've gotta go." I picked up my pants from last night, looking for my keys, but couldn't find them anywhere. "Oh crap! Where's my car? I didn't drive last night, did I?"

Skater Boy was pulling his jeans on and I felt a pang of disappointment hit my heart. *Get a grip girl. You don't even know this guy. He's got a huge tattoo of all things, a skateboard. He's bound to be trouble. Leave. Him. Alone!*

"No, we took a cab."

Suddenly, memories of last night began to fill my mind. "Crap, my car's at the pole dancing place," I said under my breath.

"The what?" Skater Boy asked pulling his shirt over his head. It was unbelievable to me how putting on a shirt could be so sexy. Usually, it was taking it off that made a girl's heart stop. Watching him get dressed was more of a turn on than anything I'd seen in a long time. *Obviously, you're still drunk.*

"She went to a pole dancing class last night." Dana answered before I could explain.

"You take pole dancing classes?" He pulled on his boots and started tying them, looking up at me with his blue eyes as he finished. "That's kinda hot, Drunk Girl. Actually, it's way hot."

"Oh you should see her."

"Shut up Dana."

"She doesn't need any lessons though. Hell, she ..."

"Dana!" I screamed. "Enough!" Two sets of eyes locked on mine but I didn't care. I was seething, I could taste the anger in my mouth, my chest almost hyperventilating with anger. I couldn't believe her. "I need to go." I looked over at Dana. "Can you give me a ride?"

"Sure. What about you, Tat? You need a ride?"

"If you're going my way, that would be great."

"Oh, I'll for sure go your way," Dana said with a playful tone.

Skater Boy stood and laughed at her as he smoothed over his clothes. "I think one missed opportunity last night is more than my delicate ego can handle right now." He wasn't exactly covert in his feelings. Obviously, he'd wanted more to happen between us last night. *Or did he?* Well, one thing was for sure, he wasn't completely repulsed by me and the realization made me happy, deep in my core.

"Give me five minutes, Dana, I'll be right back."

"I'll go put some coffee on." She left the room and suddenly, the silence between Skater Boy and I was awkward.

"Hey, I'm sorry about last night," I said pulling a skirt over my bare legs. I could feel his eyes on me but oddly enough, I didn't mind. I pulled a silk sleeveless shirt off the hanger and held it up, about to take off my tank top but now I felt self-conscious. I looked up at him and he understood my silent request.

"You're funny," he laughed as he turned his back on me.

I quickly tore off my tank top and wiggled my way into the blouse, tucking it into the skirt. "Why?" I walked over to my nightstand and picked up a brush and commenced trying to tame the mane on my head that I was sure looked hideous.

"We sleep together all night in our underwear and now you want me to turn my back so I don't see you change clothes."

"Well technically, we didn't really see each other in our underwear."

"Oh, I saw you." He turned around and his amazing eyes locked with mine. He was completely serious and suddenly, the ball of glue that had been in my mouth was now stuck in my throat, making it difficult to breath.

I turned my back on him so he couldn't see my face turn scarlet but I knew it was too late. "Yeah, about that."

"What?"

Before I knew it, he was directly behind me and I could feel his breath on my neck. His fingertips grazed the bare skin on my neck and a shock ran through my entire body. *What the hell was that? Oh God, does he want sex* now? *Please tell me this isn't happening.*

I turned around and swatted at his hand. "What the hell are you doing?"

"Your tag," he said reaching around my neck to the back of my shirt. "It was hanging out."

"You could have just told me." My voice was laced with disgust. When I finally had enough nerve to look into his eyes again, I could see I'd hurt him. *Way to go, dipshit. He brings you home, takes care of you, doesn't try to screw you, and now you're actually screaming at him. No wonder he didn't have sex with you.*

I reached out and took his hand. "I'm sorry," I said, squeezing his fingers, surprised when I felt him squeeze back. It felt so natural to be here with him, hand in hand. For a moment, we were lost in each other's gaze, his beautiful brown-blue eyes locked on mine. *There's no way this guy can be good for you, he's too hot.*

"So what, now you two are gonna finally consummate this dysfunctional relationship?" Dana's voice interrupted our moment and we dropped our hands and took a step back trying to increase the distance between us. "Come on, shake a leg ho! We have ten minutes to get you to Bitchville, USA." She left the room again and I stared straight ahead, afraid to meet his gaze.

Sensing my anxiety, Skater Boy headed toward my bedroom door but I didn't want him to leave, not yet. I had an overwhelming need to touch him so I reached out and caught him by the arm. His muscles were defined and hard and I held on longer than I should have. His eyes looked down at my hand then back up to me.

"Hey, I just wanted to say thanks for last night. I really appreciate you taking care of me." I could see him working hard, trying to figure out if I was telling the truth or not. I'd been right about his height. He was tall, over six feet, but my five foot eight stature seemed to match his perfectly.

"Why do I feel like that might have been one of the hardest things you've ever had to do?" I raised my eyebrows in disbelief, shocked at how well he already knew me. I prided myself on not needing anything from anyone so words of gratitude from me were few and far between.

"Probably because it was." I pushed past him and through the door on my way to the bathroom, feeling every bit as vulnerable now that I was fully dressed as I did lying next to him in nothing but my underwear. But somewhere deep inside, I wished I was back there, in bed with him, relishing how beautiful he was.

~

"Everybody in?" Dana shouted as she slammed the door of her fire engine red Beemer convertible.

"Nice car," Skater Boy said as he tried to fold his long lean legs into the back.

"Thanks. It was a gift from my parents." Dana winked at me as I rolled my eyes and shook my head. She was so bad.

Dana lurched her small neck around to look at Skater Boy. "Got enough room back there, One-Nighter?"

"Here, I can switch with you," I said, reaching for the door handle.

"No, forget it. I'm fine. What did you just call me?"

"Oh, uh, sorry. I still don't know you're name so I called you One-Nighter. You know, my girl's first one-night-stand."

"Dana!" I shouted, hitting her square in the arm with my fist.

I heard him laugh under his breath. "Well, I guess because we didn't actually have sex last night, you can call me Rory instead."

"Ah man, no sex." Dana pouted.

"Nope, not even a feel."

"Dammit!"

"Call me old fashioned but I prefer my one-night-stands alive and alert so we can both enjoy the evening." My mouth dropped open in shock as I turned around to see him staring at me with a smirk. I noted he was especially cute when he was mischievous. *Watch it, girlie. You don't have time for Mr. Player of the Year."*

Dana glanced in her rearview mirror as she pulled out onto the street. "I like you Rory. And your real name is much sexier than One-Nighter." I turned back to face the road, letting his name roll through my head. Rory.

"Hey Rory?" Dana asked.

"Yes?"

"I'm alive and alert and I can promise to stay that way until tonight."

He laughed so loud and so hard, I choked on the water I was drinking. He had the best laugh.

"Is she always this bad?" Rory asked with amusement.

I tried to wipe my mouth with my shoulder as I looked back at him. "Worse. Much worse."

"Wow!"

"You try being best friends with her."

"You know you love me, Drunk Girl." Dana hit me with her elbow.

"I do. Lord only knows why, but I do."

We drove the rest of the short distance to the restaurant in comfortable silence. I had to mentally prepare myself for the mess I was about to enter in to. Geneva and fifty of her closest friends were gathering for a bridal luncheon. Like she wasn't spending enough money on this mammoth wedding, my mom had insisted Geneva have a pre-wedding party, too, a luncheon for "Just the girls," as she put it to Paul. The problem was, I didn't know three-fourths of these girls and the quarter who I did know I couldn't stand.

"Hey Skater Boy, whatcha doin' tonight?" Dana asked.

"Are you asking me to be you're one-nighter?"

"You wish! Nah, I was gonna tell you that you should come to this shin-dig tonight, as Hindley's date." I stared at Dana, trying desperately to chuck daggers at her with me telepathic powers but nothing happened and she kept her gaze on the road, afraid to look at me.

"You mean Drunk Girl?"

"Why do you keep calling me Drunk Girl? I don't like it."

"Um, because you were drunk off your ass last night and I didn't know your name. I didn't think Shit Faced would be very appropriate. You seemed classier than that." Dana busted out laughing so hard, I thought she might wreck the car. *Holy shit, they've bonded. You're in trouble now Hindley.*

"Well, my name is Hindley." I tried to sound as offended as I felt. "You can call me Hindley from now on."

"Wow, what crawled up your ass all the sudden?" His audacity shocked me.

"She's just pissy 'cause this is gonna be a shit day for her. That's why I thought you being there would make it easier for her. I mean, who wouldn't feel better looking at you all day."

I rolled my eyes at Dana's statement and my stomach began to flip flop. I couldn't tell if it was the massive amounts of Tequila still in my system or the fact that what she said was true. Somehow, I did feel that having him near would make today easier for me. *And maybe, just maybe, you could finally have that one-night-stand?*

"We're here!" Dana's words clanged in my head as I felt my entire body begin to throb in pain. Unlike Dana, I wasn't used to hangovers. I could count on one hand how many times I'd gone out and gotten completely trashed and last night made night number three in my record books. My gaze drifted over to the swanky restaurant we were parked outside of. *You gotta go in, sweetheart. Can't hide out here all day.* I let my head fall back on the head rest and closed my eyes, wondering how I was going to make it through the next twelve hours of my life. This was much worse than me hanging out with a bunch of judgmental girls.

A few months ago, when my mom was in the throes of planning this wedding, she'd told me Geneva's fiancé Stanley was friends with an old boyfriend of my mine. She'd said it like I had a butt-load of beaus in my basket, but I wasn't like Geneva. I wanted more than just money and casual sex from guys I dated. My mom realized her mistake instantly when she saw my face go pale at the mention of Chris Putman's name and I had no choice but to tell her the story of how he'd humiliated me.

I'd always tried to keep my private life private from my family, mainly because I didn't want to hear my mom lecture me about my mistakes. But the minute Geneva found out Stanley's friend Chris was the one who broke my heart, she'd decided he just *had* to be in the wedding. Apparently, he and Stan were much closer friends than even Stan remembered. And because Stan wasn't going to argue with Gen about anything, he'd willing allowed her to put a semi-close, old college buddy into his wedding party. I knew she was just being a bitch about it and I'd tried not to think about it over the last few months, but now, here I sat outside this restaurant knowing that today would suck beyond words.

"Is everything okay?" Skater Boy's voice rang from the back. I'd almost forgotten he was here.

Knowing Dana would probably want to tell him everything, I cut my eyes at her and gave her a look that made it clear she better keep her mouth shut.

She began to rub my arm. "You'll be alright, sweetie. Deep breaths."

"What's wrong?" I could tell Skater Boy's question was genuine but I didn't want him to know.

"Nothing." I continued to glare at Dana, just daring her to say anything about Chris. I would kill her with my bare hands and she knew it.

"There's an ass load of high maintenance bitches inside just waiting to eat her ass alive, that's what's wrong." Although what Dana said was true, she knew that's not what had my stomach in knots right now. I was thankful she didn't share any more.

"Well, when I get nervous and I know I have to be around a bunch of douche bags, I always think of the time Timmy Dubowski pissed on himself during recess."

"What!" I shouted, laughing under my breath as Dana and I both turned in our seats to face him. I had to hear this story.

"Timmy was a douche bag. He was big, fat, and mean. He bullied everyone on the playground, stole their money, their dolls, you name it, he took it."

Dana giggled. "You had dolls?"

He crossed his arms over his broad chest and I saw the muscles in his forearms flex as his full lips twisted into a smirk. "I plead the fifth." *Skater Boy has a playful side. And forearms like Popeye the Sailor Man. He may just be what the doctor ordered after all.*

I was more curious now than ever. "So what happened to Tommy?"

"It's Timmy."

"Oh, sorry."

"You're forgiven." The playful expression he gave me lit up his face and instantly, I felt my cheeks burn. How could he affect me so quickly? *Um, 'cuz he's hot!*

"So anyway, Timmy was untouchable, or so we thought. One day after school, I heard Timmy's mom talking to the teacher. She was yelling and hollering, telling them they had to get an exterminator up there to the school as soon as possible."

"Why?"

"No one had even realized it but Timmy had been out of school for two days. The entire playground was so peaceful and calm without him there, kids were playing and laughing. Timmy wasn't there to terrorize us and it was like heaven."

"Where was he?" Dana asked, both of us lurched forward as if hearing a Pulitzer Prize winning story.

"According to his mom, Timmy was deathly afraid of spiders and he'd seen some in the classroom. He said he wouldn't go back to school until his mommy got rid of them." He scrunched up his face when he sarcastically said 'mommy' and his expression made me laugh. *Skater Boy doesn't just have a playful side. He is playful.*

"Well, right then and there, I devised a plan with my best pal, Jeremy."

I looked over at Dana and saw she was just as riveted by his story as I was. He had a way of drawing you in. "So what did you do?"

"After school that day, we went to the store and bought up a shit load of rubber spiders. I wanted to dump them all in his desk but Jeremy said that wouldn't be good enough. Only our class would see him scream. He convinced me that we needed to put them on the playground where everyone would see his reaction."

"I snuck out a few minutes early before recess the next week when Timmy finally came back to school and littered the sand-filled playscape with over a hundred spiders. I have to admit, even I was a little freaked out. I stood there waiting as I saw the kids pile out of the doors and there came Timmy thumping a kid on the head and tripping another guy next to him. He was such a jerk."

The way he said it made me realize that Skater Boy liked to protect people. He'd taken care of me last night and his story confirmed he'd been doing it most of his life. Letting someone take care of me was a foreign concept and I couldn't help but wonder if there was anyone in his life who protected him. *You like Skater Boy.* I listened intently as he continued.

"So, I screamed at him, 'Hey asshole, why don't you pick on someone your own size!' He locked eyes with me and marched over to where I was standing in the middle of the sand pit as all the other kids followed. As he got closer, I backed up a bit until he was standing directly under the play scape with no straight exit possible. Then I looked down and shouted, 'Oh my God, what the hell?' and started pointing down at the sand. I swear, it was like slow motion animation as I watched his head start to look down at the sand and his eyes get as big as the moon. He let out the most god-awful, blood curdling scream I've ever heard. He was paralyzed, couldn't move. Then that's when it happened."

"What?" I asked breathlessly.

"He peed all over himself!" Skater Boy started laughing hysterically in the back seat and Dana and I couldn't help but join him. "Oh my God, it was so funny. Priceless!" He could barely get out the words through his sobs of laughter. It was contagious.

"All the kids started pointing and laughing and screaming. I almost felt sorry for the kid. But then I saw the blood running down they boy's arm who Timmy had tripped earlier and realized it was all worth it. Once an asshole, always an asshole, I say."

I wiped the tears from my eyes as I worked hard to regain my composure from all the laughing. "That's a great story. I think it just might help me to picture Geneva peeing all over her wedding gown."

"Well, if that doesn't, you can have this." His huge hand pushed between the front seats and I saw a small plastic spider sitting in his palm.

"You actually still have them?"

"Well, not all of them. I've lost a few and given some away. You never know when you're gonna run into a Timmy Dubowski."

I looked up from his hands and stared into his eyes. They were now completely blue, no hint of brown. The compassion I saw in them was overwhelming and my heart actually ached at his act of kindness. I reached out and took the spider in my hand and brought it close to my chest. It was perhaps one of the nicest things anyone had ever done for me.

I looked down at the spider now in my hand then back up into his beautiful eyes. "Thanks."

"No problem. Everyone needs a little help now and then, right?" We sat paralyzed, locked on each other's eyes.

Suddenly, a loud banging shook the car and brought us back from whatever alternate universe our minds had just taken us to.

"What the fuck, Hindley. It's ten minutes after eleven!" I turned to look out the window and saw Geneva's face contorted into an ugly glare.

"Here we go," I sighed as I pulled on the handle and pushed the door open. Before I could even put one foot on the ground, she laid in to me.

"I ask you for one thing, Hindley, one fuckin' thing! Not to be late today! And what do you do? You screw it up and ruin my day!"

I was amazed that I just stood there and took her abuse. But what could I do? Interjecting my thoughts now would only make it worse. I just had to put my head down and suck it up for rest of the day. Maybe the less I said, the less she would say.

She continued her verbal assault on me. "Maybe if you hadn't been so busy getting completely trashed last night, this wouldn't have happened!" My head started pounding so hard again, I thought I might throw up.

"Maybe if you wouldn't have left her all alone outside some random club in the middle of nowhere in downtown Austin with some dude who wanted to rape her, this wouldn't have happened."

I turned around and saw Skater's Boys face almost as scrunched up and contorted as Geneva's. The thought that he was standing up for me made me think of Dana. She never backed down to Geneva and I always envied her. I wondered why I'd always felt the need to keep the peace.

I turned back to face Geneva and suddenly her face changed. She was now the gorgeous beauty queen, eyeballing Skater Boy from head to toe. You'd never know she was about to get married in less than six hours by the way she was molesting him with her eyes.

Geneva pushed past me so she was standing directly in front of Skater Boy. "And who might you be?" Her voice was provocative and seductive all in one. I recognized it. It was her predator voice and I knew Rory didn't stand a chance.

"I'm her date for the evening." His voice was low and commanding. I couldn't believe what he just said. Geneva's face went ashen.

"You're going with her?" Her voice was riddled with disgust. "Why?"

"Look at her." Rory waved his hand over me as his eyes perused my entire body. I inwardly sang as I saw a huge smile spread across his gorgeous face. "She's a knock out. I'm just happy she said yes to me. She's totally outta my league." His eyes locked on mine and I knew in a heartbeat that he wasn't joking. He was serious. He actually thought he wasn't good enough for me. My heart ached and I felt the need to correct him, but not here, not in front of Geneva.

Her gaze turned ugly again as she surveyed my hideous outfit. "You can't be serious. Her?"

She added, pointing to me as if to make it clear we were talking about me.

"Oh, I most certainly am serious," he said coming beside me and snaking his arm around my waist, pulling me close. I couldn't help but wrap both my arms around him, he felt so good. The moment was surreal, I was Cinderella and the Wicked Stepmother, or sister in this case, was getting kicked in the stomach by Prince Charming. The look on Geneva's face was priceless.

I could see in Skater Boy's eyes he wasn't done with Geneva yet. "Don't you have a groom or a bridesmaid or a photographer somewhere you should be bitching out now, instead of Hindley?"

I couldn't believe it, he remembered my name. His voice sounded like an instrument from heaven as my name slowly rolled off his tongue. The way he stood there, solid and sure of himself as he staked his claim to me had parts of my anatomy on fire. *Holy shit, girl. Today just got good. This one may be in your bed tonight after all.*

The look on Geneva's face was priceless, I'd never seen it before. I never wanted a camera so badly in my life, anything to capture this moment that I was sure may never happen again.

She was always used to getting her way, especially with men. She could make them do all kinds of things they never thought they would. And now, here stood this gorgeous man who wasn't affected by her beauty in the least. His arm was wrapped around me, his voice was defending me, his body was clinging to me. This had to be one of the best days of my life.

Even if Skater Boy drove off right this very second and I never saw him again, I would remember this moment forever. It was the first time I could ever recall that Geneva Barton wasn't going to have what she wanted. And what she wanted, wanted me, not her. I wrapped my arms tighter around Rory and pulled him closer as we stood there together, daring her to say another word to either one of us. Today, I was getting the prize and she was livid. If I didn't know better, I would have sworn I saw piss running down the side of her over-priced ivory linen pants.

Chapter 4

Dana's Beemer shook as I slammed the door shut. I couldn't help it, I was furious with Hindley's sister for making her feel like shit. I could tell her sister was just like Timmy Dubowski and I hoped against hope that Hindley would find a way to put that spider somewhere in that bitch's lunch.

I rubbed my cheek, trying to hold on to the spot where Hindley's lips had brushed against my skin just moments earlier, hoping the memory would help extinguish the burning embers of my temper. *Breathe in, breath out, dude. Count backwards from ten. Happy thoughts.* Dr. Fowler's words rolled through my head like the ball bearings in the wheels of my skateboard.

I closed my eyes, remembering the way Hindley's face looked as she tried to balance herself on my shoulders, stretching up to whisper words of gratitude in my ear for protecting her against her sister. I remembered the feeling of her breath on my neck as her raspy voice echoed through my mind. 'I owe you one,' she'd whispered. *It's working, you're already calmer. Maybe there is something to this girl.*

"So, you gonna go tonight?" Dana's voice interrupted my internal self-help therapy session.

"What?"

"Tonight? The wedding?"

"Oh, hmm, I don't know."

"But you just told Geneva you were Hindley's date for the evening. I think those were your exact words."

I tried to recall exactly what I'd said but all I could remember was how infuriated I was to hear anyone talk to Hindley like her sister had. Whatever came out of my mouth after that I knew I wasn't in control of and at this point, was probably going to regret.

"You have to, man. If you don't show up, Geneva will crucify her."

"Why?"

"Her step sister hates her."

"I thought they were sisters."

"By marriage only."

"Why does her sister hate her?"

"Step sister. Don't ever call Geneva Hindley's sister in front of her or she'll rip you a new one."

"Which one?"

"Either of them."

"Wow. They hate each other that much?"

"Well, Geneva hates Hindley. Always has, ever since their parents got together. I don't know why, Geneva's pretty much got everything she's ever wanted, spoiled bitch."

"I know why." Dana twisted her neck to look at me, her eyebrows scrunched together in disbelief. I thought I'd made the comment to myself but obviously she'd heard me. *Great!*

"What does that mean?" she asked.

I hadn't noticed until this moment how attractive Dana was. Her blue eyes were like glacier water you'd find deep in the Arctic Ocean and stood in stark contrast with her dark skin and jet black, curly hair. This girl was definitely hot, like Hindley's step-sister, Geneva. But neither of them even held a candle to Hindley. She was in a league all her own. As hot as Dana and Geneva both were, I was surprised to feel nothing toward them, no sexual desires at all. Not like I felt for Hindley. Even at her worst, Hindley had stirred something inside me that I couldn't explain, even if I had to.

"I don't know." I finally responded. It was a lie. I knew what I meant, but I didn't know how to put my feelings into words Dana would understand without asking more questions. Hindley was different, an unattainable woman who would never give someone like me a second thought. But for some reason, that excited me. She excited me like no other woman I'd met in a long time, if ever. I was relieved to find Dana concentrating on the road again comfortable with my response.

I liked Dana. She felt like a kindred spirit. I could see why she and Hindley were friends. She exuded fierceness and I knew if left in Dana's care last night, I would never have found Hindley in the condition I did. I may have never found her at all. Hindley had been in harm's way because of her sister, well, step sister, and suddenly I felt my pulse racing again.

~

I'd never fully committed to going to the wedding tonight but somehow, it was no surprise to find Dana at my doorstep at five o'clock to take me to the festivities. Now, here I sat in a stupid zoot-suit in the second to last row of a massive church, waiting for the nuptials to begin.

Dana reached over and straightened my tie. "You look really good. Chris is gonna have a shit fit. So is Geneva. I can't wait." Her laugh was diabolical and I couldn't help but laugh with her. It was obvious Dana hated these two.

"Chris is her ex?" She nodded. "He's really that bad?"

"He dumped her in front of half the student body in college on Valentine's Day all because she wouldn't put out. I'd call that a major douche bag, wouldn't you?"

I knew there was a time and a place to cut a woman loose, especially if she wasn't putting out, but in front of a crowd wasn't one of them. Obviously, Hindley's refusal to consummate their relationship had damaged Chris's fragile male ego and he felt the need to crush her. What better way to do that than through public humiliation. I hated bullies and that's exactly what he was. I felt in my pocket and rubbed on the spider, inside vowing to shove his dick in the dirt tonight. "A total douche bag," I finally responded.

The ceremony started and I was disappointed that I could only see the back of Hindley as she marched down the aisle along with the posse of other chicks. It made me sad to know she wouldn't even know I was there to support her.

"Holy shit!" I heard Dana say. The couple in front of us looked back and gave her an ugly face. "What?" she said with no apologies. They shook their heads and turned back around to enjoy the ceremony. "Now you know why they didn't invite me." She started laughing.

"Are we wedding crashers?"

"No, you're not. Hindley was granted permission to bring one guest."

"Are you her guest?"

"I was. But now that she brought you, I couldn't resist showing up for the show."

"What show?"

She looked me up and down and laughed under her breath. I began to get nervous, like before a competition. *Dude, you've gotten yourself into more shit with this girl than all the other chicks in your life combined. Remember Girl Rule number one? 'No Drama! This is beyond drama now.*

"I can't believe that bitch did this." Dana was so small, she was now half standing trying to look over the other guests' heads so she could get a good look at the front of the church. "She must have just changed her line-up today." She continued.

"What are you talking about?"

"Up there," she said nodding toward the front of the church. "Hindley was supposed to be the second bridesmaid in the lineup. Her mom arranged the gaggle of girls in height order. But now, she's the last bridesmaid."

"What's wrong with that?"

"Geneva paired her up with Chris."

"Who?"

"The douche bag who dumped her."

"Her sister actually knows the guy?" She cut her eyes at me as if I was the dumbest man in the world then rolled them in disgust.

"Her fiancé does, supposedly. Geneva couldn't wait to put him in the wedding party when she found out what he'd done to Hindley. That bitch did this on purpose. Now Hindley has to actually lock arms with that prick and wear a smile on her face while doing it."

Finally, the minister announced that the couple was now man and wife and they turned to the crowd as everyone cheered. They descended the stairs and rushed down the aisle toward the exit at the back of the church like it was on fire. But just as they got to our row, her sister slowed down her walk, turned toward me and winked. *What the fuck was that? This is her wedding. Did she just seriously give you a 'Sex for Sale Here' sign right in the middle of a church while standing arm-in-arm with her husband of like one minute? Dude, this chick is wacked. Run, don't walk, run away. Now.*

I watched as couple after couple filed down the aisle in long succession before Hindley finally made her way toward our pew. My entire body went still as I caught my first glimpse of her. She was literally breath taking, a real life goddess.

Her dress was the color of a brand new copper penny with a strapless corset top that showcased her perfect tits and small waist. I lost my breath at the sight of her long blonde hair falling in waves over her bare shoulders. The skirt was floor length and hid her legs but I smiled, remembering how good they looked this morning when she'd jumped out of bed in nothing but her tank top and panties. I knew they were long and lean and the way they moved under the soft material of her dress as she walked down the aisle made me think of wrapping them around every part of my body.

Everything about her was perfect, except the expression on her face. It was sullen and taut. She was trying hard not to show any emotion, good or bad, but I could still see her beauty shine through the dark mask she was wearing. Anyone who knew her could tell she was physically sick having to be so close to her ex-boyfriend and in that moment, I was glad I'd decided to come. I was overwhelmed with my need to protect her. It was a foreign feeling to me but I liked it.

As if hearing my silent thoughts, her head turned toward me, our eyes locked on one another, and I could see and feel her entire countenance change instantly. Her full lips parted into a magnificent smile that lit up her entire face and her dark brown eyes began to shine again like earlier today when she'd kissed my cheek. She was beyond beautiful. *Dude, what the hell just happened to this chick?* I knew what happened. I had affected her as much as she had me. The emotion that ran through me was indescribable, better than any drug I'd ever taken or any contest I'd ever won. I watched as her graceful form walked past me and smiled when I saw her strain her neck to look back at me before disappearing beyond the large oak doors at the back of the church.

I turned to Dana. "So, where's the reception?"

"Dude, what the hell was that?"

"What was what?"

"What the fuck just happened between the two of you?"

So it hadn't been just me who'd noticed our exchange. I felt a small smile spread across my face, knowing that what I felt for this girl was real. *This is the last thing you need right now. You've got* way *too much other shit to concentrate on besides this girl and her bat shit crazy step sister. Run!*

~

As we stepped into the grand ballroom of one of Austin's swankiest downtown hotels, I realized Dana hadn't lied. Hindley's parents had spared no expense for this wedding. I knew as a guy shouldn't say this but the place was gorgeous, not tacky, not cheap, but sophisticated. I felt all the inadequacies from my childhood surface like dead fish in a stagnant pond and a wave of fear washed over me. I seriously thought about bolting, but all I could remember was how beautiful Hindley looked coming up the aisle. How her entire body changed just at the sight of me. I had to see her one more time. *Why risk it, man? Have you not seen this place? Any minute they'll be on to you and hand you your ass on a silver platter as they escort you outta here like they always do. And trust me, this time won't be pretty. Let's go, now, and save us all the embarrassment.*

"Don't bother looking for your name," Dana said coming up behind me. "They just added you today so I'm sure you won't find it here."

"What are you talking about?"

She looked at me like I was an alien. "Your table assignment. Haven't you ever been to a wedding before?"

"Yeah, but they were mostly either at a courthouse or somebody's backyard." She laughed hysterically but I didn't see anything funny about it.

"Oh, you're serious?" she asked covering her mouth to stop her laughter. I nodded my head. Her eyes blazed with apology and I knew she wasn't trying to make fun of me, she just assumed everyone lived like this. "Come on." She took my hand and pulled me toward two tables lined with rows and rows of white place cards. "Here. Look in this row for my name and I'll look in these over on the other table. They should be in alphabetical order. It's Dana Di Grazio. D-I capital G-R..." As she began to spell out her name, my heart rate skyrocketed and I felt my palms fill with sweat.

"Uh, I gotta take a leak. I'll be right back."

"Oh, here it is!" She shouted holding up a place card. "I found it. We're at table fourteen. I'll see ya inside."

"I'll follow you in."

"I thought you had to pee."

"Well, I don't want to miss seeing Hindley come in."

"I bet you don't, Mr. One-Nighter. If y'all didn't have sex last night, you sure as hell did back in that church. How sacrilegious! I loved it! Maybe I should start going back to church."

Before I could respond, the DJ announced that the happy couple had finally arrived. The wedding party busted through the doors and immediately, I began searching for Hindley. But my anticipation was quickly washed away by a wave of panic when I saw her frantically searching across the massive room for something or someone and I wondered what was wrong. *Calm down, dude, she's looking for you. Why are you so worried about her anyway?*

Finally, her eyes found mine as if she'd heard my silent thoughts again. It was uncanny. A small smile spread across her lips as she pushed away from the bridal party and half walked, half ran to our table like she was a slave being freed after years of captivity. I found myself just as excited to take her in my arms but she stopped just short of me like she had slammed into an invisible wall.

"You came." Her words sounded unsure, like she thought I wasn't real. She let her eyes roam over my entire body from head to toe and I felt desire run through my veins from the attention she was showing me.

"Well, I had to get my spider back." She giggled and I thought it was the most soothing sound ever. "Or did you already use it?"

"I'll never tell." She moved in closer, leaning into me and I could smell her perfume. "But if I were you, I'd stay away from the wedding cake." I had to work hard not to sweep her up into my arms and run upstairs to one of the hotel rooms and have my way with her.

"You didn't!" Dana screamed. Hindley shrugged her shoulders and we all began to laugh.

I spotted a bar in the back and decided I she could probably use a little liquid courage right about now. "You guys want something to drink?"

Dana looked back and forth between the two of us. "Why don't y'all go get me the most expensive bottle of champagne they're serving."

"Come on," I said, taking Hindley's hand in mine. She looked down at our fingers as I interlocked them, her long eyelashes spread across her cheeks like black fans. Finally, her eyes rolled up my arm and slowly worked their way over my shoulder and up my neck before finally coming to rest on my face. She was drinking me in, and I loved it. Her lips parted slightly and her chest heaved up and down, accentuating her beautiful breasts in the tight corset dress as she tried to catch her breath. It was one of the most erotic things I'd ever seen or been a part of. Everything from my waist down screamed in agony.

"You two having optic copulation again?" Dana's voice broke our intimate moment yet again. This was becoming a habit of hers that I didn't like.

Hindley's brow furrowed. "Are we what?"

"Are you fuckin' each other with your eyes again?"

"Dana!"

"What? I'm not the one doin' it, unfortunately."

I started laughing but apparently, Hindley didn't see the humor. "Come on," she said, tugging on my hand, leading me back toward the bar. She swung her head over her shoulder to look back at me and I watched in slow motion as her long hair slid across her neck and tumbled down her back, golden tresses gently caressing her skin as they skimmed the top of her dress. I'd been wrong. This was the most erotic thing I'd ever seen before. Ever. *Fuck!*

Hindley nodded her heads back toward Dana. "I'm sorry about her."

I couldn't answer, I couldn't think. All the blood from my brain was now in the central part of my body. I was too mesmerized by this surreal creature. How was it possible that less than twenty-four hours ago, this gorgeous woman, who now stood before me, had been on all fours puking her guts up? And what was even more shocking to me was that I now realized she'd been just appealing to me last night drunk as a skunk as she was now.

"Rory?"

My name rolling off her tongue was like healing music, better than any song I'd ever downloaded.

"Rory!" Hindley's voice was louder now and I felt her pull on my hand.

"Oh, I'm sorry."

"This is my step-father, Paul Barton. Paul, this is Rory."

I shook my head trying to understand what she'd just said. *You. Must. Make. Blood. Return. To. Brain. Douche bag! This is her dad, for Christ's sake. Pull it outta the gutter, man.* What was I going to say? 'Hi sir, it's nice to meet you, I was just eye fuckin' your daughter two minutes ago and about to take her upstairs and screw her thirty ways to Sunday.' *No, don't say that.*

"Hello sir." I extended my hand.

He took my hand in his and gave me one solid shake that was firm but not overbearing. He was a good looking man with thick hair that was dark on top but graying along the edges. He wasn't as tall as me, but I could tell he was in good shape and could probably kick my ass, especially if he knew what I was just fantasizing about his daughter doing to my body with her puffed up little pink lips. *Douche bag alert! It's you, you're the douche bag. Put your dick back in your pants and talk to the man.*

He kept his hand in mine as his gaze drifted back to Hindley. "Does Rory have a last name?" Hindley's eyes expanded to twice their size as her eyebrows shot up in the air. He turned back to me, obviously aware that Hindley and I were only on a first name basis. I wanted to rescue her but didn't know how. I just stood in stunned silence. It all happened so fast, in a nanosecond.

Paul still had my hand in a death grip as he brought his other one up to my shoulder and squeezed it just to the point of pain. He leaned in and brought his face within inches of mine, obviously wanting to whisper something for my ears only.

"Perhaps by the end of the evening, you'd be so kind as to properly introduce yourself to my daughter before you peel that banana in your pants and try to feed it to her again, okay, player?" I stood in stunned silence, praying my mouth wasn't on the floor. This guy was good. He'd once been a player himself and I wasn't fooling him in the least. But the worst part of all was he thought Hindley and I had already slept together, without her knowing who I really was. He thought she'd had a one-night-stand with a random guy. I didn't want to ruin her reputation, especially with her father. *Again, we care because?*

He gave my hand one final shake before releasing me, turning all his attention to Hindley. He gently caressed her shoulders, taking great care with her as if she were an expensive doll. *She is, you moron, and he just reminded you of that fact.*

"You look stunning tonight, sweetheart. You're stealing the show." His words weren't cheesy or gimmicky, he was for real. Hindley was his pride and joy and I'd just fucked up royally and I wasn't sure I'd ever get back in his good graces. *Dude, you were never in his good graces. Look at her. Look at you. Enough said.* He kissed her cheek and I watched as Hindley's face lit up, similar to when she'd seen me in the church earlier. She loved her father and I knew if I didn't secure his approval, I'd never get anywhere with her. *Man, what are you saying? You're not even in the same league as her and her father just reminded you of that. Save everyone the heartache and just bow out now. You'll only hurt her in the end.*

"Don't let her drink too much, Rory," Paul said looking back at me as he let Hindley go. "She doesn't hold her liquor well."

Hindley cut her gaze to me and we both tried desperately to stifle a laugh. "I don't think I'll be drinking again for a while, Pop."

"Yes, so I heard." He winked at Hindley and I could tell he wasn't disappointed in her. In fact, he seemed tickled to know his daughter had gotten drunk last night. If he only knew the real story, he wouldn't be happy at all. He'd be furious. "Well, you two have fun tonight." Paul's gaze traveled up and down my entire body. "But not too much." He flashed a mischievous million dollar smile that honestly lit up the entire room, as cheesy as that sounds. *Dad has a sense of humor. That's a good sign.*

"Paul!" Hindley shouted. "You're as bad as Dana, I swear."

"Nobody's that bad, Hindley." We all began to laugh and I felt some of the tension between us subside. *Maybe you could win him over after all, player.* "Take care of her, Rory with no last name."

"Yes sir, I will." I stood and watched Paul Barton disappear into the mass of guests, trying desperately not to feel as tiny and insignificant as I knew I was.

"Hey." Hindley tugged on my hand. "What's wrong?" Her face was riddled with concern.

"Nothing."

"Please don't let Paul get to you. He loves intimidating people. He's really a great guy once you get to know him."

Get to know him? Dude, we don't even want to stick around for the best man's toast let alone spend time 'getting to know' her father.

"Easy for you to say."

"Well, thankfully for you, you're not asking for my hand in marriage. You're just a fill in for tonight, right?"

Her words were a sobering reminder that there was nothing between us. I was here so she wouldn't feel so bad when her jerk-wad ex-boyfriend showed up. I was her buffer. And if that's all she saw me as, that's all I'd ever be to her. *Done. Choice was just made for you, lover boy. Enjoy your dinner, eat some cake, and let's hit the road. No harm, no foul.*

Her face went soft and her eyes filled with remorse. "That came out wrong. I'm sorry."

"Sorry for what? You're right, it's not like I'm gonna ask you to marry me. Well, not tonight anyway." I let out a nervous laugh but she remained quiet. Too quiet.

"You're not just a fill-in to me, Rory. You're much more. I tried to make a joke but obviously it wasn't funny and I apologize. I hope you'll forgive me." *This girl has more class in her little finger than you do in your entire dumbass body. You'll never measure up.* "I do care about you." She continued. "And I know you care about me or you wouldn't be here tonight."

The gentle tone of her voice and the caring words that flowed from her mouth made me forget everything that had just happened with her step-father, made me forgot all my inadequacies. She had a way of making me feel better about myself and she saw something in me I didn't know I had. She said I was 'much more'. That was her gift to me and she didn't even know she'd given it to me. Or did she? *Don't let her see you like this, man. It's a woman's cue to go in for the kill.*

I didn't respond, I didn't accept her apology, but I didn't reject it either. Instead, I turned to the bartender and ordered a Heineken for Dana and two waters for me and Hindley. I could tell she didn't need any more alcohol tonight. As he placed the drinks on the bar, I handed him a fifty dollar bill.

"Thanks, but it's an open bar." He told me. I fished back into my pocket and gave him a twenty instead. Hindley looked at me with surprise, as if she wasn't expecting me to pay anything.

"That was nice."

"The guy's a bartender. That's how he makes his living."

"I know, but that was a lot of money."

"What, you think I can't afford it?" I knew my voice had more attitude than I meant for it to but I couldn't help it. As nice as she'd been to me earlier, I wouldn't let her or anyone else think I couldn't afford things. I may not be as rich as all these people, but I made a decent living doing what I loved and I could afford special things if I wanted them.

She put her hand on my arm, stroking it gently. "Hey," she whispered, waiting until she had my undivided attention. "I'm sorry. I didn't mean anything by it. I was just saying it was a nice gesture to offer him so much money, that's all."

I could see by her furrowed brow that I'd messed up, again. How could she be so nice to me when all I kept doing was screwing up with every interaction? I was letting my low self-esteem run amok and she'd misread it as anger. *It was anger, man. Quit dickin' around with her and decide already. Do you want her or not? If you want her, ease up on the psycho.*

I didn't know how to respond with words so I wrapped my arm around her waist and pulled her closer to me, silently asking her for forgiveness, too. She looked up into my eyes and gave me a soft reassuring smile before letting her head fall onto my chest. Having her cuddled next to me felt like home, a home I'd been searching for my whole life.

"Oh, crap!" She raised her head and I felt her entire body go rigid.

I immediately let her go, fearing she'd read my thoughts again. "What is it?"

"It's my ex, he's on his way over here."

I looked down and saw her face go ashen. She was scared and shutting down and I missed her already. I could sense the asshole was near so I snaked my arm around her waist again and pulled her close. Just like before, her body next to mine felt right, like she'd been designed to fit with me perfectly.

I watched as a guy at least half a foot shorter than me approached the bar. I recognized him as Hindley's partner from the wedding. He had blonde hair with an okay build but not one girls would drop their panties for. I was laughing to myself, thinking what a knucklehead this douche bag was for letting someone as beautiful as Hindley go. He would never be able to get anyone half as hot as her again, even if he lived to be a hundred.

"What brand of Chardonnay do you have?" His voice was light and airy and I couldn't help but wonder now if the guy wasn't gay. First, he dumps a hottie like Hindley and now, at an open bar, he's gonna order wine? This guy was a major pussy. This was going to be like shooting fish in a barrel.

He turned and began to examine Hindley from head to toe like he was going to buy her and resell her to cannibals. There was no lust in his eyes, like most guys would have when looking at someone as gorgeous as Hindley. He was disgusted with her, like she was miles beneath him in the social order of life. Looking around this grand ballroom and seeing all the stuck-up socialites like Douche Bag here, made me believe his social order of things was ass backward. Hindley was in a class of her own and I was gonna show this asshat what he'd missed out on.

"Thanks for walking with me today, Hindley. I know I wasn't your first choice."

"Anything for Geneva." Her attitude was cynical and rigid. I didn't like this Hindley.

I decided it was show time. "Baby, how much longer we gotta stay?" I asked in my sexiest voice.

Hindley looked over at me in complete surprise.

"I'm sorry, babe. It's just that you look so fuckin' hot in that dress, I don't know how much longer I'm gonna be able to keep my dick in my pants without blowin' a wad all over this ballroom."

I saw Douche Bag spit out his wine all over his overpriced tuxedo and costly ballroom carpet and was proud to see my verbal assault had hit him square in the nutsack. I turned to Hindley, wanting to smooth things over, afraid that my comment may have offended her. She didn't look pleased but I knew she wasn't going to argue at this point. A part of her was obviously happy her ex had been knocked down a notch.

"Rory, I don't think you've met Chris."

"Hey man." I stuck out my hand to shake his and he gave me the once over just like he did Hindley. He took a napkin off the bar and wiped his mouth and chin, chunked it back at the bartender like he was a peon, then graced me with his hand. It was small, cold, and clammy, just like I expected. "It's nice to meet you. Chris, Putz-man, is it?" I knew his real name but thought *Putz* man was a better description of him.

Hindley let out a snort and Chris and I both turned our attention to her. "Sorry." She offered trying hard not to laugh again.

"It's Putman," Douche Bag corrected me.

"Oh, yeah, sorry about that, man. I've heard a lot about you."

He gave me an arrogant smile. "Hindley still talks about me, huh?"

"No, man, Dana was fillin' me in on the way over here, telling me what a major dumbass you are."

"Excuse me?"

This was it. I was about to make him regret ever hurting Hindley. "Ya know, my dad used to take me fishin' when I was young."

"How wonderful," he said sarcastically.

I continued, unfazed by his mockery. "I always wanted to keep that first fish of the day. I would be so stoked about catching one, all the adrenaline would be surging through me." I let Douche Bag fall into my story and by the looks of it, he was becoming somewhat more interested. At least he wasn't blowing me off and that's all I needed. "But my dad was smarter than me and he'd always talk me into throwin' that first one back in, no matter how much I fought him. Ya know why, Chris?" I knew Douche Bag wasn't completely impressed with my story but I needed him to be able to relate it to his relationship with Hindley if I was going to really rub his dick in the dirt. I looked at Hindley and was surprised to see how engrossed she was by my tale. I hoped she wouldn't hate me later when she found out it never happened. I didn't even know where my real father was.

"No. Why?" Douche Bag asked.

Yes! He'd taken the bait. I continued, going in for the kill. "My dad told me that if I threw the small one back in now, in a year or two he'd grow to ten times his size. And my dad promised if I was patient, he would bring me back and we could catch that fish again and win any tournament we entered with him."

"Okay?" Douche Bag responded. "That was a riveting story." God, I wanted to punch the fuck out of this arrogant prick! "And your point is?"

"My point is you threw Hindley back in the water. You gave up too soon. But, I waited for her, I watched her, I caught her. And now she's my grand prize." I pulled Hindley in as close to me as I could. "Me and my dick thank you for being the biggest douche bag on the face of the earth. You're a complete moron. This chick is a monster in the sack and you'll never know what you threw back. But every night, I promise you, I sure do."

I turned to Hindley, knowing I'd pushed her well past her comfort zone. She was a sophisticated woman and probably completely mortified by my words. I knew she wouldn't stay quiet but I had to keep her from talking if my words were going to have the maximum effect on Douche Bag. My eyes lit up in delight as I realized the best way to keep her mouth shut was to cover it with mine.

Chapter 5

As soon as his lips touched mine I knew I was in trouble. The sane part of my brain, the one that finished college despite all the odds, the one that had been accepted into law school and passed with almost flying colors, that part said push him away, slap his face and escort him out of the hotel. But the other side of my mind, the irrational side which was rarely used, screamed 'Live in the moment Hindley, for once forget about the future and stop doing what everyone expects you to!' That side was slowly beginning to win the war raging inside me.

His lips felt like soft rose petals floating in the air, like chocolate syrup oozing down an ice cream sundae, like fresh sunshine after the rain. They felt like every delicious thing I'd ever tasted, seen, heard or experienced in my life. Sometimes people talk about *seeing* fireworks when they kiss, but that didn't happen for me. I *felt* the fireworks, the vibrations of their detonations deep in my core, and it shook my soul. Every part of my body was ignited and exploding in technicolor starbursts like The Fourth of July and I just couldn't stop myself no matter how hard I tried. I wanted this, bad, and part of me was happy about that.

Instead of fighting it, for once I just enjoyed myself, in the moment. I wrapped my arms around his neck and dug my fingers into his hair begging for more. I knew my response was polar opposite to what he expected. His moan inside my mouth was proof. That just drove me more over the edge as I parted my lips allowing him full access to everything inside me, body and soul. Suddenly our kiss went from just playing out a scene to full on lust. His arms tightened around my waist pulling me in closer to his body as if he was trying to become one with me. Soon he couldn't stop them and they roamed all over my body, one wrapped up in my hair while the other made its way down south to my butt. We couldn't get enough of each other. I knew I should stop but every fiber of my being kept me attached to him as if he was my saving grace, my only hope at peace.

"Get a room!" I heard someone shout.

Suddenly I was brought back to the present. *You're in the grand ballroom of a five star hotel for God's sake Hindley. Get ahold of yourself. Your mom's gonna kill you.*

Slowly I pulled away from him feeling drunker from one kiss with Skater Boy than I did from the ten shots of Tequila I drank the night before. I had to steady myself on his shoulders while I readjusted my dress and smoothed out my hair. After I was finally able to balance by body, I worked on refocusing my eyes again, afraid to look at him. *He probably thinks you're a horrible kisser and never wants to do that again.* I finally found the courage to raise my head and was surprised to find a smirk on his face, as if he'd just gotten away with the most despicable crime. Actually he had. I'd never kissed anyone in my life like that, let alone in a room full of crowded, stuck-up socialites. I should have been ashamed, mortified, humiliated even, but all I could think was how sensual the experience was, how seductive he made me feel, and how much I wanted to do it again. The sparkle in Rory's eyes affirmed he felt the same way and a sigh of relief escaped my lungs. I reached up to wipe away my lip gloss from his mouth, knowing it might not be such a good idea to make contact with him again. Any physical interaction between us may lead to another frenzied make out session. *Would that be so bad?* My thumb grazed across his lips wiping away the last of my pink gloss but just as I was about to pull away he took my hand in his and brought it back to his mouth, gently kissing my knuckles. It felt so divine. *Run! Go! Now!* I knew I needed to escape, get away from him now or it would all start over again.

My head fell to the floor and I stared at the bizarre design in the carpet trying desperately to avoid his gaze. "I'm just going to go to the ladies' room and freshen up my make-up," I whispered in a shaky voice. His hand caught under my chin and he slowly lifted it up trying to make our eyes meet. *Don't look him in the eyes!*

"Okay. Don't be gone long." His voice sounded like sex on a stick and I felt a tingle, down there. I had to run. I knew my face was burning with embarrassment and I was deathly afraid he'd be able to read my thoughts. "I don't know a soul here except Dana and from the looks of it she's about ready to explode on both of us."

I glanced over my shoulder and saw Dana standing by our table with one hand raised high above her head palm side up pumping it into the air while the other sported a thumbs-up sign. Her head bobbed to some imaginary music and the smirk on her face matched the smugness of this event. Through it all I could see her mouth moving and could hear her voice in my head dragging out an exaggerated "Heeeyyyy girl!" I shook my head knowing I'd never hear the end of this one.

Afraid to look Rory in the face I ducked my head and immediately made my way to the restroom hoping he wouldn't follow. I was pleasantly surprised to find it empty when I entered and I was thankful. I needed some quiet time to process that kiss. Was it real, was it fake, was it just for show? *Girl, that kiss was for real. You better watch it.*

I noticed a small Hispanic woman sitting by the vanity waiting to help guests clean their hands and offer paper towels, soap, lotion, even perfume if they wanted it. I always thought that would be a lonely job but right now I envied her.

Suddenly I heard a toilet flush from the far end of the bathroom and saw the door of the handicap stall swing open wide with Geneva, of all people, waddling out in her gargantuan dress with dumbass Wendy toting behind trying to lift the train off the floor. They looked like Lucy and Ethel in the middle of a comedy routine and I couldn't help but laugh under my breath.

"What's so funny?" Geneva asked trying to wash her hands but having a hard time through all the bows and tulle and satin surrounding her.

"Nothing." I went into one of the empty stalls near the front and stood inside, waiting for them to leave, praying their exit would come soon. I didn't need to pee but I sure wasn't going to stand there and watch Geneva primp in the mirror.

"Aren't you even going to congratulate me?" she asked from the other side of the stall.

My kiss with Rory had given me a kick of confidence. I didn't feel like playing into her bullshit tonight and I wanted to lay into her more than anything. But I reminded myself that it was her wedding so, just for tonight, I'd hold back. *You're such a liar. You always hold back. Tonight is no different. That kiss gave you gumption and now you're letting it all fly down the toilet like your vomit did last night. You're such a weenie!*

I flung the door open like I was in a Western movie and made my way to the vanity, peering at myself in the mirror as I dug around in my dress looking for my lip gloss. I wanted to be brave, I wanted to confront her, but I couldn't. My entire body sagged in defeat. *You're such a chicken.* "Congratulations," I said never diverting my gaze away from my own reflection in the mirror.

"So, who's this new love interest?" The way she said it made me hypersensitive to the fact that she didn't care about me, she never had. She was just trying to garner as much knowledge as she could to help knock me down sometime in the future. She'd probably do it tonight, right in front of Rory if she found an opening.

I kept my eyes glued to the mirror in front of me. I wasn't going to offer her any more information than I had to. "He's just a friend."

"I've never kissed a friend the way you just kissed him."

Oh shit, she saw you. How the hell do we get out of this one? Wait a second. Was that jealousy I heard in Geneva's Barton's voice?

"He's a friend, with benefits." I was proud of my comeback but wondered if Geneva would believe me. Hooking up with a guy that wasn't a full-on boyfriend wasn't my style and she knew it.

"Well good for you. Looks like hanging out with Dana is finally paying off."

I could see out of the corner of my eye she'd finished primping and was now facing me full on. I smacked my lips together, stuffed my gloss back down my dress then turned to face her, too. I promised to behave tonight for my mother's sake, but if she was ready to do battle, so was I. Rory had given me strength I'd never felt before and I was tired of being walked all over, by everyone.

"He's hot."

"Really hot," Wendy added. Geneva cut her a look and she bowed her head as if she were a child being reprimanded. Actually, she was. Geneva was domineering to everyone, even to me sometimes and I was ashamed to admit that I'd let her get away with it. Not tonight though.

"So, where'd ya meet him?"

Yeah, try and come up with a slick answer to that one that won't get you laughed outta this bathroom dumbass. Maybe you should have stayed in the stall. I didn't want her to know he'd rescued me last night but I had to tell her something. "At a bar," I finally said.

"Last night?"

I cursed at myself for being such a horrible liar. I knew there was no way I could make up a believable story that she'd buy right here on the spot.

"What's up bitches!" I turned and saw Dana standing next to the attendant. "Congrats Gen. You got you a real fine man there." I knew her words were sarcastic but she had a gift for covering her mockery so that people never really knew if she was serious or not.

"Thank you." Obviously Geneva thought they were real.

"Don't ya just love Hindley's new beau. Damn he's fine."

"He sure is," Wendy piped in again.

An evil smile spread across Geneva's face and I braced myself for another assault. "I was just asking Hindley where they met."

"Oh he's a friend of my cousins," Dana responded without missing a beat. She was a natural born liar and at times like this I was glad she had such a masterful skill. "I introduced them a few weeks back and they've been inseparable ever since."

"Why am I just now hearing about him?"

"Probably because if you met him before you got married you'd try to ride his skin bus into tuna town."

I rolled my eyes in disgust but Geneva just laughed in a smug sort of way knowing there was truth to Dana's words. It amazed me how shameless Geneva had always been in not publicly denying what a nympho she was. She was a slut and everyone knew it although most would never admit it, at least not to her face. I knew most in that ballroom were surprised that Geneva was finally settling down and willing to commit herself to just one man for the rest of her life. The only person who always seemed oblivious to Geneva's sexual proclivities was my mother.

Dana continued on her tirade. "Although this morning he pretty much told you you'd never get a ticket for that ride. Ouch! That must have hurt, huh Gen?"

Geneva's face got as red as Dana's car and she looked like she was going to blow a gasket any minute.

"He's the reason Hindley was late to your luncheon ya know." I knew where Dana was going with this so I turned and begged her with my eyes not to go any further.

"What do you mean?" Geneva was finally interested again.

"Well when I busted in on them this morning, let's just say Cinemax After Dark would have been buying the rights to their show, if ya know what I mean." She gave Geneva an innocent wink that I knew was anything but. "They were goin' at it like monkeys."

"Dana!" I shouted, her name echoing off the bathroom walls. I was more than petrified, I was furious. I didn't want anyone, let alone Geneva, to think I'd been intimate with Rory. It was untrue and it gave her too much information, information I knew she would use against me one day very soon.

"Well, look at you," Geneva said in a sultry voice letting her eyes survey me up and down like a predator sizing up its kill as she came closer to me. "You've finally taken a trip to the wild side. Although I must say I'm surprised you could do anything at all last night you were so hammered. Isadora said she saw you pukin' your guts up in the bathroom."

Oh crap. Here we go. She's on to me.

Dana started in again. I swear she should write a book or a screen play the way she made up stories so fast in her mind. "Hindley was so wasted Rory came to pick her up. He wasn't too happy with you when he got there. Couldn't believe you'd left her all alone."

"I didn't see her go outside." Geneva tried to explain.

That's a lie! Tell her Hindley, you know she's lying. She was happily being groped at the bar by two hotties when you left. Say something, call her on it!

Luckily Dana continued and saved me from making a decision. I hated confrontation.

"But apparently Rory's got some special tonic that helps with hang overs." *Oh god, please don't tell her his name!* "It obviously worked for Hindley cuz this morning he was on her like stink on dog shit and she was happy to take it all, and I mean ALL!"

"God! You're so foul Dana!" Geneva scrunched her face as if offended. I thought that was funny because Gen had a side to her that could be just as vulgar, she just never let high society see it.

"Thanks! Coming from you I consider that a compliment."

Geneva pushed past me and Dana trying to get out of the bathroom almost knocking the attendant and all of her belongings onto the floor. "Watch it you idiot!" she screamed at the woman. "If you get anything on this Mauro Adami wedding dress I'll sue this whole damn hotel and you personally. This is imported Italian silk you imbecile!"

The poor woman was frightened to death even though I doubted she could understand a word Gen was saying. Geneva had a way of evoking fear in people with just one look. Everyone except Dana Di Grazio.

"Congratulations again on your wedding!" Dana shouted as Geneva rushed through the swinging door. "I'm sure you'll be very happy!" The door swung closed as Dana turned to me. "In hell that is." She started giggling, proud she'd gotten the last word in.

"Why the hell did you tell her that?"

"Calm down."

"I can't calm done! You know she'll use it against me and it's not even true. Paul knows I don't even know his last name."

"What?"

"And now she's gonna go tell him we've been dating for weeks."

"I'll go smooth it over with your dad." I was on the verge of tears and Dana knew it. "Look, I'm sorry. You know I love to get Geneva worked up. I'm sorry it came at your expense. I'll go tell her I was yanking her chain if you want me to."

"Forget it. She'll just figure out another way to screw me over no matter what you say."

"So. Now that we've put Bitch Witch Geneva out of our hair, tell me about that kiss." Suddenly all the anxiety I'd felt over the earlier scene with Geneva vanished as I told Dana everything, just like I always did.

~

I came out of the bathroom and frantically scanned the room in search of Rory fearing in the back of my mind that Dana had riled Geneva up enough that she might actually make a play towards Rory at her own wedding. I never put anything past her. *He probably left if he had half a brain.* I sighed at the thought of him leaving and made my way back to our table hoping to find him there.

"Seems like your gentleman friend is very popular with the kids."

I looked up from the napkin I was tearing into little shreds and watched my mom sit down next to me at my table and nod towards the back of the ballroom. I glanced over my shoulder and saw Rory surrounded by at least five boys ranging in age from eight to eighteen. It looked like he was showing them some kind of technique, like he was surfing or something. *Great, he's a real mature one!* Then I saw one of the smaller boys tug on his suit jacket. He turned around and his face lit up just looking down at the kid. He got down on one knee so that he and the little boy would be eye-to-eye. The boy pulled out some type of magazine and a pen and handed it to Rory. He took it with no question and began writing on it. *That's weird. Well at least he seems to like children. That's a plus I guess.* Before he was finished with the small boy's magazine another boy shoved something in his face and he started writing on it, too.

"Not too bad with the ladies either," my mom added. I cut my eyes back at her wondering what she was talking about but saw that hers were focused on the bar now. Several women were congregated and all staring at Rory like he was a fresh piece of stripper meat. My body spiked with fever as liquid jealousy rushed through my veins. *Whoa Nelly, hold your horses. What do you think you're doing? This guy ain't yours.*

"It's alright sweetheart." My mother reached out to touch my arm. "It's obvious to everyone that you're the object of his affection tonight." My head snapped back to face her. She said it as if tonight would be it, like after tonight he'd turn his attention towards someone else.

"What is that supposed to mean?"

"That kiss was something else, huh? I haven't seen passion like that since Paul and I started going out." She'd completely ignored my question. It was a specialty of hers, sweeping things under the rug and ignoring the elephants in the room, no matter how big or bright or ugly they were. "Makes me wish I was twenty again."

She also had an uncanny way of turning every subject back around to her. No wonder she was able to relate to Geneva so well. I saw a dreamy look in her eye and knew that Paul couldn't be far away. I followed her gaze and found Paul standing a few tables away. He was a handsome man I had to admit. She'd chosen well.

I was actually jealous of my mom and Paul in many ways. The fire and passion they'd found years ago had never faded. After all this time they still acted like teenagers in love. Sometimes teens in lust was a more accurate a description. They'd embarrassed Geneva and I on many occasions growing up in the same house together. It was probably the one and only thing Gen and I agreed on. We found it highly uncomfortable watching them make out.

I waited patiently while she got her eye full of her husband. As if sensing her stare Paul's head turned to face hers, his eyes alight with a fire that seemed to promise something to her later, something sexual. *GROSS!!!!* He blew her a kiss and gave a wink but waited until she returned both gestures. They really were sappy little love-struck teens. *Jealous? Yes! Very.* Satisfied he was still hopelessly in love with her, she finally turned her attention back to me.

"So, tell me where you two met. Paul says you don't even know his last name but Geneva says you've been dating for a few weeks. Which is it?" I rolled my eyes trying to decide which story to go with. She furrowed her brow which only intensified her look. She stared at me as if I was a wanted felon and she was the interrogating officer. "Spill the beans Hindley Frances." I laughed as she said my full name, like I was in trouble.

"Truth?"

"Always."

What could I tell her that wouldn't make her freak out. Silently I wished that Dana were beside me to pull me through this mess. *Better to go with the truth. If he stays you'll have to explain and if he leaves, you'll still have to explain.*

"I got drunk as a skunk last night at Gen's Bachelorette Party."

"I heard."

"Good news travels fast doesn't it?"

"We're you alright?"

"No mom I wasn't!" She could tell that I was upset. "Geneva and her gang of misfits got me smashed then left me." My mother rolled her eyes and I knew she was only half believing my story. It was beyond my understanding why she always wanted to believe in Geneva's innocence even when she'd been shown the evidence of Gen's deceitfulness time and time again.

"Anyway!" I rolled my eyes just as she'd done but mine was in disgust. "After Geneva left me puking my guts up in the bathroom a stranger helped me outside and that's where I met Rory." I neglected to tell her about Gap Boy or the fact that Rory spent the night in my bed.

"You met him outside a bar Hindley? How could you? And bring him here?" She was disgusted with me.

"Geneva left me, mom! She left me all alone in the middle of the night on a dark city street where some guy thought it would be alright if he started rubbing his hands all over my body and throw me into the back of a cab and take me god knows where to do god knows what with me! Why do you not get that! Why do you think she's such a saint?"

"Hindley calm down, you're making a scene" she whispered, her neck twisting around the entire room trying to make sure my dysfunctional words hadn't been heard by any of the judgmental socialites in attendance. "I don't think she's a saint."

"Well, I don't really care what you think. Rory helped me when my own step sister wouldn't. That's all you guys need to know."

"Why are you getting so upset?"

Because somehow I know you're twisting this around like Rory's the bad guy, thinking he's a social nobody when in reality he's definitely somebody, somebody special, to me. I could feel tears start to burn my eyes and that pissed me off even more.

She took both my hands and held them in her lap pulling me closer to her. "I'm sorry honey, I didn't mean to upset you. It's wonderful that he took care of you and I appreciate him for that."

"Well, you should. And you should stop judging him. I know that's what you're doing."

"Honey, I just want the best things in life for you."

"How do you know this guy isn't the best thing for me?"

"Hindley, you don't even know the boy's last name. What kind of a man doesn't even tell a woman his last name? For all we know he could be a…" I knew what word she was searching for in her mind. It was an ugly word, a judgmental word, but the daggers I hurled at her with my eyes froze her mouth mid-sentence daring her to go on. I yanked my hands from hers devastated that she'd even thought about taking me back to that dark place. I'm sure Rory was no saint, but he wasn't an illicit predator.

"What do introductions have to do with anything mother? That doesn't prove what kind of man he is. I think we've both learned our lesson on that one." I wanted to cut her with my words and I watched as her wounded eyes retreated. "Look mom, he saved me last night. That's all you should be concerned about, not whether or not I know his last name or what he does or doesn't do for a living." I couldn't believe my mother was being so petty. My blood was boiling again, all the anger I felt towards Geneva over the last twenty-hours was starting to surface. I was tired and hungry and still hung over and I could feel it in my bones. My mother was about to get the brunt of my frustrations.

"I'm just saying, giving you his last name would have been the gentlemanly thing to do."

"Did you not hear me!" *Ut-oh, here we go. Hang on everybody!* "Who the hell cares what his last name is? He was there for me last night when I needed him the most. I don't give a flying fuck what his last name is! He saved me when you couldn't and Geneva WOULDN'T!" I heard her take in a sharp breath at my personal attack on her maternal skills. She knew exactly what I was referring to and I knew it would hurt her. But I didn't care. She was hurting me with her judgmental attitude.

"Good evening Mrs. Barton." I recognized the deep, sexy voice behind me and nearly passed out when I turned around and saw Rory standing behind me. Obviously he'd snuck up on both of us. I went ten shades of red wondering how much of our conversation he'd heard. My mother and I both sat in stunned silence embarrassed by my very public outburst just two seconds earlier.

He reached over to the table opposite ours and drug a chair over placing it directly next to mine. As he lowered himself into the chair I felt the material of his jacket slide against my back as he wrapped his entire arm around me and let his thumb caress my bare shoulder. Chill bumps erupted all over my body. In that one gesture I felt more protected than I ever had in my life. I felt as if with Rory by my side I could do absolutely anything.

"You're right ma'am. It was wrong of me not to properly introduce myself last night, to Hindley. And to you and your husband tonight." His words sounded genuine but his tactics were very similar to Dana's. I knew I wouldn't be able to tell if his words were genuine until he continued.

He stuck out his long hand holding it in front of my mom. "I'm Rory Gregor." My mother looked down at his hand but there was no judgment or disgust in her expression only embarrassment. She slowly put her hand in his and held it in place.

"It's nice to meet you Rory. Please, call me Caroline." My mom was staring directly into his eyes and I saw her lips curve into a small smile at his gesture. They simultaneously released their hand as we sat in silence.

"I spent the night with your daughter but we didn't do anything." I snapped my head back at Rory, shocked by his blunt honesty. "I found her outside of a bar last night completely inebriated and all alone as a young man tried to push her into a car." My mom gasped finally understanding the danger I'd been in thanks to Geneva and her dipshit friends.

Rory continued and I knew without any doubt he was being completely genuine with my mother. "Realizing how intoxicated she was I thought it best if I try and get her home to make sure no one else tried anything with her. I brought her home and with the help of her neighbor got her safely inside. I stayed only to make sure she was alright. Her friend Dana was kind enough to invite me to the wedding tonight. Your step daughter Geneva was very rude to Hindley this morning before her luncheon and I thought it best if perhaps I accompanied Hindley tonight, to make sure no one else hurt her, especially since she'd been in harm's way last night. That's truth, that's how Hindley and I met and I'm sorry if I or anyone else gave you the wrong idea about our relationship."

I stared at Rory's profile desperately trying to keep my mouth closed while I listened to his words. My mind was void of any coherent thoughts. I couldn't believe he was telling her everything. He was being so honest and open and vulnerable with no concern for himself. He'd admitted to her that we'd spent the night together and made no excuses for it. But the most touching part of his story was his courage to tell my mom exactly how Geneva had treated me today. Anyone listening knew he was just as hurt as I was and he'd issued a quiet warning to my mom, he would not put up with it anymore.

My mom stood. *Oh shit! What is she going to say?*

"Well it's very nice to meet the young man who took care of my precious daughter. I'm delighted that you came tonight and I truly hope you'll stay and enjoy the rest of the evening, as a personal friend to our family."

What the hell did she just say? He was a 'personal friend' to the family?' What the fuck did that mean???

I stood up so I could get a good look at her to make sure she was still my mother. Rory's eyes darted from me back to my mother as he decided to stand and join us. As he rose from his chair I saw it. Caroline Hagen-Barton was smitten with him. If he had been a foot shorter and fifty pounds heavier with thinning hair and a fractured face she would have had him escorted out of the building after admitting to spending the night with me while I was completely drunk. But the fact that he was basically a Greek god in a stunning charcoal gray suit and lavender shirt with an ass that wouldn't quit meant he'd been forgiven, for everything. Hell, she'd even invited him to be a part of our family. Classic Caroline. She DID judge a book by its cover. Thankfully for Rory he had a good looking cover.

"Thank you ma'am, I appreciate your hospitality but it's not necessary. I would have taken care of Hindley regardless of the reward."

They both turned their attention towards me and I was baffled by the scene playing out before me. Two minutes ago my mom had been furious with this guy and she hadn't even met him. Now here they stood, committing to be life-long friends using me as a pawn.

"Well, I'm glad to meet you and hear the real story. I wish Hindley would have felt open enough to tell me the truth." *What! She's dogging me right in front of Skater Boy. What the fuck Caroline!* "Enjoy yourself tonight Rory." She let her eyes roam over his entire body leaning forward and pressing a kiss against his cheek. When she pulled back her eyes were sparkling. *OH! MY! GOD! She is flirting with him. Get this boy out of here. Now!*

I grabbed Rory's hand staking my claim on him, disgusted that I had to do it for my mother's benefit. "Rory promised me a dance." He looked at me like I was crazy which I knew I was. He'd never promised to dance with me but I had to get him away from my mother and dancing seemed like the best way to do that.

"Nice to meet you Caroline," he said looking back over his shoulder as I yanked him out onto the floor. I pulled his hand hard and spun him around to face me. His eyebrows were pulled together forming a 'V' just above his nose. "What's wrong with you?"

"I can't believe my mother was actually flirting with you." He started laughing. "It's not funny, that's gross."

"Why, you don't think I'm attractive enough for a woman to flirt with me? Are you jealous?" I let my eyes roll so far back in my head I almost got dizzy trying to show my silent sarcasm. "Well I think she has great taste. I mean look around this ballroom, this wedding is amazing." His eyes swept over the room surveying his surroundings before finally returning to my face.

"Yes, I think she has excellent taste." I locked eyes with him. "In everything."

He smiled down at me. "Well I didn't even notice it if it makes you feel any better."

"It doesn't. But thanks." My smile didn't last long thinking about all the awkward situations my family had put me in over the years. Tonight was just one of many to add to the list.

"Something else is going on."

"I'm just tired. It's been a long day."

"Are you ready to go home?"

"I have to stay until they leave."

"Who?"

"The newlyweds," I said sarcastically.

"Why? Who cares?"

Yeah Hindley, who cares?

"My mom will have a hissy fit. It's just not worth it."

"Maybe I could talk to her." His mouth turned up in a mischievous smile and I knew he was kidding. God, I wanted to kiss him again so badly. Instead I raised my hand back and slapped his shoulder.

"That's alright. I'll suffer through thanks." He nodded his head in understanding as he continued to sweep me around the dance floor. I relished being in his strong embrace. It made me think back to our kiss and how much I longed for another. "You're a really good dancer."

"Thanks. So are you. But I'm sure taking pole dancing classes help."

"Shut up!" I hissed punching his arm and searching the room to see if anyone else heard him.

"Quit hitting me." He drew me in even closer and I watched as his eyes were drawn to my lips, staring at them as if they held some mystical powers. I could feel my breath catch as I waited, hoping he'd go in for another kiss. "So the socialites don't know about your classes?" he whispered close to my ear.

"I don't take classes. It was a party, for Geneva."

"If you say so."

"Well I do say so."

His eyes darted between mine searching for something but I didn't know what. I turned my head and gently laid my head on his shoulder quietly sighing in contentment as we continued to dance in comfortable silence until the music ended.

"Hey, who were all those kids around you earlier and what were you writing down for them?" He pulled me off the dance floor completely ignoring my question letting his fingers intertwine with mine as he led me away. He drug me past our table and out into the foyer before finally stopping in the lobby. "What's going on? Why'd you bring me all the way out here?"

"You're right. It's been a long day. I'm beat."

This was it. This was the brush off. Well, I deserved it. He'd been nothing but nice to me for the last twenty-four hours and all I seemed to do was insult him, embarrass him and hit him. *No wonder you're all alone. Maybe you should go by the animal shelter on the way home and pick up twenty cats while you're at it!*

"Oh, okay. I'm sorry."

"Why are you sorry?"

"Because." I paused trying to think of the right words. "You've done a lot for me today. Well last night, too, even though I can't remember it. I wish there was a way I could repay you."

"Stop letting Geneva get under your skin. That's how you can repay me." *What did he just say?* I was completely baffled by his comment.

"What does that mean?"

"Look Hindley, you're an amazing woman. I can tell from the short time I've known you. Someone like Geneva doesn't deserve your energy so quit giving it to her. Eventually she'll run out of steam and crash and burn all on her own."

His words were surprisingly candid yet so poignant. He knew me better in just twenty-four hours than some people I'd known my whole life, my mother included. "Wow." That's the only word that came to my mind, the only word that could express how I felt. I was shocked.

"What?"

"No one's ever put it to me like that before." I stared off behind him watching people come and go through the revolving doors at the front of the hotel. I was stuck, in a revolving door with Geneva and I had to get out. "Thank you."

"You're welcome." His voice was deep and rough and I could feel my legs turning into Jell-O. *Get a grip Hindley.* I let my eyes drink him in feeling this may be the last time I ever saw him again. His voice jolted me. "Hey maybe we could get some dinner tomorrow night or something." *He's asking you out, he's asking you out. Is this a good idea? Of COURSE it is!*

"That sounds great!" I knew I answered too quickly and my voice was too high, too enthusiastic, but I didn't care. This man had given me hope, hope in breaking free from the old me and that was something I wanted more of.

He reached inside his jacket and pulled out a cell phone tapping the screen repeatedly. "Here," he said holding it out to me.

I took the phone and saw he'd created a new contact for me called 'DG.' I looked at him with a furrowed brow in confusion.

"What's DG?"

"Drunk Girl," he laughed.

"You know I have a name."

His brown-blue eyes sparkled as a lopsided grin appeared. "I know."

I rolled my eyes and laughed as I typed in my cell phone number adding 'Hindley Hagen' in the 'Title' space, just in case he forgot who 'DG' was. Then without thinking I twisted my body around so my back was leaning against his chest and hit the 'Add Photo' button. I held the phone out in front of me at arm's length. "Say cheese." Much to my surprise he actually leaned in closer to me, his chin resting on my bare shoulder.

"Cheese," he whispered in my ear. His warm breath hit my neck and I nearly dropped the phone. It was the most erotic thing anyone had ever said to me. Parts of my body were screaming in agony and ecstasy both at the same time. *HOE-LEE SHIT!* I was so dazed and disoriented I had no idea if I'd even taken the picture or not.

He pulled the phone from my hand while I just stood there, mouth gaped open looking like a complete idiot I'm sure.

"Got it," I heard his raspy voice ring through my head. I turned and I watched as he slid his phone back inside his jacket. How was he able to make the most mundane of things sexy as hell? "Are you alright?" I heard his question but I couldn't answer. I was still intoxicated by the moment. "Hindley!"

"What!" I shouted finally comprehending he was talking to me.

"What's wrong with you?"

My eyes washed over his face and I could feel him looking straight through me. My entire body shuddered. "I'm not sure," I whispered. I knew I should have offered a more elaborate answer, but I didn't have one. All I could tell him was the truth. I had no idea what was wrong with me. *You know. You know exactly what's wrong with you. And you like it. A lot!*

"So tomorrow?"

"What?"

"Dinner?"

"Oh, yeah. That sounds good." His face lit up and I was excited to think maybe I was affecting him, too.

I closed my eyes and drew in a deep breath feeling oxygen enter my lungs again. I must have been holding my breath. The fog was lifting and I was finally able to register what he was talking about. "Oh, I forgot. I have to work most of the day tomorrow but I should be free by the evening."

"You work on Sundays? It's the Lord's day ya know." He started laughing and I felt dizzy again. *Girl, calm down!*

"Well when you get shit faced on Friday and stuck with a bunch of snotty rich people all day and night Saturday, you have to work on the Lord's day just to catch up." His smile broadened and I saw small dimples on either side of his mouth that I hadn't noticed before. He was perfect.

"Yeah, I guess those things can make taking Sunday off virtually impossible for some."

"But I'll be done by eight o'clock, I'll make sure of it." *You're too desperate. Stop begging. Men don't like that.*

"That works. What do you do anyway?"

"Oh, I'm an attorney." His smile quickly faded. "Don't tell me you hate lawyers, too," I laughed. He didn't. His face was sullen and he stood silent. Suddenly I regretted telling him. I'd found since I'd passed the bar that a lot of people hated lawyers. Usually I didn't tell anyone about my profession right away so I could avoid this type of judgment, but considering what Rory and I had been through in the last twenty-four hours I deemed myself pretty well known by him. Apparently not.

He finally spoke. "Well, I better go." He reached down and kissed my cheek barely brushing my skin with his lips. It was a far cry from the smoldering kiss we'd shared earlier. *What the hell just happened?*

"Um, okay? Take care." He gave me a small smile and without another word turned and walked towards the revolving door. "See ya tomorrow night Skater Boy," I shouted. *What an idiot. Why did you do that? He's obviously giving you the brush off. Again. You just embarrassed the hell out of yourself.*

He looked back over his shoulder and lifted one hand in farewell but his expression was bleak, as if he'd lost something. I stood in place and watched as he disappeared into the revolving door wondering what in the hell had just happened. Confused and tired I gave up and walked back to the ballroom. *Better to cut him loose now probably.*

Halfway down the corridor my body refused to go another step coming to an abrupt halt. I decided I wasn't giving up, not this easily. I wanted to know what was wrong with him and I wasn't going to wait until tomorrow night to find out. He was a good guy, he'd taken care of me and protected me and I didn't want to lose him. Not like this anyway.

I turned on my heels determined to finally live in the moment for once in my life. My stiletto shoes clicked on the marble floors as I entered the lobby. I looked at the portico outside through the large glass walls of the entrance and saw him standing next to a beautiful woman. Panic ran through me like fire. She was laughing as if she'd just heard the funniest joke ever. Rory seemed amused as well but not nearly as much as she did. He reached inside his jacket and pulled out his phone and a spark of relief ran through me thinking he might be trying to call me already. *Come on Hindley. Look at her, look at you.* He tapped on the screen multiple times before handing his phone over to her. She reached for it and I watched in agony as their hands rubbed against each other. Instantly my heart was seized with pain and I clutched my chest, but I couldn't look away. I continued to stare in horror as the woman typed in what I could only assume was her own phone number. She smiled at Rory and he reciprocated as he took the phone back and tucked it away in his jacket. I thought I might actually vomit. The scene was eerily similar to our interaction less than five minutes ago. *I told you. Once a player...*

My eyes began to sting as I turned and made my way back down the long corridor to the ballroom. I refused to cry. I'd shed too many tears on situations far worse than this in my life. Rory didn't deserve my tears. This was a reminder to me of why I wasn't spontaneous, why I kept order in my life, why I guarded myself. Rejection hurt. Especially from someone I was really starting to fall for.

Chapter 6

~RORY~

I sat in the glider on the back porch of Leif's house and took another long drag off my cigarette, inhaling deeply and hoping the nicotine would calm my nerves. I held the smoke in my lungs for as long as possible before finally exhaling, watching as the smoke disappeared into the atmosphere. But still I couldn't rid myself of that one word that had kept me up all night. Lawyer. *Lawyer!* She's a fucking lawyer. Of all the things in this world she could have done, she picked a lawyer.

In my vast experience with attorneys from the courtroom to the boardroom, they'd only been interested in three things, money, fame, or both. That's why I couldn't wrap my head around this. Hindley was too beautiful, too caring, too naive to be an attorney. She obviously let people use her, instead of using them. That went totally against the lawyer's first commandment – screw others over before they screw unto you.

I gazed out over the railing at the setting sun. It was hot as hell in Texas but I had to admit, the scenery was breathtaking. From Leif's home, you could see the rolling hills of Central Texas. They'd had a good amount of rain during the spring so everything was green and colorful, not brown and burnt like last summer when I'd come out. The temperature had reached one hundred and ten when I was visiting last year and I wondered how anyone could live in such conditions. I preferred my home in California much more. Even though it was crowded as shit, at least you didn't need to run an air conditioner ten months out of the year and you could sit on your back porch without melting.

The sky just above the hills was a glowing mix of orange and mauve and I had to admit it was nice to breath in the fresh, clean air of Austin as opposed to the dingy smog of Southern California. I smashed my cigarette into the saucer on the side table and grabbed my pack of cigarettes to pull out another one but cursed when I saw it was empty. Leif wouldn't allow smoking in his house. In fact, he didn't even have an ash tray. I'd been forced to use one of his plates. He hadn't been happy but admitted it was better than flicking my butts over the side of the house. In Texas, that was a huge violation of the law. Not just because they were all nature freaks here in Austin but because Texas had become so drought ridden in the last five years, even the slightest of embers could spark an entire forest fire. Just last year, a small town near Austin lost everything, homes, businesses, even an entire state park to a massive blaze.

Leif had felt so badly about the devastation in this small town, he and his entire crew took time out of their hectic schedule designing and building skateboard parks to volunteer with the cleanup project for a solid week. He even designed a new skatepark for the town that had lost everything to the devastating fires. Through the donations of other pro skateboarders like me and our sponsors, he was able to raise enough funds to build it free of charge for the city. That's the kind of guy he was and that's what had drawn me to him from the start.

Leif's parents had been Olympic athletes, both of them medal-winning downhill skiers. Leif had never taken to the snow but loved being on the boards so skateboarding had been a natural fit for him. By the time he was any good at it, his parents were retired from their sports and really getting into the boarding scene, pushing Leif to the extremes in his sport hoping he'd make it big. When they followed him to the local skatepark one day to watch him practice, they found me working the rails and said they knew instantly I had potential. I'd kept it a secret that I was a runaway, although I could tell they sensed my need to be cared for and had quickly taken me in, no questions asked.

Leif had learned to be giving and generous from his parents. Jack and Kara were some of the most genuine, most real, most honest people I'd ever met. They'd shown me that through my tough exterior, I actually had a protective side and I was grateful to all three for helping me develop it. Even though, at times, protecting others had landed me in trouble, I was still glad Jack and Kara Jennings had fostered that side of me. It's what led me to Hindley and I would always be indebted to them for that, and for countless other reasons.

I'd run away from my home at the age of sixteen, when my stepfather decided to teach me a lesson about 'putting my shit up,' as he'd called it. He was drunk as usual and had come home and tripped over my skateboard and decided that instead of his belt or his fists this time, my skateboard would be his weapon of choice. I don't know if I was trying to protect myself or my board but suddenly, I became the abuser and all the years of pent up frustration, of abuse, and neglect came out on him and I didn't stop beating him until the cops were on top of me, pulling me off. He was half dead when the paramedics arrived and my mom told the cops to take me away, never once telling them of the years of abuse I'd suffered at her husband's hands.

My court appointed attorney was a real gem. He told me to my face that he didn't give two shits about my punk ass, that he had a tee time to make. Instead of defending me and explaining to the judge why I'd beat my step father to a pulp, he'd decided on his own to speed the process of my trial along by showing the judge my rap sheet. I'd found out later that was totally illegal and he could have been thrown in jail. But apparently, the judge wanted to get out early that day, too because she took it into evidence. She hadn't been impressed with my priors, breaking and entering, vandalism, minor in possession, possession of a controlled substance with intent to sale. I had to admit, I wasn't proud of my past either. She called me a habitual juvenile delinquent and the prosecutor and my own defense attorney agreed. Instead of offering me help, they deemed me a menace to society and sentenced me to one year in juvie. My time spent at the youth detention center in the state of Colorado had been just as abusive as at home and when I was released after serving only four months, I left the prison and never went back home.

I liked living on my own. I liked being the one in charge of my own destiny, good or bad. But with the Jennings, I learned a new sense of what it felt like to be part of something. As much as I wanted to give in to them, most of me still considered myself a loner.

Through hard work and practice under Jack's training, I worked my way up in the amateur standings of skateboarding and by the time I was seventeen, I was getting major recognition by some big name manufacturers. On my eighteenth birthday, I celebrated by signing my first major deal and officially went pro. I also got high as shit and screwed two random chicks I met at my signing party, but I tried to forget that part. *You're a dick.*

I quickly learned that being a professional athlete brought along lots of women and that had always been a bonus for me and the guys who followed me. I'd slept with my fair share of women since I'd lost my virginity to Kalie Michaels' at the tender age of fifteen. But I'd never become serious with any one woman in particular. I didn't date women. I didn't like anyone trying to tell me how to live my life or make decisions for me or change me. I kept women at a distance. I brought them home, fucked them in all kinds of crazy ways, took down their number and promised to call, but never did. Most of the women knew I was just using them for sex but it always surprised me when some came back for more, as if I were going to change. At first I'd felt guilty about it, but early on, I'd decided they knew what they were getting into. Sex for me wasn't meaningful, it wasn't a connection. It was just sex, a way to blow off steam. If they didn't have any self-respect then I wasn't going to show it to them and I sure as hell wasn't going to feel bad about it or make any apologies.

The money and the notoriety of being a professional athlete proved to be a lethal combination and I found myself in the bottom of a jail cell more than once on my way to the top. Sponsors and endorsers don't like bailing their star athletes out of jail and I was quickly let go from most of my contracts. In the end, it proved to be more beneficial to me though. I found out through my criminal process that the attorneys my sponsors had secured for me worked very lucrative deals in their favor, not mine. Leif's father had tried to warn me but I was a dumb ass teenager, smitten with the idea that I was going to make it "big." Now, here I was at twenty-five, working hard to make a comeback in a sport that loved underdogs. I was working my ass off, training and entering every major competition I could find and it was working. My name was starting to be recognized again in the circuit and not for the bad boy I used to be. I was a really talented skateboarder and once again, companies were taking notice. Companies like River City here in Austin.

This time around I'd listened to Jack and let him help me through the process, hiring a sports agent once it was clear that I was truly on my way to a comeback. For some reason, fans loved me. They loved the bad boy turned good boy story that I possessed. Even though I'd given up the booze and drugs two years ago, I wasn't completely convinced that the bad boy in me was gone. I still had anger issues, got jealous like a red hot hornet, and used women for their bodies and not their minds. But there was still one secret that was worse than all those traits combined, a secret that could bring all my success tumbling down in an instant.

Thankfully though, River City was willing to take a chance on me and I promised myself that if I was ever given another opportunity at success, I was going to do it right and I was going to follow the rules. River City Skateboards was based here in Austin. Leif had worked with them for years and swore they were a reputable company with a long history of making quality boards and gear. He said they were an honest, family-owned company on the verge of monstrous success and felt sure they wouldn't try to screw me over like the others had when I was a teen. Just in case though, my agent hired an attorney in California to help me review all my contracts. River City and my attorney both thought it would be better if we actually came out to Austin to sign the paperwork. I had no idea why but given the fact that I was trying to make a comeback and needed this deal to stay afloat, I agreed. Plus, it gave me time to spend with my best friend, Leif, and try out one of the new skateparks he was designing down in San Antonio and take part in the pro-am tournament River City was sponsoring.

Thinking about reviewing the contract tomorrow had my palms sweating and my stomach in knots. Not because I was worried about being screwed over again. I didn't exactly have the greatest faith in my new attorney, but he was keeping my secret and I was still classified as a long shot, so I didn't have many options when it came to legal representation. It was just the fact that looking at documents, large or small, always scared me. Whether it was a letter from my grandma when I was in juvie or a one hundred page contract with a sporting goods company, words confused me and I didn't like depending on anyone for help, especially when I wasn't convinced of their loyalty. I had a secret in my life that very few people knew about and we all worked hard to keep it that way. I knew, as we reviewed the contracts tomorrow, River City may want to pull out parts of it and ask me to look over it like other companies had in the past. My attorney would be there to help keep my secret but I was still a nervous wreck. How could I admit to my new sponsor, or anyone else for that matter, that I was functionally illiterate? *You can't. It would ruin your comeback.*

I mean, I could read some, mostly small words. And usually, I could fake my way through by recognizing things like brand labels at the grocery store or street signs on the roadway, but that was only because I'd memorized them, not because I could read. My mind memorized pictures, not words. Putting bigger words and phrases together had always proven to be too difficult to me so instead of trying, I'd dropped out of school when I was released from juvie and run away, hoping no one would ever discover my secret.

Throughout the years, my friends had tried to help, especially Leif's mom, Kara, but I just never could force myself to focus or concentrate, and the techniques they used never worked. It always seemed like we were looking at two totally different things and anyone who tried to help me could never understand that, no matter how much I tried to tell them. Eventually, I just gave up. And now at twenty-five, I was too ashamed to ask for help. If I walked into an adult learning center now, potential sponsors and endorsers would drop me like a bad habit. Not to mention what social media would do. I'd be crucified.

Luckily, the people who knew I couldn't read loved me enough to help me get by and keep my secret. It wasn't easy and I have to admit, I'd surprised myself by keeping it under wraps for as long as I had. It's amazing the types of things people are willing to overlook when you're a successful athlete bringing in lots of money. But I lived in constant fear that people would find out my secret and reject me just like everyone else in my past had, even my own mother.

I leaned back in the glider, watching the sun vanish over the hills and wished I could disappear with it. I was slowly becoming obsessed with Hindley Hagen and I couldn't get her out of my mind, no matter how hard I tried. This was completely out of character for me. I was a love 'em and leave 'em type of guy. Actually, I never loved them, I just had sex with them and then left them. But Hindley had been different from the start. Our relationship hadn't started over my desire to screw her, it had started over my need to protect her, and that was totally different. And I'd known her now for over forty-eight hours and still hadn't had sex with her. That was a new concept for me, one that frightened me but also excited me. It was like I had something to live for outside of skating. *She gives you hope.* There's that word again, the word I hate, hope.

Hindley was one of the most beautiful people I'd ever seen, inside and out. She had a heart I knew was kind and loving, even if her family didn't see it or appreciate it. I couldn't stand the way her stepsister treated her and from the sounds of their conversation, it sounded like her own mother was a little bat shit crazy, too. What was it with mothers?

As much as I wanted her, I knew I couldn't have her. She'd never sleep with someone like me and even if she did, I knew I'd never be able to keep her. She was smart and sophisticated. She came from wealth and affluence. I was a runaway skater boy who could offer her nothing but heart ache and misery. Someone like Hindley deserved the best in life and I'd known from the start that would never be me. But my heart just wouldn't listen, it wouldn't let her go. I wanted to see her again. I needed to see her again. *Dude, they will eat you alive if they find out your secret. You're not even in the same social stratosphere.*

I wanted to believe that I wasn't good enough for Hindley, I wanted to walk away but deep down, I knew she was different. Even though she came from wealth, she wasn't pretentious like her sister and mother. And even though she was a lawyer, I knew she wasn't selfish and greedy. I was torn. I had a need to protect her, from everything. Especially myself. But I knew I needed her, to fill a hole deep in my core. That would require me to open up and be vulnerable again, to share all my secrets, and I just wasn't sure I could.

I pulled my phone from my back pocket and found her contact information with ease. I stared at the photo she'd taken of us, my eyes locked on her face. She was breathtaking. She drove me crazy and I could tell by her expression in our photo, she was just as captivated as I was. That one photo gave me hope. I scrolled down a little further and found the contact information from the woman I'd met outside the hotel last night. I was ashamed of myself just looking at the number. I'd met her after walking away from Hindley. *Dude, you didn't walk, you* ran *away from Hindley.* The woman had typed in her name as Mandy S. but I had no picture of her and could barely remember what she looked like. I wondered if I saw her in the street today, would I even recognize her?

By contrast, I had every facet of Hindley burned in my mind. From the way she twisted her hair when she was nervous to the dimple in her chin that formed only when smiled really big to the soft tender skin of her lips. I was infatuated with everything about her. That feeling scared me almost as much as thinking about going to my meeting tomorrow morning. My finger hovered over Hindley's number on my screen as my mind debated reasons why I shouldn't call her. *You're no good, man. What can you offer her? Look at her life. You'd never fit in.*

Then I scrolled down to Mandy's number, thinking of reasons why she'd be a better fit for me. *She's obviously into you and she gave you all the signs that said she was good for a roll in the sack. You need to relieve some of your frustration before your meeting tomorrow. Call her. Fuck her. Forget about her. Forget about Hindley. Let's move on.*

It was so much easier said than done. I scrolled back and forth between the two numbers before I finally forced my finger to hit the 'Call' button. I anxiously waited as it rang, vowing not to leave a message if she didn't answer, I would just hang up. After only one ring, I heard her voice.

"Hello."

"Hey, it's Rory. Sorry I'm late in calling you." Suddenly my voice got nervous and it irritated me. "I was wondering if you still wanted to go out this evening?"

After finalizing our plans, I went back inside glad to find that most of Leif's friends had left for the evening. I was somewhat surprised that she'd agreed so easily, especially since it was later than I realized.

"Hey man, can I borrow your motorcycle?"

"Got a hot date?"

"Maybe."

"Girls don't like to have helmet hair, ya know. Why don't you take my Stang?" Leif had an awesome 1966 vintage Mustang that he'd totally restored. It was an amazing car and there was no way I was going to take that thing out on the road. It was his baby.

"I'll just take the motorcycle, if that's alright with you." I didn't admit that I was actually meeting her, not picking her up.

"Whatever man, it's your date. I'm glad you finally called her. She sounds like a decent chick from what you've told me. You need a decent chick in your life." I laughed under my breath. "Keys are on the hook by the garage door. Drive safely."

As I pulled on the helmet and started the engine to Leif's bike, I couldn't help but think of his comment earlier. 'You need a decent chick in your life.' I wasn't sure I would know how to treat a decent chick but I wanted to try. I was afraid though. And when I was afraid, stupid things always happened.

~

I stood outside the restaurant wondering what I was doing here. Was this a good idea? Should I even go in? *Does it matter? You're already here. Go to bar, enjoy some chips and salsa, hang out for a while, and see where the evening goes. She obviously likes you. Don't screw this up.*

As soon as I pulled open the massive wooden door, I was assaulted with blaring mariachi music and the smell of stale tortilla chips. Overhead was row after row of multi-colored tissue paper banners looped across the ceiling. *Mexican food, dude. Really?*

A large Hispanic woman approached me, wearing a bright yellow Mexican dress with detailed embroidery and her hair pulled back in a slick bun. "Table for one, sir?" Her accent was heavy but thankfully, I lived in Southern California so I was used to the language barrier. I even spoke a little Spanish.

"Um, no. I'm meeting someone at the bar."

"Of course, sir." She swung her arm out in front of her motioning toward the back of the restaurant. "I'll make sure she knows you're here when she arrives. It is a woman, yes?" I laughed out loud. Austin was a mecca for gay people, not that I cared one way or the other. 'To each his own' I'd always said. Her lips parted and turned up into a secretive smile, as if she already knew the woman I was meeting was my soul mate or something. *Anything's possible, I guess.*

"Yes, a woman, thank you." I walked through the mass of tables and made my way to the bar, still laughing at her question. A woman? *Hell yeah, a woman. A* hot *woman!* I planted my elbows firmly on the cold tile of the bar as I waited for the server.

"What can I get you, sir?" the bartender asked.

"Just water."

"Tap or bottle?"

"Tap is fine."

"Comin' right up, sir."

He placed the glass down on the bar, along with a basket of tortilla chips and salsa.

"Anything else?"

"Not right now, thank you."

"Rory!" someone yelled behind me. I swiveled around on my bar stool and caught sight of her familiar face standing only a few feet away. "Thanks for calling me," she uttered.

"Sure." It obvious she was glad to see me and I felt bad. My attitude was halfhearted at best. After everything I'd experienced last night, I couldn't help shake the feeling that this was a big mistake. "I can't stay long though," I explained. "I've got an early meeting in the morning."

She closed the distance between us coming to rest comfortably in between my open legs at the edge of the bar stool I was sitting on. She gently placed one hand on my thigh just above the knee and began to rub it up and down coming dangerously close to my manhood. With her other hand, she braced herself on my shoulder leaning in so close to me that her boobs were practically in my face.

Her lips nestled close to my ear and I felt massive amounts of adrenaline start to pump through my veins. "It's alright," she whispered. I could feel her breath on my neck. "I don't need long. Not with you." I was thoroughly shocked to find that my man parts didn't respond to her overt actions. *What's wrong with you, Gregor? Have you lost your game?*

I pushed her away with both hands trying to create some type of formal distance between us before she jumped right onto my lap and started fucking me in front of the whole damn restaurant. Two days ago, that idea would have sounded entertaining to me, she was a knock-out by anyone's standards. But now, looking at her short auburn hair, her sea-green eyes and massive fake boobs, all I could think about was how different she was from Hindley and how much I wanted her to be gone. Why had I called her? *You called her because she's not a lawyer, she's not a socialite debutant, she's a hot chick who wants to give it up to you in all kinds of kinky ways.*

I cursed myself for not being remotely interested in what she was offering up so freely. Women never ceased to amaze me by how easily they threw themselves at men then acted appalled when men treated them like shit.

"What's wrong?" She was affronted by my actions and for a brief moment, I felt bad. I had led her on.

"Um, nothing."

"Ya wanna go back to my place?"

"No, I don't think so. In fact, I really shouldn't even be here."

"What?"

"I really need to go." I reached into my wallet and dug out a twenty throwing it on to the bar then shoved my hands in my jeans for the keys to Leif's motorcycle.

"Are you fuckin' with me?" She was pissed, definitely pissed, and I couldn't say as I blamed her one bit.

"What do you mean?" *Douche bag, you know exactly what she means.*

"You call me up and tell me to meet you in half an hour. I bust my ass to get ready and look halfway decent, thinking you wanted to take a roll in the sheets and now I haven't even had one drink and you say you have to go. What the fuck is up with that?" *Nice mouth, Cinderella.*

"I'm really sorry. Honestly. I should never have called you. Stay here, order whatever you want. I'll leave the bartender some cash for you."

"I don't need your fuckin' cash, you prick. I'm not a prostitute." *Oh, she's real classy, man. I can see why you picked her over Hindley now.*

"Look, all I can say is, I messed up. I made a mistake. I never should have called you. I'm sorry. Tell me if you're staying and I'll buy you a drink."

"Hell yeah, I'm staying. I didn't get all dolled up on a Sunday night just to sit at home and watch Dateline."

I waved down the bartender and gave him a fifty dollar bill. I leaned over the bar and yelled in his ear over the music. "Give her whatever she wants but make sure she takes a cab home. Make sure she gets home safe, okay?" *There you go again, giving two shits about a chick. You're totally fucked, man. Hindley has you totally fucked up.*

He looked Mandy up and down then took the fifty. "No problem, man." I turned back to say good bye. "I really am sorry. I know you're a nice girl. I just need to get up early tomorrow. Sorry I wasted your time."

She brought her Mexican Martini up to her lips and cut her eyes over the rim of the glass. "Fuck off, asshole!" Well, there you go. I judged a book by its cover and look where it got me. She seemed like a classy lady last night standing outside of one of Austin's most luxurious hotels. I'd obviously been a poor judge of character. Maybe I was wrong about Hindley, too. Maybe just because she was an attorney didn't mean she would try to take advantage of me once she found out who I really was.

As I walked out of the restaurant, I felt the cool nip of the night air. The dip in temperature was unusual for this time of month in Texas. I pulled my phone at of my pocket and looked at the time, ten twenty-eight. Shit! It's probably too late to call her. Fuck it. I pushed Hindley's number, hoping I wouldn't wake her, staring at her beautiful face on my screen as the call went through. I needed to talk to her, I needed to hear her voice. After the fifth ring, her message played.

"Hey, it's Hindley, leave a message."

I hung up and had to talk myself out of immediately calling back just to hear her voice again. *So what, now you've decided you want her after you just stood her up? Good luck with that, dude. You promised you'd call her. Not only did you* not *call her, you called some other chick. Hindley's a classy woman. No classy chick puts up with bullshit like that.*

I swung my leg over the seat of Leif's bike and started the engine, not sure where I was going as I listened to the rattling hum of the motor. I didn't even know the city that well but I did know where she lived and before I knew what happened, I found myself sitting outside a very familiar looking duplex. *Dude, its official. You are now a fuckin' stalker. What are you doing here?*

I felt like a predator lurking in the shadow just outside the light of a street lamp, completely out of sight. I knew what I was doing was wrong but I had to see her, just a glimpse of her. *Are you a Peeping Tom now, too?* I couldn't bear to believe that I'd never see her again. A small light illuminated one of the windows on her side of the duplex. She was home. I pulled out my phone and saw the time in big glowing numbers, eleven o'clock straight up. *It's way too late. Don't do it. Please.* I didn't care. I'd already gotten her under my skin and there was no way to relieve the itch until I scratched. I pushed the 'Call' button and listened as it went directly to voicemail, not even one single ring.

What the fuck! Now she was rejecting my phone call. Shit! I was pissed. *Why are you pissed? You stood her up man, remember?*

Before I knew it, I was off the bike and making my way up to her front door. *Rory, I'm seriously begging you. DON'T! DO! THIS!*

Holy shit, what am I doing? What am I gonna say? Should I knock? Should I ring the doorbell? *None of the above, you dumb ass! You should get back on that fuckin' bike and get the hell outta here. NOW!* She probably wouldn't even answer the door. She better not answer the door, it's eleven fuckin' o'clock at night.

As much as I wanted to leave, I just couldn't. Hindley was like a drug to me now and I had to get a fix. The more she eluded me, the more I wanted her. I couldn't forget anything about her, her lips, her eyes, her hair, her scent, her laugh, her voice. God, her voice was sexy. I had to see her.

I held my breath as I stepped up on the porch, hoping against hope that she'd open the door and let me in. My fist clenched in a tight ball as I stuck it out in front of me just inches away from her door. *Don't do it, man. This is gonna end badly!* I blew out my breath into the cool night air and let my knuckles brush over the door with a light tap. If she doesn't answer, I'll leave and never come back, never call her again. I promise. *That's a lie. If she doesn't answer, you'll fuckin' wait on the edge of her driveway til she runs over your ass tomorrow morning.*

I tried to look inside the small window in the door but it was covered with material. I could see movement inside though, so that gave me hope. At least I knew she was home. But suddenly, I realized, if she doesn't answer now that means she's blowing me off, on purpose. That scenario pissed me off royally. *That's because you've never been blown off. You're usually the one blowing chicks off.*

Then, an even more disturbing scenario came to mind. What if she's with someone else? What if she's got some other dude in there? The thought had my head spinning. I couldn't bear to think of another man touching her shoulders, her arms, her hair, her legs, her lips. God, those lips. I could still feel them on mine as we'd kissed last night. I'd sucked face with a lot of women, for a multitude of reasons, but none had ever made me feel so completely whole. I hadn't even fully comprehended how utterly incomplete I was until I kissed Hindley. And the best part of the entire thing was, she kissed me back, with a passion and a desire that matched mine.

The seconds ticked by as I waited for her to answer, my blood reaching dangerously high temperatures. *I can't believe you're doing this. It would serve your ass right if she calls the cops and has your ass carted off to jail. I'm sure River City Boards would love that. Come on, man, you do this to woman all the time. Doesn't feel too good now, does it, pretty boy?*

Finally, I heard the dead bolt unlock with a click and the door creak open. Her hair was in a ponytail, just like the first night I met her, and black framed glasses covered her eyes. She was wearing a t-shirt that had some type of Hello Kitty design on it with matching Hello Kitty flannel boxer shorts. Her face was void of any make up and I thought she'd never looked more beautiful. My eyes swept over her entire body, trying to memorize everything about her, fearing she may cast me off at any moment. Instead, she just stood there, staring at me, expressionless. I couldn't read her at all and it was unnerving me. I had no idea where I stood with her and I felt vulnerable, my heart on display.

"I'm sorry to come by so late but it's just that I was trying to call and you didn't answer and I started to get worried about you." *Jesus H. Christ, you sound like a pathetic pansy boy begging for a piece of ass. Grow a nut sack man and ask her why the fuck she didn't answer your calls.*

I watched her intently, as one eyebrow arched over the frames of her glasses, afraid of what her response would be. "Really?"

"What, you don't believe me?"

"Rory, what do you want? It's late and I still have a lot of work to do."

"I thought you said you'd be done by eight," I said sarcastically with a smirk on my face. I thought my words would lighten the mood but judging by her tightened lips and blatant scowl, I was obviously wrong. I looked down at my dingy boots, nervously knocking the sides into each other, trying to hide my anxiety. I couldn't even look her in the eye. "I'm sorry."

"For what?"

"For not calling you tonight like I said I would. I asked you out to dinner and then I never called you."

"Apology accepted. Now, if that's the only reason you came, I'd like you to go. It's cold out there and I'm tired."

She started backing up, preparing herself to slam the door in my face, but I wasn't ready to let her go. Not yet. I stuck my foot in between the frame and the door, effectively stopping her.

"Wait, Hindley."

"What!" she half shouted. I expected her to be disappointed with me but now, I could tell this was more than disappointment. I had wounded her. But it wasn't because of one missed call. Something else had happened.

"What's going on with you?"

"What's going on with me? What's going on with me!" she shouted again.

"Can I just come in and talk to you for a second?"

Suddenly, the porch light from next door flashed bright. Holy shit, I'd waken the neighbors. If muscle-head came over here now, I knew it wouldn't be good.

"No, you can't come in."

"Why?"

"You apologized, I accepted. We're done. You've absolved yourself, you're cleansed. Happy?"

Her head hung in what looked like defeat and I felt like the biggest asshole alive. *You did this. You're the asshole.* "No, Hindley. I'm not happy, I'm not happy at all," I whispered, my voice full of as much pain as I felt.

Finally, her gaze swept up from the floor taking in my entire being before coming to rest on my face. My insides shivered at her expression. Her eyes were full of pain. I had hurt her, really hurt her. I knew the minute I decided not to call her earlier tonight that it would, but I did it anyway and now I felt like a piece of shit. Why was it such a shock to me then, standing in front of this beautiful creature, looking into eyes that were beginning to pool with tears. I couldn't remember feeling lower in my life.

"Hindley, everything alright over there?" I heard the familiar voice of her neighbor.

Hindley pushed past me, wrapping herself up with her arms for warmth and leaned over the edge of the porch. "Yeah, I'm fine, Frannie, thanks." I saw Red's familiar face come into view.

"Oh, Lover Boy. Finally back for more, huh?" Her eyes rolled over me but not as seductively as the first time we met. I was relieved to see that muscle-head was nowhere around.

"You two know each other?" Red and I glanced at one another and nodded our heads in unison.

"Well, he's just leaving," Hindley said, ushering me off the porch with her shoulder.

"I don't think I'd let this one get away so easily, Hindley. I mean, how many guys find a totally smashed chick on the street and work their asses off trying to get them home safely without getting anything in return? He even came and banged on our door to make sure this was your address before he carried you inside."

"He did?" Hindley's eyes moved from Red over to me. The look of disgust was obvious but it was fading. *Thanks, Red!* "You carried me in?"

"Uh, yeah, he did. You were toast, Hindley." Red laughed to herself. "You couldn't have walked if you had to. Who knew you had a wild side to you?"

Hindley's expression was morphing from anger to passive. I could take that. At least she wasn't glaring at me anymore.

"Well, good night then. See ya in the morning, sunshine! Maybe you too, Lover Boy!" Red disappeared around the corner, laughing all the way. Within seconds, her porch light was extinguished. It was just Hindley and me again.

Her entire body was shivering from the cold so I reached out and began rubbing her arms up and down, trying to warm her. "Come on," I said pulling her inside. "This is ridiculous. You're freezing out here."

"I can't believe how cold it is outside," she commented. I escorted her in with surprisingly no resistance and shut the door, locking both dead bolts before slowly turning to face her.

"Why did you lock us in?" Her question took me off guard.

"Because I want to talk to you and unlike you, I'm not nearly as trusting of the human race."

"Rory, I wasn't kidding. It's late, I'm tired, and I've still got a shit load of work ahead of me." She motioned toward her dining room table and I saw her lap top at one end with piles of paper covering almost every surface. Next to her computer was a plate with several pieces of pizza piled on.

"Did I interrupt your dinner?" I tried to sound funny but suddenly realized I was supposed to take her to dinner tonight. The reason she was eating pizza was because of me. *You're a fuckin' douche bag, man!* I glanced over at her and saw she was looking down at the floor, obviously trying to avoid me. I let out a heavy sigh, resigning myself to the fact that I was now officially a douche bag.

"Look, Hindley. I just wanted to apologize to you about tonight. I needed to see you."

"That makes absolutely no sense. You said you wanted to go out with me but then you never called. Instead, you show up hours later and say, 'I need to see you.'" Her voice was deep trying to mimic my tone, and I had to bite my lip to keep from laughing.

"Was that supposed to be me?" I couldn't hold it any longer. A small laugh escaped my mouth before I could clamp my hand over it to silence myself. I tried to show a straight face but it was futile, my eyes were aglow with laughter.

She balled up her fist and swung at my arm connecting with my bicep. "Shut up!" she cursed me. She was trying to stifle her own laugh as well. A sense of relief washed over me when I realized the impending tears I saw earlier in her eyes were gone, replaced now with mixed amusement. I knew she'd kick my ass out if I gave her the option by asking so instead, I acted as if I owned the place and walked purposefully toward the kitchen bar, pulling out a piece of pizza from the box.

"What kind?" I asked as if it mattered. I could care less if dog shit was in it, I was gonna eat it if it meant I could stay here a little longer.

"What are you doing?"

"We're having dinner?"

"No. You're being a jack ass and eating *my* dinner."

"Either way, we're both hungry. Can you take a break just for ten minutes and eat with me?" Her eyes were glued to mine, penetrating through me as if she were trying to look deep into my soul. I diverted my gaze to the table, hoping that would stop her. I didn't want her to see that far inside me. I didn't want anyone to see that far inside me.

"Hold on!" She sprinted down the hallway and I couldn't help but notice her tight little ass. Man, she was hot! A chill ran down my spine and planted itself firmly in my dick. I thought about following her but a few seconds later, she reappeared wearing a huge fuzzy robe and slippers, essentially barring my ogling eyes. I noticed she'd let her hair down and I couldn't help but hope she'd done it for me. The thought that she was doing anything for me gave me hope.

I brought both of our plates over to the coffee table without even asking permission. I'd spent the night in her house already so it wasn't like I wasn't familiar with my surroundings. I plopped down on the sofa as if I'd lived here for years and picked up a piece of pepperoni pizza, not realizing how hungry I was. She was still rummaging around in the kitchen.

"So, do you own this duplex?" I shoved half the piece in my mouth, unaware of how ravenous I was. *Can't you even wait on her? God, you're such a douche.*

"Don't do this, Rory." I glanced up and she was handing me a bottle of water and a napkin.

"Do what?" I tried to get out in between bites.

"Don't start this small talk shit. It doesn't suit you."

I swallowed the entire contents of my mouth so I could reply. "What does that mean?"

She sat down on the chair opposite me, the one I'd put her down on when I'd brought her home just two nights ago. "I know who you are."

"Who am I?" I asked sarcastically before realizing there had been a level of disgust in her voice. Maybe she'd discovered I was a pro skateboarder. She probably thought that was completely beneath her. She'd made up her mind, judged me without evidence. She'd probably never give me a chance. Not that I deserved one after what I'd done tonight.

"You're a player."

"A player?"

"Yes! A player!" She pulled her pizza apart and picked at the crust. I could tell she was nervous and I knew I was the cause of it. I hated myself for being the source of any pain she had to endure. "I saw you last night, Rory. Outside the hotel with the other woman. I saw you take her number, just like you did mine."

I swallowed hard. Shit! Shit! Shit! I was prepared to grovel, I was prepared to beg, but I wasn't prepared for this. *How ya gonna get out of this one, Lover Boy?*

"You have one chance to get this right, Rory." Her tone was steady but her voice was quiet. My eyes were as wide as saucers, knowing full well she was right. If I fucked this up, it was over. Tonight. This second. How was I going to explain taking another woman's phone number and calling her instead? *You can't explain it because there is no explanation. You're a prick, plain and simple.*

"Answer me one question?"

My heart raced and I swallowed hard, my throat constricting with every breath. "Okay."

"Why did you run when I told you I was a lawyer?"

That was it? That was her one question I had to answer? My throat closed up and my heart seized as I realized that answering that question would be much more difficult for me than explaining why I took another girl's phone number.

I put my pizza back on my plate and wiped my mouth with the napkin, tossing it onto the table. I'd suddenly lost my appetite. What could I tell her? The truth? *Yeah, try that. Tell here you're a juvenile delinquent, a hot headed punk who's seen the inside of a courtroom more times than you care to count. Tell her you're a dope head and constantly have to check yourself to make sure you don't go over the edge. Try that out and see how it goes.*

My heart was pounding in my ears and I thought I might pass out. What can I say? What can I say that won't make her bolt? *Don't say a goddamm word, just get your shit and get the fuck outta here man. I'm tired of all this bullshit this chick is bringing us. She's shaking shit up inside you that you can't afford to be shaken. You've finally got your life back on track, don't derail for a piece of ass.*

I'll keep it generic, generalized. I don't want her to run, I need time, time to explain. She'll understand. *Will she?*

"I guess I've just had bad experiences with attorneys in the past and I'm a little leery."

"That's not all and you know it and I know it. If that's your answer then you need to leave. Now." She leaned back in her chair, making no attempt to escort me and I knew she was giving me another chance. She crossed her legs and I watched her robe fall open, revealing her long silky-smooth legs. I sucked in a quick breath as my heart seized with pain. I lost all thought. All I wanted was her lips on mine. "So, is that your answer?" she asked, waking me from my lurid thoughts.

"Look, Hindley, I've got a tainted past. Can we just leave it at that?"

"Why didn't you call me tonight?"

"I don't know. I guess I just figured you deserved better than me."

"Did you call her?"

"Who?"

"You know who."

Shit! You knew this was coming. I looked down at the coffee table afraid to look at her. "Yes," I whispered.

"Did you take her out today?"

"We met, for drinks."

"Oh. Well, I'm sure you had a nice time."

She stood and took both our plates and left the room. I sat with my head in my hands, knowing I'd blown it. One chance and I choked. I'd lost tournaments and competitions because of one bad trick and I'd thought that feeling was the worst in the world. I was wrong. This was. Knowing I'd lost Hindley felt like my own heart was being ripped from me. I sensed that if I lost her, I may never be able to breathe again.

When she reappeared, I didn't know whether to be ecstatic or scared shitless. She made her way directly to the door and turned the knob, pulling it open and letting a gust of cold wind spill into the room.

"It's late, Rory. You need to go."

I'd fucked up. Really fucked up. I didn't want to leave. I wasn't even sure I could leave. But she didn't want me. *Real surprise there, genius!* I'd single handedly self-sabotaged any chance I had with her. I was living out my own nightmare, creating scenarios that gave people no choice but to think the worst of me then acting surprised at their reaction.

I rose from the sofa, realizing this was it. I'd never see Drunk Girl again and my heart actually ached. I'd never felt that way before. I walked past her but couldn't leave, wouldn't leave, without touching her one more time.

I took her small hand in mine and brought it up to my mouth, brushing each knuckle with my lips. I purposely kept my gaze on her to judge her reaction. Just like last night, she was definitely affected by me. But tonight was different, there was indifference there and I wasn't entirely sure I could overcome that obstacle. I wanted to try though. As long as she didn't object, I'd push on.

I let my fingers trail over her furry robe working my way up from her hand to her shoulder. I brushed her hair back and noticed that her eyes flickered slightly. It was enough to spark me on. I snaked my hand around the nape of her neck, elated to feel her lean into me. I pulled myself even closer, my eyes locked on hers looking for any sign of opposition. When I saw none, I pulled nearer, watching her intently until my mouth slowly covered hers. My entire body seized up in pain, a delicious pain. I pushed on, taking more of her mouth inside of mine and still, I didn't feel her protest. She was actually starting to become a willing participant and my pulse accelerated to illegal speeds. She gave me more confidence so I drew her into me, trying to fuse our bodies into one. She came willingly and I could feel the heat of her hands wrap around my shoulders. Her touch was like heaven. Our kiss progressed to another level of primal hunger and I felt her succumb to all our desires. I couldn't think, couldn't breathe, I was consumed with everything about her.

Without warning, she abruptly pushed me away, a look of disgust in her eyes. My chest was heaving trying to bring oxygen back to my lungs. What happened? Had I misread her responses to my touch? *No, dude, that girl wanted you too much and she knew* it.

"Go Rory." She whispered, so low, I could barely hear her. I searched her eyes looking for an answer but found nothing, only shutters. She had effectively closed me out. I walked toward the door, knowing there was nothing more I could do. Tonight.

I stepped out on the porch, but turned to catch a glimpse of her one last time before she closed the door. I was surprised to see the corners of her delicious mouth curl into a hesitant smile just before her face disappeared. I'd affected her, it wasn't over! Two clicks echoed through the silent night as I realized she'd bolted the door. I was relieved to know she was trying to keep herself safe. Darkness suddenly engulfed me. *She turned off the porch light, dipshit. It's time to go.* I stood outside her house, all alone, with an unfamiliar feeling racing through my body. Hope.

Chapter 7

~HINDLEY~

I couldn't believe what I was looking at. I'd been staring at it for well over an hour now, my eyes growing weary from glaring at the laptop screen. Why hadn't I noticed it before? I prided myself on details. I was a contracts attorney for God's sake. Well, I was for the time being.

It wasn't like contract law or tort litigation had been my passion in law school. My desire to be a prosecutor had fueled my need to finish school, but after my first year, I interned with the local DA's office over the summer and quickly realized I'd never survive that type of law. I thought I would do some good, contribute some justice to a system that had been unjust to me. But in the end, it all became too overwhelming, the crime scene photos, the victim's statements, the police reports. It brought back too many bad memories and I'd nearly dropped out of law school entirely.

Instead, Paul talked me into starting my meds again and seeing Dr. Nelson, assuring me it would only be temporary.

I'd interned in almost every area of the law during my breaks from school, trying desperately to figure out what specialty best suit my interests and skill sets but still, after graduation, I hadn't settled on a one.

Thankfully, one of Paul's financial investors was a founding senior partner at his own law firm and overheard Paul talking about my situation at a party my mother was throwing. He introduced me to Aston Stedwick and we had an impromptu interview right there at the party. I must have impressed Mr. Stedwick because two days later, he called and offered me a position with his law firm, Stedwick and Nigh.

It was an honor to work for such a prestigious law firm, especially having just passed the bar last year. They had lots of divisions but he was creating a new section and needed attorneys to help him build it from the ground up. I'd been reluctant at first, not knowing much about contract law but in the end, I needed a job and he needed a new lackey, so I agreed. Plus, there was the added pressure of not disappointing Paul. I mean, I knew he wouldn't mind if this didn't turn out to be my cup of tea, but I couldn't just leave Mr. Stedwick high and dry if I didn't like the work. His investment was integral to Paul's company and Paul didn't let me forget about that fact. I agreed to a six month trial period, which we both decided would give us enough time to see if my skills and abilities matched what Mr. Stedwick and his firm were looking for and if this was the type of law I might be interested in pursuing.

He obviously expected this new division to be pretty lucrative because he'd started me out at a very high salary for a first year attorney. It had been enough to allow me to put a good down payment on my duplex and stash the maximum amount in my retirement account, my 401K, and a separate annuity. I was planning for the future. I'd learned my lessons by living in the moment and being careless. Every move I made now was calculated, precise, and planned. My life didn't have room for surprises.

I turned my attention from the laptop to the document on my desk, my eyes focusing on it intently, as if I thought I could use mental telepathy to change it. Seeing my efforts were in vain, I turned back to the laptop and cringed when I discovered nothing had changed. The majority of the contract was boilerplate. I'd worked really hard over the last three months drafting the verbiage with Michael and Luis, two associates who were in charge of this new division I was now a part of. We'd made sure the words were perfectly written to protect both parties involved. Today though, I wasn't concerned about anything but the name in front of me. I was peeved that I was letting my personal feelings get in the way of my professional judgment.

Why hadn't I seen it before? I'd been pouring over the contract all day yesterday, well into the night. *You know why. You were interrupted. And you liked it.* I didn't know if I was more furious that Rory had come to my house for a late night booty call, that Rory had called a complete stranger to go out instead of me, or that I had dreamt about our parting kiss until the wee hours of the morning. I was so mad at him, so hurt by his dismissal, yet in one kiss, he'd essentially wiped away all my anger and disappointment.

I clicked the internet icon on my laptop and let it toggle over to the pages I'd pulled up earlier this morning. It was him, definitely him. My eyes rolled over to the stack of papers on my desk. It was right there, literally in black and white. The title of the document was the same, 'Sponsorship Contract.' The Sponsor name was no surprise either, 'Kopra Enterprise, LLC.' We'd drafted a several legal documents for them in the past, including an Article of Incorporation when they'd decided to grow their company. This was the third sponsorship contract I'd personally worked on with them under their subsidiary company. Maybe that's why I'd skimmed over it so hastily. I wasn't representing the Sponsee, I was representing Kopra.

No, all of the rest of the text on the document was common to me, no surprise. The only thing different was the 'Sponsee Name' and it had my head spinning. The man Kopra Enterprises wanted to sponsor, the man whose name appeared before me was the only difference. Rory Gregor. *Rory fuckin' Gregor.*

I'd been sitting at my desk for over an hour, staring at Rory's name on my computer and on the physical document lying next to it, trying to decide what to do. I'd been so caught up in the particulars of the terms of the contract that I'd completely neglected to associate Rory's name with the 'Sponsee' title. How could I trust myself now with this contract, if I couldn't even notice something as major as that? What should I tell Michael and Luis? Should I even tell them I knew Rory? *Yeah, you know him, alright. You know him very well. Especially your lips.*

And what would Mr. Stedwick say? I knew he would be at the negotiations today. What if they asked *how* I knew Rory? *Better to keep this one to yourself.*

I looked down at my watch, relieved to find I still had an hour to figure out what the hell I was going to do. I needed help, so I picked up my phone and dialed Luis's extension.

"What's up, girl? You ready for the meeting?" No matter what the situation was, Luis always seemed to be upbeat and positive. And he was unbiased and nonjudgmental. Two things I needed today.

"Um, about that. I need to talk to you."

"Ut oh, that doesn't sound good. What's going on?"

"Do you have a second to talk?"

"For you, doll face, I have a lifetime. I'll be right there."

Luis Marquez was an angel fish in a sea of sharks, a beauty inside and out that I feared one day may be eaten alive by those he worked for. But he never seemed to mind. I had no idea why he'd ever pursued a law degree, he had so many other strong talents. But here at Stedwick and Nigh, he'd managed to climb his way up the corporate ladder nicely. He always told me "Girl, my taste is too expensive. I have to have a profession that can afford me."

Luis was funny, borderline hysterical, and handsome as all get out. The problem was, he knew it. His Latino blood lent him just the right amount of skin pigment to make him look edible, like melted caramel and his jet black hair and light hazel eyes made every woman and gay man in the office swoon, including me. His voice was deep and husky and his foreign accent made him sound exotic and mysterious. But the real pull to Luis, the thing that made him over the top gorgeous, was his heart. In this industry, where it was 'self first, other's never', Luis had never succumbed to that thinking. He always said his Latin culture was about family first. I thought it odd that he considered this cold, unfeeling law practice his 'family', but because his own family was still back in Brazil, I knew he needed something beyond his boyfriend to give him purpose.

"What's up, doll face?" he asked swinging open my office door with more attitude than Miss Piggy. In any other law firm or business, his actions toward me could have been construed as sexual harassment. But given the fact that one, Luis was gay and two, that was his nature, I'd grown accustomed to it. In fact, a large part of me loved that about Luis. His terms of endearment were a welcomed part of my day.

"I think I may have a problem with the Kopra contract."

"What's up?"

"I know the Sponsee," I said, pushing the front page over to him.

Luis and Michael had shown extreme trust in me over the last three months. They allowed me to draft the contracts now pretty much on my own. Michael was the closer, the negotiator and Luis dealt with the personalities, the "divas" as we liked to call them. I knew he was already familiar with both parties we'd be dealing with today. He prided himself on Intel and was good at it, really wanting this new division to prosper and grow. Despite his lackadaisical attitude, Luis had goals, and becoming a partner by the age of thirty-five was one of them.

Stedwick and Nigh was slowly trying to move its way into what they called attorney-agent representation. It brought together the best of both an attorney and an agent for the athlete, something that used to be stand alone positions. Not only was an attorney-agent someone who was familiar with all aspects of the law, they were also able to promote the athlete and stay on top of any legal issue that may surround them. It was the latest trend in sponsorship contracts and it was a very lucrative deal, with the attorney earning much more than just a standard fee. They wrote the contracts to ensure that when the athlete succeeded, so did the sponsor and the attorney-agent. To date, our firm hadn't handled any athletes, only the sponsors, but this was the area Mr. Stedwick was extremely interested in breaking into.

"So what, he's a professional athlete. Most people who haven't had their head up their ass for the last ten years know Rory Gregor. He's got like a zillion X Games medals, for God's sake."

"Well, that's just the thing, Luis. Up until an hour ago, I'd never heard of him."

"So, what's the problem now?"

"I *know* him," I answered trying to put more emphasis on the 'know' part of the sentence.

Luis perched high on the edge of his seat and covered his mouth with his hand. "Uhnt uh. Tell me you did not tap that?"

"Luis!"

"I mean, I wouldn't blame you. He is one red hot motherfucker. I would too, if I thought I stood a chance."

"I didn't 'tap that,'" I said with air quotes. "We just kissed. Twice."

"I know there's more there, girl, I can see it in your eyes. Spill!" He pushed back in the chair and folded his hands over his chest as if he were preparing for an LMN movie.

I started from the beginning, telling him about getting drunk, how Rory took care of me, how he went to the wedding with me, how he kissed me, how he screwed me over, and how he showed up at my house to apologize and ravished me, again.

Luis rubbed his dark hair with both hands as he rolled his eyes up toward the ceiling. "Holy hell, baby doll. We have us a real problem here."

"I know. I can't go into these negotiations."

"I'm not talking about that. I'm talking about you."

"What about me?"

"You're already over the moon for this guy. It shows in your face, in your whole damn countenance. Every time you say his name, your eyes sparkle and you get this adorable crinkle in your nose. I've never seen you like this before. You look good wearing a little lust on you."

I threw a paper clip at him but missed. "That's not true." I was really upset with Luis, not for his comments but because of the fact that deep down, I knew everything he said *was* true. Even after all the things I'd learned about him on the Internet, after all I'd experienced with him personally, I still felt a pang of lust deep in my belly, like I'd never felt before.

"Look, I'm not saying you can't play with him on the side. Just be careful. I think he's way beyond you though."

"What the hell does that mean?"

"Don't get defensive."

"I'm not getting defensive. First, I can't have any sort of relationship with him other than professional because that's my job. And second, I still wouldn't involve myself with him even if I didn't represent his sponsor. Have you seen all the shit he's done?" I turned my laptop around so Luis could read page after page of Rory's infractions.

He'd become pro at age eighteen, which was really remarkable apparently. But in less than four years' time, he'd managed to piss away all his money, lose four endorsement deals, be arrested twice, once for drug charge, and screw every prostitute looking bimbo in the lower forty-eight.

When it came to men, I'd never quite been sure what my 'type' was but I definitely knew what my type was *not*. Rory Gregor was not my type, *at all*, at least not on paper. But in person, I was in trouble and I knew it. I couldn't wrap my head around reconciling that the punk pretty boy I read about in countless stories on the Internet was the same man I'd met just two days before. That man was caring, kind, and protective. *Yeah, well, don't forget he also stood you up, called some other skank, then came over to YOUR house for a midnight booty call, probably after she'd rejected him.* Definitely not my type, at all!

"Yeah, I knew he was a crazy kid and did some serious damage to his reputation." Luis stared at me intently. "How did you not already know this? I mean, I know I'm the one who schmoozes the client, but you're so detail oriented. This really surprises, Hindley." I knew he wasn't reprimanding me but his words of consternation hurt. I really prided myself on my work and Luis's approval was huge to me. I knew I'd disappointed him and I couldn't hide my shame.

"I don't know. I'm worried."

"Why?" His tone was extremely sympathetic.

All I could do was shake my head.

"That bad, huh?" I glanced up and saw him turning the laptop back around to face me.

"What do you mean?"

"Baby girl. The guys a fox, solid, no doubt. He's talented as shit and poised to be the next great skateboarder of all time. He's changed."

"I don't think so. Did you not hear my story? He took another chick's phone number seconds after taking mine. He promised to call me and instead, called her. Once a player, always a player."

"That's not true. Look at me."

"You're different." I knew what Luis was talking about. He had been quite the man's man when he was single. But three years ago, he met Teddy. Teddy had been patient with Luis, watching countless times as Luis tried to sabotage their relationship. Instead of bailing, Teddy had helped Luis, shown him where his demons were, and helped put them to rest. In the end, Luis was a different person and was able to love Teddy with his whole heart. Something, apparently, he'd never been able to do before. And he credited Teddy with all of it.

"No, I'm not. I'm no different than Rory Gregor. Except he's white and straight." He laughed to himself. "I *was* a player sweetheart, plain and simple."

"Not as bad as this guy," I said pointing to my laptop.

"Trust me, if I'd been given all the money, notoriety, and free ass that boy had handed to him at eighteen, I would have been worse!" I rolled my eyes in disgust, all the while knowing, in my heart, it was true. Luis had been bad. "Look, Hindley, people change, they evolve. The guy fucked up. It doesn't mean that's who he is, that he can't change. Once upon a time, we were all Neanderthal cavemen, draggin' our knuckles across the vast terrain." He straightened his tie and pulled down on his suit jacket, completely smitten with himself. "Oh, wait, I forgot. You white people hate the word evolution." I couldn't help but laugh. Luis was anything but politically correct. "But look at us now! Civilized creatures. You'll do fine, sweetie." With his final words of wisdom, he pushed up out of my chair and headed for the door.

"Wait!" I shouted, feeling as desperate as I sounded. He turned to look at me, those hazel eyes full of hope and promise.

"Hindley, you have killer instincts, you've just never trusted them. What do your instincts say right now? What is your gut telling you?"

"I don't know."

"Yes, you do." I dropped my gaze and nervously twisted my hands, afraid to look him in the eyes. I knew exactly what my gut was telling me and it scared me to death. "Until you admit it to yourself, there is nothing I or anyone else can do to help you. If you like this guy then don't let his past stop you from at least exploring your options." I could hear the sexual innuendo in his voice and my head snapped up. He gave me a wink and a huge smile before quickly disappearing.

I loved Luis. He always knew exactly what to say. And he was right. No matter what the Internet said or what had transpired yesterday, my gut told me Rory was a good guy. He was on his way back to the top of his profession and I felt almost certain he'd learned his lesson. Last night was probably a slip up. He'd acted really squirrelly when I'd told him I was an attorney at the wedding and he admitted he didn't have a good history with them. Maybe I'd spooked him and that's why he'd turned to the other girl and blown me off.

I straightened the papers on my desk as I continued working on a few more changes I had. His attorney had drafted an original sponsorship contract but I found it was riddled with all kinds of loopholes that didn't benefit Rory or River City Skateboards at all. I wondered, several times, where this guy had gotten his law degree. Probably some miniscule island in the Caribbean.

Rory had a right to know that perhaps his attorney wasn't working in his best interest. Maybe Mr. Stedwick was right. Athletes did need better representation. But I didn't want to be responsible for Rory Gregor. I couldn't. I knew I was already developing feelings for him and there was no way I would be able to keep a clear head around him. Somewhere along the way, my personal feelings would jeopardize my professional decisions and in the end, we'd both lose.

~

"They're here." I glanced up and saw Michael's head poking through my door. "You ready?" His eyebrows shot up and I knew Luis had told him everything. Well, maybe not *everything*, but enough for Michael to be concerned.

"Yeah, I'm ready." I took a deep breath in and blew it out, trying to release the butterflies that had now taken up permanent residence in my stomach

Michael looked me up and down. "You look like you're about to throw up."

"I feel like it."

"You can't go in there like this, Hindley. Go to the bathroom and freshen up. Splash some water on your face, throw some lip gloss on or whatever it is you girls, do then meet us in the main conference room in five minutes. Luis and I are going to go in and schmooze everyone over." Michael ran his eyes over me, not in a perverse way, he was just surveying me to see if I could stand up to the challenge. I would and I could. I had to prove myself to him, show him that he could count on me, even when the situation was less than perfect. "Five minutes," he repeated, more sternly. He left the door wide open as he walked away, with Luis not far behind. I stood up and all but ran to the bathroom on legs that now felt like Jell-O.

I stood outside of the conference room, smoothing out my dress while smacking my lips together. I'd applied a light coat of gloss and a little mascara but other than that, I was au naturel. *You can do this, girl. He's just a guy. A guy who's totally hot and probably an animal in the sack, but all the same, just a guy.* I took in a deep breath and grabbed the door handle, putting on my best game face. As I turned the knob, I silently blew out my breath knowing that what lie inside may very well eat me alive.

The first person I noticed was Mr. Stedwick, the owner of the firm. Even though I was expecting him, my body went rigid, realizing this encounter was going to be different. He never attended these meetings. My eyes began to scan the room and saw Luis and Michael, their faces just as nervous as mine.

Mr. Stedwick stood and motioned toward me. My eyes were glued to his, trying to balance myself. "Gentlemen, you've met Mr. Marquez and Mr. Perkins. I'd like to introduce you to another associate here at our firm, Ms. Hindley Hagen."

My eyes slowly panned the table across from Luis and Michael. The first man I saw was wearing a short sleeve polo shirt and had light brown hair with graying around the temples and brown eyes. He looked to be about fifty or so. Very nice looking with well-defined arms that had the sleeves of his shirt pulled taught.

"I'm Jack Jennings, Rory's manager." *Why does that name sound familiar?* As he stood to extend his hand, I noticed he was wearing neatly pressed khaki pants and a black belt with an odd buckle that, for some reason, made me look twice. *Hello, Hindley, you're staring at the man's crotch.* I shook his hand but immediately diverted my gaze to the next man trying not to turn as red as my dress.

He stood and held out his hand. "I'm Eugene Albright, Rory's attorney. But you can call me Gene-O" *That's an odd nickname?*

He was much more rotund, sporting a huge beer belly and at least two chins. He was wearing a starched white shirt with a navy blue tie but no jacket. I shook his hand and it was limp and cold. Paul had always taught me to make my first impression by a person's handshake. My first impression of Gene-O was that Rory was in trouble if this guy was representing him.

I literally held my breath as I let my eyes slowly move over to the final person in the room, dreading what I might find. He was beautiful, gorgeously dressed in a blue, button down, dress shirt that matched the color of the sky outside perfectly. His hand was long and lean and I couldn't take my eyes off of it as he extended it toward me. This was it, his expression would tell me everything. Either he was going to bust me right here in front of the owner of my law firm and cast me out onto the street or he was going to play the game, act as if we'd never met. I wasn't sure which scenario would hurt me more. I secretly hoped he'd land somewhere in between and we'd all survive.

My eyes worked their way up to his face, taking so long I'm sure everyone was wondering what my problem was. I couldn't help it. Drinking in the sight of Rory Gregor was something I wanted to savor. His lips were just as round and perfect as I remembered them in my house last night when they were glued to mine. His eyes were bluer today, probably because of his shirt, but I could still see a hint of brown around his pupils. His face was difficult to read. I could tell he was shocked but he didn't seem infuriated. I put my hand in his and instantly felt a connection, a pull to him. I was glad the table separated us because I really wasn't sure if I could have restrained myself from yanking him toward me. His eyes roved over my body as if deciding which way to eat me alive first. A chill ran through me entire body, thinking of him in my bed the first night we'd met, wishing now we'd done more than just sleep.

"It's nice to see you again, Hindley," he said with no malice or hostility. Either he could care less or he was a great actor.

"Oh, you two know each other already?" Mr. Stedwick asked.

"Yes," he answered before I could. I had the pleasure of meeting Hindley Friday evening when I was out with friends."

"Well, how delightful. Perhaps that will help these proceedings to go more smoothly."

I ducked my head down, pulling my skirt flat against the back of my thighs as I took a seat next to Luis. "Nice to meet you all." I cut a glance at Rory and saw he was studying my every move. The butterflies in my stomach were turning into bees, stinging me relentlessly.

All eyes were on Mr. Stedwick as he started off the negotiations. "I'm sorry Bucky and Pena couldn't join us this morning. Apparently, their daughter was violently ill last night and had to be rushed to the hospital." My eyes grew bigger and I saw Mr. Stedwick smirk a bit at Michael, whose face remained impassive. He was lying and I didn't know why. If something had happened to Bucky or Pena or one of their children, I would be devastated, and the fact that Mr. Stedwick may be exploiting them by lying about their children had my blood boiling.

Bernard "Bucky" and Pena Kopra were the husband and wife owners of River City Boards and President and CEO of Kopra Enterprises, their parent company. They were two of the nicest people you'd ever want to meet, always more concerned about relationships than the bottom line. Kopra Enterprises was all family-owned and operated. They'd first retained our firm several years ago, when they filed for a corporation status. They could see their company was growing exponentially and wanted to protect everyone associated with them. Having worked with them twice before, I was very familiar with their company and with them personally. I would never wish harm to any one of them, least of all their children, and I certainly would never use it as leverage at the negotiation table.

"Is everything alright?" I heard Rory ask. "Is their child going to be okay?" I was surprised to hear the level of concern as Rory spoke. And he seemed just as shocked at the look on my face when I turned to stare at him.

"Yes, yes, they'll be fine." Mr. Stedwick tried to smooth things over, shocked himself to see Rory was so concerned. I could tell by his expression that he hadn't expected that response.

"That's quite alright," Gene-O said. "I don't think it's really necessary that they be here for this portion. We're still ironing out details. As long as they're present for the signing, we should be fine." He tried to sound authoritative as if he was in control of this meeting but obviously, he had no idea who Mr. Stedwick was. He'd never be in control, not sitting here in the conference room of Stedwick and Nigh, especially with the owner and senior partner personally present and sitting at the helm.

"Shall we begin, gentleman?" Michael opened up his portfolio and pulled out the contract. I stood and passed out copies to everyone at the table. As I handed Rory his copy, his eyes locked on mine and I was curious to see a look of relief on his face, as if he was glad I was here.

"I believe Ms. Hagen has made quite a few changes to your original contract, Mr. Albright. I'm going to let her review those first, then we can start our negotiations." Michael was firm and precise and his faith in me gave me confidence to begin. I wasn't as experienced as Mr. Albright, but I could tell by the verbiage in his original document I was much shrewder.

I straightened the copy in front of me and cleared my throat to begin. "As you can see, Mr. Albright, I've made quite a few changes to your original document. I felt it was lacking in specifics that would protect and benefit both of our clients." I spent the next half hour going over all the changes, trying to be as specific as I could. At sporadic intervals, I would take a breath and glance up to find Rory staring at me. He had an unnerving look of pride on his face that gave me a sense of confidence. *He believes in you,*

Hindley. Everyone does. Why don't you believe in yourself? I literally shook my head, trying to clear the thoughts before continuing.

"I think the biggest change you'll find is in the Incentives Clause on page fourteen." All the men flipped through the pages but Mr. Albright reached over and turned Rory's for him, pointing to the exact spot on the paper where we were. It wasn't unusual for athletes to be lost in these negotiations so the act didn't completely surprise me but it did seem somewhat odd for whatever reason. I let the thought go and continued. "I don't think the incentives are specific enough for either client to fully benefit."

"Are you referring to your firm benefiting, Ms. Hindley?" I was completely thrown by Gene-O's remark. Was he insinuating that we were trying to take advantage of everyone? It was his dumb ass document that was so screwed up. How dare he make it look like I was exploiting Rory or the Kopra's. *Be cool, Hindley. Don't blow a gasket right here in front of Mr. Stedwick. Douche bag will hang himself eventually.* Instead, I continued on as if I hadn't heard him.

"If Mr. Gregor continues to perform at the level he's at, we're assuming his victories will only increase over the next year." I'd done my research before the meeting and although I found lots of knocks in Rory's personal armor, professionally he was really talented. The critics made it clear on the Internet that they believed if he stayed on the path he was on, he'd really soar over the next few years. I'd also had a chance to watch videos of him skating and I had to admit he was amazing. "We believe it's in the best interest of Mr. Gregor and River City Boards to tie those victories to the incentive clause."

"Well, that's unusual." His manager's voice startled me.

"What's that, sir?" I asked looking up from the contract.

"An attorney representing the sponsor who actually tries to negotiate a better deal for the athlete."

"Although I know Mr. Gregor is currently represented by Mr. Albright, it is not River City's position to hold him back. If there is a way they can help Mr. Gregor succeed, they will. This isn't about taking from Rory, it's about being mutually beneficial to all parties. Believe me, if Mr. Gregor is successful, everyone in this room will be, too. It behooves us all to support him in any way possible. Incentivizing this contract for him only means we're allowing him to perform and be rewarded when he's successful. After all, it's he who's doing all the work, not us."

Listening to the deafening silence, I scanned the room, surprised to see all eyes on me, as if I was an alien they'd never seen before, including Mr. Stedwick. I wasn't sure if he was happy or pissed but I decided to trudge on and let them know how I truly felt. If Mr. Stedwick really wanted to be in the business of becoming attorney-agents then he needed to know that I had drafted a sound document that protected not only Kopra Enterprises but also Rory Gregor. And if I could do it for Rory, I could do it for other athletes who chose our firm. At least, I thought I could. I wasn't entirely sure that my need to make sure Rory was compensated fairly wasn't tied directly to my feelings for him as a man.

"To be honest, Mr. Albright," I continued, "I was surprised at how poorly your contract was written in Rory's favor. It is your job to not only protect Mr. Gregor but to also negotiate the best deal for him. Not only were the performance incentives lacking in specifics, but you also failed to allow Mr. Gregor to approve any and every advertisement or promotional product distributed by River City Boards. Believe me when I say River City has no intentions of maliciously harming Rory in any way. If he looks good, they look good. But I would have expected you to understand that and draft a contract that protected him regardless."

Again, all eyes were on me but this time most were big as saucers and several jaws were gaping open. Including Mr. Stedwick. *Oh, shit! He's pissed. You've done it now! Go pack your bags, you're a goner.* The one face I really concentrated on was Mr. Gene-O Albright's. It was bright red and his eyes were fuming so bad they almost crossed. If looks could have killed, I'd be dead. I'd affronted him and attacked him in front of fellow professionals and even his own client. But I couldn't help it. It was obvious this asshole didn't give a rat's crap about Rory's well-being, which was surprising to me because the better Rory did, the better he'd do if it were drafted correctly.

Michael was going to kill me. He hated insubordination with a passion. I was out of line and he would call me on it. He may even fire me as soon as I left the room. Maybe he'd do it right here in front of everyone. That would serve me right. Mr. Stedwick would probably back him, adding in his own choice words. That would have been a *huge* embarrassment especially because Paul had basically finagled me into this job. If I screwed up, it would be a reflection of him and Mr. Stedwick might pull all his backing from Paul's real estate holdings. *When are you going to learn to hold your tongue? You say Rory's a hot head. Look at you.* All I could think was, 'Please don't fire me, please don't fire me.'

I jumped when Mr. Stedwick broke the silence speaking directly to me. "I think your changes and concerns are very valid, Ms. Hagen. I'm sure Mr. Gregor and Mr. Albright appreciate your diligence to negotiate the best possible deal for all parties. Am I correct, Mr. Albright?" I heaved a huge sigh of relief, finally realizing Mr. Stedwick was on my side. I had to mask the smirk raging inside me. I'd done a good job and I deserved the praise. Gene-O's grimace faded as he realized we were not going to back down and he'd been served his ass by a lowly first year attorney and backed by her firm's owner. *Alright, Hindley!*

From the corner of my eye, I could see that Michael and Luis were both on the edge of a smile as well and it thrilled me. It was validation to me that I was well on my way to becoming a great attorney. Even if contract law hadn't been my first choice, I was at least happy to see my hard work and diligence was paying off. And it didn't hurt that the senior partner was witness to my efforts.

Suddenly, I thought about Rory and wondered what his reaction to my outburst would be. Would he be upset? Surely not, I was working a deal in his favor. I felt chills run up my neck and instantly I knew why. I had all his attention, and I liked it. Actually, I loved it. Slowly, I let my eyes sweep up to meet his gaze, worried at what I might find. Why was I suddenly concerned about what he thought of me and my abilities as a lawyer? When I finally found those bright blue eyes fixed on mine, I was lost. His expression was smug but his pride was palpable. He was impressed with my work and it meant more to me than having my superiors' approval. Why? *Because even though you won't admit it, Skater Boy matters to you. Girl, you got it bad!*

"Well, if everyone is in agreement then we'll make these changes and have a finalized version for you by tomorrow." Michael shoved the contract back into this portfolio and closed the cover. "Should we deliver it to you personally, Mr. Albright?"

Gene-O was taken aback, as if he'd never done this before. Didn't he know how contract negotiations worked? He'd obviously received his doctorate of jurisprudence in Puerto Rico as I'd suspected, if he'd even received it at all.

"You can have it delivered to our house."

Our house? Wait a minute, whose house? Did Rory have a house in Austin? That was a surprise.

"That sounds wonderful. If you'd like to stop by my assistant's desk on the way out and give her the address, we'll be sure and messenger it over tomorrow. After you have a chance to review the changes, we can schedule another meeting with all of you and Bucky and Pena to sign all the documents."

I knew I wouldn't be at that meeting. I was just needed for contract review and negotiations. Signing protocol was all Luis and Michael. I took in a deep breath and breathed out like I was giving birth, knowing I'd survived another meeting with Rory. Hopefully, for my heart's sake, this would be the last. My chest seized with pain at the realization that this might be the final time I saw him. *It's a good thing. He's a player, no good for you.*

My conversation with Luis reverberated through my head. There is hope for all of us to evolve into better human beings. Even he had experienced his own transformation, once he'd met the right person. Was I the right woman for Rory? Did I have what it took to reform him, transform him? Did I even want to? *No! Hell no! You have no time to train a dog and that's exactly what he is.* His past actions may have been animalistic but so were his kisses. A small smile emerged as my fingertips rubbed over my lips, remembering how delicious it felt when they were pressed on his.

I turned to leave, trying not to look at him again but it was futile. If this truly was the end for us then I wanted to have one last look at his gorgeous face and try to commit it to memory for all time. His physique looked so good in that shirt that my body ached for him. As he stood, I noticed he was wearing dark navy slacks that were tailor-fitted, revealing all his best assets. I gasped when I felt a warm tingle wash over my midsection. One look at him and I knew it had been a bad mistake to turn around. I felt like what's her name from the Bible, who looked back at the city and instantly turned to salt because she hadn't obeyed God. I was melting right in front of him.

Our eyes finally met and I saw a look of awe reflecting back. Was it because of me? Was he impressed with me? I couldn't image why. *Maybe because you just stood up for him. Maybe because you just negotiated the best deal he's ever had and you don't even work for him. Maybe because you look fucking awesome in your tight red dress and nude stiletto pumps.* I couldn't help but hope all those reasons were true. And when I saw him drink me in from head to toe, I knew I was right. His eyebrows lifted in a silent statement that told me in no uncertain terms I was not seeing the last of him. My body tingled in response and the butterflies that had once resided in my stomach were now flying south to other parts of my anatomy. I knew if I didn't walk out of that conference soon, I'd throw him down on the table and rip off all his clothes and beg him to make love to me in every way imaginable. His hand reached out for my arm but I instinctively pulled it into my chest and ducked my head, ashamed of my thoughts. I rushed out of the door, racing to the only place where I knew I'd be safe, the ladies' bathroom.

~

Michael and Luis took me to a celebratory lunch, talking non-stop about what a fantastic job I'd done. I was surprised that they never realized before how feisty I could be. Then, I realized, I'd never negotiated like that before. I'd really never negotiated at all. Had Rory changed my tactics, had he allowed me to tap into my never before seen predator side? I smiled, thinking about him and how delicious he looked today.

Suddenly, my office phone rang, bringing me back from my thoughts. "Hello."

"Miss Hagen, it's Donna Friar."

Donna Friar? That was Mr. Stedwick's personal assistant. What the hell did she want with me? Before I could think of any more questions, she continued.

"Mr. Stedwick would like to see you in his office at two."

"Um, okay."

"I'll let him know to expect you."

"Thank you." There was silence on the phone and I realized she'd already hung up. She carried about as much personality as a thumb tack and I was immediately intimidated by her.

At one fifty-five, I reapplied my lip gloss and made my way to the elevators, surprised to see Michael.

"You ready for this?"

"What's going on?"

"I don't know. Either we're both being fired or we're getting big fat raises. I'm thinking its raises because Mr. Stedwick never does the firing. It's always HR."

Shit, shit, shit. What have you done now, Hindley Hagen?

After waiting almost fifteen minutes outside of Mr. Stedwick's office, Donna finally escorted us in. It was huge corner office, almost as big as my side of the duplex with a breathtaking view of the Central Texas hill country on one side and downtown Austin on the other.

"Please, have a seat." He motioned in front of us to two high back leather chairs.

I couldn't wait. I had to explain myself. I had to absolve Michael. "First, I want to apologize about this morning, sir. I know I was out of line and I should have discussed the changes with Michael beforehand," I explained. "I had no right to assault Mr. Gregor's counsel. Please believe me, Michael had no idea I was going to be so forward."

"Well, if Mr. Perkins deserves none of the blame as you suggest, then it would stand to reason he deserves none of the accolades as well."

"I don't understand, sir."

"Rory's manager called me an hour after our meeting. It seems that they hadn't been happy with Mr. Gene-O Albright's performance for a while." He said the man's name sarcastically and I could tell he had no respect for the attorney either. "After hearing how passionate you were about protecting Rory, they began to rethink not only their selection in an attorney but also in their agent as well."

"So, wait a minute. You're not upset with me?"

"On the contrary, Hindley. I'm extraordinarily pleased with you. Your tenacity has proven beneficial not only to this firm but to Mr. Gregor as well. They've asked to retain our firm as their legal counsel for all contracts."

My neck snapped toward Michael and his gaze firmly planted on mine, both our mouths slightly ajar, trying desperately to hide our smiles but failing miserably.

"Don't be ashamed, Hindley. This is something to celebrate for sure. This is exactly the type of business our law firm has been trying to attract. When word spreads of your tactics to negotiate for the other side, I have no doubt that other athletes will line up behind Mr. Gregor. You've done a great job, Hindley." I could hide it no longer. Mr. Stedwick was proud of me so certainly I deserved some self-praising, too. I allowed my smile to broaden as I let the realization of my success sink in.

"Here," he said pushing an envelope toward me.

"What's this?" He remained silent, waiting for me to open the envelope. I pulled out two large laminated cards that read 'VIP Event Pass - River City Pro-Am Tournament', attached to red lanyards. "What are these?"

"Those are two passes to Rory's next competition. Actually, it's not a competition. Apparently, a friend of his designs skate parks and has his grand opening this weekend. The venue set up a pro-am tournament to showcase the new park and Rory is the headlining professional. His manager sent over two passes for the weekend event. What do you know about skateboarding, Hindley?"

"Absolutely nothing, sir. In fact, to be honest, up until this morning, I didn't even know it was a professional sport." I tried to hold back a laugh. I mean, really, skateboarding a sport? Get real. What kind of training could be involved? Bong hits and beer drinking contests?

Mr. Stedwick continued, unfazed by my answer. "They'll have a trade show at the convention center in downtown San Antonio starting Friday afternoon then the competition all day Saturday followed by a wrap party that evening. These are excellent opportunities for us. I want you to attend all three events and bring along a friend, preferably a female." *That's an odd request, a female. What's up with that?* "I want you to learn as much about the industry as you can, mix and mingle with other pro skaters, and find out who the next up-and-coming amateur athletes are. I want this firm to be representing more kids like Rory."

Skateboarding? Really? I had to learn about skateboarding for my job as an attorney? It didn't make any sense at all.

"I want you to learn this industry because we need to become stronger on the agent side as well. If we are going to represent them, we need to know how best to do that. I think Rory will be an excellent source of information for you." *Oh, shit, here we go. He wants you to hang out with Rory.*

"But why me? Why not Michael or Luis?"

"It's obvious you already know him, he said you all met last week. And it seems that he was pleased with your efforts today so I have no doubt he'll learn to trust you if he hasn't already." *Oh, he trusts you, alright. He's trying to get in your pants. And as good as he looked today, I'm thinking it might not be such a bad thing after all.*

"Why can't I take Michael or Luis?"

"I think Rory's manager is leery of attorneys right now and after Mr. Albright's abysmal performance today, I can't say as I blame him. I think the fewer attorneys present, the better. And I think fitting in as a friend rather than legal counsel will go a long way with Rory's team."

"I think Michael or Luis should go, sir, not me."

"Impossible."

"Why?"

"They specifically asked for you." *Oh, shit!*

"Who did?"

"His manager. He was impressed with your negotiating skills and made it very clear that if they retain our firm, they want you to handle all of Rory's contracts." *Oh, double shit!*

My face went ashen. I could barely think when I was around Rory Gregor and now I was going to be his legal representation. How would this work? It wouldn't! I loathed him but yearned for him all at the same time. I knew I would never be able to do this. I had to refuse. Rory Gregor would ruin me, he'd eat me alive and spit me out, and never give me a second thought.

Sensing my apprehension, Mr. Stedwick continued. "Hindley, I don't have to tell you how important this is to the firm. I'm not really asking you to do this." I got it. He was telling me. He didn't have to spell it out. If I didn't take on Rory as a client, my future here with this firm would be in jeopardy. And so would Paul's. Stedwick and Nigh were big investors in Paul's company. If I screwed up here, I ran the risk of screwing Paul over as well. *Triple shit!*

I had no choice. Once again, I'd be living my life for someone else, trying to make someone else happy instead of myself. My life would not be my own. But then again, ever since I'd seen Rory Gregor in my bed, seen that tantalizing tattoo, his mesmerizing eyes, and his rock hard body, I'd known, somewhere deep inside me, on a spiritual level, that I'd already lost myself to him. The first time his lips had touched mine, I'd felt like a polarized magnet drawn to something deep within him, a moth to a flame destined to burn alive. I'd tried to pull away but it was futile, his sexual energy was too strong for someone as naïve as me. He sent those passes to me on purpose, no doubt. In the game of sex and passion, Rory Gregor was a professional and I didn't stand a chance. My only hope for survival now was that he wouldn't completely destroy me.

I knew as soon as I left Mr. Stedwick's office, I'd have to get straight to work on my wall, that invisible wall I'd had up for years, built to protect my fragile heart. Now it had to be twice as strong and twice as high if it was going to keep me safe from the turbulent storm that threatened to kill me, the hurricane already dubiously named Rory Gregor.

Chapter 8

"Dude, will you calm the fuck the down? You're making me a nervous wreck."

"I am a nervous wreck."

"You'll be fine." Leif tried to convince me.

"I'm not nervous about that." I nodded my head toward the stage. "Well, I am."

"You know I'm here. There won't be any surprise questions, I promise."

I reached out and grabbed Leif's shoulder. "I know, man. I know."

"Then what is it?"

I sat silent, staring down at my twisted hands. Leif was a good friend, my best friend. He'd stood by me for years and held on to my deep, dark secret, protecting me ever since I'd known him. I knew the stress I put on him was unfair but I didn't know what else to do. We were like brothers and I knew he'd do anything for me.

"She'll be here, man. Relax." I nodded my head, trying to convince myself he was right. I wanted to see her so badly, it actually hurt somewhere deep inside my physical being. I'd never felt like this in my life and it scared the shit out of me.

My nerves were shot as I stood backstage with Leif and the other pro skaters here for the weekend, waiting to start the symposium River City Boards was sponsoring. The trade show floor was packed and as usual, I was ready to piss myself thinking about sitting at a table fielding God knows what questions reporters, sports broadcasters, and general fans threw at me. I knew they'd shove newspapers in front of me and ask my opinion on articles written about me or other skaters or the sport in general. Fans would hand me letters they'd written me and want me to read them out loud. The entire time on stage would be a major cluster fuck for me. It was a good thing I didn't drink anymore because if I did, I'd be three ways to shit-faced right now.

Usually Leif's dad, Jack, sat with me and interceded when any problems came my way. It looked natural to have him next to me because he was my manager. No one questioned his presence. But tonight, Leif was joining me instead. This was his big event, it was his skate park grand opening and he was leading the symposium, thankfully for me. I knew he'd never let anything or anyone get through that could jeopardize my situation.

"How do you know she'll be here?" My voice sounded like a pathetic school girl and I was actually embarrassed by myself.

"My dad made sure."

"I know he sent the passes, I asked him to. That doesn't mean she'll use them." Leif's smirk warned me that I might not want to know the whole story. "What?"

"He told the attorney guy that you specifically asked for Hindley to represent you."

"I did ask for her." I didn't trust any other asshole attorney and Hindley had more than proven herself to me in one meeting. "You should have seen her, man. She was a beast! She tore Gene-O's ass apart. I actually felt kind of bad for him. I mean, he's always been decent to me and has protected my secret with a vengeance so I never faulted him for not being the *best* attorney.

"I can't believe he was being such a dumbass about your contracts though."

"You know my reputation. I was lucky to get anyone to sponsor me right now, let alone represent me. Beggars can't be choosers."

"No, but they can at least trust their attorneys to get them the best deal possible, given their current ranking."

"I'm only ranked sixth right now."

"Only? Some kids would kill to *only* be in sixth place."

"I was on top once. Sixth place is almost like not even participating."

"Whatever!" He rolled his eyes and instantly, I felt like the douche bag I was. Leif had always loved to skate but he just didn't have the talent to compete at the pro level. I'd always thought it a blessing. He created some of the best skate parks in the world. And he made a shit load of money doing it.

"Look, I'm sorry, man." I tried to offer an apology for being so thoughtless. "I just know that skating isn't her thing. I'm afraid she won't show and I really want to see her, to thank her for..." I couldn't go on.

"What?

"For believing me. For fighting for me."

"I do all those things for you, man."

"Yeah, but you don't have long blonde hair, awesome tits, and legs to die for."

"I don't know," he said, pulling up his jeans to reveal his calf muscle. "These legs look pretty good, if you ask me." He hit my arm and we both started laughing. "Look, don't worry, man. My dad said her law firm really wants to get involved in this type of law."

"What type of law?"

"Representing sports figures."

"That's not what they do now?"

"I don't think so."

"Damn, she could have fooled me. She sounded like she'd been doing this for years. Shit, man, my dick got so hard watching her, I could barely stand up to leave, it hurt so badly."

Leif spewed Red Bull out of his mouth, all onto the stage, as he began to choke and cough. "That was graphic," he coughed out. "She must be hot."

"You have no idea, Leif." I closed my eyes, thinking back to our meeting earlier this week. How fuckin' fantastic her body looked in that tight-ass red dress she wore and those 'Come Fuck Me' pumps at the end of her shapely, toned legs. The whole outfit screamed of sex and I'd wanted to give it to her right there on the fuckin' conference table. I didn't know how any of those attorney bastards got any work done looking at her all day. I remembered the thought had seized my balls with red-hot jealousy that day. The thought of any man lusting after Hindley had my blood boiling. *Anyone but you, right, dick head?*

I cracked open a Red Bull and swallowed down half the contents in one gulp. I tried not to drink them too often because they could be addicting for someone like me. But they'd been a good sponsor in the past and I hoped maybe if I proved myself worthy, they'd support me again. I'd fucked up lots of endorsement deals when I'd gone off the deep end years before. If I wanted to keep training at the level I needed to become number one again, I would have to secure more sponsors and major endorsement deals. I trusted Hindley to do that for me, and there were very few people I trusted.

I was completely stoked to have this deal with River City Boards and I knew it was a good contract because Hindley had drafted it. But I needed at least two more major deals by the end of the summer if I wanted to keep skating. Most people never realize that it takes a butt load of money to be an individual pro athlete. I didn't have a team or a franchise backing me. If I failed, a lot of other people did, too. At least with the River City deal, they were providing all my equipment so that would definitely help with some of my expenses.

"Anyway, I'm pretty sure her law firm is foamin' at the mouth to have you. My dad told them you like her."

"What! Why the fuck did he tell them that!"

"Calm down. He told them professionally speaking."

"Oh."

"My dad said the guy wants to learn the industry, he's kind of chomping at the bit, and offered up Hindley pretty freely. Trust me, if she wants a future with her law firm, she'll be here."

"Dude, I didn't want it to go down like that."

"Like what?"

"I didn't want to force her to come. I wanted her to want to come, learn more about my sport, especially if she's going to represent me."

"Hey, whatever gets her here, right?" I shook my head in disagreement. I didn't want to force Hindley to do anything. That wasn't my style. If she felt pressure, she'd resent me and I didn't want that at all.

Leif looked down at his watch. "Dude, we gotta go. You ready?"

"I guess."

"Let's give these people a show." I laughed. It always surprised me how supportive my fans had been over the last few years as I tried to straighten my life out. People said it was because my skills were unsurpassed, but I knew it was more than that. They were pulling for me, they were there for me, and this time, I wasn't going to disappointment them. Suddenly, Leif's voice came over the PA system and broke through my thoughts. I glanced up and saw him sitting down at the table.

"Ladies and gentleman, I want to welcome you to the River City Pro-Am Tournament and Trade Show. My name is Leif Jennings, owner and lead designer of Fly By Nite Skatepark Developments. I want to extend my sincere thanks to River City Boards for sponsoring this event." Cheers and applause erupted throughout the room as people made their way closer to the stage.

River City Boards was a small skateboard manufacturing company but they were known for putting out quality products at reasonable prices. They were way into the environment and that was really hot and trendy right now so their success was growing by leaps and bounds. Mother Earth had never really been a big concern of mine but if Bucky and Pena were concerned with it, then I owed it to them to make an effort to recycle, at least every once in a while. I mean, shit, I was already giving up my cigarettes. Rome wasn't built in a day.

I listened as Leif continued. He was built for this shit. If he wasn't such a talented designer, I would definitely pegged him for PR work.

"I'd also like to thank all our pro skaters who have joined us this weekend and some up-and-coming amateurs who will also participate in this symposium. If you haven't already given your questions to Mr. Billings, please do so now. He's standing here at the front of the stage. We'll try to answer as many of them as we can." I smiled, knowing Leif had purposely had all written questions go through one person. He really did have my back.

I listened as he introduced all the skaters but continued to search the crowd for any sign of Hindley. As much as I didn't want her to be forced to come, I couldn't deny that I was happy to know she would definitely be here.

"And finally, I'd like to introduce a man who needs no introduction. Currently ranked at number six but climbing the charts by flips and bounds and now signed with our sponsor River City..."

Leif's voice suddenly faded as did all the cheers and whistling. I saw her. She stood tall, like a model, at the back of the room, her blonde hair pulled back in a ponytail. She loved those damned ponytails. And surprising to me, I loved her in those damned ponytails. I fantasized about holding on to her mane of hair as I took her in every sexual position imaginable.

Her eyes darted around the enormous convention center, looking as nervous as a whore in church. *Why is she so anxious? She should try being up here.* Suddenly, I remembered, I was standing on a stage, awaiting my introduction.

"Rory!" Leif shouted at me covering the mic.

Oh, shit, how long had he been saying my name? I walked toward the chair he was holding out for me but just before I sat down, I darted my eyes to the back of the auditorium again to make sure Hindley was still there. My heart dropped when I found the space empty. I wondered if she'd left after one look into the freak show that was skateboarding. We were an interesting bunch but we were, for lack of a better term, a family. I knew that if this girl couldn't find a way to fit into skating then anything I wanted from her would never work. *Are you trying to plan a future with this girl? Get real. Let's take this one hour at a time. Get through this silly ass talk show then go find her.*

The symposium ended and I spent the rest of the evening either signing autographs or taking pictures with fans. I didn't mind it at all, usually. But tonight, I had one mission on my mind and being with all these people in a crowded convention center wasn't one of them.

The last of the line of fans was gone and I looked up for the first time in two hours to find the show floor was almost completely deserted. I glanced down at my watch and saw it was ten thirty. The trade show ended at nine. Hindley was long gone, I was sure. I replaced all the caps back on the markers I'd used to sign posters, skate boards, helmets, and programs and stacked them in a neat pile before pushing back in my chair to leave the stage, a heavy sigh of disappointment weighing me down.

"You're a pretty popular fella." I recognized the raspy voice and Southern accent. It was Hindley and my pulse raced.

I glanced over my shoulder, surprised to find that she'd changed her outfit. Her hair that had been pulled back in a ponytail earlier now hung loose around her shoulders. She was wearing a pair of dark blue skinny jeans that showed off every great detail of her legs. Her feet were adorned with bright yellow DC brand high tops and the fitted top I'd seen her in earlier had been replaced with a loose fitting red t-shirt with the River City Boards logo on the front. She did a sweeping turn looking over her shoulder as if she were a model trying to show me all her angles. The hem of her t-shirt hung just above her magnificent ass. After staring at it long enough to seem perverted, I finally let my eyes travel up to the top of the t-shirt and saw the graphic. It read 'Skate or Die!' in a graffiti font. The silhouette of a chick with a ponytail doing a flip kick in the air was in the background. All in all, the ensemble would not have suited someone as rich and sophisticated as Hindley and I knew she was attempting to be sarcastic, but her plan had back fired. To me, she looked like heaven adorned in the costume of my lifestyle.

"You stayed."

"I wanted an autograph." She held out a black felt tip pen and I felt a low buzz in my pants. *Is she flirting with me?*

"Are you serious?"

"Oh, very. I didn't stand in line for two hours for nothing. Here." She poked the pen at me and pulled her hair to the side making room on her back for me to sign.

"You're sure?"

"Um hum," she murmured, batting her eyelashes, her huge doe eyes shining back at me. "Please." Holy shit! The low buzz in my pants was now a painful throb. *Dude, I didn't think it was possible but this chick looks even hotter in skater shit!*

I had to steady my hand around the marker as I moved closer, placing my free hand on her shoulder to anchor myself. I let my fingers caress her exposed neck and smiled when I heard her draw in a sharp breath. I affected her just as much as she did me. She smelled fuckin' awesome, and her hair felt like silk. I scribbled my name as quickly as I could, knowing if I didn't pull away from her soon, I'd throw her down and rip off all her clothes just to have myself inside her. *Dude, you are getting way crazy with these fantasies, but I love them.* My dick was rock hard and I was in serious pain. I had to divert my attention if I was going to be able to carry on a normal conversation with her.

"Are you hungry?" I tried to divert my mind. "I'm starving. All I had was a corn dog at lunch. Do you want to go get something to eat?"

"No, I had a funnel cake and shared some nachos with Dana." I looked past Hindley on the stage and saw Dana engrossed in conversation with two of the pro skaters performing tomorrow.

"Looks like she made some new friends," I said nodding my head toward Dana.

"Dana always has friends somewhere." Her eyes had a strange look, as if she was happy but disappointed at the same time. I couldn't help but wonder if it was me. Was she sad about being in my presence? I could tell there was more going behind her eyes and if I didn't act soon, I was going to lose her to some invisible force.

"She's an outgoing girl."

"I know." She looked back at Dana and half rolled her eyes. She wasn't angry, she was envious.

"You take your time getting to know people. You're not superficial. It doesn't mean one is better than the other. They're just different." She glanced back at me her eyes were filled with a haunting mix of gratitude and fear. I knew she was shocked that I'd put into words something she'd never been able to and she wanted to thank the interpreter of her thoughts. But she was also scared I'd already sized her up. She was a woman who stood behind what most had seen as insurmountable walls. To her, I'd just found a hole and the realization scared her to death. Afraid she might run, I did something stupid. I grabbed her around the shoulders and pulled her in close to me, thinking all the while she'd fight and try to escape. Instead, she let her arms wrap around my waist and laid her forehead on my chest. *You may have a chance after all, player!*

"Come on, let's go, lovers!" Once again, Dana's voice had interrupted our moment of intimacy. As if coming to her senses, Hindley pushed me away with force and glared at me, her eyes silently admonishing me as if we'd been caught doing something sordid and disgusting.

I didn't know what to say to make her feel better so instead, I acted as if nothing had happened, as if there'd been absolutely no connection. "I'll see you tomorrow?" It was cheesy I know and desperate but it was all I could seem to muster.

"Yeah, I'll be here."

I could tell by her expression and tone that being at a skateboarding exhibition wasn't anything remotely close to what she wanted to do this weekend, but I didn't care. As long as she was here, as long as she was forced to see me in action, I'd take it. She'd seen a shitload about me on the Internet I was sure and a ton of it wasn't even true. Those asshole Internet reporters blew shit out of proportion just to get readers. The look on her face when she'd walked into that conference room earlier this week reflected it and I'd been on a recon mission ever since. I just knew if she saw me in my element, successful at something and not fucking everything up, then maybe she'd give me a second chance. I couldn't rely on my own personal skills to win her back. *Win her back? You never had her, asswipe.*

"Where are y'all staying?" I asked.

"We're not. We're going back to Austin tonight and then I'm driving back down tomorrow." I glanced over at Dana then back to Hindley, surprised at her statement.

"I gotta work tomorrow, Cheater." Dana was pissed at me. That was recon number two. Last weekend, she'd been my ally. But I was certain Hindley had told her of my major fuck up with....Damn! I couldn't even remember the chick's name now. *Nice. I guess some things never change, huh, douche bag?*

"Dana!" Hindley shouted in reprimand.

"What?"

"It's okay, I deserve it."

"No, you don't." Hindley's eyes narrowed and she glared at Dana, essentially silencing her.

"Why aren't you staying?"

"Dana has to work tomorrow."

"Oh." I was genuinely surprised. I wasn't sure why I'd never thought of Dana working. She'd said her Beemer was a gift from her parents so for whatever reason, I just thought she was independently wealthy like Hindley. "Where do you work?"

"Denny's." I immediately busted out laughing.

"No, seriously. Where do you work?" I could feel the crimson flood of embarrassment cover my face as I stared back at two sets of very serious eyes. She wasn't kidding and to them this was anything but funny. "Um, sorry, I guess I just..."

"Well, that's probably your problem, player." Now Dana was pissed. I'd insulted her. If I couldn't get the best friend back on my side, I knew I would never succeed.

I let go of Hindley, surprised to find she still had one arm wrapped around me. I had to make this right and I had to do it now. I slowly made my way across the stage to Dana, stopping just in front of her. I had to strain my neck to bend down she was so tiny. "Look, Dana, I'm really sorry. You're right, I am an asshole in more ways than I'd like to admit. I made an assumption and I judged you. It's something I'm all too familiar with and I hate it when people do it to me. I never meant to insult you and I hope you'll forgive me."

She slugged my arm with her fist, catching me completely off guard by how much it hurt. This girl was packed with dynamite and I was totally afraid of her. How could someone just over five feet tall be so intimidating?

"Don't worry about it. All's forgiven, One-Nighter."

"I thought that wasn't my name any more because, you know." I nodded over to Hindley.

"Oh, yeah, that's right. You failed to seal the deal, didn't ya, Cheater." Hindley rolled her eyes in obvious embarrassment but I saw the hint of a smirk lurking just underneath. Dana stepped in closer and made it clear she had a comment for my ears only so I bent my six foot two frame down and leaned my ear toward her. "Maybe after this weekend, I'll call you All-Nighter." I stood straight up my eyes as round as saucers, not sure how to react to her comment. She winked at me in that playful way she had about her.

"What the hell did you say, Dana?!" Hindley half shouted.

"I told him to keep his dick in his pants if he didn't want me to chop it off. He has a lot of explaining to do."

"He doesn't have any explaining to do." Hindley tried to give Dana a look to shut her up but this time, it wasn't working.

"Of course he does. I mean, who does that?" She didn't have to go on. I knew she was referring to last Sunday night.

"I fucked up, Dana. Plain and simple. I wish I had a better explanation but I don't." Her eyes rolled up to mine and she gave me another wink just outside of Hindley's view. I knew instantly this show wasn't about me. Dana was trying to rile Hindley up to make her defend me and I wasn't sure if I loved Dana or loathed her for it. I was already familiar enough with Hindley to know that when she became agitated or passionate, her lips seemed to always find mine, so I settled on loving Dana.

"Dude, we need to get back to the hotel. You've got an early morning tomorrow." I glanced over my shoulder and saw Leif carrying several bags. I rushed to his side and took two off his shoulders, not knowing what was inside. They were heavy as shit.

"Leif, this is Dana," I motioned toward Dana and she stuck out her hand. Leif looked her up and down like he was afraid to touch her for fear of being attacked but eventually shook her hand.

"Cool eyes," he responded.

"Thanks."

"And this is Hindley." I let my arm swing over to Hindley and watched as Leif's expression changed. It wasn't because he felt any differently about the two women. I could tell already he'd found Dana to be just as hot as most guys did. I think he was more in awe of Hindley, to finally meet the woman who made me want to be different.

"It's nice to finally meet you, Hindley." He casually strolled toward her with his hand extended. "I've heard a lot about you."

"Well, don't believe a word of it. Unless it was good." She laughed under her breath and the vibrations of her throaty laughter made my dick throb in pain. She took his hand in hers and I knew just as I'd found an ally in Dana, Hindley had found one in my best friend, too. I felt completely vulnerable and helpless. *And horny as hell, man.*

"I'm sorry, I didn't mean to keep y'all," Hindley tried to explain. Her Texas drawl was making me crazy. I couldn't let her go.

Leif turned from Hindley then back to Dana. "Where are y'all staying?" I was happy to see he was on the same page I was.

We're actually heading back to Austin tonight," Hindley answered.

"No we're not!" Dana shouted from behind us. She held up her phone in victory, as if she'd just conquered Spain. "They just called me. Said they found a replacement. I'm good 'til Sunday morning." There was a mischievous glimmer in her eyes. I looked from her to Hindley then over to Leif, all three surprisingly calm. Was I the only one who found this change of events odd? I expected Hindley to argue but she remained silent. Dana had found a reason to stay in San Antonio. Leif.

"Where do you work?" Leif asked. *Oh, shit! She's gonna rip you a new one man.*

"Denny's." Dana's answer begged him to make fun of her. I prepared myself for World War Three, knowing she'd tear his ass up and feed it to him if he even thought of laughing.

"Oh, cool. I'm starving. Can you get us a discount if we find one here in San Antonio?" I watched as the two walked off the stage talking and laughing the whole way as if they'd been lifelong friends.

I glanced at Hindley and saw a resigned look on her face. Both eyebrows were raised and her lips were puckered to the side in dismay. "Always makes a friend wherever she goes." She laughed under her breath but I could hear the hurt.

"And you take it slow," I reminded her. Her eyes met mine and I found myself lost in the dark brown molasses staring back at me. Usually, that color of eyes would have held no appeal to me, but there was something different about hers. I saw a glow inside that lit them up in a way that was indescribable. I could sense that no one else had ever dared peer so deep. She immediately turned her head, breaking our gaze. *You went too far, dickhead. You went too fast. This girl is a slow one.* I knew it was true. Hindley was like an abused animal. If I approached too fast, she'd attack, not out of anger but in defense, in fear.

I hiked the bags on my shoulder and began walking toward the steps, letting her know I meant no harm. If she wanted to wait, I'd be patient. It went against every fiber of my being. I was an instant gratification kind of guy in every part of my life, not just sex, but for Hindley, I'd wait. *Aren't you getting a little ahead of yourself here? You really think this chick is gonna give it up to you? And you really think this is a good idea when you basically forced her to be your attorney. Business and pleasure don't mix, man. And you have too many deals worth too much money to screw this up.*

I glanced back over my shoulder. "Hey, I just wanted to thank you."

She clumsily followed me toward the edge of the stage and I could tell she was having trouble walking in her new shoes. DC shoes were big and bulky and probably weighed as much as she did. It was amazing to watch her evolve into my world right in front of my eyes. I was her Skater Boy and something inside me wondered if maybe she could be my Skater Girl.

"You're welcome." It was bizarre, I didn't have to tell her why I was grateful. She knew. She knew I was thankful for standing up for me in a way no one ever had before in business. "I owed ya one, remember?"

"Why?" I reached back, offering her my hand to help her down the stairs, watching her clunk around in her new high tops.

"Any man who holds a girl's hair back when she's vomiting, and practically makes her stepsister piss on herself from humiliation, deserves to have proper legal representation. Plus, I know you hate attorneys so I wanted you to know that we're not all ambulance chasing vultures."

We reached the bottom of the stairs and she stopped directly in front of me. I could feel her breath on my neck, her chest just inches from mine. Our eyes were locked and I could feel that pull, the one that always came right before I attacked her. *Go slow. Go slow. Go slow.*

I took a long step backward, putting distance between as I extended my hand. "We're even." Suddenly, deep creases formed between her brows and I could tell she was confused by my tactics. She'd expected me to go in for the kill but I'd resisted. She looked, disappointed. Wait? That wasn't what I was going for. Did she want me to kiss her? For the life of me, I couldn't figure this girl out. Should I step closer and try to reconnect. Should I pull her into my arms and press my body against hers with no shame?

Suddenly, Leif's father's words rolled through my head. Jack always said, "When in doubt, leave it out." He used the phrase for training purposes, reminding me that during competitions, if I wasn't completely sure about a trick, I shouldn't do it. In the end, he said I'd be rewarded for the tricks I did well and not judged for the tricks I screwed up. I'd been judged all my life for the fuck ups. I couldn't stand it if I looked on the sidelines of my life and saw Hindley lined up with all the others, thinking I was a failure. As much as I wanted to feel my body next to hers, as much as I wanted those lips on mine, our bodies naked and intertwined, I had to wait. I wasn't completely confident and I knew if I wasn't, she'd run.

I looked her up and down, taking in the entire master piece that was Hindley Hagen. She was breathtaking. "I like your Skater Girl look. It suits you."

"Really?" She pointed her toe and flexed her ankle showing both sides of her shoes then grabbed her shirt by the hem and pulled it out looking down at the graphic. "I wasn't sure if I could pull it off."

"Hindley, you could wear a garbage bag and still be the most beautiful woman in the room." Her eyes flashed up to mine and we were lost again. I hoped she could feel the sincerity in my voice. God, I wanted her so badly and it took all my strength not to drop these damn bags on my shoulders, grab her up, throw her on the stage, and screw her senseless. *That's not her style, man. Go slow.* Something in her eyes told me she felt the same way, but I wasn't one hundred percent sure. *When in doubt, leave it out.*

"So, you gonna get the Grand Slam?"

She shook her head and her eyes reeked of guilt. She was trying to erase her own fantasies from her mind but I knew she'd never admit it. *Hindley has a freaky side!* The thought gave me hope.

"What are you talking about?"

"At Denny's." I reached back and took her hand in mine. "The Grand Slam? I love that dish." I pulled her closer to me and felt an odd sense of satisfaction and familiarity as we walked out of the convention center hand in hand. I glanced down at her from the corner of my eye and saw a smile on her face. She was looking down at the floor and was oblivious to the fact I'd seen it. I laughed to myself, realizing my doubt was starting to fade. Just like when I landed a new trick, my confidence was building and I knew that soon enough, Hindley would be mine. I'd be rewarded, not judged.

Chapter 9

"I totally don't get it." Dana's words were barely audible as she spoke, her mouth stuffed with a breakfast burrito.

"What's there to get?" I turned my eyes down to deflect her gaze, taking another sip of my coffee. I didn't want her to 'get' anything.

"Don't do that." She was snappy this morning and her tone was sharp.

"Do what?"

"Play all cute and innocent like you don't know what the fuck I'm talkin' about. That shit doesn't fly with me and you know it."

I plopped my cup back down beside me on the bleachers with a thud and raised my eyes so I could look directly into hers. "What do you not get, Dana?" I didn't have to ask her, we'd been best friends since we were kids, she got me.

"First, you say Rory doesn't mean anything to you. Then you say you're totally attracted to him but you're not going to do anything with him. And now you're all upset and pouty because he didn't ravish you last night when you gave him the thumbs up."

"I'm just saying that I don't understand him."

"Do you want him or not?"

I closed my eyes and turned my face up toward the beautiful Texas sky as I let Dana's question roll through my befuddled brain. *You know the answer.*

It was a gorgeous morning perfect for the day's skating event. We sat in the VIP bleachers in the middle of the skate park Rory's friend, Leif, had designed. The park was filling up fast with spectators and fans, more than I ever thought would show. It was only 8:45am and already there were over a thousand people packed around the perimeter of the park.

"I want him," I finally blew out, unable to look at her. The revelation was more to myself than to Dana but out of the corner of my eye, I saw her nod her head in approval as she tried to stifle a laugh. She already knew my answer before I ever even thought of replying. "I want him, but I can't have him."

"Why not?" She shoved the last bite of her taco in her mouth then wrapped her lips around the straw of her cup and sucked her soda dry. Dana never ceased to amaze me. She was tiny, just over five feet tall and barely over one hundred pounds but she ate like a horse and never gained an ounce. "Is it because he's a skater boy?"

I laughed. She was right, I'd never been attracted to the 'Bad Boy' type of persona, but that wasn't why I wouldn't allow myself to even think about being with him. "I can't be with him because I represent him. We have a professional relationship now."

"So?"

"So, I could lose my job if we did anything else."

"Only if you get caught." She winked at me as she continued to suck on her straw, but it was in vain. She'd drained the cup dry moments earlier and now the sounds coming from her reminded me of a puttering motor boat with no gas. She shook her glass in disbelief before cutting her blue eyes to me. "Do you like him?"

I rolled my coffee cup back and forth in my hands, trying to think about my answer. *What's there to think about, you idiot? He's hot, he's sexy, probably the sexiest guy you've ever seen. He oozes carnal lust. Oh, yeah, you like him. You're hot for him. But you can't do a damn thing about it if you want to keep your job and advance your career. And save Paul.*

"It doesn't matter if I like him or not. To me, he has to be off limits."

"So why were you so upset that he snubbed you last night?"

"Just because I can't do anything with him doesn't mean I don't want him to want me."

She rolled her beautiful aqua eyes in disgust. "You're sick, ya know that?"

"What?"

"Did you just hear yourself? I thought you were a feminist."

"I'm a realist."

"Well, Miss Realist, reality is he's totally hot for you."

"Really?"

Dana snapped her neck at me. I knew my voice was too high and she could see right through me.

"You're pathetic."

"How do you know?"

"How do I know you're pathetic? Because you look like a giddy school girl who just found out through the playground grapevine that little Johnny has a crush on you."

"No, how do you know he's hot for me?" I tried to bat my eyes but it was futile. Dana knew me better than anyone else on earth. I *was* pathetic.

"First of all, let's get one thing straight. It is beyond me why you don't see how gorgeous you are. You still see yourself as the dorky, overweight sister of Geneva Barton but that's not who you are anymore. Hell, you were never that girl. Even back then, you were beautiful and Geneva knew it, that's why she always put shit in your head to make you feel bad about yourself."

Dana was right. In high school, I had been heavier and had always been self-conscious about it. When I was a teen, people always told me I had a beautiful face but I chose not to believe them. I knew that was something you told a fat girl to make her feel better. Sensing my insecurities, Paul invited me to compete in a father-daughter triathlon my senior year to boost my confidence. He'd been competing for years but I was reluctant, not because I didn't think I could do it but because it was for fathers and daughters. I finally agreed and three months later and thirty pounds lighter, Paul and I finished third in the competition and I'd been running, cycling, and swimming ever since.

When we crossed the finish line at our first triathlon, I made my mind up that day that I was a different person, inside and out. But here I sat, seven years later, still stuck in my fat girl persona, wondering why Rory Gregor didn't find me attractive and about to soak my misery in a huge funnel cake.

Dana's voice broke through my morbid thoughts. "Plus, Leif told me Rory was a nervous wreck yesterday waiting for you to show."

"Really?"

"Yeah. I think he wants to make a good impression with you, you know, because he fucked up so bad in the beginning. Plus, the way Leif talked, I don't think Rory feels like he's even in your league or has a right to pursue you."

"That's ridiculous."

"That's what I told him. I said, hey, if you knew *half* the shit Hindley's done, you'd say she way beneath Rory."

"No, you didn't!"

"No, I didn't. But it's true."

"Definitely. If he only knew." Truth was, I didn't want him to know what I'd been involved in, what had happened to me. I knew he'd judge me and that's why I never told anyone what I'd been through. Only my mom, Paul, and Dana knew my history and even they didn't know everything.

"You're actually perfect for each other."

"Why do you say that?"

"You're both running from your past, trying to escape being judged by people you could give a shit less about."

"That's not true."

"Yes, it is. Why won't you sleep with Rory?"

"Well, for one, because he's never asked me."

"Please. Whatever." She rolled her eyes so deep, I thought they may fall out of their sockets. "You won't sleep with him because you're afraid your law office will judge you. You're afraid Rory will judge you. It's the biggest fuckin' lose-lose scenario I've ever seen." I took in a deep breath, trying hard to comprehend what Dana was saying. I was so busy worrying about other people, my life was passing me by. "Fuck everyone else, what does *Hindley* want?" she asked, with emphasis on my name.

I laughed.

"What's so funny?"

"Luis asked me the same question."

"And what did you tell him?"

"I told him I didn't know." She shook her head as if I were a lost cause. "I know. Luis said I knew, I just wouldn't admit it to myself."

"And that is why I am clinically depressed."

"Why?"

"I'm depressed because Luis is gay. He's the perfect man for me, except the whole gay thing." Dana giggled.

"I don't know if you need Luis. It seemed like you and Leif were getting along pretty well last night."

Her eyes lit up and I couldn't help but smirk. "He is cute, isn't he?" It wasn't a question, it was a statement and I could tell she liked him and that one fact made me happy.

Dana had had a string of not so nice guys from her past. She always put out a sense of self confidence and assurance but since the death of her parents more than five years ago, she'd really acted more from a place of self-loathing than self-assurance. To most people on the outside, it looked like confidence but I knew it was a defense mechanism. She felt alone and lonely, even though most of the time she was surrounded by people. I noticed her bright blue eyes grow bigger and I followed her gaze, not surprised to see Leif walking toward the grandstand.

"Hey." He waved up to her.

"Hey," she mouthed, holding up one hand.

"Now, who's being pathetic?" I bumped her shoulder and laughed but immediately lost my breath when I saw who was following close behind Leif. It was Rory.

He was wearing blue jeans and a bright yellow t-shirt that was somewhat baggy but you could still make out his muscular physique. The shirt bore the River City Boards logo along with the black helmet he held in his hand. His shoes were black suede with a yellow DC logo, just reversed of mine and for whatever reason, the thought made me smile. I watched and waited for his eyes to connect with mine and when they finally did, he stopped in his tracks, his expression going from anxious to sheer excitement. His lips parted and spread into a giant smile full of perfect white teeth and I could see small dimples appear on each cheek. His clear blue eyes sparkled in the morning sun and I lost myself in their pull. The tingling started in my finger tips and spread through my body like wildfire. Before I knew it, he was climbing the stairs two at a time to make his way to our row high above the park, stopping in the aisle just before he reached Dana.

"Hey," he nodded his head toward her.

"Hey, man. Good luck today."

"Thanks." She held out her fist and without hesitation, he bumped his knuckles with hers. They'd bonded and I knew I didn't stand a chance with this man. She was going to help him get into my panties no matter what I did. A small smile spread across my face thinking about it, but I would never admit it, to either one of them. After what felt like an eternity, Dana finally scooted out of the way to let him slide in next to me.

"What are you doing up here?" I giggled. He wrapped one arm around my waist, the other one holding his helmet and his skateboard. Why hadn't I noticed him carrying his skateboard earlier? Before I could think, he pulled me in close to his side and dropped his head down so his lips were just inches from my mine. I took in a deep inhale and his aroma was intoxicating. I felt my knees become unstable and his arm instinctively tightened around me more.

"You look amazing." His breath caressed my neck and my skin felt like it was on fire. I panned down over my clothes, completely forgetting what I'd put on this morning, lost in his embrace. I was wearing yellow shorts with a fitted, red, spaghetti strapped tank top and tan sandals, nothing earth shattering by any means. He pulled away and his gaze followed mine, sweeping my body from head to toe. I felt like I was a piece of meat and I loved it. "Thanks for coming." His broad smile revealed to me just how grateful he was.

"I had to." Instantly, his smile faded and I knew he'd taken my comment the wrong way. "I didn't mean it like that. I wanted to come, I wanted to see you skate. I just meant…" I hesitated, trying to choose my words carefully. "I meant I had to come see you skate because I've heard how

good you are from so many people, I had to see you skate."
I put my hand on his chest and it felt like I had just been
connected to my missing piece. "I had to see you, for
myself." My voice was barely a whisper but I saw his eyes
flash with satisfaction and I knew he'd heard me, I'd
recovered. The last thing I wanted to do was upset him
before his big event.

"Well, Drunk Girl, I hope you like what you see." His
voice and his tone were laced with sexual innuendo and I
was surprised that I wasn't offended at all. He lowered his
head back to my ear. "Because I sure like what I see."
Before I could even respond or recover he was gone, flying
back down the stairs, taking a few moments to sign
autographs and pose for pictures.

"What the fuck did he just say to you because I think
you just had an ear-gasm." I shook my head, trying to make
sense of what just happened.

"What?" I heard Dana's voice but I couldn't
comprehend what she'd said. I was too lost in Rory's trance.

"He whispered something in your ear that made you
come right here in front of God and all these spectators, no
question about it!"

"Shut up!" I half shouted.

"It's true, isn't it? I bet you probably need to go change
your panties, don't you."

I searched around us, trying to ensure no one had heard
her. "Dana, shut up!"

"What? I'm jealous. I bet that man can tear it up in
bed."

"Seriously, Dana, shut up!"

"If you don't give it up, I will."

I laughed, knowing it was futile trying to shut her up
once she'd started a rant, especially when it was about sex.
She was a semi-nympho and I'd be lying if I didn't admit I
was somewhat jealous. I wasn't well versed in the art of sex.
In fact, I could only claim two conquests to my long

existence. Dana had always said there was something wrong with me and she was right, I'd been scarred. Not to mention that my last boyfriend was pretty vocal about how bad I was in the sack. I knew if Rory took me to bed, he'd be completely dissatisfied and would leave faster than he could get his boxers back up. But that didn't make me want him any less. It just meant I had to work harder to stay away from him.

The pro-am was amazing. I'd never seen anything like skateboarding. It was astonishing what these guys could do with a board and four wheels and I felt smaller than an ant for judging them the way I had. This really was a sport, no question about it and for the first time since Rory had been thrust upon me as a client, I was actually excited to learn about the skateboarding industry.

My eyes scanned the crowd and I was surprised to see it had almost tripled in size, with well over three thousand screaming fans surrounding the entire park, all of whom were yelling at the top of their lungs, chanting Rory's name. They were growing anxious to see him and so was I.

Dana bumped my arm with her elbow nodding toward the crowd. "This dude is for real. Listen to this crowd going nuts for him."

I had to admit, I felt like I was at a small rock concert. People of all ages were out watching this event. I looked around the park and saw spectators hoisting signs with Rory's name on it. My head turned and I smiled when I spotted a girl behind us maybe sixteen or seventeen holding a poster that read, 'I love U, SK8R BOY!' She'd drawn an actual heart to replace the word 'love' and plastered a huge lipstick smeared kiss inside the heart. A pang of jealousy surged through me at the thought of someone else calling Rory Skater Boy. It was my term of endearment and I was surprised at how territorial and possessive I felt.

Suddenly, someone announced Rory's name and out of nowhere, he came sliding through this enormous cement cylinder and started his run. The skate park was huge, taking up at least three acres. Half of it looked like a giant empty swimming pool, six feet deep with humps of varying shapes and sizes. The other side contained several sets of stair cases with railings and side boards. There were also cement boxes with metal edges strewn throughout the park ramps ranging from just a few feet to over five or six. I'd never seen anything like it and even though I had no idea what the skaters would do with everything Leif and his team had designed, I watched the them move throughout the park with ease and soon realized every area of the park had been carefully designed with great skill and intent. Each skater competing used almost every surface to do some type of death defying trick and Rory was no exception. The other skaters had done well performing tricks that were definitely impressive, especially the other pros. But they were nothing compared to Rory. His skills proved why he'd once been on top of this sport and there was no doubt in my mind he'd be there again. Only this time, I'd be with him.

~

"Holy shit, Hindley, look at yourself!"

"What?" I'd just stepped out of the bathroom of our hotel room wrapped in a towel and I had no idea what Dana was talking about.

"Your skin. It looks like you're on fire."

I remembered my shoulders burning a little in the shower and figured I must have gotten a little sunburn but the way Dana was talking, I must be blistered. I stepped back into the bathroom and turned on the fluorescent overhead lighting.

"Oh my god, Dana!" My entire chest was beet red except for two small white lines going over my shoulders where my spaghetti straps had been. I saw her face peer around my back in the mirror.

"Holy shit, Hindley. This is bad."

"What am I going to do, Dana? I have to go to this banquet tonight, I'm supposed to make contacts with other skaters and vendors. Mr. Stedwick will have a fit if I'm not there." I could feel the tears forming and I was unable to wish them away as one broke the bounds of my lashes and rolled down my cheek.

"Okay, calm down, Hindley. We'll figure out something." Dana put her hand to her head and left the bathroom. No longer able to look at the lobster standing before me, I followed her out and plopped down on the bed beside her. She was holding the hotel phone next to her ear. "Um, yes, do you have a pharmacy nearby?" I touched my chest and felt the heat radiating from my skin before I even made contact. "Oh, really, here in the hotel." She looked up at me with a smile. "Is it open now? Oh, great, thanks." She replaced the receiver and popped up off the bed. "They have a store here in the hotel. I'll go down and grab some aloe vera lotion and you'll be good as new."

Now that Dana had a game plan, I felt better already and smiled as I realized my tears had retreated. I bounced off the bed, strolling back to the bathroom to finish getting ready but stopped in my tracks when I heard her gasp. "What!" I shouted in fear. I turned around to look over my shoulder and saw horror spread across her face.

"Nothing," she said, heading toward the mini fridge and pillaging through the contents.

I knew she was talking about my back. It had to have been just as red. What was I thinking today? I was fairer than a sheet of paper. I knew better than to sit out in the sun all day. But I couldn't help it, Rory had mesmerized me and I didn't want to leave. I'd stayed well after the event watching him sign autographs and take photos. I'd been surprised at the sheer number of fans he had. A lot were beautiful, young girls and I'd felt a dull ache in the pit of my stomach that I didn't like, at all.

I pulled my hair down from the towel it was wrapped in and began to brush it out as Dana pushed a glass tumbler towards me, filled with an amber liquid.

"What's this?"

"It will help with the pain."

"What is it, Dana?"

"Just drink it." I knew it was some type of alcohol but I didn't care. I could already feel the burn start to ache and it would only get worse as the evening went on. I shot back the whole glass in record time.

"Now, take these and drink this whole bottle of water before I get back." I looked down and saw four burnt orange pills sitting on the marble countertop. I popped all of them in my mouth and downed them with half the water in the bottle.

"You'll be fine," she encouraged, stopping just short of patting my back. "Oh, shit."

"Dana, what am I going to do? Everyone will want to shake hands and hug." I felt tears forming again.

"Don't worry, sweetie, the alcohol and Ibuprofen will kick in soon. You'll be fine. Finish getting ready and I'll be back in two seconds."

I continued to stare at myself in the mirror surprised at how much better my face looked with a little sun. I'd been wearing a ball cap so it wasn't as blistered as my shoulders but I could still see a little color and it worked in my favor. I decided I wouldn't cover it up, instead I'd go with a more natural look tonight.

I was almost done drying my hair when I thought I heard a knock on the door. Why wouldn't Dana just let herself in, I wondered.

"Did you forget your key," I laughed swinging the door open. My eyes grew twice their size as I stared at Rory standing in front of me, looking just as delicious and hot as he did at Geneva's wedding. His suit was lighter tonight, a platinum gray and he was void of any tie which only added to his sex appeal. I could see the dark skin and small smattering of chest hair creeping through the opening of his lavender button down shirt. His suit was form-fitting and even though I'd seen almost every inch of his bare body, it was still beyond obvious that this man was ripped. All I could think about was what a fool I'd been to be so drunk with him that first night. *Mental note, no more alcohol tonight.*

"Shit, Hindley!"

His words were like a cold bucket of water on my libido and I was drawn out of my erotic fantasy much sooner than I wanted to be.

"What!"

"What were you thinking?" I knew what he was asking, why hadn't I taken better care of myself, and the question had been in the forefront of my mind already. Once again, I felt tears welling up and I had no desire for this man to see them. I turned and left him in the doorway, trying to hide my shame.

"Wait," he whispered, reaching out to grab my shoulder. I winced in pain as his hand connected to the beating red glow of my shoulder. "Oh my God, I'm so sorry." Before I could even think, he was in my hotel room, scooping me up, the look in his eyes one of sheer terror. What had happened? "I didn't mean to hurt you, I'm so sorry." I could tell he thought my tears were from the pain of the sunburn, but they weren't. It was a different pain but I wasn't going to let him know that.

He gently placed me on the bed and sat down beside me, careful not to touch me.

"Here," he said, producing a small bottle from his pocket.

"What's this?" I asked, reaching out and taking the bottle from his hand. His fingers caressed mine during the exchange and I felt more fire in my body from our contact than from my sunburn.

"It's a special lotion I use when I get too much sun. It's a mix of aloe, lidocaine, and extra emollients that will help with the pain and discomfort."

"How did you know?"

"I saw you this afternoon when you got back to the hotel. I was going to stop by earlier because I knew you'd need it. Then I ran into Dana downstairs and she told me. I'm sorry, Hindley."

My eyes cut towards his and I saw such pain. "Why?"

"I should have told you, I should have reminded you to put on sun block." I couldn't believe how hurt he seemed, but why? "Here, turn around."

"What!" It came out louder than I wanted to and I instinctively clutched at my towel, the only thing separating the two of us.

"I'll put some on your back."

"Oh." I allowed myself to relax a little but was still apprehensive about letting him touch me, not because of the physical pain it might bring but because of the desire I knew it would create.

I felt the bed rise as he stood up. "Lay down, on your stomach," he instructed. There was such authority in his voice, I immediately complied. *Holy shit, girl. You better watch out.*

Before I could even think, he was on top of me, his legs straddling my rear end. At first, I thought he would break my back because he was so much bigger than me but he was able to keep enough of his weight off of me that it felt…like heaven. We fit.

"Push up," he instructed. I couldn't comprehend his instruction. As I turned to look over my shoulder, I saw a dangerous look in his eyes. He was holding back something and I didn't know what it was. But more surprising to me was the fact that I wasn't completely sure I wanted him to hold back.

"What?"

"Push up so I can pull the towel down." Again, his voice was so strong and commanding, I immediately did as he said.

A chill ran up and down my spine as I felt the towel pull away and slowly move down my back, almost down to the crack of my ass. He gently placed his warm hand in between my shoulders and I realized he was guiding me back down. I sucked in air when I felt my bare breasts make contact with the comforter. It was a sensation I'd never felt before. I closed my eyes as I replayed the entire scene in my head, realizing there was more eroticism in that one act of removing my towel than in every sexual encounter I'd ever had in my life combined. *You are WAY out of this guy's league, Hindley. And you need to get laid, or at least get a vibrator. Getting excited by a hotel comforter is not healthy.*

The bed began to move and I felt his weight shift. My eyes darted over my shoulder, panicked at the thought he may be leaving but I was relieved to find him slowly pulling his jacket off his shoulders. I watched intently as he tossed it over onto the bed next to us then unbutton his long sleeves, rolling them up to his elbows. Slowly, his body readjusted on top of me and I closed my eyes, trying hard to extinguish the guilt and shame in my mind. As if knowing I needed reassuring, his hand gently slid across the nape of my neck and he pulled my hair to the side, completely exposing my entire back. I felt the light pressure of his palm as he spread his hand between my shoulders.

Instantly, a fire erupted in my stomach and quickly worked its way south between my legs.

"Damn, Hindley, you're hot." My eyes closed and my lips turned up in a huge smile, taking in his compliment. "I bet your body temperature is up a full degree or two with this burn."

Just as quickly as my smile came it, left and I felt my entire body go stiff when I realized he was being literal. He didn't think I was hot or beautiful or anything remotely sexy, he was referring to my core body temperature, which was definitely on the rise now that he'd insulted me or rather, now that I'd embarrassed myself. I put my hands under my chest and tried to push up but his weight was too much.

"What are you doing?"

"Just leave the lotion," I gritted out through clenched teeth. "Dana can put it on."

He pressed his entire body into mine, trapping me underneath him. Tears began to sting my eyes as I felt the buttons on his shirt push into the skin on my bare back. He slowly lowered his chin to my shoulder, the rough growth of his beard scraping my delicate skin. I should have felt pain but all my weak mind could register was the warmth of his breath on my neck. *You're pathetic, Hindley.*

"You know I think you're fuckin' hot, Hindley." My eyes rolled up into my head and I couldn't think. Hell, I could barely breathe. "Can't you feel how sexy I think you are?" He pushed his crotch into my back and finally my mind registered what he was saying as I felt his erection on the small of my back. I had affected him. A small smile washed over my face and it pissed me off that I was so affected by him, too.

"That's my Drunk Girl," he whispered in my ear. "Now relax and let me put the lotion on you." His lips caressed the area just below my ear and something exploded...down there.

What the hell was that? What did he mean, 'That's my girl?' *It means you're already lost in him, you idiot, and he knows it. You're as much as his. You might as well roll over and spread your legs wide open for him.*

I felt the tension in my body slowly melt away as his surprisingly soft hands spread lotion across my back and shoulders. It was so soothing and sensual that I think I almost had an orgasm without him being anywhere close to my private parts. I didn't have much experience with orgasms, my other two partners being much more selfish in the sack and taking from me what they could, not giving much in return. Suddenly, his weight was off me and I was surprised at how disappointed I felt.

"Roll over."

"What?"

"Roll over, so I can do your front."

I pushed myself up and wrapped the towel around my body before turning around. "Thanks, but I can do the front." I reached across and tried to take the bottle from him but he pulled it back, just out of my reach. His eyes fell down toward my lap so I followed his gaze and was paralyzed when I saw my towel barely covered my girlie parts. I was pretty sure my own gynecologist hadn't even seen that much of my hooter. I shot up like a rocket, trying to make a beeline for the bathroom but he caught me around the waist and forced me to stand between his legs, his face mesmerizingly close to my crotch. Shit, shit, shit! *Oh, hell yeah!* My entire body shuddered and I had no doubt he felt the effect he was having on me.

He put his large hand over my stomach and gently pushed me back up against the bed. Our eyes were locked on one another's and I noticed his were darker now, a deep blue mixed with brown flakes that were strangely hypnotic.

"Sit, Hindley." His voice was deep and commanding and I had no choice but to obey.

His face looked like a predator on the prowl as he climbed on top of me and straddled my hips. A quick pulse vibrated in my core and buzzed up and down my body as I clutched my towel around me tighter. I'd never felt anything like this before. I knew I should buck him off and tell him to leave but I just couldn't. I knew what he was going to do and despite my better judgment, I knew I was going to let him. For better or for worse, I was about to expose myself to this man, who'd captured me some time ago. I closed my eyes, embarrassed by how primal I was feeling but mostly ashamed of what he would see underneath my towel, what he would find, in my soul.

"Open your eyes, Hindley."

His breath hit my face and I knew he was close, closer than I wanted him. When I finally forced my eyelids open, I saw two bluish-brown eyes staring back at me, searching my face for an answer to an unspoken question. I couldn't speak.

"Do you want me to put lotion on your body, Hindley?" I had never heard anything so erotic and inviting in all my life. I was pretty sure my legs were wet and it wasn't from the shower, it was from his commanding presence. I couldn't find a voice. Instead, all I could do was nod my head. "Yes?" I nodded my head again but he still wasn't satisfied. "I need to hear your answer, Hindley. Out loud."

Oh shit, oh shit, oh shit, he likes to talk dirty. *You are screwed, little girl. You better find your funky junk and get dirty with this boy or he's gonna throw you outta your own hotel room.* I took in a deep breath and closed my eyes, not knowing if I could talk like this in my head, let alone out loud. I knew I was horrible at the act of sex itself so I was pretty confident I'd fail miserably at trying to talk dirty.

I could tell he felt my apprehension but he wasn't going to let me off the hook. He needed assurance from me but I wasn't sure I could give it to him.

"I'm only going to ask you one more time, Hindley. What do you want me to do to you?"

I blew out a breath I'd been holding on to for what seemed like a lifetime and offered up the best instructions I could muster hoping it would be good enough. "Rub lotion on me." I looked into his eyes and watched as his entire face lit up with the most evil smile.

"All you had to do was ask," he said, with a deep laugh. "Where, Hindley?"

Oh shit, please don't do this. Please, I silently begged. *Tell him, girl, you know where you want it, just say it.*

"Here," I answered, pointing to my red chest.

Finally, he complied and slowly began applying lotion to my chest, just above the towel. "Only there?"

"My arms, too." *See, this isn't so bad. And it feels fucking awesome!*

"Anything for you," he breathed out. He took each arm into his hands and held them with such care, I felt like I was a child. Never had I felt more nurtured and cared for. I was lost. After covering both arms with lotion, he gently placed them above my head and I felt the towel pop open, exposing the skin between my breasts. He leaned down on top of me so that his cheek was resting on mine, his lips softly caressing over my ear. "Anywhere else...Hindley?" My entire body convulsed and I was pretty sure I'd just had an ear-gasm with that one question. There was no stopping my body now, it was on fire and not from the sunburn.

I nodded my head. "Where?" he breathed against my neck.

I closed my eyes, petrified to look, afraid this was a dream. "Everywhere," I whispered, my eyes still screwed shut. He leaned back on my hips and I felt his fingers slowly pull my towel apart, exposing my breasts. My mind freaked and I began to panic when I realized there was no hiding myself from him. Instinctively, I pulled my arms down to cover my body but my eyes flew open in surprise when he grabbed my wrists and yanked them back above my head.

His eyes were dark and menacing, yet strangely alluring. "Don't move your arms again or I'll tie them to the bed. Do you understand?"

What the fuck? Tie them to the bed? Is this guy serious? Oh shit!

I wanted to protest, to scream in objection, but there was nothing in my being that would allow me to fight him. I wanted to please him and that one desire spurred me on. I'd never been tied up or anything kinky and I knew without a doubt he would do just that if I didn't comply. Strangely enough, I wasn't afraid of him and the thought of being restrained, by him, didn't sound as terrifying as I thought it would. I already knew enough about Rory Gregor to know I didn't want to upset him so I clasped my fingers together and slowly raised my hands back over my head. There was something so erotic in that one act.

"Good girl, Hindley." His eyes became a shade lighter and I smiled at his approval. He pulled his body off mine and immediately I felt deserted and cold. But before I could concentrate on my old ghosts from the past, he was back, his hands applying lotion between my breasts, just teasing me. "You said everywhere, right, Hindley?"

I closed my eyes, embarrassed by the answer I wanted to give but reeling from the sound of his sensual tone. "Um hmm," I choked out, nodding my head.

"Open your eyes, Hindley. I won't tell you again." My eyes shot open at his command. *This guy is a dom, a fucking dominant. He likes to be in control. Shit, girl, you are in trouble, real trouble.* I'd read about dominants and S&M stuff, I mean *Fifty Shades of Grey* had pretty much put that crap out in the open market for chicks to talk about in the grocery store check-out line. I'd never understood the fascination but here in this moment with Rory, I definitely wanted to keep going and that surprised me. I'd never thought of myself as submissive.

"Where do you want me to rub the lotion?" he whispered in my ear. "Be specific, Hindley." Shit, he's not going to let me point, that's why he put my hands up. *He wants to hear your dirty talk, girl, you better do it.* Shit, shit, shit! I couldn't do it. I wouldn't do it. This wasn't me.

My abs tensed as I began to pull myself up but suddenly, he was on top of me, his mouth covering mine, his tongue invading every open crevice he could find. He was pushing me down, keeping me under his control, and I was surprised that old instincts didn't kick in that would force me to fight back. Instead, I wrapped my arms around his neck and pulled him closer to me, my mouth matching his kiss in passion and intensity. He wanted it rough I could tell but he was holding back, for me, and I was surprised to find myself disappointed.

"Don't leave me," he whispered against my lips.

Where did that come from? Two seconds ago, he was dominating me, and now he was pleading with me. "I'm not leaving."

"I meant in here," he said, tapping my temple. "Your mind left me. It's just as important to me as your body, Hindley. I have to have both to have you." *Shit, man, this guy is good. I think he's exactly what you need.* "Where did you go?" I knew exactly what he was talking about but I had no answer and he knew he was losing me again.

Suddenly, I felt his hand splayed across my torso, flattened against my stomach and moving lower. His mouth left mine and skimmed across my burnt chest, leaving a small trail of kisses along the way before continuing down my body, pausing at my breast and seeming to take up permanent residence. He gently began to suck and lap, his tongue stroking my nipple back and forth as his teeth gently clamped down, tugging on the now puckered peak. I sucked in a breath and let out a small moan. God, it all felt so good, this man was good. I could feel a smile spread across his lips as he brought a hand to my other breast and began to roll my other nipple between his fingers. As he felt my body relax, he slowly pushed his knee up between my legs, spreading them wider. His mouth left my nipple but was quickly replaced by his other deft fingers as his lips worked their way down toward my navel.

Oh shit, oh no, not there, no!

"Rory please, no," I begged, trying to stop him, my hands pushing him away. No one had ever done this to me before and I was still in shock that so much of my naked body was on display. I felt my breathing start to increase and feared a full on panic attack.

He sat up and looked at me with such compassion. "Hindley, look at me." His voice was gentle now, full of care and concern void of any dominance. I couldn't, I couldn't look at him. I was too embarrassed and ashamed. No one had seen this much of me, physically or emotionally. His fingers wrapped around my chin and I felt him tug my face toward him. "Hindley, please look at me."

His words were so soft and gentle and his concern for me so evident, I knew I didn't have a choice. He wasn't going to stop until I opened my eyes. I slowly lifted my lids and saw his gorgeous face shining down on me. It was filled with such adoration and respect. He revered me and my heart ached like never before. His eyes roamed my entire body and I felt my lungs constrict in apprehension of what he would do next.

His thumb gently stroked under my eyes, wiping away my tears. "Hindley." He waited until my gaze was solidly on his deep blue eyes before continuing. "You. Are. Beautiful." In between each word, he leaned down and kissed my face, under my eyes, along my cheek, over my lips.

This man was a living breathing oxymoron. He was a professional skateboarder, a bonafide player of the most dangerous kind. He was a delinquent, a trouble maker, a punk and he made no excuses for it. Yet, here in this small hotel room, he was so kind and caring, offering up something I'd searched for probably my entire life, if I was honest. No doctor or therapist or counselor had ever been able to give me this. No drug or self-help book had ever provided me with this much relief from the pain, which Rory was now offering me in this moment. I'd hidden my true identity from people in hopes of escaping the demons that lived inside me. But here I was, lying completely exposed to this man both physically and emotionally, unafraid of what he would find. For the first time in my life, I felt free and that made me feel beautiful.

"There she is," he smiled. "My Drunk Girl is back." I couldn't help but giggle as his thumbs ran across my checks and down to my lips. "I don't know who's told you differently in your life but they're wrong, Hindley." He was so genuine and gentle in this moment. "You are beautiful, inside and out."

"Thank you," I whispered.

His eyes swept over my body in a predatory fashion. "I've seen the outside, Hindley." He lowered his head to my waist as a delicious smile spread across his face. I was hypnotized by his dancing eyes and I watched as he drug his lips across my abdomen. The feeling was exquisite and I couldn't remember why I'd tried to stop him. "Now I want to see the inside of you."

"I'm not on the pill!" I blurted out.

"You don't need to be on the pill for what I'm about to do."

Holy hell, girl, this guy is about to make your dreams come true. Hoo-hah!

"Wait!" I half shouted.

"Hindley, you are fuckin' hot and sexy like no one I've ever seen. Now close your mouth and lie back like a good little girl so I can eat you out and make you come so hard, you forget about everything in your life but me."

What. The. Fuck! No one had ever spoken to me like that before in my entire life and I loved it. I had no choice but to collapse back on the bed and let this man take over. Surrendering control wasn't easy for me but Rory was making it easier and easier. I covered my face with two pillows, knowing full well I'd need them to hide my beet red face and deflect my screams.

"Eyes, Hindley." His words startled me and I felt ashamed to look but slowly, I found the willpower to be brave and pulled the pillows away from my face. He sat up on his knees and I knew he was trying to look at me fully, not willing to let me cower behind my fears. "There is no shame in this body," he said, running his long fingers along my hips, "And I refuse to let you act like there is." How could he do that, how could he tell exactly what I was thinking? "You don't have to look at me, but you have to look somewhere because I know when your eyes are closed, you close yourself off from me and there's no way I'm taking you there if you're not one hundred percent with me."

Well, there you go, he'd put it out there. He wasn't going to let me run and there was a part of me that hated him for it, hated him for exposing me and making me work on my issues, especially when he was sitting between my naked legs. But it was freeing, he was freeing and I wanted that part of my life, I needed that part of my life.

A smile spread across my face as I ran my hand through his messy blonde hair. "Okay," I whispered.

"That's my Drunk Girl." I loved his term of endearment. "Now, if you'll excuse me, I believe you asked me to rub lotion, everywhere."

"Not with your tongue."

"Would you like me to use my tongue, Hindley?" I nodded. "Tell me exactly what you want me to do." I closed my eyes but only for a second, as I realized he'd bark another order at me if I did. *Do it, girl. You know you want to. Just tell him.*

"I want you to eat me out and make me come so hard that I'll forget everything but you." I fell back on the bed with a giggle and let my hands fall above my head as I felt his warm breath on my girlie parts.

"That's my Drunk Girl." I felt the smile on his face as he buried it deep inside me.

It felt like heaven, he felt like heaven and for the first time ever, I truly felt beautiful.

Chapter 10

"I can't believe you had sex with her." It was obvious from Leif's expression as he stared out the windshield that he was never going to believe a word I said.

"For the hundredth time man, I didn't sleep with her." I watched intently as his face jerked toward mine and immediately felt the daggers zing by my head. "I swear, man!" I added, holding up my hand as if under oath.

"If you screw this up Rory, so help me God."

"What?"

He shook his head in frustration and I just laughed. "Have you ever heard of anyone being allergic to latex?"

"What?"

"Latex. Have you ever heard of anyone being allergic to it?"

"What the hell does that have to do with you and Hindley having sex?"

"She can't use condoms."

Suddenly and without warning, Leif twisted the steering wheel and cut the car across three lanes of traffic as horns blew all around us. I watched helplessly as we veered off the highway and slammed to a stop on the shoulder, watching helplessly as most of the contents inside the car flew toward the windshield, including my head. Leif shoved the car into park, while simultaneously unlatching his seatbelt and before I knew what hit me, he was halfway in my seat clawing at my neck. "What the fuck, man!" Leif was small, much smaller than me, but I was surprised by the amount of strength he showed as he fought ferociously to get at my neck.

"You dumb motherfucker! I swear to God, Rory if you get that girl pregnant, I will kill you with my bare hands."

"I did not have sex with her, man!" I shouted at the top of my lungs.

"You're a fuckin' liar. I know you. That's how you operate." I wrapped my hands around his shoulders and it took almost every ounce of strength I had to shove him back into his seat.

"Well, I didn't operate like that this time." A small smirk spread across my face as I remembered Hindley's naked body sprawled out on the bed, watching her quiver and shake from my oral skills. Leif's hand immediately grabbed my throat and just like that, I was back from my erotic memories.

"Your shit eatin' grin says otherwise."

"Dude, seriously, I didn't have sex with her. Let. Me. Go!" His hand finally went limp and I felt somewhat safer. "She can't use condoms."

"What!" he screamed. "You fucked her with nothing. God, I hope she's on the pill."

"She's not on the pill either."

The words were out of my mouth before I could even think about how guilty they sounded and I knew my declaration would send him over the edge. My entire body tensed up, waiting for his first punch but instead, I heard him take in a deep breath and I watched as he settled himself back in his seat before blowing out an audible sigh. I heard a loud click as the doors unlocked and watched as he slowly reached for the handle and opened the door. My ears were instantly ringing with the sounds of the speeding cars on the interstate but were abruptly silenced again when he slammed the door closed behind him. *What in the hell is this bonehead doing?*

Without warning, my door flew open and before I could react, his hands were clutching my shirt by the collar as he worked desperately to pull me from the car. Had it been any other time, he wouldn't have been successful, but he caught me off guard and he was so pissed, his adrenaline had spiked and the next thing I knew, my ass hit the ground with a thud and I watched as he clenched his fist and raised it high into the air. Instinct and experience made my hand involuntarily fly up to stop him seconds before he connected with my face. Now I was pissed.

My free hand hit his chest and shoved him so hard he flew off of me and rebounded off the door, his back slapping it with a thud as he slid to the ground. In less than a second, I was on my feet dusting off my body.

"What the fuck was that, Leif!" I shouted above the road noise. He sat on the ground, staring out in front of him at some invisible scene. "Leif!" I yelled again but still he remained motionless. Panic hit me at the thought that I may have actually hurt my best friend. I squatted down in front of him and wrapped both hands around his shoulders, trying to jolt him back from wherever his mind had taken him. "Leif, what the fuck is wrong with you?"

"You can't do this, Rory."

"Do what?"

"You can't screw this up, man. You've got one shot. This girl is different. She's not like the others. You can't do this." These words were becoming a chorus for him and I found my insides twisting with pain. Obviously, Leif knew Hindley was out of my league, too, but the fact he verbalized it hurt me more than the realization itself. It was one thing for me to be self-loathing but for my best friend to actually say I wasn't good enough for her either confirmed what a failure I was.

"Just get in the car, man." I stood up and extended my hand to help him up. My eyes followed him as he silently walked around the car and when I felt I was out of harm's way, I finally slid back into the passenger seat. My eyes glazed over as I stared through the front windshield, thinking about how little my best friend really thought of me. The car rocked as he plopped down into the driver's seat and turned the key in the ignition, the engine roaring to life.

I stared off into vast Texas highway spanning out in front of us, hoping all the external noises would drown out the voices in my head, but it was useless. No one needed to tell me Hindley Hagen was too good for me, least of all my best friend. I'd been telling myself that since the moment her neighbor told me she wasn't "that" kind of girl.

"Look, man, I know she's out of my league, I get that." My head fell down and my eyes watched as my thumbs rubbed vicious circles on my palms, a nervous tick I'd developed years ago as an odd coping mechanism during my violent adolescent home life.

"What the fuck are you talking about, Rory?" I turned my head and saw him staring at me in disbelief.

"Hindley. I know a loser like me has no right to even look at her, let alone try and get in her panties. Don't you think I've told myself that a thousand times?"

"You're a fuckin' idiot, man."

My entire body stiffened at his comment and my lungs seized up and contracted, refusing to take in any more oxygen. *Idiot. Idiot. Idiot.* The word replayed over and over in my head. Out of all people in my life, Leif especially knew how traumatizing that word was for me. My folks had called me an idiot, among other things. My teachers had called me an idiot. The judge who sentenced me to juvie even called me an idiot a time or two. It was a red-hot button for me that conjured up all types of emotions and feelings I never wanted to have.

"I know you hate that word, but I'm not going to apologize for it because that's exactly what you're being right now," Leif explained. I was speechless. He wasn't even going to try and apologize to me. "You're being a fuckin' idiot. It is beyond me why you think any person is out of your league." He used a mocking tone and air quotes when he spoke the words 'out of your league,' and a felt a tiny spark of relief that allowed my lungs to inhale again. "That's not what I meant at all and you know it."

I let my head fall back on the head rest and closed my eyes, trying to will his comment out of my head but all I could hear was my stepfather saying I was a piece of shit and the only thing anyone would ever do with a piece of shit was flush it down the toilet.

"Don't go there, Rory. I mean it. I'll get out of this car again and kick your ass if you let that shit hole you called a stepfather bring you back down. There is no one, and I mean *no one* who is out of your league. You're in a league of your own, man. Look at you. You're talented as shit, you have money, and have the potential to make an ass load more." Even though his words were true, my stepfather's verbal berating just seemed to be louder. "And you're sexy as hell," he added. His fist hit my arm and jolted me from my dark memories. I turned my head and saw the jovial smile that I'd come to expect from my best friend. We both began to laugh and instantly, the tension was gone.

"Well, you're right about one thing."

"What, that you're sexy as hell?" I shook my head and we both continued to tease. This was the Leif I needed in my life.

"Yes, that I'm sexy as hell."

"And that you have the potential to make a shit load of money, Rory. That's what I meant."

Leif was right. I'd pissed away so much money in the last eight years, it sickened me. And now, here I sat on the edge of a comeback with the potential to make it all back, plus tons more. But money wasn't what excited me anymore. True, I needed it if I wanted to continue to compete at the professional level, but that's not why I skated. It was the thrill, the thrill of competing, the thrill of being the best at something. Skateboarding for me was liberating. Being out on the course, jumping over the rails and ramps, just me and my board soaring through the air freed my mind and allowed me to let go of all my anxieties and fears and insecurities. It was the only time I truly felt good about myself.

"That's why you can't fuck this up, man." My thoughts where a million miles away. "Rory!" Leif shouted. I jerked my head toward his. "I'm serious. Hindley is your attorney, man. She's not one of the countless bimbos you bring home, screw, and then toss out the next morning."

"I know," I whispered under my breath. I knew I couldn't fuck this up, but not for the reasons Leif thought. This girl was different and I'd known it from the moment I'd discovered those delicious blue toenails the night I undressed her when she was three sheets to the wind. Then when I'd woken up beside her the following morning and found her admiring my body, something inside me lit on fire, something I'd never felt before, that I couldn't quite explain. I didn't want to lose her, I couldn't fuck this up. Yet, somehow I knew I would.

"Her law firm is big time, man. They'll treat you right and I know they'll negotiate the best deals for you. But if you hurt Hindley, if you screw this up, the firm is likely to drop you like a hot potato and word of that will spread, like wildfire. You know that." He didn't have to tell me how fast bad news worked its way through the media. We were all acutely aware of their inaccuracies and their lack of journalistic excellence when it came to a juicy story line. "You need these endorsements to stay in the game, man."

His emphasis on the word 'need' was a sobering reminder of just how much I'd fucked up. I'd almost sold my house in California just to pay expenses, but Jack wouldn't let me saying it was an investment and he didn't want me to jeopardize my future. Instead, he took a major cut in salary just to let me keep living my dream.

Jack and Kara were good that way, they were my surrogate parents, had been for ten years and I couldn't let them down. Not this time. I knew I had the potential to make millions with some of the deals Hindley would negotiate for me and yet here I sat, selfish as ever, wondering how I would ever be able to walk away from this amazing woman who made me feel things I'd never experienced in my life.

"She's different, Leif."

"She's way different. And she's off limits, Rory. You need to get that through your thick fuckin' head."

"I know, I know. You don't have to tell me again. I know my place in this world and it's not with a girl like Hindley Hagen."

"Man, you're a …" I held up my hand threatening to punch him in the face if he said 'idiot' one more time. "Well, you're acting like one. But that's not what I mean."

"But it's true."

"What?"

"There's no way I could ever be in her world."

"What world? What are you talking about?"

"Look at her, Leif. She's beautiful, she's brilliant, she's educated, and she comes from a family of money, power, and wealth. She oozes refinement from every pore of her body. I can't even fuckin' read, man."

"Yeah, she's hot and her parents are loaded. But from what Dana told me, they're definitely not perfect and I have a feeling that her dad's money has purchased a lot of cover-up to hide their flaws."

"What does that mean? What did Dana say?"

"She didn't say anything specifically but I could tell that Hindley and her family are anything but perfect. She did say that Hindley put herself through law school and she refuses to take any money from her dad so there goes your whole loaded theory."

I sat back in my seat, trying to comprehend what Leif had just revealed, trying to let it all sink in. I'd known from the beginning Hindley was a hard worker but why wouldn't she let her father pay for law school when he obviously could? She had something to prove, just like me. The thought made me want her even more.

"Besides," Leif continued. "Even if they all were perfect, that should mean nothing to you. You totally have the right to someone like Hindley."

"Then why are you having such a shit fit?"

"Because after Tuesday's meeting, not only will she be your attorney, she'll be your agent, too. Fucking this up with Hindley doesn't mean you'll get a psycho bitch stalking you for a month. It means you could lose endorsement deals and be sued by her firm."

"I never thought about that."

"You never do. That's why I'm here."

I wanted to let Hindley go, I knew I needed to for both our sakes but all I could see were her giant, chocolate eyes from last night and the way they pierced through my hard exterior as she lay sprawled out on the bed, completely uncovered before me. All I could remember was how fucking hot she looked entering the grand ballroom later that evening in that tight, little, black dress, her ass as round and firm and juicy as a sun-ripened watermelon. All I could feel was her skin on mine as I caressed her arms in the elevator, those perfect little hips grinding into my crotch as we rode back up to our rooms after the party had ended. And all I could smell was her delicious hair as I nuzzled her neck and wrapped my arms around her waist just before she opened the door to her hotel room. I could still hear her contagious giggles when I swatted her ass and watched helplessly as she batted her eyes and gently but firmly swung the door shut in my face. There was nothing about this girl that didn't completely and totally transfix me and I knew I would never let her just walk away, no matter who she was.

"Just please tell me you didn't screw her with no protection."

"First of all, it's none of your business what I did or didn't do with her last night."

"Your business is always my business." He was right. Even though it was his father who technically was my manager, I'd always involved the entire Jennings family, Jack, Kara, and Leif, when making business decisions. Four heads were better than one, especially in my case.

"Second, we didn't do anything."

"Well, you sure as hell better not, if she's not on the pill. And what's up with the latex?"

"She's allergic to it."

"And?"

"And, condoms are made out of latex, you idiot."

"Now who's insulting who?"

"I think it's whom." We both busted out laughing, knowing I had no idea what was grammatically correct. Hell, I probably couldn't even spell 'whom.'

"So if she's not on the pill and she can't use condoms then you better really stay the fuck away from her." We drove in silence for miles as I thought about staying away from Hindley, wondering if I would ever be able to muster that much strength.

"So what does she use, for protection, I mean?"

I thought back to our conversation last night when she panicked, thinking I wanted to have sex with her. It had never been my intention in going up to her room last night,

I'd just wanted to give her the lotion. I knew firsthand how painful sunburn could be and I didn't want her to go through that, not if I could help. But when I saw her hot little body wrapped up in nothing but that towel, other parts of my anatomy took over and I just couldn't stop myself. *That's because you're a man, a weak fucking douche bag of a man.*

"Why aren't you on the pill?" I'd asked her last night.

"Me and estrogen just don't mix." My brows furrowed in confusion. "The female hormone, that's what's in the pill that stops you from ovulating," she said answering my silent question. I was actually thankful for her statement. Finding out she wasn't on any type of birth control had essentially reduced my hard-on to a limp noodle.

But then I'd removed her towel and my hands roamed all over her gorgeous body and in true Rory fashion, my stiff soldier returned for battle ten times more aggressive. I'd hoped just tasting her would be enough to sedate my boy but who was I kidding? Hindley Hagen had been a buffet that I couldn't get enough of. She tasted better than anything or anyone I'd ever had before in my life and my senses were on fire for her. My dick actually ached to be inside her. But the panic in her eyes after I'd given her the release she'd craved told me something else was going on and I had to put my One-Eyed Milkman back in the fridge.

"What's wrong, Hindley?" She sat up and yanked the towel back tight around her, as if disgusted with herself. "Hey, what's wrong?" I reached out to stroke her arm but she pulled away.

"We shouldn't have done that."

"Why?"

Her eyes darted between mine like a caged animal awaiting slaughter and I saw a hidden emotion wash over her face. It didn't look like shame, it didn't even look like regret, God, please don't let it be regret. I knelt in front of her and wrapped my arms around her waist, trying to give her some sense of safety. For the first time in my life, I had more concern for the well-being of a woman than for my selfish need to be inside her. If this wasn't what she wanted, if she didn't want to have sex with me, then it wasn't going to happen. I tried not to think about why, about how she'd probably come to her senses by now and realized what a loser I was and couldn't possibly stoop so low as to sleep with someone like me. I braced myself, preparing for her dismissal, for the inevitable rejection I knew she'd hurl at me but as I gazed up at her face, I saw something else entirely, something I wasn't prepared for. Her once bright almond eyes were now pooling with tears.

"I can't use condoms," she expelled with great effort as her head fell back and her eyes rolled up toward the ceiling.

Suddenly, I knew there was more going on inside that beautiful mind than just her fear of condoms. I couldn't tell if she was trying to avoid me or keep her tears at bay but I knew her eyes wouldn't lie to me. I had to regain their focus if I wanted the truth. I watched her face intently as I stood and put my face directly in front of hers, essentially blocking her view from anything but me as I gently and lovingly cupped her face with my hands, ensuring she couldn't look away.

"If you're not on the pill and you can't use condoms, does that mean you're not sexually active?" She slammed her eyes shut and tried to pull away from my grip but I held on tighter. I wasn't going to let her run. My heart clenched as I saw two lone tears roll down her cheeks. *Fuck, dude, is she a virgin?*

I needed to find out what was going on in her head before I lost her again and I knew I couldn't take this power position standing over her if I wanted the truth. I slowly released her face, letting my hands skim across her neck as I sat down beside her, folding in my leg so we were as close to one another as possible without touching. "Hindley, what's going on? Talk to me."

She was reluctant to speak at first, her anxiety almost palpable as I felt it seep through every pore of her body. I needed to reassure her, convince her that I wouldn't hurt her like someone else obviously had before. My stomach churned in disgust thinking about anyone intentionally hurting her. Who had it been? The ass-hat from college her sister matched her up with at the wedding? An old high school boyfriend? Shit, maybe it was even her birth father, she never talked about him. My mind reeled with the endless possibilities and I felt my fists tighten as a sense of protectiveness for her washed over me. I didn't have time to think about it though, I needed to bring her back. I reached out and slowly stroked her hair as I placed a small lock behind her ear. She was wounded and like any wild animal, I knew I had to wait and let her come to me, so I did. We sat in silence for what seemed like an eternity before she finally spoke again.

"I'm allergic to latex. I can't use regular condoms." *That's it? That's all?* Her head was hanging low and I was aching inside for the shame she obviously carried but I couldn't understand why. I caressed her jaw with my knuckles before wrapping her chin in my hand and turning her face toward mine. Her eyes were still screwed shut.

"Look at me, Hindley." She immediately complied and my dick twitched at her obedience. *Not now, boy.* Her eyes were blood shot and swollen and...mesmerizing. For a minute, I couldn't think, I couldn't breathe, I just wanted to stare at her, forever. "I don't care, Hindley," I whispered. Her face softened and I was reassured that she felt a little safer with me. "Why are you so upset?"

"Because I know you're used to woman just, like, lying down and spreading their legs for you and I'm not like that."

She swatted my hand away and I felt rejected, surprised at the dull ache in my heart at her reaction toward me.

"I never thought you were you like that, Hindley."

"But that's exactly what I just did," she sighed, her face riddled with shame. I had to wipe it clean. I couldn't sit by and let her feel this way, not when I didn't share the same sense of guilt. I took her chin in my hand and gently pulled it toward me again, inhaling sharply as I noticed her cheeks were stained with tears. I was suddenly lost in her pain, confused by my own sense of empathy.

"Hindley," I spoke gently. "Did I do something to you that you didn't want me to?" She hesitated and I held my breath, fearing there was a small chance that, perhaps in my dickheadedness, I had actually pushed her too far. But my anxiety was wiped away as a tiny smile erupted across her face and her head shook in silent denial. She'd wanted what I gave her and I couldn't help but smirk, knowing I'd satisfied some yearning desire deep inside her. My body visibly sank as all the apprehension and fear I'd held on to suddenly washed away. "Well, if I wanted to and you wanted me to, why should you feel shame?"

She shrugged her shoulders and tried to disconnect from me physically and emotionally but I wouldn't let her.

"Look, Hindley, I'm not a saint, you know that. Hell, half the world knows that. I've screwed a lot of women and I'm not proud of it."

She pulled out of my reach, turning her back toward me, staring at the wall in obvious disgust. Suddenly, I felt anger welling up inside me. The whole scene was starting to piss me off more than I wanted to admit.

"Look at me, Hindley!" I half shouted. I didn't mean to sound so demanding but there was something about her that brought out the dominant side of my personality. I needed to maintain control and order in my life. That's how I survived. Yet with this woman, I felt more out of control than I had in years. It more than scared me, it shook me to the core. Her head jerked around as her eyes snapped up at mine in submission. Unaware of my need to control her, a sick part of me loved her reaction. It excited me to know that even in her embarrassment, she wanted to obey me. I knew it shouldn't excite me but it did, that's what I needed from her, submission. *That's because you're a control freak, domineering, sick motherfucker.*

"What I just did with you is not something I make a habit of doing with every woman I sleep with." That part was true. I may be considered a certified muff-diver with the ladies but that didn't mean I ate out every chick I brought home. In fact, I couldn't remember the last time I had. "I think it's a very personal act, at least for me it is. I know you're not the type of woman who goes off and has casual sex with random men you meet at a bar. You proved that on the first night we spent together." Her eyes grew wide and I knew I'd hit a nerve I didn't mean to. Then, it finally dawned on me. *She is a fucking virgin, you douche bag.*

"Has anyone ever done that to you before, Hindley? What I just did, you know, oral sex?" She jerked away from me and tried to stand but I wouldn't let her. Instead, I grabbed her hips and forcibly pulled her back down.

"I don't want to talk about this, Rory."

"Are you a virgin, Hindley?"

"What?" she shouted. "No, I'm not a virgin, you idiot." My entire body stiffened at her offensive slur but I couldn't focus on my self-esteem issues right now. This was about her. "Why would you even ask that? This was wrong and it shouldn't have happened. I'm sorry I let it get that far."

I was losing her, I was losing my Drunk Girl and I just couldn't just sit there and watch her escape. Experience had proven that she responded to my dominant side so even though it went against my better judgment at the moment, I switched tactics. I placed my palm on her stomach and gently pushed against her until she fell backward onto the mattress. Slowly, I rolled on top of her and pressed myself against her until we were essentially one body sinking into the bed together. My eyes rolled up to meet hers and I felt confident as my mouth spread into a predatory smile.

"Are you, Hindley?

"Am I what?" she breathed out in a sultry whisper, obviously trying to sound innocent but failing miserably.

"Are you really sorry about what I did?" I rubbed my crotch against her so she could feel how much I wanted her. She needed to know I desired her, that I ached for her, that this wasn't some random act for me.

"That's what I'm talking about." She tried to shove me off but I sank deeper into her, crushing her body with mine. I could feel her chest rise and fall as her breathing accelerated. "I can't do this, Rory," she whispered.

Who was I kidding? She was so far out of my league, of course she couldn't do this. She'd never wanted me from the beginning and I was a fool, a gigantic dumbass to think I had a chance. Something in my mind snapped. *Dude, this chick doesn't want you. You don't belong here. Get off. Get off of her! NOW!*

I immediately rolled away, pushing myself off the bed to stand. Suddenly, she grabbed my wrist and pulled me back down. My dick twitched just from her touch and my pulse raced, in what? Excitement? Anticipation? No, in hope, hope that maybe I could be with her after all.

"It's not what you think," she whispered.

My whole arm felt like it was on fire where she held on to it and I tried desperately to focus on that one sensation. I didn't want to see her beautiful face, for fear it would express her rejection and remorse at what I'd done to her. But I couldn't help myself, I made up my mind that if she was going to cast me out for being beneath her, I was damn well gonna make sure she did it looking at my face. My eyes rolled over her body, my lungs holding in a breath I thought might be my last, afraid of what I would find when our eyes finally connected. As I focused on her angelic face, preparing for the worst, I was surprised to see vibrant eyes full of longing and desire staring back at me. This wasn't a rejection, this was an invitation.

"I want you. I *really* want you," she spoke softly, her emphasis on the word 'really' hard to mistake. I slowly expelled the breath I'd been holding in but a feeling of dread washed over my body as I sensed there was more she needed to say, something I didn't want to hear. "But I'm not on the pill and we can't use regular condoms so it's a no go."

Still, there was more she wasn't telling me but I refused to ask any more questions, not when she'd declared she wanted me, really wanted me. Her revelation made my heart soar and my lips wanted to spread wide in silent jubilation but I couldn't show her how elated I was. Not yet.

"If you're not on the pill and you can't use condoms, what do you use?" I was surprised by how much anxiety my question evoked in me as I waited for an answer that perhaps I didn't want to know. Just the thought of her with any other man had my entire body tensing up with jealous anger. It wasn't like me to be possessive of a woman but there was something different about Hindley and before I knew it, my mind had wondered to the dark side, wanting to pummel any man who'd ever had sex with her, let alone hurt her. The expression in her eyes was sobering and immediately, my green-eyed monster disappeared. Her face told me the memories were too difficult to speak of. She'd been scarred, damaged, just like me.

She tried to pull away again but I knew I wasn't going to let her. I wanted to be with Hindley any way I could. I wanted to protect her and comfort her and wash away all the hurt from her past. If that meant we could never have sex and all I would ever be able to do was rub lotion over her sexy body, I would be okay with that. Hell, I'd get excited about that. I just had to be with her, next to her, holding her.

What the fuck are you saying, man? No sex with this chick? Ever? That is never going to happen. Your blue-balled nut sacks will fall off. We will not let this dick go unused for the rest of your life!

I'd never had a relationship with a woman that wasn't sexual, except with Leif's mom, Kara. Suddenly, I realized just how special Hindley was becoming to me. Wanting to be with her, even if it meant we couldn't have sex, was huge for me. I wanted her, I needed her, just for her, not for what she could give me in return. *Hey, dick face, you're a selfish asshole, remember? This will never work!*

"Look, Hindley. I'd love to have sex with you, don't get me wrong. But if you can't, you can't." Her eyes were suddenly filled with pain and rejection and I cringed realizing she'd misunderstood me, again. Verbal communication was obviously not our strong point right now. "I'm sorry, that sounded bad. I just meant that with you, it's not about sex." Her eyebrows rose in confusion. "I mean it is, I want to, it's just…" Suddenly, she burst out laughing as I tried miserably to recover.

"I can have sex, Rory, God," she said, with a mischievous smile. "I just have to use special condoms, non-latex."

A giant smile washed over my face as sexual fantasies flooded my mind. I felt like a six year old on Christmas morning, looking at his brand new bicycle giddy with wild anticipation of the adventures that lay ahead of him. I coughed with embarrassment, realizing how shallow I was being. Knowing I really could have sex with this wanton Goddess was like heaven for me though, and I had a difficult time containing my joy.

"Um, where do you get these special condoms," I asked with a raised eyebrow, trying to sound coy. I didn't want to seem too eager even though my dick was throbbing like it'd been beaten with a hammer.

"I usually order them online."

"And you have some here?" Without warning, her first flew up and hit me square on the arm. "Ouch!" I yelled in actual pain, rubbing the spot where her tiny fist had had made contact. This girl was strong. *Note to self, don't piss her off.*

"Unlike you, I don't walk around with a box of condoms in my purse."

"I don't have a box of condoms in my purse," I replied sarcastically. She tilted her head and cut her eyes up at me in disbelief. "Well, I mean, I have some, but not a whole box."

"Where, in your purse?" She started laughing and instantly, our mood shifted. Her revelation was a saving grace to me. Was it possible that we could actually have sex, tonight? God I hoped so.

"So seriously," I asked.

"No, Rory, I don't have any with me."

"Did you leave them all at home?" She shook her head. "Where are they?"

"Probably still at the store."

"You don't have any of your special condoms, at all, anywhere?" She shook her head again as she pulled her dress off the rack and laid it down on the bed. *Go back to sleep, Woody, no action for you tonight.*

"Shit!" she shouted.

"What?"

"My dress."

"What's wrong?"

"My legs are beet red."

"And?"

"This dress is above the knee. I'll look like ridiculous, like I've been down on my knees all night." I tried to stifle a laugh but failed miserably. She cut her eyes and pointed at me with a stern face. "That's not happening."

"Ever?" She remained silent and her face passive but I saw her pouty lips shift ever so slightly and that's when I had confirmation. Hindley had a freaky side. Maybe no one had discovered it before, but it was there. One-Eyed Milkman was back out of the fridge and ready for action. I stalked her like a wounded animal and laughed when she stuck her palm in my face.

"No, Rory. I need to fix my dress."

I pushed her body against the wall with relative ease, holding her in place with my hips as I pressed my hands on either side of her face. Her eyes grew darker, more erotic by the second and her chest began to heave. She wanted this and I was going to give it to her. A low growl erupted from my throat as I watched her grab at her towel.

"You didn't answer me, Hindley."

"What?" she breathed out against my neck, her response barely above a whisper.

I drug my lips down to the nape of her neck ,just below her ear and let my voice wrap around her shoulders like a sexy velvet ribbon. "Are you saying your knees will never, ever be red because you knelt down in front of me and sucked me off?" Her body shivered against me and my dick got so hard I thought I might explode right there in my pants. "Well, I'm waiting for your answer, Hindley." I whispered.

Her hair rubbed against my face as she shook her head but I wasn't sure if it was an involuntary reaction to my voice or an actual answer. I drew in a deep breath, inhaling her scent, and my head began to spin from the intoxicating aroma. No woman had ever affected me like this. I was pretty sure what her answer would be but I needed to hear her say it, out loud. I felt like a predator that'd just gone in for the kill, my lips turning up in a victorious smile. "Say it, Hindley." She shook her head again. "Say it," I whispered in her ear, letting my lips rub against her soft skin.

"Say what?" she blew out her breath caressing my shoulder making it impossible for me to move with the painful throbbing in my pants.

"That you'll never get down on your knees in front of me, put your face in my crotch, and suck my dick until I come all over you." I felt her body shudder against me and could only imagine how hot and wet she was. Hell, I was about to come all over the entire hotel room if she moved against me one more time. She responded to me in a way no other woman ever had and I loved it. Slowly, I dropped my hand and let it slide up her leg, raising the towel as I went, feeling for myself just how turned on she was.

"Rory, please," she whispered.

My hand stopped just shy of the juncture between her long, lean legs as I pulled back to gauge her reaction. Was she serious, did she really want me to stop or was she just overwhelmed with desire? When I looked down at her face, I was surprised to find her eyes closed, the expression she wore one of pure ecstasy. I knew, in that moment, she was mine. I let my lips graze hers and smiled when she twitched at the sensation of our skin on skin contact. "Please what, Hindley?" I murmured as my mouth covered hers.

"Please, not tonight."

Those were my affirming words. She wasn't saying no, she was merely saying not now. My lips crushed down on her as I pulled up her leg and guided it around my waist, transported into another dimension when her arms wrapped around my neck pulling my body into hers. I knew we couldn't have sex, not tonight, but it didn't mean I didn't want to get as close to her as possible.

"Knock, knock!" Dana's voice rang out as she entered the hotel room. *This chick is the biggest fuckin' cock blocker I've ever seen in my life!*

Hindley pushed me off with such force, I bounced onto the bed, landing flat on my back. That's when I noticed her towel. It was lying on the floor. In our tango of lips and legs, it must have fallen off. I knew Hindley didn't want to look like 'that girl' so I flew up from the bed, grabbed the towel, and shoved it in her hands as I darted over to the other side of the bed trying to look as innocent as possible but knowing I was failing miserably.

"Well, well, well, what do we have here?" Dana asked, surveying the room.

"Hindley needs to fix her dress. She asked me to look for a needle and thread." My entire body clenched at the painful sound of my own voice, which was now an entire octave higher than normal. I knew I sounded juvenile and guilty as hell.

Dana's sarcastic tone didn't shock me in the least. "I'm surprised she didn't ask you to look in her suitcase where she always keeps it." I turned around and saw Dana holding up a small sewing kit with two fingers and looking from me to Hindley and back to me again with one raised eyebrow. This girl was a master and she loved everything she'd just interrupted. I wanted to hate her but her sky blue eyes and saucy attitude made it nearly impossible. All I could do was return her rueful look.

Hindley snatched the sewing kit from Dana's hand and the dress with the other as she stomped off into the bathroom and slammed the door. I didn't need anyone to tell me differently, that was my cue to exit. I'd seen a lot of girls do the walk of shame, all thanks to me. This was the first time I could ever remember having to do it myself. It felt awful and I was ashamed I'd ever made any girl feel this used and abandoned.

"We'll see ya downstairs, One-Nighter!" Dana shouted as the door closed behind me.

Hindley wasn't a random sex kind of girl and I'd known that from the beginning. I'd be damned if I was going to make her into one now, not that she'd let me. But the twitching in my crotch was making it harder and harder to abide by the rules.

"Rory!" I heard Leif shouting from the driver's side of his Mustang. "Rory!" Suddenly, I was brought back from my memories of last night.

"What!" I shouted.

"Where were you?"

"A million miles away," I said softly, under my breath.

"Please, man, don't do this."

"I know, I know, you've said it already. She's off limits. She's my attorney."

"It's not just that, man."

"I know, she's out of my league."

"She's not out of your league. Well, not for the reasons you think." I jerked my head so I could see his profile.

"What are you talking about?"

"Nothing man, forget it."

"I'm not gonna forget it, you brought it up, man. What the hell are you talking about?"

"Hindley's different for a lot of reasons."

"I know, you don't have to tell me."

"Yeah, I think I do." I stared at him aimlessly, waiting for him to continue but he didn't.

"So what? Are you going to tell me why?"

"I don't know all the reasons, Rory, not for sure. I just know that after talking to Dana, it's really clear that Hindley's been through a lot."

"A lot like what?" He didn't answer. "Just say it, Leif."

"I don't know, I can't. Dana didn't explain it, it's just a feeling I got listening to her talk about Hindley."

"What did she say?" He stared at the road and I felt my temperature rising. The thought of anyone hurting Hindley, physically or emotionally, had me sick to my stomach. "What exactly did she say?"

"She just said that Hindley's been through a lot. She emphasized a lot."

"I know the ass-hat boyfriend in college humiliated her."

"I think it's more than that man. It's like Dana was warning me, or silently asking me to warn you."

"About what?"

"Do you like her? You know, *like* her, like her."

"What are we in third grade again? Yes, I like her."

"Then leave her alone. I don't think she can handle someone like you, Rory."

What the fuck does that mean? I stared out the window as I watched car after car pass us by, surprised at my best friend's words. He had so little faith in me and the truth was, I had little faith in myself. But I had all the faith in the world in Hindley. She was strong, stronger than even Dana knew and even though I realized I shouldn't, I wanted her, I needed her and I'd never needed anyone. Ever.

Every fiber of my being shouted, 'Leave her alone!' but I knew I wouldn't. I couldn't. And that thought, more than any other, scared me to death. I'd fought addiction for years and won, but Hindley Hagen was slowly becoming my new drug of choice and even though she wasn't illegal, I had no doubt she was lethal. At least for me.

Chapter 11

~HINDLEY~

I glanced at the clock on the dining room wall and couldn't believe how long I'd been working at my sewing machine. Almost four hours! No wonder my neck was killing me. I pushed back from the table and stood up, stretching like I'd been in a cave for months. I was working on a maternity set for a girl at work. I'd never cut nor sewn maternity clothes so this one pattern was pretty stressful.

I'd been sewing since high school, more out of necessity than desire. Shopping for clothes back then was a daunting task, given the fact that I was thirty pounds heavier. Nothing ever fit right and when I couldn't pry up a zipper all the way or watched in horror as the pant sizes got bigger and bigger, it sent me spiraling in a shame game that left me shoving another big, fat cheeseburger in my mouth. One day, after spending a depressing afternoon at the mall humiliating myself at store after store, finding nothing that fit me, I schlepped back home and threw myself on my bed, silently crying so my mother wouldn't hear me. That's when I decided to try and make a few pieces of clothing on my own. I was surprised to find my mom was really supportive, she even bought me one of the nicest sewing machines on the market and the one I still used to this day. People gushed over my first shirt so much that I kept sewing and before I knew it, I had a complete wardrobe that fit me perfectly.

At first, sewing was just a hobby but as I moved into law school, it actually became a way for me to pay the bills. I'd stay up late at night and wake up early in the morning to create new looks for all kinds of clients. The work was interesting and I loved designing but sewing was much more than that for me. It was an escape, a way to forget about all the bad in my life. It gave me a sense of accomplishment and pride like nothing else ever had. I could get lost for hours on one pattern and obviously, that had happened tonight.

Even though the clock registered eight in the evening, there was still plenty of light outside, a benefit of the late spring and early summer in Texas. The scrap pieces of material strewn about the floor caught my eye and ideas began to swim around in my head about what I could make with the remnants. I hated to let anything go to waste. Maybe I'd make a baby blanket with it. I bent down under the table to pick up scraps, envisioning all the various shapes and sizes of bedspreads I could design.

I jumped at the sound of my cell phone ringing, banging my head so hard on the table's edge that my teeth literally rattled. I rubbed the tender spot on my scalp, trying to stop the instant throbbing. I was embarrassed to admit that I'd been anxiously awaiting a phone call from Rory since Dana and I returned from San Antonio earlier this morning. I felt like an idiotic girl in middle school, waiting for the boy I'd been pining for to call. In actuality, that's exactly what I was and it wasn't my proudest moment.

I can't believe you actually expect him to call. Come on, he's a player. Player's don't call after they fuck you. Bag 'em and tag 'em, and get out before you get up, its rule number one in the Player Handbook.

It wasn't like I'd actually had sex with him but we'd done plenty. We'd technically been intimate together and that was enough to have me feeling shameful and disgraced. But what really pissed me off was the fact that I'd actually lain awake in the hotel room last night, lusting over him, remembering the way his hands felt on my body and wanting it to happen again. The release he'd provided me was an escape I'd longed for and didn't even know it. I wanted that freedom again. I craved it. With Rory I wasn't afraid.

But I reminded myself that being with Rory Gregor was not a good idea. If people discovered our relationship, they'd soon delve into my past and find it just as sordid as his. I'd worked too hard and too long to overcome my past and I couldn't afford to risk it. Not now, not ever. But I'd felt a connection with him that was undeniable. I saw the demons of insecurity haunting his eyes last night. I was all too familiar with them as they held residence in mine as well.

Mr. Stedwick believed in me enough to give me this opportunity and I couldn't screw it up. True, Rory's manager had specifically asked for me but he'd done so because he'd seen me fight for Rory, for his fair compensation when he wasn't even my client. And after Tuesday's signing, if Rory and Jack agreed, I'd be fighting even harder for him. A smile slowly began to cover my face just thinking about doing battle for Rory. Something deep in my heart told me no one had ever really fought for him, not enough to make a difference anyway.

I knew it was wrong and went against all my better judgment, but I wanted him, really wanted him, in every way. I had a deep seeded desire to help ease his insecurities, to make him feel as special as he had made me feel last night. His gentle words shocked me and his mannerisms made me realize there was so much more to my Skater Boy than met the eye. I'd always feared being judged by others, especially given my past, but Rory made me feel that no matter what I'd done, I was special and deserved to be treated with the utmost care. And it was for that reason that I found myself hanging by the phone all afternoon, now late into the evening, waiting to talk to him, to feel that rush of belonging, of being treasured and cherished.

I held my breath as I frantically searched for the phone, fearing he'd hang up before I could answer. After the fourth ring, I finally found the phone hiding under piles of material. I didn't even have time to look at the caller ID before I answered.

"Hello." I sounded frantic and desperate, but I didn't care.

"Whatcha?"

I let out a disappointing sigh as I heard Dana's voice on the other end.

"Nothing."

"Still no word from Clam Diver?"

"Who?"

"Clam Diver. Muff Muncher. Furburger Flipper." I sat on the phone in silent humiliation. Perhaps it was a mistake to tell Dana everything about my life. "Ya know, Rory 'Mack the Knife' Gregor."

"I knew I shouldn't have told you what he did. You're sick. You know that right?"

"Mistake? Are you kidding me? It's been months since I've had someone munch my carpet."

"Dana!" I screamed, my entire body turning scarlet with shame.

"What? I gotta live out my fantasies through you now apparently. Who would have ever thought it?"

"This is disgusting."

"Why? Are you embarrassed because of colorful terminology or because Rory ate at the Y?"

I hung my head in defeat, rubbing my temples as I felt a migraine coming on. "Both."

"Don't be. Do you know how long you gotta be with a guy before he goes down on you?"

"Obviously, it takes way longer than any guy I've ever been with since no one's ever done that to me before." I could hear the disappointment in my own voice as I thought about all of Rory's past sexual experiences. I was just another notch on his bed post and his lack of communication was evidence of that. What had I been thinking last night? *Um, you weren't thinking, and that's why it felt fucking awesome. Don't ever think again.*

"Oh, yeah, I totally forget, your old lovers, Shit-for-Brains and Dick-Smaller-Than-My-Forefinger, never did get you off did they?"

Most times, I knew it was a mistake to tell Dana about every single sexual escapade of mine. This moment was no different. But she was my best friend and we just couldn't seem to hide things from one another. Not to mention, I was so inexperienced, I needed her help to navigate the turbulent waters I called sex. She was the one who'd explained how to put a condom on. She was the one who'd told me how to hold a guy's penis and how to work it. She was even the one who'd helped my find alternative condoms when I'd discovered I was allergic to latex.

When I was seventeen, I had my wisdom teeth removed. As soon as the oral surgeon put on the plastic gloves, I could feel something in my body react just to the smell alone but I dismissed it as nerves. Once he touched the gloves to my lips though, everything changed. Within a minute, I looked like Angelina Jolie on Botox.

Even as I prepared for my first sexual encounter with Tim Moffit in college, it had been Dana who'd reminded me of my allergy, which now included most condoms. And it had been Dana who'd taken me to the sex shop to look for alternatives.

That's where I met Regan Jackson, owner and operator of 'Sex World.' It was a small sex shop in downtown Dallas, not far from the university I attended. It specialized in anything from vibrators to party favors to latex-free condoms. I'd been embarrassed as hell to go into the store but my pending sexual escapades had required it.

I was shocked to find the store was really like any other specialty shop in downtown Dallas, minus the dildos and crotch less panties in the window. It was clean and upscale and Regan was a hardworking, honest business owner. That was the day I discovered just how judgmental I'd been my entire life and after that, I vowed never to be so sanctimonious or holier-than-though ever again. Dana and I struck up a friendship with Regan that still remained to this day. Judging Regan and what she did for a living had been an eye opener for me. *But, wait, isn't that exactly what you're doing to Rory right now?*

You'd think after all these years of having a friend like Regan in the sex shop industry, I'd have been more comfortable with the act of sex itself by now, but I wasn't. I had too much to overcome. She'd rant and rave about what a beauty I was and how a girl who looked like me with the type of body I had should be up on stage making money with it.

I thought about Rory and what a mistake this was to get involved but laughed as Regan's words of advice from years ago rattled through my mind. "Honey, if it feels good, it's legal and don't hurt nobody, then get on board and take the ride." She was a mentor and a hero to me in so many ways and I laughed thinking about her words of wisdom.

"What's so funny?" Dana's voice brought me back.

"Regan."

"What about her?"

"I was just thinking what a hoot she would get out of me. Knowing so much about sex but still being so embarrassed at Rory's act."

"You can't even say it, can you?"

"Say what?"

"What he did to you."

"No, I can't." My body flamed with embarrassment from her comment. "Why is that such a big deal to you?"

"Oh, it ain't a big deal to me. But judging by what you said he wanted last night, you better start getting comfortable with talking dirty."

"Why do I tell you everything?"

"Because you love me."

"I do love you, but there's gotta be a better reason than that, to go through the humiliation you're putting me through."

"Ah, I'm sorry, Hindley. You know I'm just bustin' your chops. I love the fact that you've found a guy who's obviously willing to put your needs above his own. And it sounds like he's pretty well versed in the art of…"

"Stop! Don't say it anymore." I heard her giggle on the other end and I couldn't help but laugh with her. "You know I can't do this."

"Why?"

"You know why."

"Oh, the whole, I'm his lawyer thing? Whatever."

"It's not whatever. I took an oath."

"No, you didn't."

Okay, she was right, I didn't take an oath per se, but there was the whole hypocritical oath thing, not to mention the loss of my job if this came out. "Dana, I could lose my job."

"So? You're not that crazy about it anyway. Look, I'm telling you from experience, Hindley, if you can find a guy who one, is willing to go down on you, and two, does it with super skills as you said Rory did, then you better keep him. Or at least ship him over to me when you're done."

"Rory doesn't keep women, he uses them."

"I know, Leif said."

Dana shared some of the conversations she'd had with Leif over the weekend with me on the drive home this morning. He'd confirmed to her that Rory was a player and he had never been in a committed relationship. It hurt my heart and made me feel cheap and used. But could I really judge? I mean, I knew going into it he was a player. And it wasn't like I was asking him for forever. I just wanted for-right-now, and that's what he'd given me.

"I didn't mean to upset you, Hindley."

"You didn't. I'm a big girl and I took it for what it was."

"And what was it exactly?"

"It felt good, no one got hurt, and it wasn't illegal so I went along for the ride."

Dana laughed as Regan's words rolled off my tongue with ease. "That's true. But I know you, Hindley. You don't just buy a ticket for one ride. You want a season pass to the whole frickin' park, don't you?"

I nodded my head in silent agreement, frustrated that she knew me so well. I wasn't looking for Mr. Right Now, I was looking for Mr. Right. I knew Rory didn't fit that bill but it didn't mean I wanted to get off the ride, not yet anyway, and that one thought scared the shit out of me.

This guy was different in so many ways and I knew he had the potential to not only hurt me but completely destroy me, if I let him. I was hiding under the facade that this relationship was about work, that I was letting him into my life because I now represented him. But the sobering truth was, I was falling for him, fast. I was on the edge of a high cliff about to jump into a dangerous sea that would beat me, tatter me, and throw me mercilessly into the jagged rocks below. Instead of fleeing, all I could think about were his beautiful blue eyes, his amazing body, his shaggy, dirty blonde hair, his adorable dimples, and his tattoo. Oh, that tattoo. My Skater Boy. It was wrong to claim him so early on, but who was I kidding? I was already hopelessly lost.

"Just take it slow, Hindley. Maybe Leif was wrong. Maybe he just hasn't met the right girl yet."

"Yeah, right. You've dated tons of players like Rory Gregor. Has one of them ever stopped their promiscuous ways to settle down and make you an honest woman?" She laughed nervously and we both knew the answer. Once a player...

Suddenly, my other line beeped.

"Hold on." I pulled the phone away and sucked in a breath. "Holy shit, it's Rory! What should I do?"

"Do you want to talk to him?"

"I don't know."

"Yes, you do." I sat in silence. I knew, I just didn't want to admit it to myself. "I'll talk to you tomorrow," she finally answered for me and without another word, the line switched over and immediately, I heard his deep raspy voice.

"Hello? Hindley?" I held my breath, afraid that he would hear me breathe. *Ride the ride, Hindley.*

"Hello?" I finally responded. I tried to act as if I didn't know who it was but my voice was broken and shaky and I knew I was failing miserably.

"Oh, uh, hey. It's Rory. I wasn't sure if you were there or not."

"Oh, sorry. I was on the other line."

"Do you need to go? I can call you back. Or you can call me back. Whatever works for you." I laughed to myself. He was nervous and it rang through the phone line like an echo in a gymnasium. The thought that Rory Gregor was nervous talking to a woman, to me, made my heart sing and opened up a window of ideas for our future. I thought of what Dana just said, 'Maybe he just hasn't found the right girl.'

"No, we're good. It was just Dana."

"Oh, okay. How is she?" I laughed, thinking of all the vulgar ways she'd described Rory's actions last night. If he only knew. "What's so funny?"

"Dana."

"Let me guess. You told her about last night and she was being sick and twisted about it, like only Dana can be." I giggled in acknowledgment. "There's nothing more lovely than the sound of your laughter, Hindley." His comment took me totally by surprise. "So how many different ways did she describe cunnilingus?"

"What!" I screamed. Old Rory was back.

"That many, huh?"

"You guys are sick." His deep rich laugh reverberated through the air and I felt my thighs clench just at the sound of him. *Hoe-lee-shit, girl.*

"So, what are you doing?"

"Right now?"

"No, ten minutes ago, dipstick." He didn't give me time to answer his smart-ass remark and I was shocked at how unoffended I was. "Yes, I mean right now."

I wasn't sure how far into my life I wanted Rory Gregor to travel but letting him know about my hobby seemed innocent enough.

"I'm sewing."

"You sew?"

"No, dipstick, I just said I'm sewing when, in fact, I don't sew." The phone was silent and for a split second, I thought I might have offended him.

"I see I have my hands full with you, Hindley."

His growling laugh did things to me I wasn't sure I was all too comfortable with, but it felt so right. I was a sheep and he was a wolf and it was only a matter of time before he devoured me. *Um, hello, he pretty much did that last night.* My lips twitched at the memory. I decided to play his game. It was a dangerous one and I risked being hurt but for once in my life, I was going to try and get the upper hand.

"Yes, you do, Rory. You'll always have your hands full with me."

He let out a sexy moan and I could feel my insides tighten with desire. "Oh, God, I hope so," his deep voice rumbled in response. I closed my eyes, letting his words wash over me as my entire body began to throb with a deep pulse, especially down there. There was silence as we both tried to compose ourselves. "Do you want to get something to eat?"

Okay, it went against every fiber of my being but I couldn't help it. I was on the ride with this wolf and I didn't want it to be over. Not yet anyway. I drew in a deep breath, trying to push past my anxiety as I felt the roller coaster reach the summit and plummet down that first hill.

"I have something you can eat." *Oh, my God, girl, did you just say that? No, you didn't. Hoe-lee-shit. This guy is gonna literally eat you alive.*

I heard an audible gasp on the other end of the phone and could only imagine what he was thinking. I couldn't believe what I'd just said. It came out with no thought. Well, okay, there'd been thought, but it just came out. I'd never talked like that with anyone, ever.

I had to reel it back in. Before he could respond, I shouted out. "Pizza!" I shouted, panting in anticipation of his response, knowing this could possibly go horribly wrong. *Girl, you are playing with fire here. You better be careful or you're gonna spontaneously combust.*

"I don't want pizza." His voice was low and rough and sexy as hell. "I had something entirely different in mind, Hindley." Oh my God, the way he said my name made my legs feel like jelly and I swear I almost had an orgasm on my sofa.

"Well, all I have is pizza and that's all you'll get from me." I wanted to add 'tonight' but I knew I'd taken him too far already and to be honest, he was completely out of my league.

"So can I come over?"

Oh, shit. I have him so revved up. If he comes over now, I know he'll try to start something and I'm not sure if I can say no again. *I don't think you want to say no again.*

"That's probably not a good idea."

"Why?"

"I'm your attorney and it would be wrong for us to…" I couldn't even finish my own sentence.

"I believe we crossed that line last night in your hotel room." I didn't know whether to be thrilled or embarrassed by his revelation. From the tone in his voice, it was obvious he enjoyed it too.

"It shouldn't happen again."

"But you know it will."

He was right. Even as I said it, even as I tried to push him away, I was already more brave with him than I'd ever been with anyone else in my life and that power was intoxicating. I wanted to push past my limits, not just sexually. Rory made me…brave. I was tired of being afraid of sex, of my job, of people, of life in general. Getting involved with Rory wasn't technically illegal but it was definitely frowned upon. If word got out that we were involved in a relationship, it could ruin both of us.

"This isn't a good idea for either one of us, Rory."

"Why?"

"I could lose my job and you could lose millions of dollars in endorsement deals if anyone finds out. Sponsors don't like to see their star athletes dipping their pen in the company ink."

"Did you just say that?"

"Yes, I did just say that." I know it sounded cliché but I meant it.

"No one will find out, Hindley."

"How do you know?"

"You taste too good for me to ever jeopardize one moment with you." I knew a lot of girls would probably be offended by his statement but to me, it was one of the sweetest, most erotic things anyone had ever said to me. I wanted to say yes, my body was screaming for the kind of relief this man could offer but my brain was in the way. *Fuck your brain, girl, you need this. You need a break, you need a distraction. You need him.* I caved.

"Pick up some food on your way over. I'm starving." I could hear his lips spread wide with a mischievous smile and desire washed over me as I pictured his beautiful expression, full of stubble and dimples and all kinds of sexy.

"So am I," he purred in a dirty, provocative voice that sounded so lustful. My body literally shook from head to toe and I thought I might drop the phone from the tingling his words evoked between my legs. "I'll see you soon." Without another word, the line went dead and my heart raced with anticipation and fear. I'd just invited the Big Bad Wolf over for dinner and I had a feeling I was the main course.

~

"So, what are you working on?" Rory asked as he walked around my table, picking up pieces of fabric and inspecting them.

"A woman at work is pregnant. I'm trying my hand at a maternity top for her."

"That's cool."

I pushed the material aside and cleared a spot for us at the end of the table as I sat down our plates and water. "What's cool?"

"That you're making something for her. You know, using your talent for someone else."

"You do it too, don't you?" I remembered reading about Rory's generous donations through the years to various children's organizations ranging from cancer treatment to afterschool programs for at-risk youth. It was another facet to him that drew me in. Somewhere beneath the bad boy facade laid a generous man and I wanted to draw him at.

"What?"

"Donate your money."

"How did you know about that?" Suddenly, he sounded defensive and I wondered if it was something I should have mentioned.

"I read it, on the Internet."

"You can't believe everything you read on the Internet."

"I didn't read it. I saw photos."

"It's not that big of a deal." He was modest, almost shy. Nothing was fitting the bad boy image and I could feel my pull toward him intensify. "Anyway, what do you want, beef with broccoli or Kung Pao chicken?"

"Is the chicken spicy?"

He picked up a piece and popped it in his mouth sucking off the sauce on his fingers as he pulled them out. I thought I was going to melt right there on the spot. *Girl, you got it BEE. AY. DEE. BAD! This guy can't even eat without you having an orgasm.*

"It's pretty spicy."

"I'll have the beef then."

"You don't like spicy?"

"I do, but my stomach doesn't."

"Why?"

"I had ulcers as a kid."

"I didn't know kids got ulcers. You must have worried a lot."

"I guess I did. I still do."

"Why?"

"I don't know."

"You're a control freak."

"Me? Don't you have that backward?" I sat down in the chair and motioned for him to take a seat next to me.

"What do you mean?"

"You were pretty domineering in the hotel room last night." I wanted to wait for a more opportune time to discuss this issue of dominance he had but I'd brought it up so maybe we should just go ahead and get it over with now. There was no way I was going to be put on a leash and whipped or caned.

"I can be."

"So are you into that, you know the whole bondage, S&M stuff."

"You girls read too much *Fifty Shades of Grey*."

"You didn't answer my question."

"Define 'into it.'"

"I mean, do you get off to beating chicks, tying them up, leading them around on a leash? You know, that sort of stuff."

"Why, would that turn you off?" he asked with a playful smile.

"Well, it wouldn't exactly turn me on, being led around like an animal."

"But you'd like to be spanked?" He started laughing and I knew he was mocking me.

"I'm just saying I'm not into that shit so if that's what you need to get your rocks off then you can forget it." My tone was one of obvious defiance and I felt old emotions coming to the surface. *Don't you dare cry, girl. Don't let him see this side of you or all kinds of crazy shit will happen.*

He reached across the table for my hand but I bolted up and half walked, half ran into the kitchen, trying to calm myself. I wondered around aimlessly, fully aware that even from his vantage point at the table, he could still see my movements. I flipped open cabinet door after cabinet door as if I were searching for something, listening to my heart race like I was on a ten mile run.

Suddenly, I felt arms slide around my waist and a familiar scent invade my senses. His rough whiskers skimmed my still sunburned shoulders as his nose nuzzled up to my neck from behind.

"Hey," he whispered in a drawn out syllable, as if he were trying to calm me. I was surprised at how quickly his technique worked. Within seconds, I felt myself melt against his body as my arms slid down from the open cabinet door to settle on his hands, now locked around my stomach. It was amazing to me just how right this position felt to me, how perfectly I fit with him and I couldn't help but wonder if he felt it too.

His chest rose with a deep inhale as I stood still, trying to feel every movement of his body as it pressed against mine. He held his breath and I wondered if he might pass out. But then, slowly yet intently, he began to exhale and I reveled in the feel of his chest relaxing beneath me as my body sank deeper into his. Instantly, I was filled with a sense of contentment, his contentment. I was right where I belonged and I knew in the center of my being he felt the same way, even if he never verbalized it.

"I'm sorry," he whispered in my ear, his breath caressing my neck.

His words were a salve to my injured soul. I hadn't heard apologies much in my life and certainly not from the people who'd actually hurt me. Somehow, those two words coming from his mouth filled a need in me I hadn't ever realized I had. I felt…almost whole again. Rory was filling up the void in my life and giving me the confidence and the freedom to be who I'd always wanted to be, even though I still wasn't sure exactly who that was yet. *That makes absolutely no sense. 'He's making you be who you want to be but you don't know who you want to be?' You are such a goner for this guy.*

I turned around to face him, keeping my hands solidly planted on his, which now rested on the small of my back. My new position forced my chest to press into his and the sensations of my breasts rubbing against him with only a thin t-shirt and bra separating us brought lurid thoughts to my mind. Me being tied up, him doing God knows what. *Oh. My. God. Do you really want to do this shit? Hoo-ray, it's about damn time you turned on the kinky switch.*

My eyes focused on his neck, on his large Adam's apple, and I watched as it bobbed up and down. He was nervous, even a little afraid, I could sense it. I leaned my head down and kissed the hollow in his neck just between his collar bones and scrunched my nose when I felt his chest hairs tickle my chin. I'd never felt anything more glorious in all my life. I worked my way up his neck, spreading kisses along the way, surprised to realize his head was rolling back to give me easier access. I released my hands from behind me and ran them up his muscular arms, all the way to the nape of his neck, letting my fingers run through his unruly hair. It was like heaven, every sensory organ I had was awakening for the first time.

"Don't be sorry," I whispered in his ear.

"If you don't have any condoms and you're not on the pill, I'm really gonna be sorry if you don't stop what you're doing right now."

He ground his pelvis into my crotch and I could feel the huge erection promising to present itself soon. I giggled and without stopping to think, he grabbed me around the waist and threw me up on the counter, spreading my legs open as he pressed himself against me. His hands thrust into my hair and his lips came down hard on mine. I wrapped my legs around his waist as one of his hands slid down my shoulder. I winced in pain.

"Oh, God, I'm sorry, I forgot about the sunburn."

For once, I didn't want this exchange to stop so instead of acknowledging his apology, I wrapped my arm around his neck and yanked him back toward me, trying to melt our bodies into one another's again. His hand ran up the back of my shirt and I felt him playing with my bra for a fraction of a second before he popped it loose. *Where in the hell do guys learn how to do that so fast? Experience, girl. Be careful.*

I pulled at the hem of his shirt and was surprised at how quickly I was able to remove it with as little experience as I'd had with the opposite sex. His vexing smile said he was quite pleased with me as well and it sparked me on. I placed my palms on his chest and moved down toward his tattoo, letting my fingers trace the shape of the board on display across his ribs.

I peeked up over my lashes and watched in fascination as his eyes glazed over with an emotion that seemed unusual for him. It looked like awe. Was he in awe of me? Whatever it was, it threatened to stop our scene and I didn't want it to end, not yet.

"My Skater Boy," I whispered in a sultry, sexy voice as my fingers lightly traced the words on his ribs.

Suddenly he pulled away and left me sitting on the counter all alone, panting like a hot animal on a summer's day. His eyes dropped from my gaze and sank to the floor.

"We can't do this," he explained, pulling his shirt back over his head as he continued to back away from me. I was hit with the most humiliating rejection I'd ever felt in my life. Without warning, hot tears began rolling down my face in silent shame.

Had I misread him? Something happened to him after called him 'my Skater Boy' but I didn't have time to analyze the scene, I just wanted to escape, to crawl into the first hole I could find and die. I refastened my bra and slid down the counter, trying to make my exit but he caught my arm just as I was halfway through the doorway.

"Let me go!" I shouted, yanking on his hand with such force that mine slung out of his hand and hit the door frame, sending shooting pain all the way up my arm. I recoiled and pulled it toward my body, curling into myself as I silently cursed the pain. I would be damned if he was going to see just how much he'd hurt me, physically and emotionally.

"Oh my God!" His voice echoed through my tiny kitchen. "Hindley, I'm so sorry."

Another apology. How many was he going to extend tonight?

"Let me see it," he snapped back, reaching for my hand. He tried to turn me toward him but I shook him off and pushed past him toward the refrigerator. I riffled through the freezer until I found a bag of mixed vegetables. I gently laid the bag over my hand and slammed the door shut with my elbow, trying to secretly plan an escape route. Rory looked like a giant in my tiny kitchen and I knew he wasn't going to let me leave, not without a struggle and I didn't know what to do. I just didn't have any fight left in me. He reached for the bag but I tugged on it, almost ripping it in two.

"Hindley, stop!" He screamed.

Is this douche bag actually yelling at you? Oh, hell no, girl! My ego was crushed and my hand throbbing, all because of this jackass and rather than try and soothe me, he actually had the nerve to yell at me.

"What the fuck!" I shouted back. "You did this to me, asshole. Let me have the goddamn bag!" As soon as the words rolled off my tongue, I was sorry I'd retaliated. I'd cut him deeply and pain was carved all over his face. He wasn't an abuser. I'd never thought that but somehow, that's how he'd registered my words.

"You can't put that directly on your skin, it will burn it." His words were quiet and defeated and I felt completely responsible. "Here, let me wrap it in this towel and then you can put it back on your hand."

He took the bag from me, uncovering my hand and we both gasped in horror. There was a purple line running from my middle knuckle to my wrist matching the angle of the door frame exactly. I snatched the towel from his grasp and quickly covered the frozen bag before placing it back over my hand, trying to hide the bruise before he passed out. I wanted him to feel bad, but not this bad. He shuffled away from me, his eyes full of horror as if he were trying to protect me from himself, like he was a vampire and I was fresh blood.

"It's not your fault." I didn't know what else to say. It sort of was his fault but he didn't do it on purpose. "It was an accident."

His eyes told me he was about to run and something inside me wanted to stop him, I needed him to stay. Even though he'd rejected me physically, it didn't feel like he'd rejected me as a person, just the idea of me. His logic was completely off, I could feel it radiating from his entire being. Somehow, he'd gotten the ridiculous idea that he wasn't good enough for me, that I deserved better, and the thought made me literally laugh out loud. I was instantly sorry I did. He'd taken my laughter as an insult, as if I were mocking him and I watched helplessly as his eyes grew darker. I had to do something, anything to get my Skater Boy back, but I was clueless as to what I should do. Part of me wondered if I really even wanted to get him back. *Are you shitting me? Of course you want him back.*

"You didn't do this to me, I'm sorry I said that." I walked closer to him, thankful he didn't back away but disappointed his impassive face showed no emotion. "Will you please stay? Please have dinner with me."

Now he was the one who looked like a captured animal, his eyes darting back and forth. I could almost hear his thoughts racing, trying to convince himself that he didn't belong with me.

"I don't think that's a good idea, Hindley." He tried to turn but I reached out and stopped him with my free hand, letting the bag of frozen vegetables fall to the floor.

"Why?"

"I'm not good for you. Just look at your hand." He knelt down and picked up the bag, re-wrapping it in the towel, and holding it back up to me but I wouldn't take it. Instead, I held out my hand, silently asking him to take care of me, again. When he didn't stand, I slowly sank to my knees so that I could look deep inside him, willing him to come back to me.

"Stay," I begged. "We can review your contract. It will be a business dinner." I could tell my words were slowly starting to break through his self-deprecating thoughts. "You really need to look at it anyway, right?" Then as quickly as the relief in his eyes came, it left, replaced with a new emotion. Fear, genuine fear. Now I was the one trying to apply salve to his fragile soul. Slowly, I rose and stood above him, hoping he'd rise with me but he didn't. He remained squatted on the ground, his face glued to the floor. I reached down and slid my hand under his jaw, raising it up to meet mine but still his eyes were down turned.

"Rory, look at me." His eyes stayed motionless. "Rory. Look at me. I won't ask you again." The domineering words felt so powerful and I was taken aback by how easily they'd rolled off my tongue, as if I were meant to be this person. His eyes darted up to mine and I was instantly satisfied, that in my dominance, I held as much power over him as his did me. "Stand up." My voice was flat and low and...sexy as hell. Cautiously, his six foot three stature rolled up off the floor, towering over me but I wouldn't let that affect me. My technique was working, even if I didn't one hundred percent believe in myself.

"You're right. We can't do this." I saw disappointment in his eyes. "I'm your attorney, you're my client. Any relationship other than that would be inappropriate, right?" He nodded his head. "That is the only, and I repeat, the only reason this relationship would be inappropriate, do you understand that?" People had trampled on him his whole life. He had a damaged soul and I knew exactly what that felt like. But unlike me, he'd fought back, using woman, booze, drugs, fame, even money to ease his pain. We were birds of a feather but our coping skills were different. I couldn't let him leave, not like this. I took his hand in mine and pulled him toward the table.

"Now, have a seat." I walked him around to the table and pulled out his chair. "Do you like hard copy or screen version?"

"What?"

"Your contract. Is it better for you to look at it in hard copy or on the computer?" His eyes literally bulged and I could tell I was losing him again, but why? What had happened?

"Just email it to me and I'll look at it when I get home tonight." He tried to push away from the table but I wouldn't let him. It took all my power but I was able to keep his chair shoved in.

"No. I'm *your* attorney. There are several points we need to review together, not on your own. I'm sure you've read lots of contracts before but this one is different, a lot different."

I marched over to the living room table and picked up the file marked 'Gregor, Rory – Attorney/Agent' and carried it back to the dining table.

"Scoot over," I nudged him, pulling my chair over so we were sitting side-by-side, our arms brushing against one another. Just the touch of his skin on mine made my heart ache and my entire body tingle. *What is with this guy?* I still wanted him.

I tried to remember his rejection earlier, of how much it hurt. I would embrace it and allow the painful memory to keep me strong, keep me away from this delicious man. Even though we couldn't be together, I didn't want him to ever think it was because he wasn't good enough for me or worthy of me . He was worthy of so much more, he was worthy of love, great love, even if it could never came from me. Somewhere out there was a great love just waiting for him and he deserved to know he was worthy of it.

Taking in a deep breath and resolved to put the past behind me, I pulled out the large contract and saw him squirm out of the corner of my eye. "What's wrong?"

"It's just…Jack usually reviews these for me."

"You don't review your own contracts?"

"No."

"Why?"

"I just get…"

He couldn't go on and I saw sweat forming on his brow.

"Rory, what's wrong?"

"It's just all confusing, you know, the legal-ease shit."

"I know exactly what you mean," I laughed, remembering how lost I was the first year of law school. It was beyond me why they felt compelled to add in so much language to documents. I always had a sense that they were purposely trying to confuse people and, in the end, it usually worked.

"Understanding legal documents takes time," I tried to explain. "Hell, I've been to law school and this crap still doesn't make sense to me sometimes. That's why I've drafted yours so it's not so confusing. This is actually my first attorney/agent contract I've written it so, of course, I'm quite proud of it." I glanced up at him and saw his face was still pensive. "Hey," I said putting my hand on top of his. "I'm *your* attorney." I tried to put emphasis on 'your'. "I'm here to help you Rory, not confuse you. If something doesn't make sense then tell me and together, we'll sort it out. That's why I'm here, to protect you." I knew he thought I meant protect him legally, but I really meant much more than that. Even though he'd hurt me with his rejection earlier, I could sense he hadn't done it from lack of desire but rather from an internal need to protect me, from himself. The funny part was, I wanted to protect him, too, physically, mentally, emotionally, in every way possible.

His eyes roamed over our hands lying on top of one another and suddenly, his entire body stiffened. I glanced down and realized it was the hand I'd hit on the door and the bruise was now becoming a deep purple. I jerked it away, trying to hide it from him but he pulled it back and gently laid it in the palm of his. My hand looked so small and delicate compared to his mammoth-sized one. Never breaking our gaze, he brought my hand up to his lips and pressed feathery light kisses all over the ever growing bruise. I closed my eyes, trying to hide the fact they were rolling into the back of my head with sheer ecstasy. Everything this man did turned me on like no one I'd ever met.

"I hurt you." His words were achingly sad and I felt my heart clench in physical pain at his torment. "I'll always hurt you, Hindley. In the end." I forced my eyes open, surprised to find I didn't recognize the man sitting next to me at all. Where was my Skater Boy?

"What does that mean?" I tried to pull back but he wouldn't let me go. Instead, he held my hand like it was a precious jewel, like it was sacred and held special powers.

"I fuck up everything I touch," he explained, never taking his eyes off my hand.

"All the more reason to work harder this time, Rory." I knew he thought I meant the skating but I also meant me, maybe he could try harder, with me.

"If I hurt you again, like this," he continued, holding my hand up for me to see, "I'll never forgive myself, Hindley. Ever."

I yanked my hand away from his, upset at how I'd been reading this whole scene. Maybe I was wrong, maybe he'd never wanted me at all.

"Look, Rory, I don't know what's happened in your life to make you feel so shitty about yourself but trust me when I say I know exactly how you feel. If you hurt me, I'm a big girl, I can take it. What I can't take is your on again, off again shit." I was seething with anger and he knew it. His eyes searched mine, looking for something I wasn't sure I could offer. Permission? Rejection? Slowly, his hand slid into my hair as he pulled my face close to his, his now infamous predatory smile spreading across his face.

"Who knew Drunk Girl could be so forceful," he whispered against my lips.

"Who knew Skater Boy could be so sensitive," I smiled, pressing my lips into his.

This kiss was different, not as passionate or as desperate as our other kisses. I wasn't sure if that was a good thing or a bad thing. Part of it felt like a new beginning but part of it felt like good-bye. There was something inside our embrace, an indescribable feeling that filled me down to my soul. This man was different and I knew it with every fiber of my being. I just had to figure out what different meant, to me.

Before I could think, he pulled away and just like that, our moment was over. He brushed away a piece of my hair that had fallen onto my forehead, tracing the entire strand with his eyes. "I think I should probably get going." I tried not to be disappointed. I tried not to let my old insecurities spike but it was futile. This was good-bye and I knew it.

"All right." That's all I could offer without my voice breaking. I pushed my chair back and went to walk him out. This thing between us, whatever it was, wasn't going to happen and I realized it was for the best. I was his attorney. He was my client. But I was still a woman deeply moved by this sexy, vibrant, virile man and most of me couldn't help but feel disappointed and hurt by his rejection. Again.

"Here," I said, shoving the contract at him. He looked down at the document like it was a snake ready to strike him. "You really need to read over it, Rory, before you sign."

"That's what I pay you for," he said with a nervous laugh that I knew was meant to mask a deeper emotion.

And there it was, spelled out for me in plain English. 'That's what I pay you for.' He was paying me. I was an employee. Nothing less, nothing more.

"Even still, you should read it over and let me know if you have questions. But if you still don't want to, even after

I've advised you to, you'll find I've labeled it with idiot proof tags at all the places you need to sign. But don't sign until Tuesday though. We need witnesses and a notary."

He yanked the contract from my hand and folded it in half, shoving it into his back pocket. His brows were furrowed as darkness enveloped his eyes with an anger I'd never seen before.

"What's wrong?"

He jerked open the door. "Nothing!" he threw out with venom as he walked out onto the porch. "I'll see you Tuesday." I followed, trying to escort him out but before I could reach the door, he'd slammed it shut in my face. *What the hell was that?*

My eyes stung and I could feel the tears coming. I didn't have to ask myself that question twice. That was rejection in its purest form. And it had come from a man I'd mistakenly saw as a catalyst for me, someone who might actually change my life and make me start living it for once, instead of just existing. I picked up the phone as the tears streamed down my face and listened as the ringing echoed in my now throbbing head.

"What the fuck happened now?" I heard Dana's raspy voice on the other end.

"Nothing." My sobs came rolling out.

"I'll be over in ten."

The line went dead and I rolled over on the couch, burying my head in the cushions as my insecurities came crashing out. How had I let this man get into my head? I'd been doing so well for so long and now, within the span of a week, I was right back where I started, flailing like a wounded duck on the verge of spiraling out of control again.

I sat straight up, willing myself to be strong. I dialed Dana's number again, waiting for her to answer.

"I'm just headed out. Are you hungry?"

"Don't come over."

"Why?"

"I need to do this on my own, Dana. I need to learn how to fight back by myself."

"Are you sure? You know I love you, I'll be there in a heartbeat if you need me."

"I know and I love you for it but I've gotta learn how to do this on my own, without help, ya know?" "I know sweetie, and I'm proud of you. I'm just worried about you, that's all."

"Don't be."

"Why? Have you been watching Doctor Phil again?"

I laughed. "No. I've just been letting one guy get into my head and even though he just crushed my heart, he also made me feel brave and confident."

"Even though he's the reason you called me tonight?"

"Yep, even though he's the reason I broke down. Ironic, huh?"

"Ironic that this little prick would be the one to help you get over his own douchey maneuvers? Yeah, I'd call that pretty damn ironic." We both started laughing. "I'm proud of you, Hindley. You are brave and strong and smart. So many things I wish I was, and probably everything Rory wishes he were, too."

"But you are. You both are all those things."

"And so are you, sweetie." I smiled, realizing, for once, that maybe she was right, maybe Rory was right. "So did y'all do the nasty? Is that why you're so upset? It was horrible?"

"No!" I shouted. I doubted very much that doing the nasty with Rory would be anything but horrible.

"Yeah, I'm sure he knows exactly what he's doing in the bedroom. Especially if he macks the muff as well as you said he did."

"I don't know why I even told you."

"Because you tell me everything." I snorted, knowing she was right. "You wanna talk about it?"

"There's not much to say. I know he wants to be with me. He works so hard at making me feel special and beautiful and all the things a girl wants to be. But then, I don't know, it's like he pulls away."

"It's probably better this way, don't you think?"

"Why? You don't think I can handle him?"

"Why would you say that?"

"Because I wonder if I could handle him. I'm pretty inexperienced and it's all over the Internet that he's been with tons of women. What could I offer?"

"I thought you said you were going to work on yourself. Putting yourself down doesn't help anything."

"You're right. But it's true. I don't have much experience."

"Then let him teach you."

"You just said it's better if we don't get involved."

"Well, that's the whole attorney-client thing. But the more I think about it, the more exciting it sounds. Like a Cinemax After Dark movie or something."

"Why do you love that channel so much?"

"Because I don't have a love interest in my life right now. I haven't had sex in weeks and it's killing me. Do you know how much it sucks that I have to live through you now? I never thought I'd see the day."

"What about Leif?"

"Leif's gay."

"What! He told you that?"

"No, he didn't have to."

"So what makes you say that?"

"Experience."

"Just because he didn't try to get in your panties in the first twenty-four hours of meeting you doesn't make him gay."

"No, but it's definitely a mark against him."

"I think you're just saying that because you like him and you're afraid because he's not pursuing you."

"Maybe, we'll see. Time always tells with the homos."

"Dana, that's awful."

"What? It's true."

"I'm talking about calling him a homo."

"Why, that's what he is."

"First of all, you don't know that Leif is gay. Second of all, that's a derogatory term. You wouldn't like it if someone called you a WOP."

"Wow, you are being feisty aren't you. I like the effect Rory is having on you. Even though he's making you cry your eyes out tonight."

"I'm not crying my eyes out."

"Not now."

"That's why I called you. I knew you'd make me feel better." Mid-sentence, I heard a beep and pulled the phone back only to see Rory's gorgeous face appear on my screen along with the name I'd put in my contacts 'Skater Boy' Gregor. "Shit!"

"What's wrong?"

"It's Rory."

"Are you gonna answer?"

"I don't know. I'm still pretty raw right now."

"Well, if you need me, call me. I'm not doing anything except changing out all the batteries in my vibrators." I smiled thinking about it, realizing she was probably telling the truth.

"Love ya, Dana."

"Love you too, Hindley. Tell Douche Bag I said hi!"

Chapter 12

~RORY~

"Fuck, fuck, fuck!" I shouted, banging the door closed and flinging Leif's keys on the table in the entryway.

"I take it dinner didn't go so well?" Leif laughed, in a sarcastic tone similar to Dana's. Those two were made for each other.

"I totally fucked up, man." Leif switched off the television and turned around to face me.

"Want a drink?" He held up a tumbler filled with an amber liquid. I threw my head back, my face riddled with disgust. Leif knew I hadn't had a drink in over two years. "Relax, man. It's just apple juice."

I ran both my hands through my hair and let out a deep sigh, falling down onto the plush leather sofa. "Don't fuck with me right now, man. I'm a nervous wreck."

"What happened?"

"I hurt her."

"Well, we knew that was coming. That's why I told you to leave her alone, fuck-face!" I cut my eyes at him in silent warning. "Well, I did!"

"Whatever, man! No, I mean, I physically hurt her."

"What!" he screamed, jumping up from the sofa.

"It was an accident, man. But still, she hurt her hand."

"Shit! You fuckin' idiot!"

I couldn't take it anymore. Something inside me snapped and I flew toward Leif in a nanosecond, jumping on top of him about to beat the shit out of his fat mouth when I felt someone's hand wrap around my arm and pull me off. There was only one person who would dare touch me when I flew into a rage and I knew without even turning around it was Leif's father, Jack Jennings.

"Rory, what are you doing?!" Kara Jennings screamed. I immediately retreated at the sound of disappointment and distress in her voice. Leif's mother and father had been surrogate parents to me and the fact that they'd just found me about to pummel their son was more humiliation than I could take.

I flew off the couch and threw open the back door, slamming it behind me as I paced around the deck. Not even the beautiful night sky lit up by the full moon and bright stars could calm me down. I leaned over the railing, lifting up a silent prayer to no one in particular, wondering what in the hell was going on with my life. I hadn't felt this out of control in a long time.

Suddenly, I felt the warm imprint of a tiny hand burning into my back and I knew that Kara had followed me out. She was the only person who could calm me down when my brain exploded. She didn't say a word, she didn't have to. She'd been talking me down off the ledge for years. Any other mother would have knocked the shit out of me for almost beating their son, but not Kara. I was just as much a son to her as her own and I knew there was nothing she would ever do to break my fragile soul. She'd worked years, trying tirelessly to build up my self-worth and up until this moment, had done a pretty good job of it. But the fact that I'd hurt Hindley physically, and probably mentally, had me in knots like I'd never felt before. And now, after trying to go after her own son, it was a wonder she wasn't hurling me over this railing, sending me plummeting to my deserving death. Without lifting my head or turning to face her, I finally spoke.

"I hurt her, Kara. Physically." She was silent and I was thankful. "I'm pretty sure I hurt her emotionally, too." Still, she remained quiet, just letting me empty my conscience with no judgment or pretense, her hand never leaving my back. She'd always offered me unconditional love but I still had a hard time believing I deserved it.

"I didn't mean to, Kara," I continued. "It was an accident, but still." All at once, I felt something welling up in my throat, it felt like a cry but I hadn't cried in, well, ever. I tried to push down whatever it was caught in my chest but before I knew it, tears were running down my face and my body was convulsing uncontrollably.

I twisted around to face Kara, not surprised when she took me into her tiny arms, holding me close as my soul emptied out years of pent up anger, frustration, and hostility. She remained silent, her welcome hands rubbing my shoulders back and forth feeling me shudder beneath her hold. She didn't try to soothe me, quiet me, or stop me. She just held me until the tears subsided and the tension in my body released. When I finally pulled away and tried to focus on her face, I was shocked to find her eyes riddled with tears and pain just like mine. Well, shit! Now I could add Kara to my growing list of people I'd hurt tonight. She reached up and stroked my cheek, trying to wipe away the stains left by my grieving.

"I think we both needed that," she said quietly, pulling me toward the glider. "Sit," she commanded, nodding to the spot beside her.

I nestled in beside her and watched as she extended her tiny arm across my back, folding her legs underneath her so she could look directly at me, all the while giving me the time I needed to process everything I'd just experienced. That was her way. Kara never pushed me, she knew I was a wounded animal just like Hindley and she'd always taken the wait and watch approach when it came to me. When everyone else in my outer circle of friends poked and prodded me to uncover my demons, Kara was the opposite. She'd found a way to reach me ten years ago. My only regret was letting her down by pissing my life away. Not once had she ever fussed, complained, or even acknowledged that she was disappointed in me. She knew I had enough self-loathing to last a lifetime. I'd spent many an hour wondering just how different my life would have been if Kara Jennings had been my mother from the start.

"She's different, Kara." I blew out a breath I'd been holding since I left Hindley's. "I don't know how to explain it other than that she's different." I cut my eyes toward her and saw a small smile spread across her face. "What?"

"Nothing."

"That smile is definitely something."

"I'm just waiting. I want to hear more about this girl who's so different."

"What's up with the smile?"

"Can't I be happy you've finally met someone who's different?" I'd never really stopped to think of Kara wanting me to find someone special. I'd just always assumed she was resigned to the fact I'd be a 'One-Nighter', as Dana always called me.

"You want me to find someone, don't you? Someone to settle down with?"

She reached out across her legs and took my hand in hers. "Rory, I just want you to be fulfilled, mentally, physically and spiritually." Kara and Jack weren't religious fanatics but they did believe in spiritual gifts and atonements. I'd never really swung one way or another but I'd always noticed how content they were and I knew, at some point in my life, I wanted to know how they'd achieved that. That time was probably now.

"How do I get that? Fulfillment?"

"Only you can answer that one, sweetheart."

"A likely answer."

"What? It's true."

"Says the woman who's fulfilled."

"I can't argue that."

She looked up at the heavens and closed her eyes, taking in a deep breath. I envied her and Jack so much. They had peace, something I'd never even knew existed before I'd met them.

"What?" she asked, never opening her eyes. Her question was confirmation that she'd heard my silent thoughts.

I'd always found it strangely familiar how attune Kara was to me. She and I were connected and I'd known that since the first day I'd met her. Maybe not by blood but by spirit and that thought had always brought me some semblance of comfort during my darkest times.

"I like her, Kara."

"I know you do, sweetheart. You didn't have to tell me that," she responded, finally opening her eyes and turning her attention back to me. "It's written all over your poor, pathetic little face." Her lips curled up into an empathetic smile.

"Whatever!" I spewed out sarcastically, thankful to hear her laughter ring through the night air.

"So, tell me about her, this girl who's so different. Why do you like her, Rory?"

I'd never slowed down enough over the week since I'd met Hindley to think about why I liked her. Maybe answering Kara's question would help my find some sort of peace when it came to my life.

"Rory, close your eyes," she instructed. I knew I'd never escape until I followed her command so I did as she asked without complaint, lifting my head toward the sky and letting my eyelids slowly fall. "Picture the first time you saw her." I immediately began to laugh. "What's so funny?"

"She was drunk as a skunk when I met her. I called her Drunk Girl because she was too smashed to even tell me her name." I continued to snort but I knew where Kara's mind was going. My eyes popped open as I quickly tried to explain. "I didn't do anything with her, Kara, I swear. I took her home and made sure she was safe." The smile on her face was a salve to my weary heart. Her silent expression was telling me how proud she was of me, as if all her hard work had paid off.

"That's why she's different to you."

"Why?"

"You want to take care of her, don't you?" I thought about Kara's words and knew they were true. I got a strange high from taking care of Hindley, from tending to her needs. "And tonight, you hurt her. It goes against everything you feel for her." My head fell forward in shame as I pictured Hindley's hand splattered with the bluish purple bruise I'd created. "Rory, we all hurt each other. Jack has torn my heart to shreds numerous times, as I have his. It's just part of the process of love."

"Love!" I shouted, catapulting back from her as if she were diseased. "I don't love her."

"Not yet," she whispered.

"What does that mean?"

"It means that this is the first girl you've ever seen potential in. The girls you've been with in the past have been superficial so it's been easy to escape unharmed. You've never let them in so they never had the chance to hurt you. Right?" I nodded. "But now you've met this woman, who wants more, who you want more with, and it's scary and exciting all rolled up into one." Kara's explanation was spot on. "And all your insecurities of the past are floating up to the surface just like I'm sure hers are."

I'd never really thought about Hindley having the same types of feelings for me. And I certainly hadn't thought about her feeling insecure. She seemed so confident and self-assured.

"No one's perfect, Rory, no matter how it looks from the outside. Trust me. And I'm sure if you got to know her better you'd find she's just as self-conscious and vulnerable as you are. If you hurt her tonight then those insecurities are going to drown her until you make it right."

"What does that mean?"

"It means that she probably has low self esteem so anything you've done tonight to prove her self-deprecating image is right the more she'll beat herself up. You have the power to really hurt her. You should know that better than anyone. Even if you don't like her or don't see it going any farther than it is right now, you have to make this right with her or she'll beat herself up all night."

"She's stronger than that, way stronger. Trust me, she doesn't need a guy like me to make her feel better about herself."

"That is bullshit and you know it, Rory Gregor!" she shouted at me. I reared back in disbelief. Kara never cussed. In fact, she hated it when Leif and I went at it, and she definitely never raised her voice in anger. "I did not raise you to think so little of yourself and it offends me that you would. Now you get on that phone and make this right with that girl or I will come back out here and beat you senseless, which by the sounds of it won't take long." She stomped past me and headed for the door.

"She's my attorney, Kara." The revelation felt humiliating and freeing all at once. I was scattering my insecurities out into the universe as I stared off blankly into the night sky. Within seconds, Kara was back at my side, her hand resting softly on my shoulder. I didn't have to explain the weight of my words to her, she knew me.

"First and foremost, she's a woman, Rory, and she has needs and desires, just like all of us." I turned to look up at her face, not surprised by the motherly love and affection I saw radiating from her eyes. "Attorneys are a dime a dozen. A girl who makes you feel different, who makes you question everything in the past, isn't. You owe it to yourself and to her to find out why." She reached down and cupped my face in her small hand. "And you are just as worthy of love as she is, my dear. Don't ever let anyone make you think differently."

"But I can't read, Kara." I felt awkward and alone as her hand fell from my face.

"Then tell her."

"I can't."

"Why?"

"If she laughs at me, if she leaves me because I'm stupid, I'm not sure I could take it." She grabbed my chin in her hands and yanked my face toward hers.

"You are not stupid, Rory. Why do you think so little of yourself and this girl?" I shrugged my shoulders. She pushed my face away in obvious frustration. "If she does any of those things then that will give you the answer you're looking for. From the look in your eyes and the way you're fretting though, I don't think that's the reaction you'll get from her. But you'll never know unless you tell her." I pulled my gaze away from her, embarrassed by my own illiteracy and lack of education. "Rory Gregor, look at me!" Kara was in no mood to be fooled with tonight, I could tell by her tone. I snapped my neck back, preparing myself for her wrath. "Reading does not make you a man worthy of a woman's love, do you understand me? Did you ever stop to think maybe this girl needs you?"

"She doesn't need anything, Kara. She's rich and beautiful and smart."

"Maybe she needs more. Maybe she needs purpose, confidence, and self-assurance, just like you. Maybe you can give that to each other." Her hand gently stroked my cheek up and down before she let it fall, coming to rest on my shoulder. "Rory, you can't sit on the sidelines wondering 'what if.' You have taken risks your whole life, most of which have paid off in the end. Don't stop taking chances now just because you feel inadequate, not with this girl anyway. She's different, right?" She punched my shoulder. "Let her prove it to you. Let her show you just how different she really is. She sounds amazing and I think you'll be surprised at just how much she needs you." She pushed off the glider, signaling her silent exit.

"Kara." I called out, just as she'd reached the door.

She gazed back at me. "Yeah, sweetie?"

"Thanks."

"You know I'm always here for you, Rory. Always have been, always will be."

"I know. Thanks." She nodded her head in silent acknowledgment before closing the door behind her.

I pulled my phone out from my pocket and ran through the contacts list until I saw her beautiful face. I didn't feel worthy of her, especially right now, knowing that I'd hurt her physically and emotionally. My self-esteem was at an all time low so I figured now was as good a time as any to face her assured rejection. I mean, come on, how much more could I hurt, if she judged me unworthy? *Who are you kidding, douche bag? This girl could completely destroy you if she rejects you.* Kara was right, I couldn't sit on the sidelines and wonder. This was a chance I had to be willing to take. I inhaled deeply as my finger pressed her name.

~

The endless ringing on the other end of the phone was grating my last nerve and I felt my anxiety growing higher and higher. Abruptly, the ringing stopped and I was deafened by the silence. No dial tone, no voicemail. What the hell?

"Hello?" I offered a silent plea but there was nothing on the other end. I pulled the phone away from my face, shocked to see the call was still connected. "Hindley?" Still nothing. I was just about to hang up and try again when I heard her raspy voice.

"What, Rory?" The disgust in her voice was palpable. *Oh shit! You fucked up big time, man.* She remained silent and my stomach churned with fear.

"Um, hi." The silence from her end spoke volumes to me. I had a lot of ground to make up for. "Did I disturb you?"

"No, I was just talking to Dana."

Dana! Oh shit, man, you're dead.

"Well, I can call you back if you want. Or you could call me back." *You sound like a pathetic seventh grader making a prank call to his middle school crush. Just grow some juevos and tell her already.*

"No, I hung up with her already." Still silence. This can't be good. *Say something, douche bag, before she hangs up on you.*

"I just wanted to call and tell you I was sorry."

"For what?" For what?, I repeated her words in my head. Where should I start? There were so many things.

"First, I'm sorry about your hand. I truly am." I could feel the emotions choking my throat and I had to pull the phone away to compose myself before I could go on. *Man, what is going on with you? Crying? On the phone? With a chick? Pussy!* "Does it feel better? I mean, is it still sore?"

"It's alright. I took some Advil."

"You should really keep ice on it to help with the swelling."

"You're speaking from experience?"

"I've had more bruises, contusions, concussions, and broken bones than I want to remember."

"Really?" I was shocked to hear genuine concern in her voice.

"Oh, yeah."

"How many bones?"

"Well, let's see." I let out a long sigh and leaned back in the glider, kicking my feet out in front of me as I put my hand up on my head, trying to remember.

"That many, huh?"

"Oh, yeah. Comes with the territory, I'm afraid. I still can't bend my left pinky."

"What happened?"

"Came down wrong from a spin on a half pipe and landed on my hand. Hyper extended my pinky."

"Stop!" she shouted.

"What?"

"Oh, that is so gross. Don't tell me anymore. That just made me want to vomit."

"I'm sorry. You asked."

"I know. I just get queasy from stuff like that."

"Then you probably shouldn't come to any competitions 'cause stuff like that happens all the time."

"I know. I saw the videos. Plus some of those amateurs bit it big time yesterday at the Grand Am."

"That's because they're knuckle heads."

"What makes you say that?"

"They shouldn't be trying out stupid shit like that for a show. The fans didn't come to watch us fall on our asses."

"What's wrong with falling?"

"Nothing, when you're legitimately skating. But a Grand Am is for the spectators, not a time for us to practice new moves."

"Well, I kind of liked the fact that they went all out."

"I thought you said you didn't like watching stuff like that, people breaking their fingers and arms and wrists and…"

"Stop!" A slow laugh escaped my lips before I could silence myself. "Why do you enjoy upsetting me so much?" Her question took me off guard, I couldn't tell if she was serious or just being quirky.

"I didn't know I was upsetting you."

"Yes, you did. You totally did. And you love doing it."

"No, I don't." My words were more somber than I'd intended but I wanted her to understand that I never felt good upsetting her. "If I upset you, it's never on purpose, Hindley. Ever." There was a long pause and I didn't know how to recover. I needed her light-heartedness if I was ever going to tell her the truth. "Are you still there?"

"I'm here."

"What are you thinking?"

"What an oxymoron you are."

I wasn't sure what an oxymoron was but I knew it had the word moron in it and I was seething. "I'm not an idiot, Hindley."

"I never said you were."

"I'm not a moron either!"

"I never said that you were, God, calm down, Rory. I said you were an *oxy*moron. You know, a paradox."

A what? What the fuck is she even talking about, man? There's no way I can tell her, her thought process is so above me, she'll never understand me. I sure as hell will never understand her. Suddenly, her words interrupted my internal struggle.

"I mean, you're a walking, talking contradiction Rory."

"What the fuck is that supposed to mean?" Now I was really getting upset. I didn't mean to sound so abrupt but I felt personally attacked and I couldn't help it.

"Don't get pissed off. I just meant that at any given time, you can be kind and caring and sensitive then in a split second you can be mean and selfish and shout out profanities that would make a customer at a biker bar red with embarrassment. Like now, what you just did."

"Are you making fun of me?"

"Dude, what is wrong with you?"

"What?"

"First, you come over here and get me all sexed up on my own kitchen counter, then you pull away and storm out of my house, pissed off like I've done something to offend you. I think it was pretty obvious I was literally puttin' my junk out there for you to take and instead, you…"

"I can't read!" I shouted out, stopping her mid sentence.

"What?" I could hear panic in her voice.

"I can't read."

"At all?"

"I can read *some* stuff, but not much. It's the longer more complicated stuff that's confusing. You know like books, newspapers, and websites."

"And contracts?"

"Yes. Contracts. Especially contracts."

"Is that what this has all been about?"

"What?"

"You, acting like I'm above you or something, like you don't deserve me."

"Yes. Well, that's part of it, I guess."

"What's the other part?"

"I'm still trying to figure that one out."

"Well, when you figure it out, let me know so I can act accordingly." There was a long silence and I didn't know if I was losing her. "How can you have survived this long without reading?" I sat on the glider, staring up at the stars, wondering how I had actually gotten by without knowing how to read all these years. "That came out wrong, Rory, I'm sorry."

"Don't be, I know what you meant. You'd be surprised how far an insane amount of money and talent can get you."

"How did you graduate high school, if you couldn't read?"

"I didn't."

"You didn't graduate high school?" I shook my head silently, knowing she already knew the answer. "So, that's it." Her words sounded like her own self-realization and suddenly, I was scared shitless.

"That's what?"

"I graduated college and law school. That's why you feel inferior, isn't it?"

"You're also talented, achingly gorgeous, rich, and smart."

"Please, don't let me stop you," she giggled. Her laughter was sweet music to my anxiety-ridden ears, an indicator that perhaps she wouldn't banish me completely.

"You're kind and sweet and sexy and funny and beautiful."

"Okay, now you're making me blush."

"Why?"

"'Cause I'm pretty sure half that stuff isn't true."

"Why do you do that?"

"Do what?"

"Put yourself down?"

"Same reason you do, I guess." We sat in comfortable silence, both trying to process why we were so self-loathing.

"Have you tried to read, you know, since you became an adult."

"I've tried. Leif's mom, Kara, really worked with me for awhile but I just couldn't concentrate."

"What do you mean?"

"It was like we were looking at two different things. Like I was seeing a square and she was trying to make me see a circle. I just ended up confused and more frustrated than when we started. Eventually, I gave up and she didn't push me."

"How do you get by, I mean, when you have stuff you need to read?"

"Leif and his parents help a lot. And my attorney. The one you got fired."

"I didn't fire him. He sucked. Your manager fired him."

"Well, good or bad, he held my secret for years so I have give him props for that."

"Aren't you scared?"

"Of what?"

"Of someone finding out?"

"Terrified."

"Were you afraid of me finding out?"

"Afraid doesn't even begin to explain how I felt about you finding out. Paralyzed with fear could sum it up."

"So why did you tell me?"

"Kara told me to."

"Who's Kara?" I heard an echo of jealousy laced in her words and I couldn't help but smile.

"Leif's mom, my manager's wife, Leif and Jack and Kara Jennings. They're my family, my surrogate family."

"What about *your* family? Your mom and dad?"

"Long story."

"So what did Kara say that made you tell me tonight?"

What could I say? How could I answer her without giving away everything and exposing myself to heartache and ridicule? "She said I had to take a chance. On you."

"And?"

"And what?"

"Are you glad you told me?"

"That depends."

"On what?"

"On how you act toward me, now that you know."

"Well, I haven't slammed down the phone so that has to count for something, right?"

"I guess."

"I'm just in awe of you."

"Why?"

"I just can't imagine how difficult this has been on you, all these years. Reading is something I've taken for granted. I'll never do it again." I heard something in her voice but I tried to convince myself it wasn't pity. "So, how do you get by?"

"Like how?"

"Like at the grocery store or at a restaurant or at an autograph signing? I'm sure people put stuff in front of you to read all the time."

"For grocery stores and stuff like that, it's pretty easy. There are enough pictures and I have them memorized so I know how to tell a can of soup from a can of dog food." We both started laughing and immediately, I felt calmer, my anxiety beginning to melt away.

"I can read a little, just not long, complicated sentences and stories with big words. But there's always Google Translator."

"Really?"

"Yeah, Leif installed it on my phone. If I need to send a text or email, I just talk into it. It types it out for me then I just cut and paste it. Or if someone writes to me, I cut and paste it into Google Translator and it speaks it for me."

"That's kind of cool, I guess."

"Not really. It's stressful as hell. I try to avoid situations where I think that might happen but if I can't, I make sure I have Leif , Jack, or Kara with me."

"Who else knows?"

"Besides you? Just the Jennings and Gene-O?"

"Really? That's it?"

"That's it."

"What about your agent back in California?"

"He probably knows but it's not something I've ever confessed like I am with you."

"So why are you telling me?"

"Because you're my attorney and eventually, it's going to come up."

"Like tonight, when I tried to get you to review the contract?"

"Yeah, stuff like that."

"Why did you leave all mad?"

"That's a different story."

"You called me."

I took in a deep breath, wondering if I really wanted to share all my secrets with her tonight. Deep inside, where no one had ever ventured before, I knew I trusted her but she didn't trust me, not yet. Being vulnerable, opening myself up to her with no guarantees scared the shit out of me. Suddenly, I realized what I was afraid of. This girl had the power to destroy me.

"Look, Hindley, I don't trust a lot of people."

"I can tell."

"How?"

"You're ability to go from zero to a hundred in about two seconds is one of them. I wish I could run as fast as your mind does."

"You run?"

"Don't change the subject, Rory. Why don't you trust people and why are you taking a chance on me?"

"It's hard to be vulnerable."

"You don't have to tell me."

"So tell me something."

"What?"

"Tell me something that makes you vulnerable to me. I've shared something, now it's your turn." I could hear the hesitation in her voice but I knew she wanted to speak to me.

"I'm not as experienced as you are. Sexually. And that scares me. I don't know why."

That was a revelation. Nothing in our past make-out sessions would have ever indicated she was anything but experienced. Shy, maybe, but inexperienced, no.

"Really?"

"What does that mean?" I didn't like that she was getting defensive.

"First of all, don't do that."

"Do what?" I could picture her sassy little lips puckering up, getting ready to fight.

"Don't get defensive. We're being vulnerable here so cut me some slack." I waited for her rebuttal but when I heard none, I forged on. "I meant that, to me, I have found you anything but lacking in the sexuality department."

"Really?" Now she was being coy and it split my lips apart into a massive grin.

"You really have no idea, do you?"

"What?"

"Hindley, you're fuckin' sexy as hell and you kiss like a prisoner on death row."

"That was a visual," she giggled.

My chest seized in apprehension. Her laughter did something inside of me, it evoked alarming foreign emotions. The sensations were heartwarming but intensely frightening at the same time. I was discovering that her voice, in any form, calmed me. It was like a silk ribbon wrapping around my fragile self-image, protecting me from myself.

"I hope that's a compliment," she interrogated.

"Yes, that's a compliment. The way you move your body is..." I didn't know how to finish. "Let's just say that my dick gets hard just thinking about you."

"Like right now?"

"Uh huh." The melodious sounds of her continued laughter had my crotch throbbing in pain. I was relieved to feel the confidence in her voice and couldn't help but feel partially responsible. I'd helped her believe in herself and that was foreign to me.

Her voice broke through my sorted thoughts. "So what if I helped you."

"Helped me? With my dick? Yeah, you could come over here and relieve the pressure under my zipper." The air between us echoed with her laughter, filling me with much needed self-assurance. I knew, without a doubt, this girl needed me and I needed her. *That's a first. We could get used to that feeling.*

"Tempting but no. I meant, maybe I could help you learn to read."

"Doubtful."

"Why?"

"Kara is one of the most patient people in the world. If she couldn't help me, then there's no way you can."

"I did some tutoring when I was in college. You might just be dyslexic."

"They already tested me for that."

"Who did?"

"My high school."

"You can never trust their tests. They're skewed to give false answers. There are more than thirty different learning styles. Those tests only pick up a few types of dyslexia. Most can never really be discovered through standard tests, if at all."

"You sound pretty knowledgeable about it."

"I don't know if I'm knowledgeable, but I know a little. And I have a thing for learning about new stuff."

"Does it bother you?"

"What?"

"The fact that I can't read."

"No." She replied with no hesitation and it made my heart flutter with relief. But I sensed fear in her voice and I knew there was something she wasn't saying.

"But?"

"I can only imagine how stressful this is for you and that makes me sad. I don't want you to feel that way. I want you to see yourself the way everyone does. The way I do."

"And how is that?"

"Confident, charismatic, charming, talented."

"Go on," I laughed, repeating her words.

"Sexy, sensual, hot as hell."

"You think I'm hot as hell?" Her statement floored me. "Well, Miss Hagen, I believe you're becoming braver, aren't you?"

"Sounds like you're rubbing off on me."

I didn't have to explain, she knew what I was talking about. I wanted her to feel as confident in her body as she wanted me to feel in mine. We both had something to prove, if to no one else but ourselves. She'd opened herself to all types of replies and my wicked self just couldn't resist engaging her more.

"Oh, I'd like to rub off on you, trust me, Hindley." Her voice bubbled over with laughter and my soul felt lighter, like I was alive, maybe for the first time ever. "Alright," I breathed out.

"You'll let me try? Really?" I was surprised by the excitement in her words.

"As long as you stop when I say stop and you don't judge me."

"I'm not a judgmental person, Rory."

"I know. That's why I told you."

"Thank you. Thank you for trusting me with your secret. I swear, I'll never tell anyone, unless you want me to."

She didn't have to confess her loyalty, I knew she would hold my secret close to her heart. That's the reason I'd shared it with her. But it touched me immensely to know she was grateful for my trust.

"Hey, Rory."

"Yeah?"

"You know I'm not as perfect as you seem to think I am. Please stop putting me up on that pedestal because I can guarantee you, I'll fall. And when I do, it will hurt both of us."

"I'll try, Hindley. That's all I can promise."

"That's enough. For now."

"Good night, Drunk Girl."

"Good night, Skater Boy."

I sat on the phone, waiting for her to hang up but silently hoping she wouldn't.

"Are you going to hang up?" she asked.

"I was waiting for you to."

"Where are you?"

"At Leif's, on his back porch."

"You're outside?"

"Yeah. It's a gorgeous night." We sat in comfortable silence. "I wish you were here."

"Me, too. What would you do if I was there?"

Ah, she wanted to talk dirty. I was okay with this, if she was.

"I'd sit you on top of my lap so you could feel how hard my dick's been since I left your house. Do you know how fucking difficult it is to ride a motorcycle with a chubby?"

"A what?"

"A boner, a trouser tent, a throbbing meat whistle." Her instant snorting and subsequent laughter gave me all the confidence and hope I needed. I knew without a doubt that eventually, I'd have this girl talking all kinds of nasty to me.

"You've been hard that long?"

"Yes."

"How's that possible?"

"I have no idea but it hurts like hell."

"Well, if I were there, I would kiss it and make it all better." A moan escaped from my mouth as my body seized in need.

"You keep talking like that and I'm gonna jump back on that motorcycle and drive over to your house and drop you to your knees like a sinner in church."

"Maybe you should."

"Hindley?"

"Yes, Rory?"

"Good night."

"Good night, Skater Boy."

Without another word, the phone went dead and my dick throbbed so hard I thought it might actually explode.

For better or for worse, I was committed to her now. My secret had been revealed and I felt a sense of relief and satisfaction flow through my veins. I could finally breathe with no fear of rejection or humiliation from the one person who could destroy me. My admission hadn't even fazed her. In fact, she wanted to help me. She wanted to protect me from everything and everyone who threatened to humiliate me. She was actually concerned for my well-being and had nothing to gain personally by doing so. I was in awe of her, again.

Kara was right. Hindley and I needed each other and I couldn't ever remember needing anything or anyone before in my life. I thought the feeling would provoke fear and anxiety, but instead, I felt a deep sense of completeness, as if Hindley was my cure for all things that ailed me in life. I just hoped I could be the same for her and not totally fuck this up in the process.

I knew it would be almost impossible to beat these feelings of inadequacy deep inside me. They were so ingrained in my way of thinking, it felt unlikely I could change. But the alternative wasn't an option. I refused to put her in any dangerous position. *What if that danger is you, my friend?*

My heart stopped. Would I be able to pull myself away from her, if, one day, we both discovered I was the one thing that could hurt her? I let the thought evaporate from my mind as I pushed back into the glider and looked up at the dark sky, wishing that she was with me, praying I'd never have to answer that question.

Chapter 13

"What'cha looking at, doll face?" I jumped in my chair at Luis's words. "What's wrong?" he asked, genuinely concerned that he'd frightened me. I quickly minimized the Google web search page I was looking at, 'How to teach adult learners to read.'

"Nothing," I shrilled, my voice laced with the same guilt I was convinced my face expressed. He arched one eyebrow in distrust but didn't say any more.

"So are you ready for tomorrow's signing? You ready to become a sports agent?" His smile broadened as he used air quotes around my new title.

"I'm still an attorney, Luis."

"Yes, you are that indeed." He sauntered around the chair in front of my desk with grace and ease then suddenly flopped down like a wayward teen. He was such a contradiction, suave and refined one minute then brassy and uncouth the next. "So what are you looking at? Market research for skateboarding?"

"Yes." It wasn't a total lie. One of my web page tabs was on various market strategies for extreme sports products, including snowboarding, moto-cross and skate boarding. I had no idea there so many facets to this industry, and so much buying potential.

"And?"

"And, what?"

"You were obviously looking at something else. What gives? Doing more Rory research?" he asked with cunning smile.

"He *is* my client, isn't he?" Suddenly my phone pinged with an incoming email. I grabbed it from my desk and punched in my password, surprisingly giddy when I realized the new message was from Rory. It was short and simple and I wasn't surprised.

<lunch?>

"Who is it?" I didn't answer. "Let me guess. Rory?" My eyes rolled up to meet Luis's and I saw a small amount of judgment in his eyes. "He wants to have lunch today, right?"

I didn't want to divulge any information that might jeopardize my job but I was a hopeless liar. Besides, it was just lunch, between an attorney and her client, what could be wrong with that? *Yeah right, JUST lunch...and then maybe a roll in the sack for dinner?*

"How did you know?"

"That goofy ass smile on your face for one. I was a player too, remember Hindley?"

"Do you think he's playing me?" my voice shallow, breathy, and...desperate. After last night's admission, I really felt like Rory's feelings for me were genuine but Luis was a certified, if reformed, player and if anyone would know the signs, it would be him.

"No. I think he's probably just nervous about tomorrow."

"Really?" I was embarrassed at how relieved I felt. Maybe Luis didn't realize where our relationship was headed. He let out a wry laugh as his forefinger rubbed against his chin in speculation. *Uh, I think he does, dumbass.* "Why would Rory be nervous?" I asked, trying to change the subject and hide my anxiety.

"The boy has the potential to earn millions and he's putting all his eggs in your basket, so to speak." His raised eyebrow made me blush. "Oh, God, Hindley, tell me his breakfast sausage has not been in your biscuit."

"No!" I shouted.

"Oh, thank God." He sighed and leaned back in his chair in obvious relief.

"Why?"

"Because this is business, Hindley. Serious business. This could cost the firm and Rory millions if you're not careful."

"I'm surprised, Luis. I expected you of all people would support me if I wanted to give my biscuit away."

Luis had badgered me constantly over the three months I'd been at the firm, wondering how someone like me could be sexual inactive. "It's a crime against nature and human sexuality for you not to be doing the horizontal hula on a regular basis," he'd offered in jest.

"Believe me, I'd love for you to give your biscuit away to any eligible man in the world, you know that," Luis explained. "Just not to Rory Gregor." I slumped in my chair, sighing in disappointment at Luis's disapproval. "When's he going back?" Luis's question brought me back to the bleak present situation I was now facing. What did our future hold? Was there even a future for us?

"I don't know. I assume tomorrow after he signs the paperwork."

Luis pushed out of my chair and knocked his knuckles on my desk. "Just think about what I told you, doll face. I'd hate to see you holding your broken heart in the unemployment line when all of this is said and done."

I rolled my eyes toward the ceiling, trying to put Luis's comment into perspective but reminding myself he didn't know Rory like I did. His warning did make sense though and I couldn't ignore it, not completely. "I hear you, boss. Loud and clear," I whispered, rubbing my hands together nervously.

"Hindley." He paused at the door until he had my undivided attention, his caramel brown eyes fixated on mine as he stood in the threshold of my doorway. "I just don't want to see you get hurt, baby girl, financially or emotionally."

"I'm fine." His face showed he wasn't convinced. "I promise."

"Good. Stay that way, beautiful." He nodded his head and gave me a classic panty-dropping Luis Marquez megawatt smile and playful wink before closing my door.

My gaze returned to the phone still clutched possessively in my hand. I exhaled deeply, not even aware that I'd been holding my breath. Rory couldn't read, well, not much, so my response had to be short, something he could decipher in Google Translator.

<Busy. Sorry.>

Thirty seconds later, I heard another ding.

<What are you wearing?>

'What am I wearing?' Where did that come from?

<Clothes. Why?>

I sat patiently waiting, surprised at how anxious I was for his response.

<Hello Kitty?>

Hello Kitty? Where the hell did that come from? And how did he know how to spell Hello Kitty? I reminded myself that he did know some words so 'hello' and 'kitty' wouldn't be surprising.

<Why do you think I'm wearing Hello Kitty?>

<UR pajamas>

My pajamas? Oh those goofy ass Hello Kitty PJ set Dana gave me for Christmas. I'd completely forgotten I'd had them on when he came to my house the other night after standing me up and taking out some other bimbo.

<Why, do you like Hello Kitty?>

<I like your hello kitty>

Oh my God. This was a company phone, every call and email completely traceable and stored on the law firm's computer server. I frantically searched my office as if someone were standing over my shoulder, reading his overt sexual messages, fearing our IT department would come busting through my door at any minute. I had to respond.

<This is a work phone. This is my work email. This is a law firm. All messages are recorded and saved.>

I wasn't sure if any of that would fit into Google Translator but I had to let him know there was no way he could send me stuff like that at work, even though his comment made my center tingle with unmatched sensations I'd never felt before. A devilish grin slowly spread across my face at the revelation that he liked my kitty. Then suddenly, the ringing of my cell phone brought me back from my erotic thoughts and my face flushed as I saw our picture appear on my screen along with the nickname I'd given him on my phone, 'Skater Boy'.

"You can't send stuff like that to my work email, Rory." I whispered in a hushed tone as if I were being taped. Suddenly, panic ripped through my body at the thought of being videotaped. *Stay calm, Hindley. Breathe.*

"What? No hello...kitty?" His voice was raspy and deep and sexy as hell.

"Rory, this is a work cell phone, too."

"So, what, is everything in your office is bugged?"

"Pretty much."

"How's a guy supposed to talk dirty to his girl?"

'His girl?' Since when had I become 'His girl?'

"First of all, I'm not your girl. Second of all, you shouldn't be talking sexy to me. Not at work."

"You are my girl, my Drunk Girl. I think I established that when I put you in bed three sheets to the wind. And if I can't talk dirty to you at work, then what's the point?" I stifled a giggle, thinking of his erotic words. "So are you going to answer me?"

"What?"

"What are you wearing?"

"Rory, I'm serious."

"Then have lunch with me so I can see you."

"I'm busy. I have a high maintenance client that I'm dealing with. He can be a real jerk."

"That sucks."

"Yes, it does."

"Maybe you should have lunch with him, to put him in his place."

"No lunch." I could hear the disappointment in his silence and I hated it. "What about dinner?"

"I can't do dinner tonight. I'm going over to Bucky and Pena's house."

"Oh, that will be fun."

"You should come."

"I wasn't invited."

"I'm inviting you."

"It's not your place to invite me. Besides, I'll probably be here late getting all your paperwork together for tomorrow. And I have tons of research I need to do."

"Maybe I could come by later and help you."

"Something tells me that you being here with me would not help at all."

"It would help me."

"We need to talk."

"Ut oh. Am I in trouble?"

"We just need rules."

"I don't like setting rules. I like breaking them."

"There are some we can't break, Rory. I'm serious."

"I know." The defeat in his voice was unnerving.

"We both could lose a lot if this goes wrong."

"I know, Hindley, I already told you, I get it." His tone was clipped and bitter.

"Why are you mad at me?"

"I'm not mad at you. I'm…" I could tell he was trying to form his answer carefully. "Frustrated," he finally concluded.

"Call me tonight after your dinner and we'll talk."

"You just told me I can't talk dirty to you on this phone. Give me your home phone number."

"Shit!"

"What?"

"They cut off my home phone last week."

"Why? Couldn't pay the bills?" The smile in his voice was audible.

"I wasn't using it much and decided last week to cancel the service and use my work phone exclusively."

"So, you do use your work phone for some personal conversations?" Hope rang through his revelation.

"I guess so, yes."

"I could come see you after dinner." His voice was dripping with sexual innuendo and I felt my center spasm.

"I don't think that's a good idea."

"Why?"

There was more erotic promise in that one word than I'd ever heard in my life and my head began to spin as I desperately searched for a reason why he couldn't at least stop by my house after his dinner with the Kopra's.

"You know why." His defeat was palpable and part of me felt bad. "Look, just let me get through our meeting tomorrow. Mr. Stedwick is expecting a lot out of me and I need to make sure I'm completely prepared. We can have dinner tomorrow night, okay?"

"I can't. I'm leaving tomorrow afternoon shortly after our meeting."

"Oh." I tried to hide the disappointment that racked my entire being but failed miserably. I was a hopeless bullshitter.

"Are you sad?" he asked with mock anticipation.

"Yes." It came out before I could even stop myself.

"Maybe even disappointed?"

"Very." Shit! Again, my response was automatic, impulsive, with no thought and no filter. *Way to go. No, you don't sound desperate at all.*

"So you really do want to see me?" I could see him smirking in my mind.

Calm down. Slow your response. Don't sound so pathetic and needy. "Of course I want to see you." I tried to calm my voice but was pretty sure my reply sounded lonely and pathetic.

"I lied," he finally admitted.

"About what?"

"I'm not leaving until Wednesday morning."

"Are you serious?" The excited shrill in my voice I'm sure left little doubt in his mind of just how much I wanted to see him. *DESS-prit, LOAN-lee, PAH-THEH-tic.*

"Well, I was supposed to leave on Tuesday evening but I just wanted to make sure you really did want to see me. I'll change my ticket to Wednesday morning, if you want me to stay."

"Shit!" I realized this was a company phone and I couldn't reveal anymore.

"What?"

"Company phone."

"Yes or no?"

"I'm not sure what the question is."

"Should we meet Tuesday evening to discuss my contract and a marketing strategy for me, now that you're my agent, too?" God, he was good.

"Yes."

"I'll see you tomorrow morning, Miss Hagen."

"I'll see you then, Mr. Gregor."

Suddenly, the line went dead and I felt a wave of relief wash over me, knowing I was no longer in danger. At least, not with the firm's telecommunications department. But, the feeling quickly faded when a painful chill of disappointment wrapped around me as I realized I wouldn't see him for another twenty-four hours. Memories of his mouth covering my lips, my face, my neck, my entire body, flooded my mind and sent a powerful surge of heat exploding throughout my innermost being. His skin on mine was like heaven to me. I laughed out loud, realizing my brain wouldn't be worth shit as long as images of his beautiful, sexy face were floating around in it.

~

I rubbed my tired eyes, trying to focus on the neon green clock on my microwave. 10:14pm. Why did I feel so empty inside? *Maybe because you told Rory to stop contacting you...and he did.* Or maybe it was the overwhelming inadequacies beginning to choke my mind again.

I'd been relentless in my exhaustive research on extreme sports over the last forty-eight hours. I couldn't remember studying this hard since law school and yet, I still felt completely incompetent. How in the hell had I convinced myself I'd be any good at being a sports agent? *Um, hello, you're still not a hundred percent sold on the idea that you're any good at being a lawyer either. What else is new?*

I'd also spent a great deal of time researching adult illiteracy, the causes and the hundreds of ways to instruct an adult unable to read. I wanted to teach Rory, I really did, but the emptiness inside me was lethal as I questioned my own abilities. By his own admission, he'd tried for years and had never learned yet. Why did I think I could do any better? I wasn't a teacher. Hell, I didn't even feel like a real lawyer sometimes. And where would that leave me if I couldn't help him learn to read? Where would that leave us?

I slowly removed the cellophane wrapper from the popcorn and pulled the microwave door open, placing the bag in the center of the glass plate. *What is wrong with you? You told him to leave you alone. You could have had dinner with him and would probably be rollin' around in your bed about right now screaming out his name in ecstasy. Popcorn? Laptop? Really?* I shook my head, trying to rid myself of these maddening questions as I hit the 'start' button on the panel.

A low buzzing tone broke through my thoughts and I turned my head in confusion, surprised to see the microwave still cooking. *It's your phone, dumb ass.* Rory? Suddenly, my heart raced and I felt giddy. *Idiot!* I desperately searched through the stack of papers on the kitchen counter like a mad person until I found it behind the toaster. I gasped in horror. Three missed texts from Rory. Shit!

9:42pm *<R u home>*
9:50pm *<R u ignoring me>*
10:17pm *<Good night DG. C u tomorrow.>*

Oh, crap. Should I text him back? Should I call? I didn't want him to think I was ignoring him. That would be rude. I knew I shouldn't but I wanted to hear his voice. We'll just talk about business stuff, prepare for tomorrow's meeting I tried to convince myself. *Yeah, that's it, that's why you want to call him.* Without trying to talk myself out of it, I scrolled through my contact list and hit the photo with his beautiful face.

"This is Rory Gregor." I stifled a laugh at his flat tone. He was keeping this professional and I couldn't help but smile.

"Good evening, Mr. Gregor. This is Hindley Hagen, your legal counsel. I hope I'm not calling you too late."

"Oh no, Miss Hagen, I'm glad to hear from you. I definitely need counseling." His voice was so erotic and sensual, I had a hard time focusing on why I'd called him. *Professional. Business. Contract. Attorney. Hello? Any of this ring a bell, Miss Sexy Pants?*

"Well I guess it's a good thing I called. Are you ready for tomorrow's meeting?"

"I think so. Are you?" he asked.

"I'm not sure."

"Why?"

"I've never done this before."

"What? Phone sex?"

"Rory!" I shouted.

"Ooops, sorry."

"No."

"No what? Phone sex?"

"Rory."

"Just asking."

"I've never been someone's agent. It's kind of scary."

"Why?"

"I want to do the best job I can for you."

"And you don't think you will?"

"Not yet."

"But?"

"But I'll try."

"Then that's all I can ask for." There was an uncomfortable silence between us and suddenly, I realized that calling him had been a bad idea. "Look, Hindley, I know there is nothing you can't accomplish that you put your mind to. You're that kind of person." His words were so refreshing. "I believe in you. That should be enough."

"It should be."

"It will have to be. Trust me, you'll do fine." The silence dragged on between us but this time, I was thankful for it. It gave me time to process all he was saying, the confidence he was bestowing on me.

"I better let you go. I've got a meeting in the morning with a really hot chick and I want to look my very best."

"Rory!"

"What? I need my beauty rest. I wasn't born this adorable, you know."

"No, I didn't know that."

"Good night," he stopped himself abruptly. "Miss Hagen."

"Good night, Mr. Gregor."

"I look forward to seeing you tomorrow. And trust me, you'll be fine. I would never have hired you if I thought any different."

"Thank you, for your confidence. It means a lot to me." I blushed, finding it impossible to wipe off the silly-ass grin that had been plastered on my face the entire conversation.

"You're welcome. Sweet dreams, Hindley."

Before I could respond, the line went dead and my mind was once again filled with memories of Rory Gregor's mouth, all over my body.

~

"So, I think you'll find that we've drafted a solid contract for you, Rory." Mr. Stedwick's voice boomed throughout the conference room. I laughed to myself at his insinuation that he'd had anything to do with the drafting of this attorney/agent contract. It had been my tireless work, not his and it infuriated me that he was trying to take credit. Rory's slight hint of a smirk reassured me of his gratitude for the tireless work he knew I'd done on his behalf.

"Yes, I have no doubt you drafted a very fine contract, sir." Rory's sarcasm was barely noticeable to anyone else in the room but I heard it loud and clear and had to duck my head, fearing I might burst out laughing at any moment.

"Ms. Hagen, I hate to interrupt you," the receptionist's voice rang through the intercom.

"We're in a meeting," Mr. Stedwick half shouted, his irritation made clearer by his vehement scowl.

"Yes, sir, I know and I'm so sorry." Her voice was quivering with apprehension. "But Ms. Hagen has a delivery and the company is insistent that she sign for it. Now."

"What in God's name is this about Hindley?" His voice was laced with controlled hostility and I couldn't help but feel like a reprimanded child. I glanced up at Rory and saw something flash across his face. Was it sympathy? Protection? No, this was something else, something that made my stomach flip.

"She'll be there in a moment," he bellowed, banging the intercom button so hard, he nearly flipped the entire phone over. His glacial stare nearly froze me in my spot. I knew I was turning three shades of red from his humiliating behavior toward me. *What the hell, man? It's not like I did this on purpose, you asshole. First you take credit for MY hard work and now you totally want to humiliate me in front of clients and colleagues after all the hours of work I've put into this one contract. Fuck off!*

I searched the room, trying to offer up silent apologies. "I'm sorry gentlemen. If you'll excuse me, I'll be right back." My eyes grew in surprise as Rory stood preparing for my exit. *Gentleman. Nice surprise. Who knew?* He cleared his throat and extended a mischievous smirk.

"Take your time, Hindley. We'll be here." I surveyed the room and watched in shock as the rest of the men took his cue and stood.

I rushed through the double doors toward reception, thankful for the escape of Mr. Stedwick wondering what on earth was waiting for me.

"This better be something good, Vanessa because I basically had my ass handed to me in the conference room by Mr. Stedwick." Her lips were pressed in a fine line and her eyebrows rose as she nodded to a gentleman sitting in the waiting area. "Oh, shit," I whispered. "Is that him?"

"Uh, yeah."

"He doesn't look like a delivery guy." He was dressed in a full suit void of a tie.

"That's what I thought but he insisted he had a delivery for you and said it had to be delivered precisely at 9:47am." I looked down at my watch and saw it was now 9:50am.

"9:47am?"

"I know. Weird, right?"

"What is it?"

"Beats me?" she sighed shrugging her shoulders. "He's got a box."

"Do you know his name?" She shook her head and I knew she'd be of no further help to me. I walked around the furniture to stand beside him. "Excuse me, sir, I'm Hindley Hagen. You have a package for me?"

"Yes," he stood. "Would you please sign here?" he asked, pointing to a small clipboard. I was surprised to see a single sheet of paper with one solitary line with my name and a space for the date. *That's weird.*

"What delivery service are you with?" I asked as I quickly scribbled my signature. He looked down at my name, satisfied with the result.

"Thank you," he responded, finally handing me the package. It was white and roughly the size of a shirt box, only deeper. Every edge was sealed with clear tape making it impossible to get into without some kind of sharp object. What the hell?

"What is it?" Vanessa stood and joined me in the reception area.

"I have no idea."

"Well, open it," she encouraged.

My mind raced at ideas of what could possibly be inside. I inspected the exterior but found no return address. Even my name and address gave nothing away as it was printed from a computer label.

"Thanks, Vanessa." I walked toward the double doors, heading for my office. There was no way I was going to open this in front of her. She was the biggest gossip in the law firm. I knew instinctively that whatever was inside was meant for my eyes only.

"Ah, come on, Hindley," I heard her beg as the doors shut behind me.

When I was safely in the confines of my office, I pulled a pair of scissors from my desk drawer and worked feverishly to cut through the thick tape sealing the box. Once all the edges were freed I removed the top shocked to find the bock entirely stuffed with tissue paper. *What the hell?* I pulled each piece out one at a time, cautious of what lie underneath. I gasped in horror as I finally reached the contents. The first item was a pair of Hello Kitty thong panties. I couldn't stifle a laugh any longer and I cupped my mouth, trying to quiet my shameful excitement.

"Oh my God," I whispered. That asshole! He'd purposely had it delivered during our meeting. He knew this box was coming and he sat there in that fucking conference room with that smug-ass smile and watched me leave, knowing I'd have to return. Asshole!

I pulled the panties from the box, staring at the huge Hello Kitty face covering the crotch. He's an idiot. I was surprised to find a note attached.

I love your hello kitty!

What the fuck! This guy has serious balls. Not that you'd know. Yet.

I shook with apprehension, afraid to look further, scared of what I would find inside the Naughty Box. I almost screamed in horror. Beneath the underwear was a box labeled Trojan Supra BareSkin Non-Latex Condoms. *A fuckin' box of condoms! Non-latex! Hell yeah!* The contents revealed 150 condoms inside.   What was he thinking! A similar note was attached.

A good start, don't you think?

What the fuck! This man is insane! *Marry him, marry him right now!*

The final item was a small white box with the words 'iPhone 5' written on the side. Oh my God, he bought me a phone. Another note was attached, no surprise there.

So we can talk dirty.

I plopped down in my chair in disbelief. I didn't know whether to be flattered or offended, excited or appalled. I think at that moment, I was all of them wrapped into one.

"Hindley, what's going on?" I jumped at the sound of Michael's voice.

"Oh, um, I'm sorry, Michael." I shoved the contents back in the box and bolted to the other side of my desk shoving it into my bottom drawer, praying he hadn't seen anything.

"Is everything alright?"

"Yes it's fine."

"Can you get back to the meeting? We're about to sign."

"Of course. I'm sorry." My heart was racing, knowing I was about to come face to face with my not-so-secret admirer. I would have to sit, ball-faced and watch in silence as he signed a contract, basically tying the two of us together for the next twelve months. Suddenly, all I could picture were those Hello Kitty panties covering my pounding crotch.

"Are you sure you're alright?"

"Yes!" I shouted, blinking my eyes rapidly. I was lying. I'd never been so aroused in my whole life. Just imagining what we'd do together had my mind reeling. *This is wrong, Hindley. Don't do it.* Wait, weren't you just cheering on the box of condoms. *Oh, yeah, I forgot. Yeah, Rory! Do it!* I was as confused as my subconscious but only had seconds to compose myself.

Michael opened the door to the conference room and held it open for me. I kept my head glued to the floor, trying desperately to avoid Rory's gaze as I made my way back to my chair.

"Everything alright, Miss Hagen?" his voice echoed with subtle sexual undertones.

I wanted to ignore him, have no contact with him whatsoever but professional protocol wouldn't allow me. "Yes, fine, thank you," I finally stuttered, still staring down at my fingers, praying everyone in the room was oblivious to the sexual tension between us. My insides were on fire with desire and I was pretty sure it was visibly oozing out of every pore of my body.

The masochist in me longed to see his face, even though I knew better than to chance it. After sitting still for what seemed like hours, I could stand it no longer and finally allowed my eyes to seek him out. I slowly slipped my gaze across the table, letting them wander up his chest, before peering up at his eyes underneath my fluttering lashes. His were molten hot and completely consumed with me. *Fuck! Calm down, girl. Breathe.*

His yellow, button down shirt encapsulated the most defined male torso I'd ever seen and made his bright blue eyes sparkle with flecks of light brown highlights. The contrasting glow of his hard, dark skin next to the soft light fabric of his shirt made my insides ache with longing. All I could think of was ripping it off so I could attack and devour every inch of the sexy tattoo that I knew from personal experience lay underneath.   He was beautiful, sexy, confident, any and everything a girl like me could ever hope for. *Except for one thing. He's you're client, or soon will be.*

I watched in helpless abandon as one side of his mouth curled wickedly into a devious, delicious smile. My breath caught in my throat and my mouth went desert dry.   *This man is gonna eat you alive. Oh, wait, he already has. Hang on, girl, client or no client, you are in for one unbelievable ride.*

~

"I can't believe you did that, Rory!" I shouted into my new phone.

"What?"

"Sending me that box. And then delivering it all to work? Mr. Stedwick almost had me for lunch."

"Yeah, that guy's a real dick." I nodded in silent agreement, remembering his less than professional response to the interruption of our meeting. "And then he tries to take credit for your work. Super douche in my book." I smiled at Rory's defense of me. I'd really never seen that side of Mr. Stedwick before and I have to say it really did surprise me.

"And then Michael almost caught me with the contents in my office," I continued, turning as red as I had earlier today.

"What can I say? I'm crass."

"That's beyond crass. Do you know how much trouble I could have been in?"

"Do you know how much trouble you're going to be in?"

"None!" I huffed as I plopped down on my sofa.

"Why?"

"Because I'm not seeing you tonight."

"At all?"

"No, not after that stunt you pulled this morning."

"Well as my attorney and agent, I'm requesting a meeting with you."

"Fine. You can call my office in the morning and we can schedule..." Suddenly, my doorbell rang, cutting off our conversation. "Hold on."

"Is someone at the door? Did you order something? More panties?" His deviant chuckle from the other end of the phone was much more telling.

"Rory Gregor, please tell me you haven't had another box of sex toys and gadgets delivered to me."

"Why, would you be happy or disappointed?"

I trampled toward my front door but stayed quiet, surprised by the realization that I'd actually be excited with that type of delivery. I chastised myself for my silence to his question, which I knew gave away my answer. Lost in my own erotic fantasies, I flung open the door without checking the peephole and almost dropped the phone.

"You really should at least ask 'Who's there' before you open your door, Hindley," he growled.

Rory leaned against the outside wall of my porch, arms and legs crossed with a deep scowl wiped across his face as he stood in righteous indignation, reprimanding me for my lack of self-preservation. Somehow, I found the whole scene...hot.

He was dressed in the same light yellow, button down shirt from earlier today. God, he looked good in that shirt. *He'd look better OUT of that shirt.* No arguments there. He'd changed into lightly faded jeans that had obviously seen better days. They hung perfectly on his hips like a priceless work of art. It should be illegal to look this good when I knew he wasn't even trying.

He was holding a bag of groceries in one hand and a bottle of sparkling water in the other. *Water?* Instincts told me if he crossed through that threshold, I'd be letting him in to more than just my home.

"I believe I have a meeting with you, Miss Hagen." He tilted his head to the side, raising an eyebrow, his face covered in a predatory smile. *He's gonna eat you alive, girlie girl, eat you alive!*

I tucked away my new phone into my pocket and tried to put on a game face. "I told you to call my office, Mr. Gregor."

"Oh, I'm afraid this couldn't wait, Miss Hagen." How could he make one simple sentence sound like a cry for the best sexual tryst known to womankind?

Okay, I'll play along. "What's so important that it couldn't wait until tomorrow, Mr. Gregor?"

"I have groceries here that could melt in this hot Texas sun if you don't let me in."

"I believe after your contract signing today, you'll have more than enough money at your disposal to buy additional groceries should those spoil as you wait outside." I surprised Rory and even myself at my sassy response. "You'll have to come up with a *much* better reason than that if you want to meet with me tonight, Mr. Gregor."

"I want to cook for you." He literally took my breath away. No man had ever made me dinner. In fact, I couldn't remember a man making my anything, except mad. "Then I want to feed you." *Oh, holy hell, girl.* "Then I'm going to take you to bed and start making good use of the other two presents I sent you today." I blushed at his inference, standing stunned and speechless. "May I come...in...Hindley?"

His prolonged annunciation of each word was not lost on me. My heart rate accelerated as the female hormones in the center of my body began to spike. Without saying another word, I stepped back and let the Big Bad Wolf enter my home. Again.

~

"I thought you were going to feed me," I laughed, while cleaning up the last of our dinner dishes.

"I did. I made you dinner. That's feeding you, isn't it?" I nodded my head in silent disappointment. "What, were you expecting something else?" he asked in his shy voice I was growing to love. I rolled my eyes, trying to suppress my smile as I returned to the dishes. Suddenly, his snake like hands wrapped around my waist and his chin rested on my shoulder. "I have another meal planned for you but it's not in the kitchen. Trust me, Hindley, I will feed you. Tonight."

I closed my eyes, pretty sure they'd rolled out of my skull as I floated away in glorious anticipation. It was beyond me how this man could make any and everything sound so damn sexy. No one had ever affected me on such a visceral level as Rory did.

"We shouldn't," I whispered, not fully believing myself. Suddenly, he dropped his hands from my waist and pulled away, leaving me cold and wanting.

"Whatever you say, Hindley."

Whatever I say? That's not what I wanted? *What do you want then, girl?* My hands were still sudsy from the dishwater but that didn't stop the sweat from breaking out across my palms. How in the world was I going to tell this sex god that I was horrible in bed? Guys want adventurous girls, confident girls, experienced girls and I was none of those. I was horrible at sex and had been told so by my last boyfriend and to be honest, I hadn't been surprised by his revelation. In fact, it was to be expected, given my history.

Without even realizing it, my back was now resting on the sink, my eyes staring off into space as my hands dripped water all over the floor, soaking the hardwood below.

"What's wrong, Hindley?" He rushed to my side, slowly drying my hands with a dish towel.

My eyes glazed over lost in a dark void, watching a horror movie play over and over in my own mind. I was miles away from the kitchen and in the end of the film, Rory always left unsatisfied and I lay in bed crying until sunrise.

Slowly, his warm touch brought me back as his hand cupped my chin and raised my face to his. "Hey," he whispered. I could feel his breath on my skin and I slowly began to search his eyes, looking for some semblance that he'd appreciate my dilemma. But I knew a man as experienced as Rory would never understand the depths of my distress. "Talk to me," he said softly.

Hot tears burned the back of my eyes and it infuriated me that I was so weak. I held on to a silent sob as I felt droplets of despair breach the damn and roll down my cheek.

"Hey. Hindley, what in the world is going on?" he asked, his voice laced with desperation and fear. He tried to pull me into a hug but I pushed him away. If I was going to tell him my secret then I had to see his face, gauge his reaction. No time like the present, I guess.

"I'm bad at sex, Rory. Really bad." I blew out.

"What?" he half laughed, half shouted as he backed away from me.

"I know you're experienced and used to a certain kind of woman. That's just not me. I'm not good in bed."

"Says who?"

"Says my last boyfriend."

"Who? Douche bag from the wedding?"

"No. I never slept with him."

"Was it someone before him?" I nodded my head. I wanted to spare him the details of just how fucked up I was. If he knew the whole story, not only would he leave my house, he'd fire me as his attorney as well. He tossed the dish towel onto the counter and began rubbing his palms up and down on the front of his jeans. *He's nervous.* There was a long pause as he formulated a response. "Prove it," he finally answered, resting his hands on his hips.

"Prove what?"

"That you're bad at sex. Prove it to me."

"What does that mean?"

"It means I want to find out, first hand, just how bad you are."

I shook my head at his preposterous idea, unable to hold in my laughter.

"You see, Hindley," he said, slowly stalking back toward me. "I don't believe for a minute that you're bad at this." His hand waved between us. "You're too damn sexy to be bad in bed. And the way you screamed when I went down on you this weekend leads me to believe an entirely different story about you and your sexual skills." Before I realized it, he was within inches of me.

"But I think you'll need to prove it to me." His cheek was grazing mine and I could feel the small growth of stubble on his face as his lips caressed my ear. "Will you do that, Hindley? For me?"

I swallowed the jar of cotton balls stuck in my mouth and slowly nodded my head. *Girl, what the fuck are you doing? He's gonna leave once he finds out how fucked up you are.* I think we've already established that fact.

"What would you do first?" he whispered in my ear. I didn't understand his question so I pulled back slightly to look at his face, mine riddled with concern.

"What do you mean?"

"If you were going to have sex with me, what would you do first?" I shook my head, still not understanding. He took a long step back and I was grateful for the space. "If you told me you were a bad cook, I'd have you cook for me so I could judge for myself." *Okay, that makes sense, I guess. Let's see where he's going with this.* "If you're as bad at sex as someone has obviously made you believe, I think I have the right to find out for myself. I have the right to make an informed decision, don't I?"

"What if he's right, what if I am bad?" I blew out, with panic oozing from every pore. He quickly closed the gap between us and took my arms in his hands.

"Hindley, it's been my experience that women are usually never bad at sex, it's the men who are. I suspect you've just been with the wrong man. But I'm willing to make sacrifices, go through the grueling task of having sex with you, just to find out for myself." His deep chuckle made me tingle as he pushed against me, his body crushing mine against the kitchen sink. "Now. For the last time." His voice was just a whisper. "Show me what you would do to me before I bend you over this counter and show you myself that you're anything but bad at sex." *Oh, holy shit bomb, fuck!*

My entire body trembled at his command and I closed my eyes, preparing for my task at hand. I'd never really been in control of my sexual experiences before. They'd just…happened. This time, I to had put thought and purpose to my actions and already I felt more empowered.

"I'm waiting," he demanded, pushing off the counter and backing away from me. I reached out and grabbed him around the waist, pulling him back toward me.

"First, I'd kiss you." I let my hands roam up his chest and around his neck, slowly tugging on his shaggy hair and pulling his head down to mine. I looked into his eyes just before our lips touched and saw a sense of pride that washed away my insecurities.

Our kiss was light at first, like we were reacquainting ourselves with one another. But within seconds, it become more impassioned as our lips and tongues fought for more of one another. Before I could make sense of what was happening, Rory pulled away and panic invaded my being, thinking I'd done something wrong. I tried to search his eyes to decipher what he was thinking but they were closed, a look of sheer satisfaction washed across his face. Slowly, he raised his lids and I saw his eyes were much darker now, a deep blue like the ocean.

"I'd say this old boyfriend must have you confused with someone else, Hindley." I couldn't mask my prideful smile. "Anyone who can kiss like that cannot be bad in bed." I puckered my lips in silent jubilation. "What would you do next?"

What would I do next? What would I do next, I wondered. I mustered my most provocative voice and was surprised at how sultry I sounded. "I'd undress you." *Whoa! You go, girl!* This man made me bold. He raised both eyebrows and gave me a crooked grin in wild anticipation, raising both his arms to the side in silent permission. I let my hands travel over his shirt again, feeling every detail of his lean and sculpted chest. As I reached the top button, I slowly undid it, exposing a small patch of hair just under his collar bone. Lifting up slightly, I pressed a kiss in the hollow of his neck and smiled silently as I heard him gasp. *Maybe you're not so bad at this stuff after all, girl.*

I worked my way down his shirt, uncovering the large muscles underneath. As I opened the shirt tail at his abdomen, I was struck by just how different our skin was. Mine light and fair, his dark and rough. It was just like our personalities and our lives. After I'd undone every button, I parted the shirt like the Red Sea and wrapped my arms around his torso, making my way halfway up his back, scratching and pawing the entire way. The look on his face was shear ecstasy and I couldn't remember ever feeling more satisfied. Slowly, I worked my hands back up his chest, pushing the shirt off his shoulders, watching with sultry eyes as it fell to the kitchen floor. My eyes were immediately drawn to the tattoo on his torso that extended down his side, disappearing into his pants. I'd never seen the entire tattoo and something inside me pushed me on, knowing it was the one and only thing I hungered for at that exact moment.

I bent down and slowly began to trace the line of the skateboard with my finger, placing light breathy kisses along the way. I felt his body tense at my touch and wondered if I'd done something wrong. I slowly began to lick the tattoo, tracing the outside border with my tongue, stopping at his waistband, unable to go on.

"Looks like something's in your way," he said with controlled excitement. *Oh, girl, he is so turned on right now. You are doing it! I always said you were a closet horn dog.*

Taking my cue, I ran my index finger just inside his waistband of his jeans, making my way to the center belt buckle. His mouth closed up into a pucker as he drew in a breath and I heard a low moan escape his throat. I could tell he was trying to rein in his own desire and I couldn't help but grin.

My hands nimbly worked at his buckle and before I realized it, I had completely pulled off his belt and cast it down on the floor with his shirt. I watched his face intently as my fingers sank further into his pants and quickly undid his first button. His eyes popped open and I was relieved to see hunger burning inside. Or, was it fear? For the first time, I was the predator and he the prey. He was making me confident and bold and I loved every second of it.

I eased down the zipper, not surprised to feel his erection lying in wait. Damn, it felt huge! I saw the elastic of his boxers and wiggled the jeans over his hips, careful to keep his underwear in place. He liked this game. I liked this game. And I was going to prolong it as long as I could. Without prompting, he kicked off his shoes and socks and I knelt down, pulling his jeans down to his ankles. His hand rested on my shoulder for balance as he lifted first one leg, then the other, out of the jeans and watched me in silent hunger as I cast them over with the other discarded clothing and turned my attention back to his manhood. Holy shit, his dick was huge and standing at full attention. I tried not to focus on that part of his anatomy but it was so hard, literally. It was the tattoo I'd been looking for.

I knelt on my knees, wrapping my hands around his muscular legs for support. Oh my God, his thighs were huge and suddenly my mind was filled with images of them wrapped around my body. I couldn't help myself, I ran both hands up and down his legs, just going ever so slightly underneath his boxers. His hands grabbed onto my shoulders for support and I knew, in that moment, he was lost in me. I rolled my eyes up toward his face, staring over my lashes trying to be as erotic and sensual as possible. His beautiful lips turned up in a mischievous smile and I knew I was succeeding in my mission. I rose up on my knees and mirrored his expression as I reached for his waist band and slowly pulled it down off his hip to expose the remainder of the tattoo. It was huge, running just below his hip bone. God, it looked so sexy on him. It was the most beautiful tattoo I'd ever seen.

I let my tongue continue its relentless pursuit, slowly licking the outside border trailing over his hip bone then down and around, just skimming his back. Suddenly, I felt his whole body shudder and my face lit up like the Fourth of July. I felt wanton and sexy and a hunger enveloped my body, not for food but for Rory Gregor. He made me feel...alive.

I let my fingers glide back around the waistband of his underwear, just skimming the trail of hair under his belly button. He took in a deep breath and it fueled my hunger for this man. I'd never done this before. Never had a man, in my mouth. But with Rory, it just felt right. I pulled his boxers down ever so slightly and before I could even realize what I'd done, his erection sprung out in front of my face. *HOE-LEE hell, girl, that thing is massive and is gonna be soooo good, I can tell.* I'd never really looked at a penis before, not this close and in person. It was...beautiful? Was that even possible?

"Hindley," Rory admonished.

Suddenly, I became scared. Had I done something wrong? I leaned back, gazing up at his face through my lashes, trying to decipher what was wrong. I was surprised to find his eyes remained closed and his hand, that had once been on my shoulder, was now wrapped around my neck. I knew what he wanted. I wanted it too and without another thought, I took him in my mouth. The feeling was exquisite, a mixture of hard and soft skin filling me and driving me on.

"Oh, shit," I heard him moan. His cries fueled me, making me brave and bold. I wasn't sure exactly what I was doing but I knew he loved it so far so I had no intention of stopping now.

I let my tongue swirl around his dick as my head went back and forth, covering him with my mouth. His hands dug hard into my hair and it drove me on, giving me courage as I took him in completely until my nose was against his abdomen smelling his erotic scent. Oh, God, this was so good. I had no idea it was possible for a woman to get turned on by giving a blow job. He was incredible. *Baby girl, YOU'RE incredible. Look at you go, you slut!*

I felt his hips move against my mouth and a few times his movements nearly gagged me but I continued on, unfazed. He was going crazy. This was incredible. The way I felt, the way I was making him feel. I couldn't believe it could be like this. I forged on, taking in his entire being, listening to the soft moans escaping from his throat.

"Hindley, I'm gonna come."

I didn't care, there was no way I was going to stop. I'd heard horror stories about swallowing during a blow job but quickly cast them aside. The only thought in my mind was pleasing this man, which, in turn, aroused me and made me wet with desire.

"Hindley!" he shouted in warning. "Oh, fuuucccckkk," he blew out in a deep guttural tone that sounded like a wild animal. He tried to pull away but I held him in place, pounding relentlessly against him until I felt him shudder and hot liquid shoot down my throat. I swallowed as quickly as I could, trying desperately not to gag. It wasn't the best tasting thing in the world but it certainly wasn't as bad as others had said. And if it gave so much satisfaction and pleasure to Rory, I knew I'd do it again and again.

He released my head but I didn't pull him out of my mouth until I was sure the aftershocks of his orgasm were completely finished. When I finally felt him still, I sat back on my heels, staring up through my lashes at his beautiful face, with a shit eating grin on mine.

"Holy fuck, Hindley!" He ran both hands roughly through his hair. I wiped my mouth clean with the back of my hand and stood to face him. He was glowing with sheer delight. *Girl, you did good! You're first blow job. Success!* "Where in the hell did you learn to suck a dick like that? Wait, no, don't tell me. I don't even want to think about you going down on other guys." I laughed out loud at his ignorance. "What?"

"Nothing." I didn't want him to know how inexperienced I was. If he'd thought I'd done a good job, then that's all he needed to know. "So, you liked it?" I asked in my most demure voice.

"Like it? Fuck, Hindley, I've never felt anything like that."

"Really?" I thought his comment would bring satisfaction to me but instead, it caused great anxiety.

He pulled is boxers back up and saw the worry in my face. "Hindley. That was incredible. I don't know who this fuckin' asshat of a boyfriend is who said you were bad in bed, but he was a fuckin' moron. If you sucked his dick half as good as you just did mine, then he must be gay as shit to say you're no good at sex."

I laughed at his colorful answer.

"But," he continued. *Oh shit, girl, here it comes.* "Technically, you haven't shown me that you're no good at sex, so..." Before I could comment, he swept me up in his arms and carried me down the hall. "This one?" I knew what he was asking and without answering or thinking, I kicked open my bedroom door, ushering us inside. He threw me onto the mattress and I flopped around like I was on a trampoline, laughing like a school girl before I finally came to rest in the middle of the bed. Rory crawled on top of me, gently stroking my hair as he bent down and placed a light kiss on my lips. It was over far too soon and my hello kitty was begging for more.

"Why, Miss Hagen, I believe you're overdressed for this meeting," he reprimand in a low growl. I was still wearing my work clothes, the same outfit I'd had on earlier for our signing at the law firm. Without taking my eyes off of his, I gently pulled on the bow around my satin blouse, exposing a large portion of my chest. He lavished kisses down my cheek, my jaw, my throat, and down my collar bones, finally stopping at the first button.

Even though he'd seen me naked before, something about this time felt different. I was more brazen, I wasn't ashamed. I lifted straight up and slowly began to undo each button in slow motion, watching as his eyes burned with desire and need. I untucked my blouse from my skirt and lay back on the comforter, opening it wide, exposing my breasts and abdomen as I let the back of my hands drag along my neck up to my jaw and into my hair, fanning out my thick tresses over the pillow.

"Oh, Miss Hagen, aren't you brave tonight," he purred.

I tilted my head to the side and twisted my lips up in a sly smile. "Yes, Mr. Gregor, it appears that, with you, I am much braver." My heart welled with pride as I realized that was perhaps the most honest statement I'd ever made in my life.

Chapter 14

~RORY~

"Does that always happen?" Hindley asked in earnest, her chin resting on my chest as her cocoa colored eyes revealed an innocent seeking knowledge.

"Does what happen?" I continued to twist her hair around my index finger, wondering how in the world anyone could have told this amazing creature she was bad at anything, especially sex.

"An orgasm. You know, during sex."

My eyes furrowed at her question. "I should sincerely hope so. Why? Has that not been your experience, Miss Hagen?" She buried her face into my chest, embarrassed by my assumption. "Hey," I whispered, pulling her hair.

"Ow. That hurt." She rubbed her scalp and I leaned down to kiss her golden locks.

"I'm sorry."

"No, you're not."

Her eyes met mine and I was relieved to find them bright with amusement. I couldn't afford to lose her. Not after the mind-blowing sex we'd just had. I mean, I'd been with a lot of women but as soon as I'd entered Hindley, everything felt completely different, strangely unique in a way that I couldn't even explain, let alone comprehend. She felt like home to me. She fit me, molded to me perfectly in more ways than just sexually.

"You've never had an orgasm during sex?" She shook her head again. I couldn't help but puff my chest out in supreme arrogance, knowing I'd brought her satisfaction in a way she'd never experienced.

"You're quite proud of yourself, aren't you, Mr. Gregor?" Her fingers rubbed through the hair on my chest and I felt my dick twitch.

"Quite," I answered, smiling down at her.

"So, is it normal? Does it always happen?"

"Not always. But it's something I aspire to." My smile was wicked and deviant and I was completely caught off guard to see her face mirroring my expression. She had a growing appetite for my sexual prowess and I didn't remember a time when I'd felt more flattered. "I swear, you're insatiable, Miss Hagen."

"What can I say, I'm addicted."

"Are you saying I'm a drug?" She nodded and I laughed inside at how ironic her words were. I felt the same way about her. "Well, in that case, do you want another fix?" She nodded again like an excited child, rolling her lips inwardly, silently pleading. I motioned to the three opened and discarded condom packages on the floor. "So I guess buying the jumbo pack of condoms was a good idea?" She reached up and caressed my neck with her lips, making her way up to my ear.

"Um hum," she moaned.

Her words were my undoing. I grabbed her waist and flipped her up on top of me.

"What are you doing?"

"Well, Miss Hagan, I'm afraid you have thoroughly worn me out. This time you're working."

"What?"

Her innocent face was mesmerizing and I felt captivated by everything about her. My eyes wondered down to her perfect breasts already puckered in anticipation. Her stomach was heaving in and out and I knew she was wild with desire. I put my hands on her hips and pushed her away so my dick was just in front of her beautifully landscaped mound as I reached over to the box and produced another condom. These were different, much thinner and part of me worried that they may not be as strong. But remembering how good it felt to be buried inside of Hindley Hagen, I let my fear pass.

"Here, doll." I held out the package, waiting in wild anticipation at what she'd do next. It was obvious she was inexperienced sexually but I'd not found her lacking in any way. She was a natural vixen and my face curled up in a wicked smile knowing she'd no doubt deliver.

"What?"

"You," I replied, reaching up to wrap my hands around her neck, stroking her throat with my thumbs. Slowly, my fingers fell down her chest, caressing her collar bone then down lower to her chest, lightly tracing the curve of her perfect breasts. "You. Are beautiful, Hindley." She laughed in obvious disbelief. "Hey." I grabbed her chin more forcefully than I'd intended. Her eyes were dulled with doubt and it made my chest grip with pain that she actually believed she was anything but perfect. *Some asshole did a real number on her. Go easy.*

"Hindley," I encouraged, happy to see her returning to me. "Just because you don't believe you're beautiful doesn't mean it's not true. And I'm going to make you believe me, if it's the last thing on earth I do." Her eyes went wide in shock. Somewhere inside, I saw her crack. She was at least going to give me a chance and that's all I needed. "Are you going to rub on that packet all night or are you going to put it on me so I can bury myself inside you and make you scream my name in ecstasy." She giggled and I realized that if I didn't get inside of her soon, I would explode.

I took the packet out of her hand and put it on in record time. "Now, Hindley," I whispered. She put both hands on my chest, balancing as she rose above me, her hair cascading around her face like a veil. She looked like an angel, my angel. *Yeah, but she fucks like the devil.* As she eased down on me, my head fell back onto the pillow, my eyes rolling back in my head. In no time, she found her natural rhythm and I felt every erotic fantasy I'd ever had since I was thirteen come true in this beautiful, gorgeous, insanely sexy woman.

"Fuck, Hindley," I blew out. "God, you feel so fuckin' good."

"Really?" Her question caught me off guard. Did she really think she was bad at this? My eyes flew open and I saw how erotic she felt.

I wrapped my hands around her hips, moving mine with hers as we slowly began to grind in perfect harmony. I let my thumb work its way down to her special spot and smirked as her moans escaped.

"Oh, Rory, please."

"Please, what?"

"Please, don't stop."

"Never." I felt her entire body begin to tighten in preparation for her release. "Not yet, baby. Wait for me."

"I can't," she panted.

"Slow, Hindley," I drew out. "Control."

Her eyes flew open and found mine. She was so fucking hot and sexy, it propelled me to my peak and I felt myself start to crumble. "Now, baby, now!" I shouted. We spiraled into an alternate universe together, the feeling euphoric, sedating, and exhilarating, all in one. I'd never felt anything like it. Our bodies shook in unison as we moaned unintelligible words that echoed throughout the room.

After what felt like hours, maybe even days, we returned from our magical high and I realized we were still on planet earth, lying atop her mattress. She collapsed onto my chest, utterly spent and exhausted, and I instinctively wrapped my arms around her, letting my hands slowly and lovingly caress her back. "Sleep, baby," I whispered in her hair. She moaned against my chest as I continued to stroke her hair and for the first time in my life, I felt complete. I felt like I had a purpose. I'd finally found someone who's happiness I would put above my own. I wasn't sure if that was good or bad but tonight, it felt perfect.

~

The arena was packed and for some bizarre reason, I felt nervous for the first time since…well, forever. *You know why.* I frantically searched the crowd for the now too familiar face, panicked that she was nowhere in sight. *Dude, what is your problem? You better fuckin' focus on your skating or you won't even make it into the finals tomorrow.*

Hindley's plane was supposed to arrive early this morning in California, just in time for the start of the Dopa Mash-Up Pro Pool Party. I'd been registered for several months but it wasn't until I'd discovered she'd actually be in attendance that I'd started really gearing up for the event, practicing every day, working out religiously, watching my caloric intake. I was good, I knew that. But Hindley was my attorney, my representative, and I had to prove to her that I was worthy of all the hard work she'd been doing for me. For some bizarre reason, I wanted to make her proud of me.

"Hey, what's going on, man?" Jack's voice brought me back to the present.

"Oh, uh, nothing."

"Who were you looking for?"

"Um, no one."

"So I guess you won't want to see this little lady?"

Jack stepped back, revealing Hindley standing directly behind him. She was wearing the same red t-shirt with the River City logo she'd worn in San Antonio at the Pro Am, only this time, it was gathered to the side and bunched in a small knot revealing a portion the precious white skin around her midsection. I wasn't entirely sure I was happy about others seeing any part of her, let alone an area I'd devoured over and over again and claimed as my own like the Pilgrims at Plymouth Rock. *Dude, what the fuck is that? Are you actually being territorial?* The feeling was completely foreign to me.

"Hey," she said softly.

"Hey." I felt like a total blockhead, standing there dumbstruck by her devastatingly dangerous beauty.

"Like my shirt?" She twirled around slowly in front of me, her hands stretched out like a graceful bird. "It has your signature. See?" She pointed over her shoulder and my dick pulsed when her eyes slowly rolled up to meet mine. She looked like a fuckin' dessert, everything about her delicious and enticing. The expression on her face told me she was slowly beginning to understand the effect she was having on me. "Are you ready?" she asked. I heard her raspy voice but my mind couldn't make my mouth respond, my tongue was too swollen, along with other parts of my body. "Rory."

"Um, yeah." I literally shook my head in an attempt to bring blood back to my brain, trying to rid my mind of the elicit memories of our last night together. *Focus, you dipshit!*

"Are you ready, for today?" she repeated.

It'd been over a week since I'd seen her naked body rubbing against mine and all I could think about was ripping that shirt off her and throwing her down right here in front of God and everyone, just to bury myself inside her. *Dude, what is your problem? You have a major competition to get through. Get your fuckin' head in the game, man.*

"Uh, yeah, I think so," I sighed. "Hopefully, we'll see."

"I'm gonna go grab a seat." She lifted up on her tip toes and grabbed my neck in a seemingly innocent embrace. I wrapped on arm around her tiny waist and nearly fell out as her lips quickly grazed my ear. "I wish I could grab your seat though," she whispered, her breath caressing my entire neck. God, she smelled amazing. Without another word, she pushed off me and made her way through the crowd, looking back at me briefly, offering a smile that promised more, leaving me bewitched and horny as hell. How the fuck was I supposed to skate now with a hard on as big as the state of California itself?

My eyes locked on her as she parted the sea of pro skaters and spectators, their heads turning to watch her plump little ass swish off like I was. Suddenly, an explosion of anger seared through my chest, radiating out to all my limbs. *What the fuck was that?*

"Alright, man, do you have your skating plan mapped out?" I barely registered Jack's words, still lost in Hindley's erotic words and this intense burning fury running wild throughout my entire body.

"Yeah, I've got it," I barked out, sick to my stomach.

"Rory!" he half shouted, grabbing my shoulders.

"What!"

"Focus."

"Okay, I'm with it." *Competition. Skate. Impress Hindley. Remember?* "Sorry, man."

"Manny's gonna be bringin' his A-game today. He's still pissed about last month's disqualification in Brazil." I chuckled out loud, remembering Manny Morales cussing out one of the foreign judges during the competition. He thought cursing him in Spanish would make his words unintelligible to most but in his own fury, he'd forgotten he was actually in a Latin country. The broadcasters had a hell of a time covering up his expletives and the governing board voted unanimously to disqualify him.

"Rory!" Jack shouted. "Focus! Please."

"Alright, sorry. You have to admit though, it was funny as hell. I mean, come on. Spanish, in Brazil?" Jack finally let his scowl fade into a small smile.

"He's dangerous today, Rory, so just keep an eye on him." Jack was right, Manny could be lethal when he was out for revenge. "Okay, you also need to watch out for Smitty. He's fresh off an injury and word is he's looking for a comeback just as bad as you are."

Charlie Smith, aka Smitty, dislocated his right shoulder in a fall earlier this year. Rather than rest it like the doctors and his manager had insisted, he'd decided to skate a week later and tore the shit out of major ligaments and tendons. His recovery had been slow and painful but I was pretty confident he still wouldn't be one hundred percent today.

"You've totally got Jake and Buzz, especially on your aerials." *Fuckin' A! You've got the best aerials in all of skating, dude.*

I was totally secure in my back flips, slides, grinds and aerials. But now I was working really hard to perfect a new trick, one I'd informally called 'The Helly.' It was a seriously complicated trick and dangerous as hell, hence the name, but I knew it would be totally worth every point I'd get once I pulled it off! The trick required me to suspend myself in the air while balancing and rotating on only one arm. I held the board flush to my feet with the other hand, while making two complete revolutions on my free hand, my skateboard spinning like the rotors on a helicopter. The name of the trick came from the effect the skateboard gave, looking like a helicopter. But I'd also called it 'The Helly' because I'd fallen so damn hard and so many times, it hurt like hell the next day.

"Don't even think about trying it. Not today, Rory." Jack didn't even have to say it, he meant The Helly. There was no way I was doing that trick today. It still wasn't perfect and I didn't perform any trick I wasn't a master of. Plus, there was absolutely no way I was going to fall today, not in front of Hindley. Something weird churned in my stomach at the thought of embarrassing myself in front of her.

"You alright?" Jack put his hand on my shoulder, his brows furrowed.

"I'm fine, just going over my routine in my mind."

"Well, you know you need to watch Axel in your rearview mirror."

Axel Pretorius, aka Pretty Boy, had literally been a pain in my ass for the last five years. I'd first met him at a Pro Am invitational similar to the one Leif and River City just hosted. Back then, Axel was just a snot-nosed amie, our nick name for amateurs. I'd known from the very beginning he was a total dick though and he'd proved me right ever since. But the pinnacle of our relationship came last August. I was working on a comeback in the industry and he loved to rub it in my face, how far I'd fallen and how I continued to chase his sorry little ass on my climb back up to the podium. I'd been standing in line on the deck, waiting for my ride when the dipshit took a side rail turn and completely clipped me at the ankles, buckling my entire six foot three body and bringing me flat on my ass. He told the judges it was an accident but everyone on the pro circuit knew he'd done it intentionally. That's just the kind of prick he was. They'd nearly disqualified him from the competition once they discovered my tailbone was actually bruised. But I wouldn't give him the satisfaction. I skated against him the next day in the finals and kicked his ass. I wished it had been literal and since then, I worked hard every time I saw him to keep my composure. I couldn't afford to fuck up, especially not today.

Right on cue, I heard his weasel-ass voice ring in my ear. "Nice agent, Gregor." Just the thought of him looking at Hindley had bile rising in my throat and my fists clenching.

"Do you mind, Axel? Rory and I are discussing our game plan," Jack cast him off.

"Oh, for sure. Please don't let me stop you." He held up his hands in innocence but Jack and I both knew he was anything but. "I think I'll go introduce myself to the little beauty."

"Don't you even dare think about it, asshole!" I shouted. The words were out of my mouth before I could even think.

"Whoa, sounds like someone's pretty attached to their agent," he laughed. "From what I hear, she's a smart one, too. So, tell me Rory Gregor, what the hell is she doing with a dumb ass like you?"

My arms pulsed with fury and rage as adrenaline surged through my entire body. *He's just trying to provoke you, man, don't let him do it. Blow him off. Deep breath, deep breath, deep breath. Beat his ass in the pool.*

I tried to steady my breathing, turning my attention back toward the course. This competition was being held on a pool skatepark, named for the hollow hole in the ground that resembled a drained pool. The course was eight to twelve feet deep with various bumps and humps on the bottom and surrounded by a two inch steel railing that skaters could ride for extra points. I remembered the last competition how Axel had fallen on his smart little ass when he tried to ride it for a fraction of a second too long. Much to everyone's surprise though, he'd recovered and impressed the judges to land in first place. *Fucker!*

Mentally, I ran through my skating plan that Jack and I had devised the prior evening, trying desperately to ignore the little prick, who was still standing way to close for his own safety. Although skating left a lot of room for improvising, I'd always found it important to have some basic plan in place to make sure I covered all the various tricks in my repertoire.

"Well, well, well, if it ain't Axel 'Pretty Boy' Pretorius as I live and breathe." I was thankful to hear Buzz Dahlke's voice ring from behind Axel. He and I were soul brothers and confidants in the skating circuit and everyone knew it. When I'd taken a turn for the worse and my career nose-dived, it had been Buzzy who'd stood by me, encouraging me to come back to the sport I loved. He despised Axel more than I did and had no problems showing it.

"What's up, dick face," Axel nodded.

"Ah, dick face, how original, Pretty Boy. Remind me again why they call you that?" Buzz snorted.

Axel remained frozen. Pretty Boy was a nickname other skaters had given him years before. He thought it was an innocent play on his last name, Pretorius. But actually, we all called him that because of his constant need to primp just before skating. He was from Australia and apparently was a sports legend in his home country. No one in the world thought Axel Pretorius was better looking than Axel 'Pretty Boy' Pretorius himself and if you didn't believe him, all you had to do was ask him again and he'd tell you. It really ate my shit that it was true though. He was a good looking guy. Girls would shout out his name at competitions and ask for him to throw any article of clothing or other item that had actually touched him into the stands. *Dude, they do that shit to you, too. Its fuckin' annoying, by the way, you know that, right?*

Most of the girls who followed the skating circuit had done the horizontal hump dance with him on more than one occasion. He was notorious for it. It was rumored that there were at least four little Pretty Boy babies out there around the world but he'd never claimed a one of them.

But what worried me the most about him getting close to Hindley were the most recent rumors surfacing around the tour. Apparently, not every girl Axel was bedding was a willing participant. In the past six months he'd had two girls accuse him of some type of assault, sexual and physical. No charges had been formally filed but the governing board wasn't happy. Real or not, the threat was there and I wasn't going to take any chances when it came to Hindley's safety.

"What are you doing over here harassing the winner of this competition?" Buzz antagonized him.

"Winner?" Axel spit out in disgust.

"Yeah. I said winner," Buzz repeated.

"Aren't you kind of putting yourself down already, Buzz, declaring that he's going to beat you? Of course, my grandmother could beat you on a bad day and she's on a walker." Axel laughed at his own joke but the rest of us remained silent.

Unfortunately, what Axel said was true, Buzz was on his way down the leader board. I'd told him for the last year he should retire when he was on top but he couldn't let go of the glory days. I'd changed my stance and decided to back him, no matter how I felt about his professional skills.

"Whatever, dick head. As long as he wipes the pool with your dumb ass, I don't mind comin' in last place if it means I get to watch your fuckin' face pucker up tighter than your shit shooter with humiliation."

"Come on, guys, let's take this out in the pool," Jack intervened, stepping between Buzz and Axel.

Axel was much smaller in stature than me and Buzz but no matter the size, he'd always stand shoulder to chest to both of us. I had to give him credit, he had tons of self-esteem. More than me.

"With pleasure," Axel ended our confrontation, bumping Buzz's shoulder as he pushed through the mass of people now gathered around the skater's platform.

"Tell your Granny she's gotta sweet little mouth and she can suck my dick again tonight if she wants to!" Buzz yelled out toward Axel as he walked away. I wasn't surprised to see Axel flip him off as he disappeared into the mass of skaters.

"Buzz, why do you insist on antagonizing him?" Jack was obviously perturbed with the entire situation.

"Calm down, Jack, it's all part of my master plan," he explained.

"And what's your master plan, Buzz?" Jack inquired with mild interest. "Have him so pissed off and pumped up that he'll beat your ass?"

"Something like that," he laughed before turning his attention towards me. "Hey, who was the hottie wrapped around your neck earlier? Rumor has it she's your new agent. Wish my agent had an ass like that." Even though Buzz and I were friends, it still infuriated me that he pictured Hindley in that way. "Ease up, man, I was just kidding," he laughed, his hands in the air. "You look like you ate a bowl of lemons."

Dude, get a hold of yourself. You're being too territorial over this chick. No one can find out about you two or it will ruin Hindley.

"I just don't want anyone thinking of her like that," I finally answered. "I mean, she's smart and talented, as an attorney and an agent." *And a sordid minx in the sack!*

"Well, sorry dude, the chick is way too hot for any red-blooded dude not to picture her ass naked in bed."

My fists balled up again and I felt that same explosion firing deep within my chest sizzling my veins. *What the fuck is this, man?* Buzz was my friend, a good friend, but I wasn't really sure I could hold back my rage. He leaned in closer, resting his hand on my shoulder obviously wanting to tell me something for my ears only.

"Dude, are you fuckin' her?" he growled lowly.

"What!" I shouted in mock surprise. Okay, it wasn't mock, I really was worried as shit that he could tell and even more petrified that he'd actually voiced his concern.

"I mean, it's okay, I'm not gonna judge you. You know that."

My heart started pounding like I was running with the bulls in Spain and sweat beads broke out all over my body. *Shit! You're giving yourself away, dumb ass. Be cool.*

"No, I'm not fuckin' her, man." Technically, it was true. I'd fucked a lot of woman and I could say, without a doubt, what Hindley and I were doing was anything but fucking. *If it ain't fuckin' then what is it? Making love?* Absolutely not!

"Mind if I give it a try then?" Buzz laughed as he nudged my shoulder with his fist. I could feel my chest heave as I drew in a deep breath, fighting against my natural urge to knock the fuck out of him. "Dude, I'm just kidding. Calm down."

"She's good, Buzz, really good. I don't want to fuck this up."

"Look, I get it, man. You've been working hard. You deserve the best. And from what I can tell from her back side, she is the best." I listened with silent fury as he bellowed with laughter before turning on his heel to make his way to the platform.

Dude, this is never gonna work. Ever! You wanna know what you're feeling? It's fuckin' jealousy and it's gonna rip through you and fuck up any chance you have at winning this year. End it with this chick. End it now before you kill someone and destroy her reputation in the process.

I knew what was right, what I should do, but I was a weak motherfucker and even my conscience knew it. I scanned the packed auditorium, searching for her, thankful this was a covered event. I didn't want her to get burned again. *Why are you worrying about her? Do you even know what your skate plan is? Get a grip, man.*

I pulled a piece of paper out of my back pocket and reviewed all the graphics, trying to familiarize myself with all the tricks I wanted to perform, trying to drown out the echoes in my head telling me to walk away from Hindley Hagen. Not even the voice of the announcer on the PA system proclaiming the start of the event could drown out the vicious warning rattling in my mind. *End it, Rory. End it. NOW!*

~

"Oh my God, Rory, that was amazing!" Hindley's accolades did nothing to dissuade me from scooping her up in my arms and throwing her onto my bed, but I had to let the thought go. She was dressed in a tight purple halter top and short-as-shit black mini skirt that showed off every delicious detail of her amazing legs. My dick instantly stood at attention. *You're so pathetic, dickweed.* She reached out for my waist but I pulled away, opening my hotel room door further to reveal Jack sitting on the couch in the living area of my suite. "Oh," she whispered, "Sorry." I shook my head, more in disgust of my own weak restraint, knowing full well when he left my room, I'd have her stripped down and spread out across my bed if I wasn't careful.

"Rory did a great job this weekend, didn't he, Jack?!" Hindley gushed, plopping down on the couch next to him. Jack rolled his eyes. He was pissed at me, way pissed. Yesterday, during the semi-finals, Kara called and informed him of my true feelings for Hindley. He'd lectured me well into the night after the first round of competitions about how hard I'd worked to make a comeback. He sounded just like Leif, a broken record stuck on the 'Stay Away from Hindley' anthem that even my own mind couldn't take off the fuckin' player.

"I mean, come on, second place. That's awesome!" she continued.

Second place? Second place is shit man!

"It's not first," Jack seethed. Normally, he wasn't into where I ranked but rather how I skated or, more importantly, how I felt about how I skated. This time he knew I hadn't performed at my best and my second place title was proof of it. He was more upset about why I didn't skate to my potential. I was hung up on Hindley and he knew it.

"I know you like her, Rory and I'm happy for that, especially if she's as different as you've told Kara," he'd explained last night after the first round of competition was over. "But you have to keep your head in the game. X Games are in three months and you've got to pull some serious tricks out of your bag to make it there."

His words had played over and over again in my head last night as I'd tried but failed to find solace in sleep. His words had been like a cold shower raining down over my dick, forcing me to say no to Hindley last night when she'd come knocking on my door after dinner. I knew by the expression her face she was ready for a replay of our time in her bedroom. I'd fended off her advances, claiming that I needed to stay focused but in the end, I'd ended up with my dick in an ice bucket, trying to ease the massive woody she'd given me with her mouthwatering good-bye kisses. God, that girl knew how to suck face. She was disappointed last night, even a little hurt, I could tell. But I had to stay away from her, I had to let her go, for both our sakes.

Hindley's eyes darted from Jack's to mine then back to Jack's again, her face registering the unspoken tension in the air.

"Um, well, I just came up to tell you I've got a meeting downstairs, in the lounge." The hairs on my neck stood on end and I felt my eyes stinging with jealousy. *This is what I'm talking about man. Let her go.*

She pulled herself up from the sofa and slowly walked toward the door, her long lean legs flexing with every step. I blocked her way, forcing her to stop just inches in front of me.

"Meeting with who?" My words were much more accusatory than I wanted, but I couldn't help it. Even though I knew I shouldn't, I wanted her, bad. And the thought that she was leaving me to be with someone else had me seething.

"Matt Davis."

"Who?"

"He's with Sonara Water. I met him during the finals today. Apparently, his company is quite taken with your comeback story."

I knew I should be excited that Hindley was working deals for me but I wasn't. I was pissed. She was mine and I had an urgent need to show her. *Jack's here.* Shit! I relinquished and stepped aside, letting her pass by. Her chocolate eyes roamed over me and I saw pain flash across her face. I was disappointing her, confusing her, and I'd promised myself I wouldn't be that person, the one who hurt her again.

I slowly walked to the door, following behind her to pull it open. She made her way to the threshold, turning to face me just as I caught a hint of her intoxicating scent. That was it, I was lost. I leaned in closer. "I'll see you later?" I wasn't sure if my words were a statement, a question, or a plea. *I think it's called desperation, jackass.*

Her eyes darted toward Jack and I glanced over my shoulder, only to find him buried in his laptop reviewing videos of my performances this weekend. I turned back to face her and saw a small nod. I wasn't convinced she truly wanted to see me, but it was enough. I reached down and wrapped my fingers just under her ear as my thumb lightly caressed her cheek. I was thrilled to feel her head lean in toward my touch, her eyes filled with the promise I'd been looking for since the last time I'd been inside her.

"You've got some work to do on your 720 but you landed it so that was enough today." Jack's voice pulled me away from Hindley's eyes. He was slumped over the computer, deep in thought.

"Later," Hindley whispered, her words full of promise as she pulled the door from my grasp and quietly closed it behind her.

I trudged back to the sofa, slumping down next to him, mentally preparing myself for the debriefing I knew was inevitable. All I could see was Hindley though, sitting in the lounge downstairs in her fuckin' flimsy excuse for a skirt with some strange man probably ogling her, staring at her, fantasizing about her like I was. Fuck! My blood started boiling as my eyes rolled up toward the ceiling and my hands raked through my hair, wondering what he looked like, did he make a lot of money, was he smart? *Of course he's smart, you asswipe, he's an executive.* One thing was for sure, the dickhead could read and that was probably a much bigger turn on for Hindley than any skating trick I'd ever pulled off in my life. He was better for Hindley than I was and the thought ran dangerously deep ruts and divots in my mind. There was no other way. This would never work. I would have to let her go. Thankfully, Jack's constant nagging distracted me, for the moment.

An hour later, when we were finished watching frame after frame of this weekend's competition videos, Jack packed up his laptop and headed out toward the door. My mind was racing with all types of elicit things Hindley could have done with Mr. Executive all this time I was stuck in this god awful room with Jack.

"Just one last thing, Rory." Jack stood in front of my door, laptop tucked under his arm, his other hand resting on the door knob. "You're worthy of her. Don't ever doubt that." His comment took me totally by surprise. It seemed like now Jack possessed the uncanny ability to read my thoughts as well. "But being worthy comes with responsibilities. If you like her, if she is different, then you have to treat her differently. I'm not saying you can't pursue her, I'm just saying you can't be reckless, like you've been in the past."

I took in a deep breath, trying to let his words soak in. It wasn't anything I hadn't been telling myself since I'd bedded her. "She's good for you, good for your career," he continued. "If you can't treat her right then stop what you're doing. Right now."

"I want to treat her right, Jack, I just don't have much experience."

"You know you can't go public with this relationship, don't you? Not right now anyway."

"I know. We both do."

"You're worthy of her, Rory. Stop trying to convince yourself differently. Just be prepared."

"For what?"

"For the wrath of the entire Jennings family to come down on you if you hurt her." I laughed at his comment but realized he wasn't joking.

"I promise, I'll pull away if I feel my dickheadedness starts to take over." He chuckled, opening the door.

"Good, because I think Kara will beat the snot out of you if you hurt Hindley. Be careful with her, Rory. It's just a meeting. She's doing her job, for you. Don't go down to the lounge and go all Rory Gregor on her."

"What does that mean?"

"It means you'd probably be better off to stay in your room tonight and let her do her job. That's what she does now, she represents you. And that's what she's doing right now." I cut my eyes at Jack. "That's all she's doing, Rory." I knew what Jack was up to, he was trying to quiet the voices in my head. He was taking over for Kara but I wasn't so sure he was doing a good job of it.

"I'll stay here, I promise." He raised his eyebrow in obvious uncertainty. "If I go down, I promise to keep it professional." His eyebrow stayed glued in place. "What?"

"Just be careful, Rory. She's different. Way different. You're on your way back up. Don't hurt her and ruin both of your reputations and careers in the process." Suddenly, the door shut in my face, leaving me alone with my self-loathing thoughts.

~

The elevator doors slid open and suddenly, my palms began to sweat as my heart throbbed in anxious anticipation. I'd convinced myself that I was only traveling to the lounge to make sure Hindley stayed safe, to make sure she was out of harm's way. It was a valid concern, considering how we'd first met.

I trudged across the lobby, barely able to lift my feet off the smooth marble floor on my way to the lounge, when someone caught my arm and pulled me to the side.

"Hey." I high pitched voiced pierced my brain. "I saw you skate today. You were sooooo awesome," she drug out. "You totally should have won." I looked down and saw a petite girl, maybe nineteen or twenty, with short auburn hair, bright green hazel eyes, and tits the size of Mount Rushmore. I tried not to look but they were almost as big as her head and I couldn't help it. *Dick!*

Back in the day, this was exactly the type of girl I would have taken back to my room and fucked all kind of kinky ways, so hard that she'd walk like a cripple for the next week. And by the look in her eyes, I could see she would come willingly. But tonight, I looked closer, examining her as a person. She was young, fragile, and alone. Why hadn't I ever noticed that in women before?

"Um, thanks, I appreciate that." I wiggled my arm out of her grip.

"You are just as hot up close as you are from down in the pool." My eyes were looking over her, scanning the entrance to the lounge looking for Hindley, when suddenly I felt the girl's hand on my chest. I involuntarily took a step back and jerked my head toward her. "Would you sign my bra," she asked, licking her lips as she began to raise her tight shirt. *What the fuck!*

"Uh, no." I forcefully pulled her shirt back down but she took advantage of my close proximity, pulling me into her embrace trying to kiss me. I regained my balance seconds before her big, bright red glossy lips met mine. At the last second, I was able to dart my head the other way so they hit my cheek instead. I closed my eyes, trying to figure out what to do next. *Push her off, man, push her off.* Her arms were wrapped around my waist like an octopus, stronger than I ever thought possible. I grabbed her wrists now twisted behind my back and began to pry them away, realizing that her lips were still stuck to my cheek and working their way toward my lips. I scanned the lobby, looking for something, anything, anyone to help. I froze instantly when my eyes landed on the lounge entrance and saw Hindley standing paralyzed, her coffee colored eyes locked on mine and blazing with fury. *Fuck! Get her off, get her off, now!* I hadn't wanted to get physical with this girl but I could tell from Hindley's glacial stare, I had to separate myself from her, and fast. I gently but firmly grasped the woman by the shoulders and lifted her off the floor as I slid her an arm's length away from me.

"Thanks for your support," I ducked away trying to move to Hindley's side as quickly as I could.

The lobby was massive and as I weaved through the unusual amount of people mingling around this late at night, I saw a man exit the lounge and wrap his hand around her waist. My heart stopped and pain radiated from my core out to ever nerve cell in my extremities. Her eyes were still ice cold and firmly planted on mine until the man's touch broke her trance. Thankfully, she backed out of his touch but turned toward him with such a beautiful, warm smile that was as genuine as she was. She liked this guy and it made me sick to my stomach. I couldn't make my way to them fast enough.

"Here he is now," her voice rang through the air, cryptic and cool. "Rory Gregor, I'd like you to meet Matt Davis with Sonora Water. *Sonora Water? Where have we heard of that? Oh, yeah, it's that water company that's all earth friendly supposedly filled with all kinds of extra vitamins and bullshit stuff so they can charge you a shitload more money.*

"Matt, this is Rory." Her hand swept from her waist out toward me like she was Vanna White, presenting the next letter on Wheel of Fortune. All I could do was stare at her face. She was so fucking beautiful, my heart actually ached. What was she thinking, it was killing me. Suddenly, her brows furrowed as she gently nodded toward Dipshit.

I cut my eyes from Hindley's face and turned to survey the man standing beside her. He was tall, as tall as me, clean cut, All-American, probably even played football in high school and college and went out with the prom queen. *Fucker!* He was wearing a dark suit with a super starched shirt that was opened one button too many for my taste. He had perfectly placed black hair that he spent way more time on than most girls he'd ever fucked. His shit-eating grin revealed super white, super straight teeth and I could hear the silent words he wanted to say to me but couldn't because Hindley was next to him. 'Yeah, you idiot, that's right,' he boasted silently to me with his green eyes and smug smirk. 'I'm what she wants, what she needs, you illiterate fucker, so why don't you just get the hell out of here, you pathetic loser.' At least, that's probably what I'd tell me, if our roles were reversed.

I hated him instantly, despised him, even loathed him, and he hadn't even uttered one fuckin' word. Dick!

"It's nice to finally meet you, Rory," Dipshit said, extending his hand out to me. I let my eyes travel down the rest of his body until it came to rest on his perfectly manicured hand. He'd probably never done a hard day's work in his life. *Just Hindley's type.* He was probably an MBA or an attorney from Harvard just like her. *That's the*

kind of guy she deserves, the kind of guy she should be with.
Well, tough shit, asshole, she's with me. Tonight.

"It's nice to meet you, Matt," I finally responded, taking
his hand in mine, giving him the best man-shake I could
muster. He had a decent grip and strong hands. *Shit, this
guy is an actual contender.*

"I was just telling Hindley how much we at Sonora have
enjoyed your comeback story. We believe it rings true to
our own story of recycling, taking the best of the worst and
making something new with it, something that sustains us."

*What the fuck did he just say? Did this ass hat just call
you the best of the worst? Was that a compliment or an
insult?* Probably both. I looked over to Hindley, her
eyebrows were raised in warning. *Oh, shit! Rein it in, big
guy.*

"Um, thanks, I guess." I released his hand and watched
helplessly as he reached up to hold Hindley's elbow. *Dude,
quit fucking touching her or I'll throw you into that
goddamn fish tank in the middle of the lobby.* Hindley
graciously stepped out of his reach, coming to stand next to
me on the steps. *Well thank fuck for that!*

"Matt said that Sonora may be interested in signing a
deal with you for a national ad campaign they're launching
soon." Finally, Hindley's soothing voice washed over me,
bringing me a moment of peace, calming the crazy shit
flying around in my head. "Especially if you're able to
make it to the X Games," she continued.

I vaguely heard Hindley say something about ads and X
Games but all my mind could really focus on was the douche
bag standing directly in front of me, who thought it was
alright to put his hands on my woman. *No one knows she's
your woman, dumbass. This relationship is under wraps and
it has to stay that way so don't do anything stupid you'll
regret.*

"Isn't that great news, Rory?" I felt Hindley's elbow in
my side and suddenly realized I needed to respond.

"Oh, yes, sorry. That sounds great."

"Their corporate office is in San Diego so I'm going to fly down on Monday morning and meet with their team to talk about specifics."

"We could drive," I offered, looking longingly into Hindley's questioning eyes. Taking a nice drive down the Pacific Coast Highway with Hindley sounded like the perfect way to spend a Sunday afternoon. "San Diego is only about an hour and a half away from my house."

"Oh, you don't need to be at the meeting Rory," Matt answered too quickly in mock concern. "I'm sure negotiations are much too tedious and boring for athletes, just a lot of big mumbo-jumbo documents. You need to focus on your skating right now." He gave me a joking jab on my upper arm and I had to fight back with every fiber of my being to not knock the fuck out of him.

"Actually," Hindley interjected, putting herself between the two of us. She could obviously sense my brewing hostility. "Rory is very involved in all aspects of his career, contract negotiations being one of them."

Matt raised his eyebrows and shifted his neck back in genuine surprise. "Wonderful. Then we'll see both of you on Monday. I'll email you the details, Hindley." He reached in and kissed her cheek and I almost kicked him in the nutsack. "Until Monday, Rory." He stuck out his hand and stared at me with some type of smirk on his face. *What the fuck is your problem, dude? I'm about to take her upstairs and fuck her until she's hoarse from screamin' my name in ecstasy, you fuckwad. You ain't got shit on me.* Unless this is the kind of guy Hindley really wants.

"Monday." I whimpered, stepping aside as Matt walked down the remaining stairs, heading toward the lobby. *Fuck, now this douche bag thinks he won.* I couldn't let this happen. I wrapped my arm around Hindley's tiny waist and raised my hand in the air. "Monday, Matt! Can't wait." He turned to look back over his shoulder and I waved like the douche bag I was. He gave a slight smile but I knew the fucker was knocked down at least a notch, maybe two. *That's right, she's mine motherfucker even though no one's supposed to know it.* My lips curled up in glorious victory smile. Rory, one, Dipshit Water Boy, zero.

"What the hell was that, Rory?" Hindley's hand dug deep into my ribs, pushing me away from her side. "Damn it!" She was pissed. Really pissed. But I didn't care. *That's a total lie. You care, more than you should.*

"What?" I asked, following her down the steps.

"Why did you do that?"

"He wants you and I wanted him to know that you're not available."

"Well, you may have just jeopardized this deal."

"I don't give a fuck about the deal, Hindley."

She stopped abruptly and whipped her body around to face me, hair flying sideways, falling gracefully over one shoulder. Damn, she was hot all mussed up and fuming.

"Well, you should care," she seethed between clenched teeth.

"I don't even like that fuckin' water."

"Who cares?"

"I care. I'm not going to endorse something I don't like."

"What do you even know about them?"

"I know a douche bag works in their marketing department and he's trying to get into my girl's panties."

"Seriously, Rory? That's your come back?" Her face was scrunched and contorted but she still looked adorable. "And for the record, I'm not *your* girl." My face fell, losing all the manly testosterone buzz it once had. She grabbed my arm and yanked me into an alcove. "You know what I mean," she whispered more discreetly.

"No, I guess I don't."

"Look, you're the one who said no to me last night when I came to your room so I don't want to hear anything from you."

"Maybe you should try again tonight," I smiled.

"It's late. I can't be seen going into your room at this hour."

I looked down at my phone. "It's just a little after midnight."

"Well, still. Do you really want to go to their offices with me on Monday?" She was trying to change the subject and for once, I welcomed the diversion.

"Sure. We can drive down to my house tomorrow, spend the night, then head down to San Diego early Monday morning." I took in a deep breath and blew out a hard sigh, realizing I was fucking this up, bad. "Look, Hindley, I could give a rat's ass about the meeting. I just want to spend some time alone with you, just the two of us." I gave her my most alluring, drop-your-panties smile I could muster. She balled up her fist and hit me in the chest. "Shit, Hindley, that hurt!" I rubbed on the point of impact, trying to soothe the throbbing. Damn, she was strong!

"Good!" She flipped back around and headed for the bank of elevators.

"So?" I asked quietly nudging her shoulder as we waited.

"So what?"

"Are you stopping by?"

"No."

"Why?"

"It's late. We can't be seen like that. It's important to me." I couldn't help but feel that maybe this wasn't about us staying stealth but her not wanting me at all. "Stop!" she scolded me.

"What?"

"He holds no appeal to me, Rory."

"Who?" The elevator doors opened and I stepped back, allowing her to enter first. She rolled her eyes at me.

"Matt Davis."

"Only me?" I smirked.

"Only you." She reached up and rubbed my cheek, brushing my bottom lip with her thumb as the doors slid closed. *Alright!* My palm flattened on her hip and moved down toward her ass.

Suddenly a hand popped through the closing elevator doors stopping the seal and my stomach clenched when I heard the sickening familiar voice.

"Hold the elevator, please." Axel 'Pretty Boy' Pretorius. His prick little body scooted through the doors just in time.

Fuck! Could my night get any better?

"Thanks, man." He looked up at me like I'd saved his life. "Oh, hey, Rory, didn't know it was you." *Liar. He knew it was us. Prick.* "You must be Rory's new agent. I'm Axel Pretorius." He extended his hand as his eyes surveyed her from the top of her perfect head to bottom of her delectable toes, drinking in every drop of her glorious body. *I'm gonna kill this fucker!*

"It's nice to meet you, Axel. I'm Hindley Hagen." Her tone was friendly and professional, void of the sultry rasp she used when we were in bed together.

"She's also my attorney," I added.

"Oh, that's impressive, Ms. Hagen."

"Please, call me Hindley," she insisted.

"Certainly, Hindley." *This guy is such a putz.*

"I love your accent," she said, catching me totally off guard. My eyes cut down towards Hindley not understanding her compliment. *Please tell me she did not just say she loved something about Pretty Boy.* "Where are you from?" she added.

"I'm from Australia. Brisbane to be exact."

"Cool." Cool? *What the fuck was that? Was she actually interested in this prick?* "You know, I've always wanted to go to Australia," she added. Oh my God, my night was going from bad to worse. *We'll take her to the Land Down Under before jerk-off will. Maybe even tonight, if she's lucky. Tell her that!*

"You know my agent's contract is up in a few months and I may be in need of a new one. Do you have any cards?"

No. Fuckin'. Way! This is not happening, dude!

"I'm sorry, I don't have any on me."

Thank fuck for that!

"I'll just add you to my phone right now." *Fuck!* "What's your number?" I stood stark still, like a cement statue as she rattled off her number to him. Heat was radiating out of every orifice of my body. I probably looked like a cartoon character, turning red from my toes building all the way up to my head just waiting for it to blow off.

Bing!

Thankfully, the doors finally opened onto our floor.

"Oh, you're on the sixth floor, too," he asked, as if he gave a shit. "After you." He stood outside the elevator, holding the doors for her like he was the most chivalrous man on earth. I made my way past the door and stared down at him, silently marking my territory. Much to my surprise, the little fucker actually winked at me. *Dude, don't do it. Think of Hindley. She's with you.* It took everything inside me not to punch him straight in the face and scoop up Hindley and saunter down the hall with her like a caveman.

"Nice to meet you, Hindley," Axel shouted behind us. Hindley slowly turned her head back toward him and I saw her face light up in a way I wasn't comfortable with.

"You too, Axel. Call me if you need anything."

Need anything? What the fuck did that mean?

"Oh, I will," he yelled back sarcastically.

I knew I should keep my cool. I knew I shouldn't worry about this little prick. I knew, I knew, I knew. But I couldn't help myself. I had to put this little fucker in his place.

"She'll be pretty tied up with me for a while though," I shouted back at him, giving him a single wave and an all-knowing nod of my head. *What the fuck did you just do, dick head? You gave valuable info to the enemy, you dumb motherfucker.* Shit! Shit! Shit! *Don't look at her, don't look at her.*

I finally found the courage to peek down at Hindley and I gasped as my body was gripped with fear, real fear as it swept through me when I saw her face. I'd destroyed her, I'd hurt her and I'd promised I wouldn't.

"I'm sorry," I whispered.

"Good night, Rory," she hissed, putting the card in her hotel door and pushing it open. She turned and looked me square in the face. "You might want to wipe off that tacky ass lip gloss from your face before you go to bed."

"Hindley," I tried to explain but I didn't have a chance. The door slammed in my face before I could say another word. I was smack dab in the middle of The Wrath of Hindley and it was a fuckin' category five hurricane. A giant wave of panic and anxiety washed over me as I realized I'd never been so scared in all my life. *Of what?* Of hurting her, of disappointing her...of losing her.

THANKS FOR READING

Skater Boy

Be sure to turn the page for a sneak peak
at the conclusion to *Skater Boy*

My Skater Boy

The dramatic conclusion to
Hindley and Rory's love story

As their need to protect one another grows to escalating
heights with deadly consequences, will Hindley and Rory
finally find a future together that they so richly deserve? Or
will they discover the one thing that could destroy them both
forever is actually each other?

If you enjoyed *Skater Boy* please....

1. Write a review! It's SO important to my work!

2. Tell your family and friends about my book.

3. Visit my website, sign up for my newsletter and send
   me an email. I love to hear from my readers!
   www.kaymanis.com

4. Join my Facebook Fan Page at:
   www.facebook.com/kaymanisauthor1

Excerpt from

My Skater Boy

~HINDLEY~

Well, well, well, the chickens have come home to roost haven't they, my dear. Once a player, always a player. I tried to tell you about Rory Gregor, but noooo, you wouldn't listen.

I stood at the sink, my knuckles white where I gripped the counter as I stared at my reflection in the mirror, trying hard to keep my tears at bay. What the hell had Rory just done? First, he was about to lock lips with some skank right in the middle of the lobby. Did I really mean that little to him? Then, he gets into a pissing match with a potential endorser. It wasn't like Matt Davis from Sonora Water was putting the moves on me. Or was he? *He was awfully touchy for a business associate.* That's ridiculous. Even if it were true, Rory still had no right to act like a jack ass.

Then, there was the issue with Axel Pretorius, a fellow skater, someone I would see constantly if I toured with Rory as Mr. Stedwick, the owner of my law firm, had asked me to. *Are you sure you can do that now?* No. Why didn't Rory understand that I needed new clients if I want to make a go of this new career and keep my firm happy? *Don't you mean keep Mr. Stedwick happy so he doesn't ditch your stepfather, Paul's investment midway through the deal?*

I shook my head and rolled my eyes as Rory's dumb ass words rang through my head. 'She'll be pretty tied up for a while.' Why the hell did he say that to Axel and what the hell did that mean? There was no doubt in my mind, if Axel had half a brain, he'd assume there was more going on between me and Rory than just a purely professional relationship. How dare Rory! How dare he jeopardize not only my professional but also my personal reputation! For what? For some male testosterone showdown? Fuck that!

I pulled off my mini skirt and ripped off my halter top as I reached for my toothbrush and paste. Maybe I could scrub this disgusting taste out of my mouth. *Doubtful.* I stood by the basin, rubbing my gums raw with my toothbrush, laughing as I looked in the mirror at the Hello Kitty panties I was wearing, the ones he'd sent me at the office. I thought I'd surprise Rory tonight and have them on when he undressed me. *Looks like the joke was on you tonight, sweetheart.*

Well, I'm definitely not going to sleep in them, that's for damn sure. I walked out of the bathroom with foaming toothpaste still filling my mouth as I stalked toward the closet to dig out new panties from my suitcase. I was fuming mad as I tugged out a pair of regular old Granny panties from my bag and spun toward to the bathroom to rinse my mouth of the mounting suds, and the sour taste of Rory Gregor. Suddenly, I saw something move out of the corner of my eye and I jerked my head toward the bed. I tried to scream but it just came out as gargled moans through all the foam in my mouth. I dropped my toothbrush on the ground and my hands instinctively clutched my boobs to cover myself as I realized I was only wearing panties. My eyes flew open in shock as I saw Rory Gregor laying across my bed in nothing but his boxer briefs, his gaze fixed on mine, showing no emotion or regret. As my screams of terror finally reached my vocal cords and wailing could be heard throughout my room, he sailed off the bed, trying to quiet me.

I backed away, narrowly escaping his grasp. "What the fuck are you doing in my room, Rory?" I shrieked, nearly choking on all the foam still in my mouth.

"What did you say?" he asked, trying to stifle a laugh.

I was in no mood for his bullshit, not tonight. I offered him the gravest of expressions and sighed in relief, thankful to see him retreat. I cut my eyes at him, turning on my heel to spit out my toothpaste in the sink. After rinsing my mouth out for what seemed like hours, trying to regain my resolve, I wiped my mouth with the hand towel and stared at myself passively in the mirror. *Keep strong, girl. You can do this.* Feeling braver and more in control, I chucked the towel in the sink, vowing to give him a no-holds-barred piece of my mind.

I turned off the light and rounded the corner, quickly pulling out a t-shirt from my suitcase and pulling it over my half naked body. Feeling brave and strong and fully armored with my breasts covered, I whipped around to confront him, disappointed with myself when I felt my stomach drop at the sight of him. He was casually leaning against the head board, hands behind his head, flexing his muscular arms, his chest pulled taut and showcasing ever single muscle in his torso. My mouth went dry at the sight of him. Why did he affect me so much? *God, you're pathetic.* My mind, once filled with all types of words and accusations ready to fire at him, was now rendered useless. *Well, shit, what are we gonna do now, princess?*

"Sorry I scared you." His face looked anything but repentant. In fact, I was pretty sure I saw a glimmer of amusement and what? Hope? Get real, jackass, this will never happen. *Yeah right.*

I crossed my arms over my chest in defiance. "You need to leave, Rory. I can't have people seeing you come out of my hotel room late at night. How the hell did you get in here anyway?"

"Magic door," he responded with a conspiratory wink.

"I don't know what the hell you're up to, but you need to get out of here." He remained impassive. "Now, Rory!" I shouted. He slowly pushed off the bed and I watched in wonder as his muscles contracted and released with ease as he stalked toward me. *Shit, shit, shit. Stay strong, girl.* Suddenly, my body was overcome with his scent and his proximity. He slowly grazed by me as he made his way toward another door in the wall next to my TV stand, which I'd never noticed before.

"We have adjoining rooms." His words were low and seductive and I felt everything south of my navel quiver. *Come on, Hindley, get it together. This guy just humiliated you and jeopardized your professional reputation, more than once!* "Did you know that, Hindley?" he continued, oblivious to the ethical struggles going on in my mind. "I requested it, specifically so I could come, and go, as I pleased." He took a step toward me. "With you," he blew out. His sexy saunter was overwhelming as he made his way back to me. I instantly held my breath, hoping that maybe if I didn't inhale, he wouldn't affect me. I screwed my eyes shut tight, realizing my own visions of him were making it nearly impossible to stay mad at him. "I really am sorry, Hindley," he whispered, his breath washing over me. When I finally opened my eyes, he was standing within inches of me, his hand hovering next to my neck as the pad of his thumb brushed back and forth on my cheek. Well, shit. I finally expelled the breath I'd been holding for what felt like an eternity. It had been pointless. There was no where I could run, no place safe for me to hide from Rory Gregor's pull on me.

"What are you sorry for?" I whispered so quietly I could barely hear myself.

"For embarrassing you." His lips grazed my jaw. *Fuuuuuck.* "For being jealous." His mouth clamped down on my ear lobe. I tried desperately to fight my body's natural urge to moan but cursed silently as I felt my resolve slipping away. His lips moved along my ear as he spoke. "For coming into your room unannounced." His breath cascaded around my neck and my entire body quivered with desire. "For being a total jackass." His lips puckered and trailed kisses down my neck as his body brushed flush against mine, pushing it toward the bed. *Wait, wait, wait!* I felt myself falling, falling fast.

"Stop!" I shouted, pushing him off me. His hands dropped to my wrists, his eyes guarded but barely fazed by my command. He was searching mine, beseeching me to accept his request for forgiveness. *Don't give it to him, girl. You'll be flat on your back on top of this bed, doing the horizontal monkey dance with this guy if you do.*

His hands slowly slid up my arms, skimming over my shoulders and wrapping loosely around my neck, his thumbs caressing my jaw. Chills erupted across my skin. His eyes were darker tonight, less blue and with darker flakes of brown near the center. They were mesmerizing and I couldn't pull myself away from their hypnotic pull.

"I really am sorry, Hindley. I don't know what happened to me tonight." His words were quiet and sincere, void of any sexual innuendos or intimidation. He dropped his fingers from my face and let them skid down my arm, stopping just as he reached my hands, taking them wholly in his as he slowly and methodically began rubbing my palms with his thumbs. He looked like he was in a trance.

"You could have jeopardized everything, Rory, everything I've been working for. For you." He let go of my hands and I watched, in pain, as he slowly sank down on the bed. He looked hopeless, helpless, lost.

"I knew this would happen," he sighed.

"What?"

He turned his face up to mine. "I knew I'd fuck this up. I don't deserve you, Hindley."

My remorse quickly faded to annoyance at his continued insistence that I was better than him. *Tell him.* No!

"Why do you do that?" I asked, pushing my own thoughts to the back of my consciousness.

"Do what?"

I slid down beside him on the bed, tucking my hands under my thighs. "Put yourself down. Or rather, hold me up higher than yourself, like I'm better than you."

"I just think you deserve someone who can give you everything. Someone like Dipshit."

"You mean Matt?" I asked with a hidden smirk. He was jealous and for some reason it made me...happy.

"Whatever."

"Look, Rory, you and I are just..." I couldn't go on. What were we doing here? Rory and I weren't dating, we weren't even seeing each other, outside of the bedroom and boardroom. *You're fucking, that's what it's called. Plain and simple.* The realization horrified me and I jumped off the bed as if it were on fire. "Hey, if you don't want to do this," I motioned my long finger between us, "That's fine. But don't sit there and act like..."

Before I could even finish, he was up and had me captured in his arms, his hand pulling at the back of my neck as his lips crushed mine. I knew it was a mistake to continue my involvement with him, but I'd never felt more alive with anyone than I did with Rory Gregor. I opened my mouth to allow him access and he became greedy, needy, and I felt so hot and desired that I kissed him back with a fury I'd never felt before. Before I could even process it all, he whipped me around and threw me on the bed.

"Well, well, well," he said in such a sexy, smoldering voice. "Who do we have here?" I followed his gaze and realized he was looking right at my crotch. *Hello Kitty panties. Oh, shit!* I pushed back toward the headboard, trying to cover myself with my t-shirt but before I could make it out of his reach, he grabbed both of my ankles and yanked me back down the bed. His eyes were aglow with mischief and desire and I'd never felt so wanton in my life. I felt a chill around my chest and looked down horrified to find my shirt had ridden up over my breasts. I was fully exposed to his predatory stare and I instinctively tried to pull my shirt down to cover myself but Rory was on me in a nanosecond, pinning my wrists down next to my head, rendering me helpless. Part of me wanted to fight, I shouldn't like this aggressive behavior from a man. But the majority of me loved his sexual prowess and I couldn't hide the expectant smile.

"Oh, no you don't, Miss Hagen. I want to look at these all night." He leaned down, his bare chest making contact with my breasts as he began to kiss and lick and suck my ear, then my neck, then my throat, then...I continued to fight and buck but mostly because his tongue working over my breasts was so damn intoxicating and arousing that my body felt like it was on fire. "Stay still," he whispered against my skin. I moaned deep in my throat and he raised his head, his eyes piercing mine with a victorious smile. "Does Hindley like?" I tilted my head to the side, trying to put on the best innocent face I could muster but my body betrayed me and he knew it. His mouth continued its savage work down south and I was surprised to find he was still able to keep my hands restrained even as he moved further, down, *there*.

"Well. Hello. Kitty," he laughed as he kissed every inch of my underwear, the underwear *he* bought me. *You wore them, dipshit. He told you he liked your hello kitty so don't be all shocked and virginal now that he's reintroducing himself to her.*

"Oh, shit," I moaned, my head falling back against the mattress as I closed my eyes and tried to absorb all the sensations this man brought me. But wait, I'm supposed to be mad at him. "Rory, you can't do this."

He raised his head out of my crotch and looked at me with such boyish curiosity, his brow furrowed as he tried to decipher what exactly I meant.

"I mean, I'm upset. We need to talk about what just happened."

"We'll talk later," he chuckled as his head returned to my panties. And just like that, I knew our conversation was over, for now.

~

"So you wanted to talk?" Rory asked lying on his side next to me, his head propped up by his hand as he leaned on his elbow, staring down at me.

"Um," was all I could muster. This man was lethal in bed and I couldn't help but smile. I rolled over away from him trying to pull my wits about me and silently laughed as I looked at several discarded condom wrappers strewn about the floor next to the bed, along with my t-shirt and a shredded pair of Hello Kitty underwear. "You owe me some new panties," I snorted. His arm wrapped around my waist as he pulled me close to his chest and nuzzled my hair. It felt like heaven being in his arms and for the life of me, I couldn't remember why I'd been upset.

"I think I can arrange that, Miss Hagen. I definitely don't want you going panty-less. Unless it's with me." His lips made contact with my neck, just below my ear. The sensation of his warm breath along my skin made me giggle uncontrollably. "God, I love your laugh." His voice was a low, growling moan against my neck and I felt desire course through my veins all over again. *Damn, girl, how much sex CAN two people have in one night?* "I'm ready whenever you are," he answered my silent question, grinding his hips into my backside. *That is the freakiest thing. How the hell does he do that? I am officially creeped out.*

I rolled over in his arms to face him, staring directly into the deep pocket of his throat. I let my finger rub around the divot as I contemplated what I wanted to say.

"Hey," he asked reaching under my chin and raising my head to his. "What's going on in there?" He tapped my temple lightly. "Come back to me. I miss you," he said, placing a soft kiss along my lips.

Rory was attuned to me, it was as simple as that. He knew me, inside and out, and I'd never experienced that before. We were drawn to each other for reasons I had yet to identify, but I knew we belonged together, even if just for a little while.

"Hey," he admonished. "Stop."

"Stop what?"

"Over-thinking this."

"Over-thinking what?"

"Us."

"You're the one who got heavy earlier."

"I know, I'm sorry."

"Do you really think I want Matt?"

"He wants you."

"That's ridiculous." Did Matt want me? *He was awfully touchy feely tonight.*

"He's perfect for you."

"What does that mean?"

"His sophisticated, probably went to Harvard or Yale, comes from money, knows which fork to use at dinner."

Now I was worried about losing Rory. I pushed up on my arm so we were eye to eye.

"Look at me!" I half shouted. His head snapped to face me. "Stop this bullshit. Now! If I wanted someone like Matt, I would be with someone like him. I hate fancy parties and debutant bullshit. I went to a crap ass college and an even crappier-ass law school. And I prefer hamburgers to five-course meals so I could give a shit less if there are any forks on the table or not. I'm with you, Rory Gregor."

He pushed me back onto the mattress as his body covered mine, his lips finding their now seemingly permanent home on my lips. I wrapped my arms around his lean torso, running my fingers up and down his back as our tongues and teeth collided and intertwined in passionate abandon. I was lost in Rory Gregor once more, but in the back of my mind I knew we had bigger issues to talk about. Issues that ultimately could tear us apart.

To find out the dramatic conclusion to Rory and Hindley's story purchase

Available now!

Acknowledgements

Please read – I know acknowledgement pages are usually crappy and no one gives a rat's ass about who helped them reach their goals, but I love these people and want to thank them publicly!!

I found out, not quite by accident, that when you write a book (or two or three), there are a lot of people to thank along the way.

Tony Manis, my husband – You've been my best friend and one of my biggest supporters throughout this process. Your belief in me has spiked my confidence enough to be able to take this crazy-ass journey into the unknown world called writing. Your financial and emotional support has allowed me the freedom to pursue a dream I never thought possible. I love you.

Melody Bennett, one of my bestest friends in the world – I gave you my first baby, my fledging novel, in 2012 and you read it with love and care knowing your critique might very well end our friendship and my career as a writer. Then I gave you these two new and very different novels in my series, X-Treme Boys, and you were just as brutally honest and insightful. I can honestly say this with no doubt; if it weren't for your belief that I could do this, and your words of encouragement to continue, there would never be a writer named Kay Manis or a series called X-Treme Boys. I wuv you!

Christina Collins, my crazy niece – You offered to do a dry read through on the first novel and never put it down, offering me all kinds of information that I never would have received anywhere else. Thank you for believing in me and helping me become a better writer with thicker skin. I guess

I should also thank Zachary Parker Collins who was in-utero during your read through. I love you both!

Elizabeth Swanson, editor extraordinaire and gem of a find – Along with everyone else here, your words of encouragement meant a lot. Your insight into the crazy English language was a life saver. And, I, can, never, thank, you, enough, for, teaching, me, the, importance, of, commas!

And finally, Kimberly Manis, my daughter, a girl who's more like me than she'll ever admit – You were the first person to ever believe in me, not just in writing, but in life. It was easy to write Rory and Hindley's stories because I related so much to their own self-deprecating thoughts. But my intense, late night therapy sessions with you, an insightful young teenager, really was the reason I reached the point where I am today; a published author!!! Can you believe it! I can't thank you enough for making me believe in myself. If sales go well, I see a 1966 vintage Ford Mustang, just like Leif's, in your future. I love you shoo-gee and wish you much success in your own musical journey. I hope I can be there for you as much and as often as you have for me!

~

There is nothing more powerful than living your dream. I hope one day each of you, as readers and fans, will find people in your own life who will give you the courage not only to dream big, but to try! If you ever need a kind word of encouragement, don't ever hesitate to email me! I'd be honored to be your voice of encouragement.

A Note from the Author

People ask me all the time, "Where in the world did you come up with the idea to write a story about a skateboarder?" No I'm not a skater or extreme sport participant. Honestly, it came from Rob Dyrdek, the host of MTV's hit show, *Ridiculousness*. It's a hysterical show similar to *America's Funniest Videos*, except Rob's show has much more painful clips of people doing insane-o things. Oh yeah, and Rob is much funnier.

I saw Rob one day on the show and thought to myself, "He's so successful and so talented, but so ghetto." Hey, don't get me wrong, I grew up in the ghetto, I speak ghetto. But I wondered if he ever dealt with issues of self-esteem and how he would feel if he ever met a girl that he thought was unattainable yet irresistible. Viola! There's the story and it sparked a whole series of extreme sports leading men.

My daughter thinks I fashioned Rory after Rob and maybe I did. It wasn't intentional. She thinks I have a crush on him, which I probably do but will never admit to her. He's cute, he's talented, he's funny as hell...so sue me. But the idea from the story wasn't Rob himself, it was the character who I saw Rob becoming in my mind. I saw Rory. That probably makes no sense but hey, that's me!

My goal after finishing *Skater Boy* and *My Skater Boy* is to have Rob personally endorse my books. I mean, how cool would that be. So if you liked the book and the series, send Rob a message on Facebook, Instagram, Twitter or his website and tell him to read my damn book!!!

Thanks so much for coming along on this wonderful ride with me as I embark on my new journey. I hope to keep you interested, intrigued, engaged and entertained!

-Kay

Printed in Great Britain
by Amazon.co.uk, Ltd.,
Marston Gate.